1-22-19

Shakti Rising

Albie,
Thank you for all your help and encouragement along the way.
love,
Ann

Ann Beltran

This book is a work of fiction. References to real people, events, establishments, organizations, or locales are intended only to provide a sense of authenticity, and are used fictitiously. All other characters, and all incidents and dialogue, are drawn from the author's imagination and are not to be construed as real.

Shakti Rising. Copyright © 2018 by Ann Beltran. All rights reserved. Printed in the United States of America. No part of this book may be used or reproduced in any manner whatsoever without written permission except in the case of brief quotations embodied in critical articles and reviews.

Cover illustration by Ying Liang. Aymi.ying@gmail.com ying.virb.com

ISBN 978-1536981100

This book is dedicated to
the divine feminine force of the universe

Acknowledgements

What a journey writing a trilogy! Without fellow travelers I wonder if I could have made it. With no literary agent or editor, I've relied on my friends to help me do this. Some have been there for all three books – Albie Beannacht, Lisa Lungren, Elisa Ortiz, and Cheryl Ryan – while others joined along the way – Catherine Bradshaw, Dee Endelman, and Nicole Walter. Your support has been invaluable at times in causing me to rethink material and add or change sections.

With each book I've wanted to include an outside work that has inspired me. This time around it's the transformative work of Eckhart Tolle. When I left Seattle years ago, it was his focus on the power of now, that helped me move into a present of new work, new friends, and new family.

The evolution of Liv's nonprofit career owes so much to the Leadership Institute experiences I had directing it and working with passionate nonprofit people in the Redmond area. Thanks to the remarkable people who were my Board, hard-working volunteers, and dedicated participants. You taught me important lessons about nonprofits.

Carlo Voli, thank you! Thank you for your life commitment to climate justice. Thank you for every pipeline protest you've mobilized, for your presence at Standing Rock, for the kayak protest in Seattle of Shell No! My admiration for you made its way into this book. Readers, join me in contributing to 350 Seattle (http://350seattle.org/) which was co-founded by Carlo and has become the most effective grassroots organization in the Northwest fighting for climate justice and a livable planet.

The citizen-advocacy organization RESULTS has taught me so much about microfinance over the years. The dedication of Sam Daley-Harris, its founder, to the field gave me the pleasure of learning about the successes of Jamii Bora in Kenya and its amazing foundress, Ingrid Munro. Author Ben Rawlence provided the sad details of life in the Dabaab refugee camp in *City of Thorns*. And what would a modern writer seeking historical facts do without the Internet!

And Sara Bareilles, thank you for your haunting ethereal voice that opens my heart. Words are so flat on a page. I encourage all my readers to listen to her song, *I choose you*.

Lastly, it was fun to be with fond memories of Lonavala, India where my husband and I met in 1994, at an Institute of Cultural Affairs conference. Thank you, ICA!

> "Always say 'yes' to the present moment."
>
> ~Eckhart Tolle, *The Power of Now*

Sunday, November 8, 2015

The soft sound of the bowl-shaped gong grew stronger as the meditation leader increased her pressure on the mallet.

Where was I? Liv ever so slowly pulled her mind into consciousness of her body and the surrounding space of the meditation hall, becoming aware again of the slight residue of incense. She didn't want to open her eyes.

The meditation leader's calm, comforting voice caressed Liv's ears. "Slowly, bring yourself back into this space and time. Become aware of your breath. When you're ready, you can open your eyes."

Liv became aware of her lotus posture on the thick moss-colored carpet. Feeling the need to move, she inhaled deeply, then pressed her palms to her eyes. Lifting her wide eyelids, the leader's gentle smile floated in as her first impression.

"Take time to make some notes in your journal about your meditation experience. And then we'll take a half-hour pause. Light refreshments are available in the lobby. Remember to keep your silence."

The image that visited in this last meditation of the retreat was of her kayaking in a stream that ran near but deviated from a river. The folk on the river were many, they'd wave when they saw her, enjoying reunions where only sandbars and islands between the stream and river separated them. But always she went back to her rivulet where other odd souls occasionally paddled too. Were these voyagers who chose solitary people-powered craft over speedboats and larger leisure boats that populated the river, were her kind in the stream of slow learners? She didn't think so. But there was comfort in the narrow shallow pathways near forests, that let her drift under magnanimous willow tree boughs hanging wide and low and providing dappled secluded spots. The mainstream? No, she hadn't foregone an abortion fifteen years ago to preserve a bright future in the river. Nor had she given up the baby. And she hadn't compromised by marrying a non-medal winner in the husband and father competition who would have required constant concessions by her and Shakti. No, in those ways she hadn't settled one bit, swerving out instead from the traditional promise of the big water - a perfect career life for a single attractive girl followed by the ideal match – no, she'd explored other byways of life.

Not that there wasn't a clear pattern to her existence that one might call 'settled': a comfortable life style as a single mom, a way of being that mostly worked, albeit forsaking vague dreams and aspirations to work internationally. Not that she didn't put forth effort to achieve either; indeed, she'd pushed herself relentlessly to excel at her local nonprofit fundraising work. At thirty-seven, she was by others' standards successful in her choices, weathering the consequences of them daily in good spirits, skilled in her capacity to mother, to work, and to be a solid family member and friend.

And yet, in her meditation, floating in a backwater of slow current seemed to be aging her, the image being an older woman in the kayak. Had she been out of the mainstream too long? She'd been living in her brother Ryan's household in the lower flat for seven years, engaged in collective child raising with his wife Mimi and their two kids. Liv's desire to cross cultures had played out in strange ways as she reflected on comparable harem-like existences throughout the world. Take away the sex of course, and she inhabited a two-mother, one father family. They'd grown so comfortable with it, they joked about it on occasion: the harem, the Mormon polygamist compound, the Muslim man's entitlement to four wives. When Ryan would wax romantic and seek more action in bed than his tired wife might be up for, she'd tease him about the need to add another wife. When Liv would retire from a family gathering upstairs to her apartment below, she'd laugh with Mimi about being the unloved wife, the retired wife who spent her nights alone.

Of course, Liv pursued romantic interests. How long was it now? Two years going on three since Marco had come into her life? It was good. True enough, her early adulation of him for his environmental activist career had waned into a more reasoned respect, accepting less enthusiastically his living in a bedroom he built in his garage while he rented out the house. Yes, there had come a time when Liv's parents' assessment of her downward mobility become more pungent. But the strong connection between Shakti and Marco's son Cezar created a familial context and glue that made a break-up of their parents unthinkable. And the sex was always great - when Marco was focused on her and not totally into the next protest he was organizing.

His ten years seniority over Liv, coupled with their relationship being a third priority to his work and son, she had come to judge as helpful. It provided chunks of time to work longer hours. She'd excelled last year at the YWCA and exceeded the most recent capital campaign's bold multi-million-dollar goal.

Liv picked up the beautifully bound journal she'd bought for this retreat. Handmade and covered in deep blue silk it offered unlined pages to accommodate the images she liked to draw. She sought to capture the stream and the river, adding a small backwater offshoot from her stream where she placed her kayak. The reflective nature of the space prompted questions that she wrote down. *Am I stuck? Or simply settled into patterns that work? Is there something I'm missing out on over there in the river?*

She stretched her arms and pushed herself up, then rubbed her neck as she tilted it to one side and the other. While bending her back backwards and to each side, she looked around the group of twenty who were attending this three-day weekend retreat, fellow travelers in their loose, white and beige comfort clothes, all familiar to her in the precious space of enforced silence.

During this last break, she relished the quiet of not having to share her experience. It was enough to smile at the faces she knew from coming to programs at this spiritual living center for the past months. Yvonne at work suggested she come here about the time Shakti graduated from middle school last spring. While she'd always been an unruly child, for many years the brother/sister, Ryan/Liv, parenting duo had channeled Shakti's strong will into productive behaviors, including helping with Ryan's younger kids. But a fresh undercurrent of anger had surfaced. Shakti had spent a weekend in seventh grade at her girlfriend Natalie's house where she lived with her mom but spent every Sunday with her dad. That bit of normal divorced parenting had fueled an explosion when Shakti returned home: why can't I see my dad like Natalie does?

When Shakti turned fourteen last November, the fireworks really began. She had opinions on everything that she shared at inappropriate times, refusing to back down in losing arguments, and prone to increasing her volume to get her way. Liv could mostly still manage to tap into their deep bond, connect, and nudge her into a better space; but this year had definitely taken a huge toll on Liv's patience, straining her capability for compassion. Marco, who had no interest in exercising the authority of a father, supported Liv, counseled her, and encouraged Cezar to tame Shakti. Which helped. But still. Recalling those rough waters during the program break made Liv wonder, God, why do I think I'm settled or stuck? Shakti is unsettling me on a regular basis. An inner voice emanating from the meditative space was not persuaded: you are aging and getting left behind.

As Liv sat for the last afternoon portion of the retreat, and in an unacknowledged way began her re-entry into real life, her energy changed. There was something unsettling that she needed to deal with when she returned to work.

A new board member at the Y would be her challenge tomorrow. Liv had joined the YWCA staff in 2010, landing a higher paid, more responsible position in fundraising and communication after putting in her years at the Family Multi-Service Center and finishing her grad work in marketing at the University of Washington. She'd opted for that degree with an emphasis on communications instead of going for a nonprofit management certificate at Seattle U. She knew she wasn't leadership material. No, where she excelled was in really identifying with her clients' stories, writing them in engaging ways, and sharing them in fundraisers that caused donors to dig deeper into their resources and give more. She'd even choked up at the last event, recounting a particularly harsh story of a woman they'd rescued out of poverty.

In her time at the Y, she'd moved up to manage the multiplicity of fundraising activities, from direct mail to events to cultivating donor relationships, while learning some management skills in the trenches as she went. She was good at what she did. Executives praised her work, especially most recently on the huge capital campaign to expand their physical facilities for families. No one labored harder at meeting the $40 million goal that included not only donations, but leveraged funds from the city.

Now, a new sun named Ian was dimming the glow of her success. The Board had recruited a handful of fresh members over the summer, and put one of them, a high-level director from Amazon, on the fundraising committee. The guy oozed money, not in his informal dress but in his commentary, and boasted of his wealthy workplace connections. Liv was shocked initially to experience a new controlling force above her, especially a man. She preferred the world of female nonprofit leaders, and he was a new rooster strutting around the hen house, ruffling her feathers. Yet to board members, Ian's presence was desirable. His ability to cultivate new high-tech contributors matched with their vision of building a training site for young women, one with a strong focus on skills useful in the technology field.

The first time Liv saw him, she sensed an aura surrounding him that was trouble inchoate. And so it was playing out. Liv wasn't alone - her whole department was rankling under Ian's latest ideas that were pushing their way out of the Board room into staff meetings. Tomorrow, he was actually sitting in on one, ostensibly to learn more. The department was in an uproar over their fear of a Board member micro-managing staff, and clearly labeled it an 'orientation' session to acquaint Ian with the important work they did. Liv was one of those who had to brief him on operations. She knew already what to expect: the interruptions, the suggestions to try something else, the phony pep talk laying out Ian's version of the training center. While Liv was ready to interview focus groups of clients about the types of training they wanted – she recalled only too well the diverse business successes of women in her former employer's microcredit loan program – Cynthia, her department head, had already warned them to expect a heavy tech training focus for the new site.

Driving home from the meditation center, Liv dreaded tomorrow's session. Yet, pulling up in front of her Phinney Ridge home, her thoughts turned to prepare herself for the vibe she'd be walking into. Would Shakti be sitting doing her homework as she was supposed to be doing this time of day? Would she perhaps have started making dinner, seized by an increasingly rare whim to please her mother? What mood would she be in? Liv reminded herself that she'd just spent the bulk of three days in quiet reflection, and that she needed to bring that spirit of openness and calm into her home.

Halfway down the walk way to their lower level entry, Liv heard Kelly Clarkson beating out Shakti's latest favorite, "Catch my breath…." As Liv entered, no smell of cooking greeted her, nor a

teenager at the table with her laptop doing homework. Her daughter was lying on the worn sofa with her smartphone in her hand, texting. Liv decided not to turn down the short-of-blaring music, at least not first thing.
Oh well, so it goes. "Hi! How was your day, sweetie?"
Shakti finished her text before acknowledging Liv's greeting. Looking up, "Ah, the meditator returns. What wonderful images did you think about today?" The sarcasm was so frequently present these days that Liv integrated it as an annoying pattern structuring their conversations. Pinpricks she refused to let draw blood.
Just ignore it and don't engage. "It was good. Thanks for asking. How did the days with Marco go?"
"Oh, he dragged Cezar and me to a meeting of some Black Lives Matter people."
"That's interesting, usually his meetings are more oriented to the environment."
"He's got so many friends and contacts who are into so many things – he lectured us in the car on the relationship between social justice and environmental justice. We were younger than everyone else so after a while Cezar and I just hung around outside doing our own thing, while people were arguing about where and when to protest."
"Got it." Liv looked around, noticing a book opened on the floor near the sofa. "What have you been reading? Is it homework?"
"English class, it's about a girl raised in Africa." Abruptly coming to life, Shakti sat up. "Here's what I don't get, Mom...."
As the forceful, compelling musical voice energized the room with 'THIS IS MY LIFE!' Liv stiffened at Shakti's lead-in, one of several familiar cues that would raise Liv's defenses in anticipation of attack. "What do you not get?"
"You. And how you've made all these decisions about how I have to live my life."
Liv recalled the day's guidance about breathing deeply. "What decisions do you want to talk about?" Liv counseled herself to keep the conversation focused, specific, and limited to one thing at a time.
"All of them – well, forget that you decided to have me. But why is it I listen to all these kids talk about their divorced parents, and hear – and even sometimes go with them on stuff

with one parent one weekend and the other parent the next - and you won't let me connect with my father? Why? I just don't get it."

"You know the reasons, Shakti. We've talked about this before." They were carefully rehearsed explanations Liv adhered to after seeing a counselor last year. The advice was not to introduce an absent parent at the difficult time of teenage rebellion. Wait until Shakti was at least sixteen, if not eighteen, and more mature and capable of handling all the feelings it would bring up. Like having a father bringing up his other children but not her. Assuming he'd even agree to meet Shakti. The blows to Shakti's esteem could be immense. Liv herself also hated the idea of moving in that direction, preferring that Shakti initiate it when she'd grown up, if that's what she still wanted.

Shakti turned down the music. "Like I'm just not grown up enough to handle it? Give me a break, Mom! Why has it been okay for a little kid to grow up not knowing her father when you know who he is? Look at other kids, my limited number of friends for example, they handle divorce and all kinds of ugly arguments. Adults are always doing bad stuff to kids – yet heaven forbid I should want to face something, then it's like I'm too young and delicate. REALLY? Let's face it Mom, you slept with him and made me. I know that. I've got an unwed single mother, I mean that's worse than divorce. I have to live with that. But I'm not old enough to meet my father?" Shakti was gesturing emphatically, throwing her arms out, picking up things and slamming them down. "Your reasons suck!"

Liv could take the back talk up to a point, when it involved things they did, what they ate, who they spent time with, what they watched, well, mostly everything. But a personal attack quickly diminished her ability to manage the conversation in a constructive way. "Look here..." she began, trying to gauge how real the pain on Shakti's face was. Eye to eye as they were now in height, Liv was confronting a thin, scrawny girl with developing breasts under a tight t-shirt and a head of hair, long and tangled, that suggested she led an untamed life. The haunting blue eyes in a thin caramel colored face were filling with tears. Liv wanted to pull Shakti close, pull back those Irish curls and press their cheeks together.

"I'm waiting." Spear-headed words as pointed as Shakti's glare. Except her glares were never that good because her eyes were just too round for a truly harsh look.

"Let's sit down together."

"I don't want to sit down! I don't want to make nice. Mom, I'm reading a book about a girl brought up in Africa – how come I wasn't brought up in India? Kids at school are flying everywhere with their parents, vacations in Hawaii, trips back to China and Japan. There are airplanes, Mom, like thousands of airplanes going everywhere every day. I could go to India. It's no big deal." She swiveled around and picked up her laptop. "Facetime, Mom! SKYPE. Whatever. There are kids with dads in war zones who get to talk to them on their computers and phones. What's the big fucking obstacle in your mind? Nobody gets it."

"Who did you talk with about this?" Liv came closer, her arms crossed and voice low. "You have no right to be out there talking this up with your friends, making me look…"

"I have NO RIGHT?" With that Shakti threw the laptop at the sofa. "Yes, I'm out there talking to my friends and nobody understands what your problem is. You're beyond weird."

Liv was stunned, her blood pounding as it circled through her body, her mind numbed by the emotional outpour aimed at her. She held the table edge as she lowered herself into the chair. Her instinctive behaviors kicked in. *Shut up. Don't fan the flames. Withdraw.*

"I'm waiting. I can outwait you Mother. You owe me an answer."

Liv reached inside for the personal mantra she'd been coached to craft during the retreat. *Seek light. Create joy.* Her mind was grappling with the sequence of the silent reflective days she'd just spent and the life she walked back into. Tears started to roll down her cheeks.

"Don't do that Mom! Don't cry on me. You know I can't stand it when you cry."

"Then don't look."

A loud, long 'ugh-agh' sound came out of Shakti's mouth. She pounded her feet as a three-year-old might in a temper tantrum. Minutes passed. Shakti sat back down on the couch, stealing looks at her mom. She hated seeing her so upset, she loved her so much. With an exasperated sigh she rose and sat next to Liv at the table, bringing her chair close and hugging her mother. "Okay, I know I shouldn't have said some of those things to you. And it's not like I really talk about this stuff to anyone but

Cezar and Natalie. Well, maybe Sophie too. But Mom, please, honestly...."
 Liv leaned into Shakti's embrace. "I know, sweetie. When you say how crazy it seems to you, I do hear you. I'm getting it. You are more grown up – I mean it's happening so fast, especially with high school now. The world is different than when I was your age." Liv raised her eyes to her daughter's, seeking communion. Arguing about seeing Shakti's father, Liv was reminded, as so many times before, of the mystery of the recessive gene match to hers in Rama's family tree.
 "I already know what you're going to say," Shakti continued in a gentler voice, pulling back and assuming a dreamy face. "Let me think about it." Shakti frowned.
 "I will, honey, I promise, I will think about how you've changed, and we'll talk some more soon. Promise."
 With that, the storm passed, they cooked, ate dinner, and Shakti got on with her homework.

Liv texted Elyse, let's facetime tonight. When they connected, each's first thought crossed in communication. "What's the matter?"
 What Elyse was seeing beyond the still somewhat puffy face and lack of makeup was how Liv's recent haircut was not flattering and made her look like an aging woman who didn't know what the hell to do with curly hair. The droopy waves Liv was re-enforcing each morning either weren't long enough to be sexy, or too tightly done. Her hair color had dulled, and she needed highlights. Liv saw Elyse's extra layer of skin fat that appeared with this her fourth month of pregnancy. And her roots were showing in an unflattering way, which Elyse was determined to endure to protect her baby from chemicals. As though that would do it, Liv would point out in her Marco-inspired bursts of anti-pollution rhetoric. Meanwhile, Elyse was shoveling the food in and packing on the weight.
 Elyse fessed up first. "I just got on the scale this morning – I'm already ten pounds more than I should be. Cory said on Halloween night that I should have just draped some orange cloth over myself and become the Great Pumpkin."
 "Oh, it's not such a big deal. Remember how I was with Shakti, I packed it on early too. It'll all come off."

"Maybe. But you were a lot younger and it's easier then. Plus, you had more leisure time at your folks to breast feed a long time. I'm not sure with work that I'll make it past six months."

"Elyse, just be happy you're finally prego."

She and Cory had been trying for over two years when finally, she conceived. Workaholics and career-focused, their stress levels were usually high and their downtime for relaxing short – assuming they even relaxed together. It took the long planned two-week vacation to the Caribbean to create the desired result. Elyse was in fact grateful, extremely grateful. Her expressed priority of wanting kids had been undercut for years by her own deep, competing priority of building a foundation for a long political career. Finally, she'd reached the point, indeed gone beyond it, where she'd learned what she needed about city hall and county council. She knew all the players and had an enviable web of connections, including most neighborhood leaders. She was in her prime to run for city council. At the same time, she didn't want to press her luck and put off baby-making any longer, the idea being to squeeze one in before her first campaign, and then a few years later, go for number two. As she'd known before they married, Cory would be of little help. Although now that he had several substantial civil rights wins under his belt, he too was established and thinking more expansively about life.

Liv felt so much older than Elyse, especially now that she was pregnant, while Liv had made it through almost fifteen years of parenting. Yet Elyse had been a reliable companion all those years, even as jobs came to consume more time. In her visits since Shakti started high school in September, she bore witness to the ongoing changes in the girl's attitude and language. Elyse was the beneficiary however of the common dynamic where every adult who is not a parent is given credit for more smarts, more cool, and if not that, at least the malleability to be convinced to side with a teen against the parent and help make their arguments.

"I AM happy I'm pregnant." A phony smile appeared which grew into a sincere one. "Very happy. Now I get to share in all your bliss."

"Right, wait till you hear today's attack on me."

"She went after you personally?"

"Oh yeah. I am now this hopelessly weird mother who won't let her meet her father in India. You should have heard her yelling at me about all the airplanes that could take her there, all the facetime she could be having with him, just like all her friends with divorced parents. Who, by the way, she's confided in about this situation."

Elyse grimaced. "Nasty."

"I'm half-tempted just to throw it all back at her, give her what she wants and let my 'sophisticated young woman' – she dropped that one on me last week – let her deal with whatever happens."

"Well…what are you afraid of? You're always so good at cataloguing your litany of fears. I mean obviously he might reject her, that's number one. Could she handle that?"

"It's a big concern. The child psychologist I saw a while back talked about how in these early teen years, they're such a mix of child and adult. What they say is not what they feel necessarily – as if we adults get that right all the time – but the thing is, she thinks she's ready. But if she's not and he says no, it could really affect her development. She may think I screwed up her life, but at least she knows I really wanted her; and no one has ever rejected her. What a blow to her vulnerable female psyche if her dad rejects her."

"In a way I lived some of that with my dad not being around much. It's hard, really hard to overcome that sense of unworthiness. On the other hand, it made me an over-achiever compared to others."

"Yeah, well, next on my list of fears, say we get beyond that, he doesn't reject her. I take her to India, we go to meet him. Rama's married with sons, Elyse. Arita says his wife is very sweet. He's not going to tell her. We'd have to meet on the side. Somehow."

"That's not so bad really, is it? Cleaner."

Liv didn't know how to say the next thing, so paused.

"So, what else?"

"Okay, I know this is selfish. But what about me having to be there. I always imagined I'd help set it up when she was eighteen or older and she'd travel alone. I don't like that I'd have to go too."

"Why? Afraid you'd get re-attracted?"

"A little, I mean I don't think about him really at all, I haven't since the first few years. Why do I have to expose myself to him now?"

"Especially with that bad hair you've got right now."
Elyse could never resist.

Liv stuck her tongue out across their virtual space.

"Liv, you can deal with that. We've all changed. He'll have grown into someone you hardly relate to. And you'll feel for the wife and kids." Elyse checked her battery. "Hey, let me plug in, I'm almost out of charge."

"Then there's one other thing which is as hard as him rejecting her."

"That she rejects you because he's the amazing one now?"

"Exactly. The counselor said it was preferable to not interject a missing parent until after the worst of the rebellious years pass. Seizing on Rama - who God knows, might give her encouragement, gifts - attaching to him while I'm still the bad parent enforcing homework, curfews, and discipline, that could shift her loyalties. It would hurt, big time. It's been hard enough this past year without bringing him into our quarrels."

"I get that. Teens can be manipulative and given Ms. Shakti's track record in that sport, yeah, it's a real fear."

"So what do I do?"

Elyse, the continually decisive partner in their friendship was quiet. A rare response surfaced: "Keep thinking about it. Maybe something else needs to happen to help you decide."

"Like what?"

"I have no idea. But focus on it as you are so good in doing, and I bet something new will happen to move your thinking."

Liv was skeptical. "It's just weird to hear you say that."

"Yeah, well, hey, I've got to go. Cory just came in. I'll call soon, or you call me."

"Ciao."

That evening as Liv studied her image in the mirror, wondering what to do next with her hair, she realized she hadn't given any more thought to the big meeting tomorrow. That meant getting to work early to do another round of psychological prepping. All her materials were ready, it was just the dealing with Ian issue that she wanted to brace herself for.

She knocked on Shakti's door, knowing she'd still be awake, either with a book or her phone.

"What? I'm almost asleep."

Liv peeked in to Shakti's room, no longer a place of sunshine as it'd been in the first years, but with two red walls now covered with posters ready to peel off and littered on the floor with books and props from plays. Liv called it 'the dive.' Shakti scrambled to hide the phone and scoot under her sheet.

"Sorry, I just wanted to let you know I'll be leaving extra early tomorrow. So don't ignore your alarm. I'll let Mimi know too, and she can come down and make sure you're up, okay? And I'll leave some breakfast out on the counter."

"Okay." As Liv started to back out, Shakti said in a soft embarrassed voice, "Mom, aren't you going to give me a kiss goodnight?"

Liv welcomed the chance to revert to a loving routine that was growing out of style. As they snuggled in a hug, Shakti volunteered, "Mom, I know it's a really big deal to decide about meeting my father, it is scary, sometimes to me. But let's talk it through again, okay?"

"For sure. And I'll be thinking about it."

Monday, November 9

She arrived early as planned at the downtown headquarters of the YWCA. An old brick building centrally located in the city, it showed its age, appearing dowdy compared to all the newer highrise construction surrounding it. Sitting in her tiny ninth floor office – no remodeling expense spent here to create a cubicle environment – she used her quiet time and space to review her PowerPoint one more time and mentally prepare herself to be challenged. She and her boss Cynthia agreed that the most compelling way to brief a newcomer to the Y's Board on the operations of fundraising and development was to tell the story of what was both their most recent and largest success story: the Family Village project. It demonstrated how a well thought-out, three-year plan had been followed, including major events interfaced with direct mail using their long list of past generous donors, and networking in more personal ways by gathering their input and feedback in mixed focus groups with clients. Those had been highly successful as the donors enjoyed the personal contact and listening to the women's stories of how the Y had helped them and could do even better in the future, while the women clients had enjoyed the attention and being listened to. In short, Liv's department had been outstandingly effective.

But facing her was not some warm, fuzzy, gushing new board member. She and Cynthia knew they would be encountering a different mindset than what they were accustomed to. Neither was a stranger to the news stories of Amazon's culture and operations. Amazon which had gobbled up south Lake Union to create tech sweat shops populated by predominantly 'brogrammers', often young Chinese men who then rented nearby 'apodments' of dorm-room size and ate every meal at their desks or nearby restaurants. Those who lasted and were not part of the disposable people syndrome, those who made it to some higher level of management and operations, they had the real money, due to their success in a culture shaped heavily by fear and greed. Liv heard stories from her mom and dad, who'd spent decades at Microsoft and in consulting work with tech clients, stories followed by their 'Thank God, we're out of it' remarks as they both retired. Both were used to the techie culture, but as her dad consulted occasionally or subcontracted with Amazon, he'd say, 'it's brutal, I'm so glad I don't have to make a living there.' Her mom had worked with some of Amazon's disposable people, the ones who only lasted a year. They seemed to be marked for life by the experience, grateful to be out of it and into a more civil culture, and yet tempted to get ahead by importing tactics and behavior they'd experienced. Katherine said it was like transplanting a liver and watching the system accept or reject the new organ. Her fear remained that as the disposables streamed out of Amazon, over time the entire tech environment in Seattle would become polluted. She and Gary once had imagined moving back into the city from Redmond when they retired, but for now there was so much change rolling through the city, they decided to wait longer to watch the scene shake out. Cynthia heard similar accounts from her brother-in-law who worked at Oracle and would shake his head in amazement at the fifty thousand new employees Amazon was bringing into Seattle.

    That was Ian's environment. A successful manager of cloud-based projects, he'd adapted well to the culture. He'd chosen the Y for his philanthropy due to his sister's own impoverished beginnings, the sister who'd raised him. The Y had given her help when she needed it; now she ran the IT department of the largest bank in town overseeing thousands of workers. First, he'd been a sizeable donor to the Y; and then he'd given a decent speech at an event about why he gave and felt so strongly about helping young women make it in the world. The Board Chair invited him to join them, undoubtedly for his monied connections.

    The pep talk Liv delivered to herself was to stay grounded in her story, and to take non-verbal cues from Cynthia if there were hiccups. If Ian came on strong on an issue where Liv disagreed – because they fully anticipated that he would attempt to micromanage them – she would find a polite way to acknowledge it without obsequiously agreeing.

    Cynthia decided against bringing along the entire department team, so only Liv's counterpart in communications, Kevin, a sweet young gay guy, and the Hispanic public relations guru, Cristina, were joining them. Each had a well-prepared presentation. As they walked upstairs to the conference room where they were meeting Ian, Cynthia connected with each one of them expressing her confidence and support. All of them had briefly met Ian at the event where he spoke, but Cynthia who attended Board meetings had the most experience observing him in action. Hence, she warned about 'rough going,' but shared her husband's joke that it was hardly the clash of civilizations, simply different approaches to setting goals and work plans.

Ian was in the dated conference room already, his face focused on his Samsung. He looked up as they entered. Liv's first reaction was shit, this is trouble. She sometimes reacted to people's auras, and boy, did his make her uncomfortable. It wasn't just the bald, close-shaved head look that she disliked intensely, nor the smallish dark eyes set in an overweight face on a thick neck atop a maroon t-shirt. She knew without looking he had khaki knee-length cargo pants on, bulging calves and flip flops despite the cooler weather. She hated the look. But it wasn't really that at all – just more that she felt in personal danger.

The staff looked silly as they were all dressed professionally, out of respect for his position. Everyone got situated around Ian, Cynthia across from him, while Liv set up her laptop at the front of the room.

"Just need to finish this text," Ian said moving his fingers rapidly. "God, the one day I don't show up at the crack of dawn, things start heading south." Cristina stiffened, bristling at the political incorrectness of it. Well, at least she's feeling it too, thought Liv.

When he finally laid his phone on the table in front of him, Cynthia smiled and launched, first noting the sanctioning of this untoward mixture of staff and board member by their Executive Director Maureen Larson. Cynthia had pushed back on this, but Maureen had insisted because the Board Chair was making nice to Ian. "I understand Ian that you want to contribute your efforts to our next campaign for the training center, and that you wanted to get a handle on how we operate."

Ian pushed back into the chair, tipping it slightly on its back legs. "Yeah, exactly. I've got a lot of friends in hi-tech who have money and I want to see some of that come here."

"That's great and exciting to hear. And we know that training in technology jobs will be a huge piece of the new center's operations, so this is a perfect match."

"Right."

"I asked my key staff to brief you on what we do, and how we do it. Liv Anderson will be leading off. I think you met briefly at an event last year."

Ian looked at her, not recognizing her, probably because of the haircut. "Not sure. But nice to meet you Liv. That's Swedish right?"

"Yes, yes it is."

"I went to Stockholm once on a big job. Nice place."

Liv was anxious to get this over with, and her usual calm demeanor looked rattled to those who knew her. "I know your time is valuable so what I pulled together were a few slides to illustrate how we exceeded our goals in our last campaign that raised over $40 million."

Ian interjected, "If you exceeded your goals, maybe you set them too low to begin with." A statement, not a question.

Liv dodged that bullet and stepped aside with her clicker, so he could see the slides. "It all began with focus groups with both our clients and our donors to talk about what the facility should be." The slide showed an enthusiastic group, mostly women seated in a large circle. "Board members of course looked at all the data we gathered and from there constructed a tentative set of specifications for the architectural firm to work on. Next…"

"Probably in this case we can move faster. A tech training center is a tech training center."

Liv hated being interrupted. It wasn't part of any work culture she'd been in. And it made her lose track of her prepared remarks. She took a deep breath and turned a bit to face him more. She made herself look into those beady eyes with as much civility as she could. "I'm sure that's true. And we're also interested in non-tech training opportunities we can provide. For example, I used to support a micro-credit program…"

"Why would you want to move women into small, low paying work when you can give them tech skills they can use to make real money?"

Liv paused looking at Cynthia who had her eyes down at that moment, gathering her own thoughts. "Well, not every woman we help wants to get into that kind of career…"

"So you can always have a couple of smaller rooms to help them in some other way, but honestly, a lot of those things they get into with micro-credit go nowhere."

Liv was visualizing the kitchen she'd hoped would be part of the center. A lot of the women she knew from the Washington CASH program had wanted to market jams, sauces, cookies, and spice mixes. Having a real test kitchen would be so encouraging for them. She'd imagined guest chefs coming in too to help them with low-cost nutritious meals. She'd also wondered if they should have a basic lab to introduce them to the biotech industry. Or a small gym maybe to train personal trainers?

"Liv, why don't you move on to some of the other things we did in the campaign?" Cynthia looked at her with a supportive smile.

Ian looked at his smartphone. "Just a minute, I need to get this." He rose and stepped to a corner of the room and had a brief commanding exchange, then returned to the table, with a "Sorry, it couldn't wait."

"Sure," Cynthia countered, thinking let's just get him out of here. "How much time do you have? Each of the staff prepared a ten-minute presentation on what we do."

"Honestly, I get the event piece. You get a lot of rich people in a room, serve them food and alcohol, and ask them to pony up. What else is there?"

Liv jumped in. "Actually, there are a couple of other areas that take quite a bit of time and effort. One is all the individual meetings with really key donors, and the other is all the direct mail..."

"Junk mail? Really, do you think anyone reads that stuff? Nobody I know is going to open an envelope and give because of some words on a page. You have to use social media." In a snarkier voice, he added, "You DO use social media, don't you?"

Liv's face was gaining color. Her Irish genes were starting to emerge from their DNA encoding. "Yes, of course we do. AND about ten percent of our goal was reached through traditional mail going to the Y's substantial base of older donors who aren't into Twitter or Instagram or Facebook."

Ian sat back again, looking at Liv hard. "Why would you put all that manpower and cost into mail, when with one good introduction to the right person, you could get it all in a fifteen-minute meeting?"

Liv was infuriated, ready to punch his lights out for all the rude interruptions, and for trying to nail her in front of others. *The guy's a bully.* She couldn't totally squelch a certain sharp edginess coming over her, raising the pitch of her voice, and narrowing her eyes to sharp slits. "You probably aren't aware being new to the Board that the Y is one of Seattle's oldest community organizations – women in this city love us."

Cynthia knew she had to rescue this situation and drew on her calming skill to retake the reins at this point. "Yes, there's no reason to leave money on the table so to speak, and many of these people would actually be hurt not to be included. They like having their name in publications showing they gave. They like feeling part of our family."

Ian looked at her as though she were an alien needing deportation. "Look, I don't have endless time to give this. I know what we need to build, and I can get most of the money, if not all, you need. If you want..." he paused looking back at Liv, "lf you want to diddle around wasting time on the Y's budget, well so be it. But I can make this work if you get out of my way. We could even set up..." Ian looked toward Kevin, the young communications guy, "What's your name again?"

"Kevin."

"Kevin, you get social media I'm sure. So we could set you up in a cubicle at Amazon and get going right away." Ian cocked his eye, turning to Cynthia for approval. Suppressing her shock as best she could, her eyes saying 'unbelievable,' she forced her mouth to say, "Let me talk about it with our ED." She desperately wanted Ian gone now. "Thanks for your time this morning. We get how busy you are."

"Sure." He checked his phone again. "Yeah, I've got to go." With that he rose, nodded his head to them and left the room with a "Think about my offer."

They were all stunned. Liv closed the laptop and leaned forward towards her boss. "Evil, really evil."

Cynthia swiveled her head toward her. "That attitude is not going to help us."

That hurt. Liv felt tears coming. She picked up her computer and excused herself quietly, returning quickly to her office, holding herself back from slamming the door.

The tears slithered out of her eyes down her hot cheeks. She peeled off her long flowing sweater. "Shit. Fuck that bastard!" No one had ever treated her like that before. Except that jerk she'd dated years ago, Eric.

She pulled out her phone to call her mom, but Cynthia opened the door, closed it again, and sat in the chair next to Liv's desk. "That was the worst experience in my fifteen years here. Actually, the worst experience in my professional life."

Liv resisted firing back that her attitude was not going to help them. She knew inside that Cynthia was every bit as disturbed by Ian as she was. "What an asshole – I can't imagine putting up with that every day."

"Yeah, it's really scary that that's what success looks like today."

"I did my best to be respectful, to not be confrontational, despite his despicably rude behavior."

"I know. You did fine." Cynthia became quiet and leaned back in the chair.

"What do we do now?" Liv wanted to resign on the spot. No way would she put up with this guy telling them how to do their jobs.

"I honestly don't know. I can't let him run this campaign. Even incorporating an on-the-site link is dangerous. We could wind up with two separate processes that collide. I need to talk to Maureen about this. But first, I need to let the reality soak in, to think some on it. I've got to solve this, and then sell my solution to Maureen before he takes her and the Board over." She rose and placed her hand on Liv's shoulder and squeezed it. "Let's talk again Thursday morning after I'm back from my Spokane trip over Veterans' Day."

Liv's phone buzzed with a text from her mom. "What's up? I'm grocery shopping." Liv didn't know what to tell her now. All of a sudden, her job went to hell and she saw the devil. *My job as I knew it is over.* Liv texted back for Katherine to call when she got home. Then she checked next on her message thread to Marco, asking to come over for dinner that night, saying she needed to get her bearings.

As her glance turned to her desktop screen, she saw the stickie she'd placed on it just this morning, 'See light, create joy.' Had she been in an alternative universe these past days? How could she have felt like she was in a peaceful backwater as life passed her by? Her life was tumultuous now as though a flash flood had ripped through her valley and thrust her into some rough water crashing around rocks. And then yesterday, Shakti too, challenging her, rocking her boat. *It's more like I'm in the rapids now!* Forces were pushing her into the unknown faster than she could paddle, that's the new image she would have drawn today in her journal.

The phone buzzed with Marco's response: "Sure, come over, but bring something to eat as I don't have much at home. I want to hear all about your retreat."

Ancient history now.

Liv and Shakti parked near Marco's driveway leading to his Ballard house. Even the short trip up the walkway chilled her weakened immune system. Liv had filled Shakti in on having a totally bad day, and fortunately, she was more subdued, focused on memorizing lines for a skit she and Cezar were creating for their drama class at Ballard High School. Liv had left work early to make a sweet potato stew they could all enjoy, including Marco's long-time tenants, Mike and Angela.

Liv and Shakti ate most of their dinners with family or pseudo-family, either at home with Mimi, Ryan and their kids, or here with Marco, Cezar and his renters, now friends. People traded off cooking and cleanup which suited them all and ensured dinners were a lively event that kept them all connected.

What a surprise it had been three years ago when Katherine's prediction that Liv would meet a single dad at school materialized. Shakti and Cezar made it happen once they realized that they were destined to be friends, indeed feeling more like brother and sister. Cezar valued a trustworthy confidante whom he could talk to about his sexual preferences, which at this point seemed open, except maybe he really was gay and not bi. For now, it wasn't a big deal to him, compared to writing, acting, and having fun with friends. Cezar with his engaging personality was popular at school, into plays, improvisation, and music. Her creative side responded to him. She was choosy about friends, and perhaps because of her missing father, she valued all her family relationships above the ebb and flow of most girlfriends. Some saw her as aloof, snobby. She'd say, not true, just focused on the people who mean the most to me. Hanging out with a cute guy had boosted her status in others' eyes, removed her from some of the daily pettiness of their social media, and helped her rise above it. The successful introduction of their single parents meant Cezar had an especially important place in her life. And he came with fun, while his dad was a caring match for her mom. Shakti and Cezar even discussed the marriage possibility between their parents and how great it would be if all of them lived together.

In contrast, every time Katherine and Gary, Liv's parents, were around Marco they would give each other 'the look.' His activist career was of small interest to them. What they disapproved of was his lifestyle and the narrow comfort it would provide to their beloved daughter over the long term. They had a point.

Not so many years ago, but before Marco came into Liv's life, he'd worked as a sonar salesman pitching products to commercial fishermen in Latin America and negotiating with fishing fleets. His native Spanish birth coupled with his London School of Economics degree crafted strong credentials. But, from the outset, Marco had opted for an alternative lifestyle, first trying to make eco-agriculture work in a corrupt Nicaragua. There he married a Sandinista and fathered Cezar. As corruption made his efforts futile, he changed direction and resettled in Seattle, where his American grandmother lived. His mom, while on a foreign study program in Spain had met his dad, a transplanted Italian. Their sons were as sleekly good looking as Italian designed cars, and their daughter as chic as a designer's dress from Milan. Marco's soft wavy hair, tawny skin, and kind and sympathetic brown eyes made the heart of any woman flutter just to look at him. His strong values about the environment would not be suppressed. He hated selling sonar equipment and once his son was in middle school and his ex-wife transplanted too, with financial stability in her life as a nurse, Marco quit his job to follow his passion. He rearranged his own financial obligations made even more pressing by the rising rate of his subprime mortgage and chose to instill his values into every aspect of his life.

Thus, the room in the garage. Cezar's room was in the house, but the rest of it was rented out to people who shared Marco's commitment to sustainable living. Mike and Angela had settled in successfully and been there over two years now. Together they planted vegetable gardens in the large front yard, raised chickens in the backyard until the neighbors complained, and used a solar cooker for some meals. They deleted red meat from their diets and focused on their eggs, produce, tofu, and fruits and vegetables, frequently experimenting with specialty foods carried by the co-op.

Marco built community in the neighborhood, getting people involved in tree plantings, collective gardens, and joining with one, then another, in protests against environmental degradation. His hope initially was that his activities would find some organic connection to paying work he believed in. For now, he was part of a small group of community supported organizers who were able to modestly translate others' respect and admiration for commited activism into monthly online contributions.

His arrest record was impressive and boasted good company: police had taken him and other protesters, including George Clooney, his dad, and elderly nuns, off to be booked one time in D.C. Other media coverage included the Occupy protests, the Keystone Pipeline protest, the hazardous railroad freight protests, and most spectacularly, garnering New York Times coverage, the kayaker protest in Seattle's harbor against the Shell drilling rig being sent to the Arctic Sea. 'Shell No!' it was called. He'd exhausted himself in the organizing effort and the battle was still on-going. Liv and Shakti had been there among the kayakers supporting the effort.

This week Marco granted himself some time off, at least in the evenings. Assuming people whose causes he supported didn't decide suddenly to throw a meeting.

As Liv walked towards the front door, she passed the remains of the vegetable garden soon to be victim to the first frost. Stepping into the sixties home with big picture windows, the interior was a cross between what her mom would have called hippie living and functionality. Next to dated poster art were plants suspended from the ceiling in macramé baskets. Attention had been given to creating tidy spaces that worked for small group seating areas you might see in a café.

Holding her inner turmoil in check, she knew it wouldn't be till later that she could speak freely with Marco alone in his garage abode. They met in the kitchen where he was setting the table and cooking some brown rice for the casserole. Putting it down, he welcomed her arms around his waist. "Hi."

Laughing lightly, Marco could tell she'd had an emotional day as he took in her tense, serious and heavy looking features. "What happened? You went to a meditation retreat that I really want to hear about – I imagined you'd float in here, not look so down." Already his lightly accented melodic voice began its soothing magic.

"I'm disturbed, deeply disturbed. So please, can we have some time alone tonight?"

"Of course, let's take a walk around the neighborhood right after dinner."

Shakti and Cezar were happy to hang out and practice their skit once dinner was over. Marco and Liv had no responsibility to clean up, so they were out the door quickly after the peach cobbler dessert he'd made. They'd picked those peaches together and canned a basketful for the winter.

"Tell me. I don't want you to burst." Marco conveyed both sympathy and detachment in a way that made people think he was wise. At forty-six, he had almost ten years on Liv. His libido was more – what? Controlled? Regulated? In service to the rest of his life? It made their separate communal lifestyles more doable somehow. Life was about people and issues and the kids, not making each time together about sex. Letting the kids be happy with them came first. They fit in their love-making organically as it might happen with a couple married for years.

Liv had already done the Ian tirade once with Katherine by phone, and a truncated version with Mimi at home before they left for Marco's. In talking it through, her thoughts began to settle. "So, basically, we have this new board member, Ian from Amazon..." Marco nodded his head in recognition of what that meant "...and he wants to micro-manage our next campaign to raise money for a women's training center. Besides being incredibly rude to me in front of Cynthia and the team, constantly interrupting me, he thinks he knows better than the women we help what they need, that they should all become techies, and go out and compete with all those single-minded tech assholes who eat each other alive. Forget our women have kids, forget they may not even like computers, and forget they are people with their own lives and interests. The guy is an insult to humanity."

"Wow. Not the people I usually meet at your fundraisers. Why is he even on the Board?"

Liv turned to face him squarely under a street light. "Money. Pure and simple. He gave a bundle and he knows people who will give bundles too. It infuriates me to think we would change who we are to meet his demands."

"What kind of demands?" He took his hand from hers and laid his arm on her shoulder as they began walking again.

"He thought I was worthless so get rid of me for one thing. He wants to run the fundraising out of a cubicle at Amazon with Kevin manning it."

"Cynthia will never agree to that. You know that. What is she saying?"

"I'll hear tomorrow. She was as upset as me."

"I'll bet." They walked a way further till they hit more trafficked streets and then turned around. Liv cringed with the dampness which counteracted her intention to breathe and calm down.

"So there went your retreat, I suppose. Is there anything from it you can use or hang on to?"

"I came up with a mantra, 'seek light, create joy.'" No life left in that, she mentally observed.

"Nice."

When they arrived back, the kids were still going at it with changing lines, laughing, and being silly. After boiling some tea water and scraping clean the cobbler dish, Marco and Liv headed for his room. The garage could generously hold two cars and a work space, providing room for Marco to construct a fifteen by fifteen room set in the back corner. The rest of the building was filled with tools, camping equipment, and left-over wood from constructing raised veggie gardens, the chicken coop, and his room. They all parked their cars in the driveway. He'd created a raised carpeted floor and ceiling for the enclosed room and put in electric heating. Two windows looked out on the back deck and trees behind them. The furnishings were all used, but pleasant. What caught attention were all the artifacts from Marco's life, activities, and protests that formed the décor on the amber colored walls: one area by the computer desk had blow-ups of him getting arrested. The kayak protest photos overlay older ones now. There were a few of Liv and Shakti with him and Cezar. Above the futon sofa was a large banner from the Occupy movement: 'we are the 99%.' Near his new double bed in one corner – recently Liv made him upgrade the mattress by making him take her old one and buying a new expensive airbed for herself – there were baskets, hats, and weavings from Central America hanging on the wall along with the iconic Che poster. It was here, gradually, that Liv had learned about much of Marco's history, simply by choosing an object or photo and saying, tell me about it. She was especially fond of poems and sayings he had pinned up in a scattered fashion. Next to the computer was a poem by Goethe that attracted her yet once again, both identifying with it and feeling it challenge her current status quo.

"Whatever you can do, or dream you can, begin it.

Until one is committed there is hesitancy, the chance to draw back, always ineffectiveness.

Concerning all acts of initiative there is one elementary truth, the ignorance of which kills countless ideas and endless plans.

That the moment one definitely commits oneself then providence moves too.

All sorts of things occur to help one that would never have otherwise occurred.

A whole stream of events issue from the decision, raising in one's favor all manner of unforeseen incidents, and meetings and material assistance which no man could have dreamed would come his way.

Whatever you can do, or dream you can, begin it. Boldness has genius, power and magic in it.

Begin it now.

But I have no dream, do I, was her reaction tonight, only the need to cope. "There's something else that came up too that I need your advice on."
"What's that?"
"When I arrived home yesterday - I can't believe it was only yesterday – Shakti launched a major attack on me about meeting her father."
Marco's body energy shifted as did his torso to watch her more closely. He'd guessed this was coming. When they'd met at the Salish Sea event that the kids cleverly had brought each of them to, all either knew of the other was the parental relationship

to their child's friend. Liv had dragged her feet about going to an enviro group event, always fearing she'd run into her college boyfriend Devin that she'd walked out on when she was pregnant by Rama. Actually, she'd kicked Devin out of her life. He was married now, as was his best friend Steve who was leading the 'become-a-father-trek' among the old climbing group that included Cory, Elyse's husband – and which meant less time for real trekking.

With her guard up, she went to the event at Gasworks Park north of Lake Union on a Saturday afternoon. The kids had planned the meet up point so that within minutes of arriving, she was looking up into a pair of soft brown eyes which caused her protective shield to fall. Marco had laughed, "At last, I get to meet the incredible Shakti's mother!"

As outings of the foursome grew in regularity, Liv knew she was falling for Marco but hid her feelings behind a concern of Shakti's crush on Cezar. If Shakti was having a first puppy love interest as she approached twelve, Liv was not about to complicate it by her own actions. Most of that middle school year passed with them all growing closer and more comfortable with each other. Marco had just quit his job and was totally absorbed in his personal quest to create the future he wanted. He'd been attracted to Liv from the first, finding her womanly in a way that was more mature and thoughtful than other American girls he'd met, more global in her interests, and very sympatica in her work with others.

As Shakti and Cezar's relationship turned more familial, Liv considered inviting Marco into her life. She became flirtatious in her remarks, wore sexier clothes around him, and made dinners at her place a regular part of their week.

However sweaty or rumpled Marco might appear after a protest, his innate elegance made his moves graceful. When it became clear to him that Liv was inviting him to touch her, his instinctive moves were assuring and gentle: a touch of her elbow first, a hand on her back as they moved through a crowd, an arm around the back of the sofa where she sat after dinner. When the kids were nearby in another room, a sweet stolen kiss. It was only when Ryan and Mimi took a three day get-away leaving Jeff and Margot in Liv's care, that Shakti and Cezar took control of the upstairs house, and they all worked out a night of mutual non-interference. Liv and Marco had her unit to themselves. Amid laughs and a few worries, Liv finally relaxed into love-making with Marco that was skillfully attuned to each other's thoughts and needs. When Elyse probed about their blossoming love affair, Liv would blush and giggle, and deliver her signature sunray smile that had been missing in action for years. Elyse exploded, "At last, a real Latin lover who's glued to Seattle!"

Liv and Marco matched their strides and interests to each other's gait in life, as can happen in a mature relationship. Each had been content with brief accounts of how the other's child had come into the world – how is it that Shakti is half-Indian? Why are you and your ex, Claudia, no longer together? They moved on from those inquiries with no further consideration. Here they were, an incredible foursome that met a full spectrum of needs for love, community, and enjoyment.

When Liv brought up Shakti's demand to meet her father, 'the attack,' Marco was unperturbed and sympathetic. Neither he nor Liv tried or were interested in being surrogate parents to each other's child. That worked well for everyone, not only because Claudia was very present in Cezar's life, but also because it never occurred to Marco to be anything other than a caring adult in Shakti's life.

"That must have hurt for sure." He cuddled with her on his bed. "But...do you really object to her meeting her father? I don't really know the situation as we've had no reason to talk about it before."

His soft, smooth ways kept Liv's defenses subdued, so that she too could think more objectively. "I'm not sure what I think. I've promised her to reconsider my position that now is not the right time."

"You'd prefer waiting then, not really standing in the way of it?"

"Right. I'd been of a mind that it would be better when she's eighteen, graduated, more emotionally developed. I'd like her to have more of a sense of power within herself."

"Hmm. I understand that. What do you know, if anything about how her father would react?"

"Only a little." Liv pushed herself up now as the topic pushed out any desire for physical connection in the moment. "Before she was born, I sent him a letter telling him I was pregnant, and that whether I kept the baby or gave it up, I wanted him to know in real time that a child of his existed." Liv appreciated Marco's deep interest as he held her in a steady gaze. "He responded. I have a letter from him in a sealed envelope that says, 'for my child.'"

"That's amazing. Really wonderful, when you think about it. That recognition. Have you read the letter?"

"No, so I just don't know what kind of reception she'd get from him. Plus, it's fifteen years later. He's married, has a wife and kids."

"Yes, but the fact that he didn't ignore your letter, that he wrote back a letter FOR HIS CHILD – to my mind, there's only one meaning to it." Liv was wide-eyed concentrating on what he said. "A man doesn't write 'to my child' unless there's something very sweet in the letter. Accepting. Most likely, offering assistance whenever she needs it."

"You're that sure about it?"

"Yes, definitely. It would be very affirming for Shakti to read it."

"And then what? What if you're right – although I worry about the passage of time – but what if you're right and then she says, I want to meet him now?"

"Is now a problem?"

Liv sat back against the wall that bordered the bed. She was quiet. For the first time, she began to relax with the situation. *Shakti won't be rejected. We'd set up the logistics through Arita. I'd see him and so what? I've got Marco. What could happen that would be so bad?* "What if she meets him and then is hurt that he's with his other children, but not her? Or what if she gets these ideas that she'd rather live with him than me? You know how the unobtainable can look better than your current reality. What then?"

Marco embraced her and quieted her into a laying position, pressing their bodies together, melding into one. "Then you would keep on being the wonderful mother you are. You'd see her through all the challenges. And, even if she attacks you again, as I know she can do at this age, when it all settles out? She'll be fine. She'll love you as much as she always has." With that he petted down her hair and brushed her eyelids with his lips. "Love requires openness for the beloved to breathe...and the lover's capacity to adapt."

Liv lay quiet, reflecting, then kissed him softly and whispered, "Let's pull the curtains closed, and lock the door."

When he returned to her, she said, "I have to tell you one more thing about my retreat. Even when I supposedly meditated, my body would get energized and I'd want you so much."

A quick routine worked for nights like this when they had to get back to the kids. As they dressed again, Marco raised a travel topic they'd been discussing for months. The idea was that she and possibly Shakti would join him and Cezar to visit his parents in Madrid over Thanksgiving. Liv and Marco would then go to the Climate Conference in Paris together, leaving the kids in Madrid for a few days. "Where are you on coming on the trip? You really need to decide if you want to get decently priced tickets."

Liv had barely focused on it, despite her initial enthusiasm. She was embarrassed she hadn't checked fares in at least ten days. "Marco, I've been so out of it with the retreat, and Shakti's attack, and now this thing at work, I need to see if any cheap deals are out there – except what if I need to change my job? I'm so sorry, right now I feel like a pinball that's just been bouncing off the boards, a little out of control."

"I understand, and it's not too late to decide unless the airfares skyrocketed. You know my parents would love to show you two Madrid."

Liv had met them several times now on their visits to Seattle where Marco's mother was from. Sadly, one time when the grandmother died; other times when they liked to escape the hot Spanish summers. Cezar had already been to Spain over ten times and wanted to show Shakti his favorite places. But now, Liv was already moving on to potential expenses if they went to meet Rama. "I'd love to see them too. And see Spain. And experience the conference protest with you." She looked lovingly at him, touching his face. "The money is potentially an issue now. Let me check fares tonight. I'll decide by Shakti's birthday party this Saturday."

Ann Beltran

Thursday, November 12

Liv walked into work the next day sporting a new protective shell both literally, her forest green fall coat purchased yesterday at a holiday sale, and figuratively, in terms of fresh thoughts about dealing with Ian. Placing her tired leather purse in a low desk drawer, she vowed to continue upgrading her appearance this winter. Liv headed down the hall to Cynthia's. They'd agreed to wait to meet until this morning to provide soak time on the 'Ian problem' and accommodate Cynthia's mid-week travel to visit with YWCA staff in Spokane. The door was open, her boss looked up. "I know what we need to do. At least for now."

Cynthia was an inclusive director who always welcomed staff input. "Me too. You say your idea first."

"So, it hit me this morning. If we follow our basic project timeline as with the building we just finished, there's got to be at least six months, likely more, at the front end when the joint Board and staff committee look for the site. We know that finding space in Seattle that's well-served by public transit, centrally located – or maybe not, depending on our assessment of users - that all takes time. And just like last time, I can be running focus groups on potential users to develop our understanding of needs to be served. Fundraising like Ian talked about won't even begin until we know the site expenses, have an estimate of the facility costs, and set a campaign, goal, right?"

"Absolutely. My thoughts exactly. For now, Ian is a blip on the radar screen. He probably won't think about us for three months until the next Board meeting. By then, Maureen and the Executive Committee members, along with the site selection committee, will already be at work and making their first report to the full Board of Directors. They'll put Ian in his place on the timeline." Cynthia paused and came around her desk to stand near Liv. "But one thing, we should take him up on his offer to have a fundraising link to Amazon when the time is right."

Liv's mouth turned down.

"I know. Kevin came in here yesterday afternoon and offered to do that, which I think would be great. Why not give it a try? United Way embeds a partner in some organizations for a few weeks? And Kevin actually thinks it would be a growth

experience for him to get inside Amazon for a while and see firsthand what our up and coming wealthy audience reacts to."
    Liv liked the idea of reconnaissance too but felt protective of Kevin. Hanging out in the female-dominated environment of the Y seemed to suit Kevin's personality, but it didn't offer him any opportunities to meet other guys. Her image of the typical Amazon guy however was not what she thought Kevin deserved. *Stop being motherly!* "Okay, I see the value in that too." A tremor of anxiety followed: what if Kevin wound up being the hero of this fundraising campaign and Liv was sidelined? Would he be the center of Board accolades and supportive praise they showered upon her last time around? Is one new Board member all it would take to undermine her role? No way though that she would be the Amazon contact, that was very clear.
    "What? You look uneasy. We've got a good handle on this now." Cynthia intuited Liv's concern. "Honestly, we need your magic in understanding our clients and matching their needs with our large donors. I want to get on with the first story about this for our next quarterly newsletter, okay?"
    The compliment elicited Liv's positive energy and she mustered a hearty, "Sure, I'll get on it."
    Returning to her office, her body sensed unsteady ground beneath it. Yes, the Ian thing was a blip that had to be respected and dealt with. They had a reasonable plan to do that. And with any luck, Maureen and other Board members would soften his edges a bit – or be as alienated as she was by the guy. As she started to draft the introductory story on the new campaign, she couldn't mask to herself that her energy for the project was diluted. She'd been in the working environment long enough to learn an important lesson - plus hearing it too from her parents, and even now Elyse: success on the job comes and goes. Just when you think you have a great team, someone leaves, a new energy joins the group, and the team has to renew itself. What worked three years ago won't necessarily work anymore: you need to constantly adapt to changes around you. Liv had a good run with the last campaign, but that was yesterday's victory. *Isn't it enough I have Shakti to deal with, why do I have to be stressed at work too? What if Ian becomes a Board hero?*
    She attempted to focus on the newsletter story to get the evil one off her brain. She searched for the campaign story she'd done four years ago. As she read it on her monitor she

experienced that familiar sensation of liking her own writing. She'd had such fresh newcomer energy and passion at the time that emanated from the article. She'd embedded news of the coming site in the Y's historic context and transmitted genuine enthusiasm for this next milestone in its distinguished list of accomplishments. Liv began to copy and paste from the prior story into a new document, all too aware of her current lack of spirit for the task. No passion, no fun. *Is this what happens to people at work? Do they just keep redoing their work and settle into a 'same old, same old' mentality?* She didn't want to be that kind of worker, that kind of person. Nor did Elyse, who'd complained of getting stuck in the mundane status quo, while her energy to run for public office was growing. *Maybe I need to take a new leap too?* That thought intrigued her more than the task before her. *Is the Ian blip a sign it's time for me to find my next challenge that I can pour heart and meaning into? Seek light, create joy?*

That night Liv, Mimi, and the kids found their groove in the habits of their household: Margot and Jeff setting the table, Shakti helping with the rice, while Mimi focused on the chicken, and Liv, tonight's dishwasher, got to sit out for now. They enjoyed this routine, talking over the day while the smells of food permeated the kitchen, fresh ingredients constructing the flavor of stews and casseroles. In the same way, conversations mingled to produce their own creative directions.

"Maybe I should start thinking about a new job. I've got this success story to tell. The new campaign is just about to launch so I wouldn't be leaving unfinished work. The timing is good for me to at least look at other opportunities."

"I don't get that." Mimi was adding chopped tomatoes, onions, and spinach to her sauce for the chicken. "God, when I have my lesson plans down, it's so great to have those as a foundation. Then I can focus more on the kids. Liv, now you can run on autopilot with the mundane stuff, and spend more time understanding your clients and donors."

"Right. I'd been thinking that too, that this time around, I'd come up with a few new ideas, work with some new people, and do an even better job. Which I could do of course. But it's interesting to think about options."

"Like what options? The Y is a huge organization helping women, I mean what would be better for you to work on given your interests?"

"I got to wondering about start-ups, about what some women social entrepreneurs might be doing. Like that woman who got 'Girls Run' going. I'd enjoy helping to create a new nonprofit."

"Yeah, but aren't you the one who explained to me once how fundraising staff in small nonprofits often have to 'sing for their supper?'"

"That's true. I might have to take a pay cut to get involved with a new operation."

Shakti was listening in on this, removing one earbud and then finally pausing her smartphone. "Mom, this is not a good time to think about making less money. Remember me? College? I thought that was why I wasn't getting my own TV?"

Liv left her stool on the sidelines and went close to her daughter. "Thank you, sweetie, for reminding me that my life is not my own. What COULD I have been thinking!" She didn't often engage in sarcasm but now and then it slipped out like steam from a subway vent.

"Not funny." With that Shakti stuck her buds back in her ears and started toward the stairway down. "Rice will be done in fifteen minutes."

As they finished dinner with some store-bought chocolate-chip cookies, Liv silently thanked the universe for her family. Often at dinner gratitude rose up, thankfulness for her relations, for having enough to eat and wonderful people to eat with. Jeff was still a fun kid at nine, into writing, and eager to make plays, which of course Mimi, former theater producer, encouraged. Margot, now six, bore Ryan's imprint more strongly, always in motion, wanting to run and bike and help on the boat. While both were mixtures created by a wide genetic pool, together, as their features become more articulated, they looked to be a reversal of their parents, the boy slightly Asian in his thin frame, coloring, and eyes, and the girl more Hispanic, and a bit chunkier like Ryan. While Liv roamed in a momentary space of contentment, Ryan mentioned that he'd like to talk with her before she went downstairs. They peeled off into the living room after she and Shakti finished the clean-up.

Liv had grown to truly love her half-brother, her rock in so many ways. When the mortgage crisis came around, they'd all pulled together to make the higher payments. They'd figured out ways to let Grandpa stay with them for a week at a time to perk up his life after Grandma died. Despite all the bedroom versions of musical chairs, it had been fun. And she admired the way Ryan eventually supported her kicking Eric the Viking out of her life, while being fair to him and letting him grow the business. Ryan had become a family diplomat, tending to a web of relationships that kept everything copasetic.

"What's up Bro? Anything wrong?"

"No, not wrong. It's just that Mimi told me you were thinking of a job change."

"That's stronger than I'd put it. But it might be a good time for me to maybe think about it."

"Okay. Well, I just wanted to bring you up to speed on some developments with my dad so that we all have the same things to think about."

"Why, what's going on with him?" Liv's body tensed, feeling cold, and wanting a sweat shirt.

"He's got some medical issues. It might be dementia, we don't know yet. Maybe Mimi told you about him leaving the burners on more than once at his house. And then this weekend, we were talking, and he kept asking the same questions over and over."

"I hate hearing that, it's so sad. He shouldn't be living alone anymore even though I know he likes it that way."

"Exactly. We may be getting to the point we just have to insist on his not living alone."

Liv's mind raced now. "You mean you'd move in with him?"

"That's one option on the table. What we need though is to think this through on a long-term basis. We need an immediate fix, but then we have to watch his money, his assets, with a view to what if he lives another fifteen or twenty years. What if he becomes a wanderer who leaves the house? Or isn't able to do his daily basic activities? Long-term care in facilities is extremely expensive, several thousand a month. All those things are keeping me awake at night."

Liv reached across the ottoman between their chairs to touch her brother. "This is so hard! Thank you for telling me. How can I help?" Her own personal fear rustled beneath her spoken sentiments.

"I don't know. I need to talk to Katherine and Gary too. They know other people going through this."

"That's true. Take Sam. Aunt El thinks he's getting dementia or Alzheimer's. God, what a terrible way to be living, knowing your life, who you are, is slipping away."

Ryan's face contorted. "I know. It hurt so bad to see my dad keep recycling the same questions."

They sat quietly and then Mimi joined them. "Bad, really bad, what happens." Mimi sat on the arm of the sofa and laid her hand on Ryan's shoulder, afraid Ryan might cry again like he had Sunday night. "One option is we move into Eric's place on Queen Anne. Another..." and she made herself look right into Liv's eyes, "...another that is really hard for us to bring up is that..." Liv was searching Mimi's eyes for what was so difficult to say. "Well, we were wondering what with you being stable with your job..." Mimi grimaced alluding to their pre-dinner conversation, "...and with Marco and you and the kids seeming so much a family - just whether there's any reason you would want to change...." Mimi couldn't bring herself to finish.

Liv sparked forward, as though she'd guessed a charade clue. "Oh, I see, I move out and make space for Ryan's dad to move in! Oh, I see, yeah, I do see, that could be an option. I see why that's come up." Having put it out there, her shoulders slumped and curled forward as she watched for their reaction.

"We're all in this together, Liv, you know that. There's so many ways we help each other, we don't want to not have you and Shakti here. It's just we need to open up to all the possible re-arrangements of our lives. Just like we shifted kids in beds when Grandpa would stay with us."

Liv's mouth twisted as her forehead stretched higher. "Let's be honest, Grandpa was one thing, with one of us sleeping on the sofa for a week. But this would be way different, a total move in. There's no way that Shakti and I could stay."

Mimi seconded that. "Another option is to put him in a facility right away. We have to consider that too. I mean even though I'm usually home with the kids before five, that's a full day he'd be left alone in the house, could walk off on his own, worse, burn it down. And that's true whichever house we live in." Mimi looked at Ryan. "I know you're also wondering if we could afford for me to leave my job to watch over things here. But with the kids getting older, what would I do here by myself? I don't think I could be a daily caregiver for him listening to the same questions repeated over and over."

Ryan, sitting forward with his elbows on his knees, brought his hands up, folded them, and let his chin rest there. "It just seems so harsh and uncaring not to be there for him while he still has his mind. Plus, there's the money thing. He has a monthly retirement income, but we would need to sell whichever house we're not living in if he went into a facility."

Liv looked from one to the other. "This is so complicated. What happens next?"

Ryan spoke. "I'm taking a morning off work to take him to a doctor for an evaluation. While he's still very much with us, I want him to have a say in this. He's been in denial, but I spent time with him Sunday reminding him of how we see his mind behaving."

"That must have been awful."

"Yep. Definitely denial. He needs to hear it from a doctor."

Liv's mind was working hard. "You know, whatever you guys think the best solution is, if it turns out it's giving him our apartment, so be it. I'm making decent money and it's time Shakti worked a few hours a week too. Somehow we'd find an affordable place."

"Yeah, but it might be farther out. Rents are skyrocketing."

"Somehow my clients have places to live. There's always the Rainier Valley."

"Come on, Sis, I'd worry if you were down there."

"We're not going to figure it out tonight." Liv found herself on the verge of laughing. "God, it's been a crazy few days! It's funny almost. There was a point on Sunday in the retreat when I felt so settled, almost stuck. And no sooner do I get home, then Shakti wants to meet her father, my job is jeopardized at least momentarily, and now my living situation is up in the air. I guess the universe is starting a conversation with me about change." Liv saw both Mimi's and Ryan's eyes raise at the reference to Shakti. "I know, we need to talk about that. Just not tonight. I'm still mulling over what Marco said." Liv rose, gave each a hug, and then headed down the stairs, pausing mid-way feeling dizzy. *Change comes fast. How in the world can we take a trip to Madrid or India if I have to find a new apartment with a security deposit and higher rent?*

A wave of exhaustion came over Liv and a need to veg out. When she turned on the TV, it was CNN coverage of refugees. Liv had been fixating on news coverage of the issue for months, first the drowning episodes of African refugees crossing to Italy, then all the Syrian people cramming into inflatable boats to cross to Lesbos. Then the border scenes in Hungary and all the EU discussion of what to do. Once Shakti found Liv crying in front of the TV. She tried to make teaching opportunities out of this to the extent Shakti would still listen to her. As the months passed, Shakti converted her own outrage at the events happening to young people into anger, not tears. "Mom, don't cry, do something. What's the point of crying?" Liv reminded her that for several years she'd tried to do something, working for the International Rescue Committee. "Well, let's raise money for them." And, to her mother's surprise, Shakti and a few others began a fundraiser at her school, sending photos via Facebook and Instagram, and tweeting. She even set up a Pay Pal account for the project and was on her way to a goal of $500 that she would send to the IRC.

Tonight, refugees were shown trying to make it in Germany, their experiences contrasted with those still in the camps in Lebanon. She saw aid workers with IRC logos on their vests handing out water bottles and paper-thin silvery thermal blankets. Liv longed to be there doing that work, straining against her commitments to Shakti. The time simply was not right. As she clicked off the screen, she thought, maybe next summer she and Shakti could do something to help together. Which would require travel dollars so she better start saving now. Not a good time to change jobs either with housing up in the air. Nope, that trip to Madrid with Marco to visit his parents was not going to happen.

She noticed Shakti applying herself to homework. *Thank goodness!* The girl was an achiever and wasn't creating the homework wars beginning to unfold with Jeff upstairs. Liv needed some air, so despite the chill, she zipped on a hoodie and went out for a short walk. Stepping into the backyard through the sliding glass door, the fresh cool air coupled with the distant lights sparkling on the water brought an image from the past, so many years ago. The night she and David had sat out there. When their souls merged.

He'd been on her mind. The refugee news brought him into her dreams, and even into conversations with Shakti who remembered him as someone she loved. David felt the need to connect too. Now in Amsterdam working at the International Court, his emails picked up again as the humanitarian catastrophes followed each other in quick succession.

David. He still owned a piece of her heart. She'd never felt more attuned, more like one, with any other man. So many years ago, she'd welcomed him at the airport when he and others had arrived from the Kakuma refugee camp in Kenya. She was one of their Rescue Committee resources for resettlement. David grew from being a heroic figure, leading other children out of South Sudan on their thousand-mile trek, first to Ethiopia and then Kenya, into a poster child for refugee success. His losses and tribulations forged determination, total resolve to punish the ultimate perpetrator of the carnage to his village, Omar al-Bashir, President of Sudan. David poured every bit of mental and emotional strength into becoming a legal avenger. First, his law degree won him a one-year grant position in Nairobi investigating and documenting stories in the camps. He also used that time to search for confirmation of his mother and sister's fates following the armed attack on their village. Then, with the connections he'd made with both the Kenyan legal community and South Sudanese political groups, he'd landed a permanent investigative position with the International Court. His base then became The Hague in Amsterdam, where the Court's offices were located. He traveled frequently back to Africa to meet with people and conduct inquiries. The Court's goal was to indict Bashir for war crimes and it became the one and only focus of David's life.

As Liv walked alone in the hilly neighborhood of Phinney Ridge she loved, the zoo was near, its resident exotic animals not infrequently reminding her of Kenya and visiting the animal preserves with David. The experience had become the most treasured film of her life, starring the Liv that she wanted to be, and weaving the themes of her life into her 'second tropical romance' as Elyse liked to call it, teasing her mercilessly when Liv returned about all the hot places she had yet to place her mark upon.

After the autumn evening years ago, when Liv and David locked souls, he left for Nairobi. For the better part of a year, they wrote long emails back and forth and occasionally skyped as David was able. His days were packed with meeting and interviewing people and exploring connections. He lived with non-local, usually European, IRC staff in shared housing. Guys would crash when they had a week off from projects at the refugee camps, mostly at Dadaab but also Kakuma. They were a strong support group for each other as they dealt with challenges at the camps, from food distribution and water and sewage systems, to indoctrinating a new generation of Africans in western cultural norms of democracy and women's rights.

    David had spent years in Kakuma camp, arriving at about age sixteen, and not being resettled to Seattle until the summer of 2001 in his mid-twenties. Those camp years were so incredibly depressing as he watched his youth slip away. Day after day spent in repetitive activities of survival: getting his rations of food and water; trading food for goods brought to the camp like a pair of sneakers or shorts; or simply hanging about with others who also had no work to do. Older guys who drove the trucks to and from Nairobi talked of the broader world out there of which David was so ignorant. So often he was bored and detested it, longing for time he could spend in making a real life in some other place like Nairobi. Fortunately, someone now and then, another refugee, a camp teacher, a cleric, someone would lift his spirits. Eventually, he came under the wing of a fellow Dinka who ran a small store. David became his helper, alerting him to goods that just arrived, bringing loads from the trucks, or running errands for customers. He hoped to go to the city when he was older. Learning became his saving grace. And then a Rescue Committee guy told him he might be resettled. Which meant waiting and more waiting. David forged his goal in those years of misery and frequent despair: he would avenge his family and get Bashir. That kept him going, learning English, studying whatever he could.

    And then the rescue, the journey to Seattle, to a cold damp place where he attended real schools and made every day count. Disciplined and focused on his goal, he finished law school in Seattle in 2007. The time had finally come to begin his family search in country and seek revenge.

It broke his heart to go back into the camp and know what all these people were missing: women pretending thorn tree tents were home, kids becoming aware through technology that there was real life outside, men sinking into the crushing despair of little or no work and their inability to live a simple life on the land as their ancestors had. His first time back, meeting staff, thinking about the interviews he wanted to do, he'd left and walked to the outskirts of the camp where he cried and pounded the side of a building with his fist, burning with outrage at how political leaders could destroy hundreds of thousands of lives for decades. His anger became as encapsulated as a bullet: I am going to get this guy. He channeled anger and sadness into energy to do the best he could to be a champion for these people and to find additional evidence for the indictment and conviction of Bashir for war crimes.

He was also driven to learn what had become of his mother and sister. His story was one of so many that he felt selfish pursuing it. After six months of work, and the indictment of Bashir, he took a break to begin his search. Renting a jeep, he drove with two others involved in the war still going on in South Sudan. To say the state of the roads was terrible was to suggest you'd call most of what they traveled on 'roads.' Initially, he wanted to begin his search from the area of his village where his dad was shot, and his mother and sister disappeared. But it was too dangerous for that. His companions told him how to circumvent south of the worst of it, and drive toward Chad. There were over ten refugee camps in that direction filled predominantly with refugees from Darfur. Nonetheless, he'd concluded they offered the last unexplored hope that his family might have fled east that devastating day.

Liv had knots in her stomach for a month while he was out searching and there was no communication. Eventually she'd heard the outcome, but it was only with her trip to Nairobi in the fall of 2008, that she learned all that happened.

She'd arrived at the airport where David picked her up. He looked the same, yet different, leaner in body, harder in the eyes than she recalled. In this setting, she was the outlier with her ivory skin. They were awkward with each other, their cosmic connection from a year ago in Seattle blocked by so many interfering signals. Each felt surreal in the other's company.

He arranged for her to use one of the rooms in the IRC house while she was there, as two in the group who shared bunkbeds were up in Dadaab camp for two weeks. Not until breakfast did they begin to feel amazement that she'd come. They lingered over coffee at a cafe, more present to each other. He wanted to show her a little of the city's better features, the Museum and arts center, while she adjusted to the time change and being in Nairobi. As they moved about, he would do a double-take at turning and finding Liv in his now familiar environs. "This is so weird that you are here."

Liv knew the lost in transit feeling from her trip to India in 2000, when her openness to new experience resulted in becoming pregnant with Shakti. She was more aware of how this journey might affect her as she moved through an unfamiliar culture, visiting a large urban area, again like Mumbai, yet similarly situated with the destitute poverty of Africa's largest slum, Kibera, three miles away. The sweat on her body accompanied an internal state of melting away, of losing her identity. Look at these well-dressed professional men and women who likely make more money than I do, enjoying the stimulations and pace of standard metropolitan life. Just like Seattle basically – but with the dominant skin color changed making her more the oddity, the invader, the one who didn't belong. Looking at a beautiful mango and papaya salad over lunch in a downtown outdoor restaurant, she identified with a solitary fly who landed for a moment on her fruit – *that's me, I'm a tourist in David's territory. Is there any way I could belong here?*

That evening, after sharing a group dinner at the house and telling her stories of resettling David in Seattle, and David once again telling his story of the angel who greeted him at the airport, she began learning more about the camp workers and their backgrounds. Her presence afforded each an opportunity to tell his own story afresh. The four others who shared the house with David were either expats or volunteers in their gap year before entering university. Joel, a permanent IRC staffer, was from the States and oversaw basic water and sewage for a section of Dadaab, the world's largest refugee camp. He'd been there three years now. "When my wife said she wanted a divorce, I signed up for this. It works for me a lot better than being some low-paid manager in a New York office while she climbs the investment company ladder to success." The other expat was from Denmark. Soren kept trying to make sense of why Liv was there as David had revealed nothing but their prior relationship at the IRC in Seattle. Liv was used to this by now as she'd been trying to explain to those at home her bond to David, without really getting into it. "I spent a lot of time when I worked at the IRC assisting people coming from camps, and it's as if I only got to see the middle of a film. I haven't really seen where they come from - and with almost all of them I'll never know how they end up. I came hoping to actually visit a camp, but David's objected to that."

They all nodded assent, with one of the gap year young guys saying, "There's no point in going to Dadaab or Kakuma if you're not going to do the work. If you just come to look, you could wind up making some of the girls and women feel bad. Like you're a tourist of others' misfortunes? Weird."

Liv sensed a misplaced judgment in that. "David said I should see the Kibera slum instead if my travel agenda is to wade into human suffering. I don't want to be a tourist...or inappropriate, I just want to have more understanding of the truth, of reality. Although I imagine Kibera will be like sections outside Mumbai I've seen." She wanted to establish her credibility as someone with more substance than they were implying.

Soren looked at David. "So, you've prepared her not to gawk – or cry? She'll look enough like a tourist as it is."

"I was two months in Mumbai and believe me I've seen some real urban slums."

Soren dropped his condescending tone. "Well, okay, but Kibera makes Dadaab look good by comparison." Turning again to David, "Be sure to take her over to meet Ingrid at Jamii Bora, to see the work she's doing. That's at least an upper."

"Good idea," David said. "There's a microcredit organization this lady from Sweden got going from nothing and she's getting some amazing results. It's one of the largest microfinance organizations in East Africa."

"I would love to learn more about that – we actually run a microfinance program at the family service center where I work now." There, she thought, that should help ground me with these guys. She was also enthused that the visit to the Swedish lady would connect her with some women here. Maybe she'd return home with a great story to share.

Her questions that night kept coming. She wanted to know the tribes of the Kenyan people inhabiting Kibera and their differences, the politics behind it all, how the fifty percent of people who lived there were employed, how kids were educated, how people spent their time. She learned a lot about Changaa, the cheap alcohol that dominated many people's days in the slum, and the rise of drugs and glue sniffing.

Mid-morning the next day, Liv and David took a bus and then walked to Kibera moving step by step from relative well-being into the conditions of extreme poverty where about a quarter of a million Kenyans lived, well over ten percent of the entire city of Nairobi. The passage of time had dimmed her past experiences; being in the presence of the real thing was overwhelming again, the incredible density of the living space crowded with people speaking in languages she didn't understand. David knew a couple of the international medical aid workers there, and one took some precious moments to answer Liv's questions. Yes, those room-sized mud shacks provided sleeping quarters for up to ten people. Yes, there's finally been some progress on the water supply. No, not much electricity. A stream of pregnant girls looking about Shakti's age filed through the *Medicins sans Frontieres* facility while Liv queried the aid worker. But she couldn't spare much time. Liv handed her a donation and they left. Men drifting in the streets stared at her, and she stared down the trashy alleyways seeing mostly men passed out from drink. The combination of the multi-dimensional impact of all the trash and rubble with the density of inhabitants intensely confronted her. And the stench! The smell of sewage was repulsive, and charcoal pollution burned her nose and throat. She found she didn't want to linger, save for when she saw children. They were like children anywhere, intrigued when they saw her, shy, bold, smiling. Trying not to stare herself, she was watching some teenage girls when David whispered in her ear "They face the choice my sister did, marry young or become a prostitute."

After an hour in Kibera, a shell-shocked Liv was acknowledging she shouldn't have come. It was a mistake to go and imbibe the inhumanity of the conditions and the sense of the immutability of it all: those young girls would turn into old women there, and their children would walk the same path. *What is the point of trying to do anything?*

They walked and walked in quiet despondency until they reached the *Jamaii Bora* bank location. Here was an antidote for the despondency of slum residents, and truly for anyone seeking to make the world a better place. Founded by Ingrid Munro in 1999, it now served hundreds of thousands of members using microcredit loans to better themselves and pull their families out of slum existence. Liv knew the history of microcredit beginning with Muhammed Yunus in Bangladesh, and how it had reached even her own family resource center. To walk into do-gooders actually making a difference, many of them who'd participated in the program and now worked there, slowly buoyed her and David's spirits. She learned the Swahili word for hope, 'tumaini.' They spoke with a woman who used to live in the slum but had worked her way out with her market stall funded by microcredit. Liv found some paper in her purse and started making notes for a story for her own nonprofit's newsletter. She found herself wishing she could stay and help with the work somehow.

When they departed, again after making a donation, her inner state began to cohere again, to make sense of working to make things better for others. Perhaps it was hopeless in the awful reality of an over-populated, corrupt world, but she felt re-inspired to try, to at least try for a few sinking souls. *I know I do nonprofit lite work compared to this infinity of need. But it's what I can do for now.* The only other choice was to turn her back on it as disconnected from her own actions and choices in life. But that wasn't who she was. Better to accept the truth of reality, and then find a small way to face up to it.

David chose a local place for them to eat and try some *ugali*, a maize porridge, with a couple of chunks of beef, along with *irio*, mashed vegetable balls to be dipped in the stew. He was a fan of the latter and shared his attempts to make them himself – which then reconnected them to shared memories of his learning to cook in Seattle. Over lunch, he pulled out his map of Nairobi, and showed her where they were and how they would be taking a bus over to the other side of the capital city to a place called Eastleigh, which was the neighborhood Somali refugees populated. He had a friend there he'd look up. Maybe Liv could learn a little more about refugee prospects from him. "While there's a slum there too, really it's a very different place. Fifty years ago it had some wealth, but more recently with the exodus of people from Somalia and the growth of the camps up north, the spillover here has resulted in Eastleigh being called 'little Mogadishu.'"

The urban development of wealthy Somalis on top of the older Kenyan and Asian wealth resulted in a vibrant community despite its impoverished sections and struggling refugees seeking work. They missed connecting with David's friend, but Liv's visual impressions helped her understand that many refugees left their countries with resources that enabled them to establish livelihoods on their own provided they were given decent space to do that. She was reminded of refugees she'd met in her own experience who had professional degrees, but at first had to settle for menial jobs in Seattle until their English improved. It puzzled her why the Kenyan government couldn't transform the Kibera slum where its own citizens lived. David's uniform answer to any questions about the government was, "Corruption."

That night there was no group dinner, so she and David could simply sit and talk in the house. They'd quietly eaten some left-overs and then collapsed on a dirty, navy blue chintz patterned loveseat that an expat had donated when she returned to England. Rips at the arms now sported grey duct tape. "Liv, what are you thinking? Talk to me."

"Oh, I'm not thinking. I'm exhausted. Or maybe, it's more totally emotionally and psychologically drained from trying to put myself in the shoes of all those people. Do you think they, the slum dwellers, are just so used to it that the everydayness of it enables survival?"

David shook his head. "Used to it? I lived in something like that, maybe not as terrible, for all those years. It's deadening and that's why so many get drunk - to escape. But the half who get out to work? They have that hope still of betterment, of the possibility of leaving. Perhaps they are in a family relationship that keeps them going. For me now, having lived in the States, having experienced all the wealth of food and housing and education that I did, now even living here…I can't accept it. I can't accept these two worlds so shockingly different co-exist so closely, whether it's slums or refugee camps." He rearranged his long limbs to sit straighter, as fire returned to his thoughts. "It's especially hard for me that my sister and her children, are still in a camp in Chad, and here I am freely moving around the globe. I would love to make things better for them, and soon I hope to - but her husband is calling the shots and taking his time moving them back to South Sudan. Which I guess I agree is best since the war is still going on."

Liv knew. That startling email when David simply said, 'I've found my sister.' Then the other emails and a phone call with more information. But now she wanted the whole story. "Tell me about her David, about finding her, I want to hear it all."

"I rented a jeep, and thanks to these two guys going back to fight, I got better information about the geography of the war. Ultimately, I made it to Chad and the refugee camps located there."

He hadn't really hoped to learn what became of his mother and sister. Twenty years had passed since the vicious attack on his village, government helicopters mowing his kinsmen down from above while the murderous Janjaweed on camels and horses killed them eye to eye. What drove David was a duty to try. He owed it to them, to their spirits, that he bring closure. He held a question of what unfolded that day their family was destroyed: while he and others headed east to Ethiopia, had his mother and Amer, perhaps as part of a small group, been drawn westward ultimately to Chad? He'd spent years in the U.S. getting access to and checking International Red Cross and U.N. refugee records of inhabitants in the camps there. Even if they had fled west, he knew the most likely thing was that one or both might have been killed outside a camp while getting firewood, or because of sporadic violence within the camp.

"I began with the camps closest to the border. In my second week, and fourth camp, the pointlessness of it all was grinding me down. In addition to all the other reasons I wasn't going to find them, I was learning how many refugees were now starting to return – imagine Liv, at one point there were over 600,000 people in those camps, but now scores of thousands were leaving. I didn't really think they'd go back if war was still going on, but what if my sister had married someone from Darfur or some other place where her husband had taken her?"

He paused as he recollected that time. "There was also the whole problem of simply recognizing each other. I was sure somehow, I'd know my mother if I saw her – but what if she had died, how would I know Amer? It was crazy– yet I believed I'd see my mother or father in her.

"I was walking around looking from side to side at the women, trying to find people from my village or nearby, letting people know about my search so they could spread the word. I stopped to fill my water bottle where women were filling their big plastic yellow containers. As I looked around, pausing to gaze at each woman, testing images of what Amer might look like as a young woman, trying to recall what my mother looked like, I saw a face that held my eyes. She looked like my mother, but even with the early wrinkles, I knew the woman wasn't that old. I moved closer to her and as she noticed my attention, she looked away, embarrassed. But then she looked back, this time intently. Coming closer, she whispered, 'Dut? Dut, is that you?' We came face to face. I knew in a way I can't explain that I was looking at Amer. She dropped her container and I clutched her so hard I must have bruised her – I was stunned and in shock! It was SO unreal, I can't express what it was like for me."

"What happened to your mother?"

"I asked right away, 'is mother here too?' Amer whispered no, she'd died. We embraced each other so tightly then, and I cried so hard, Liv."

Liv reached her hand to his, the first they really touched each other since their awkward airport embrace. He looked ready to cry again. "Go on, David. Tell me the rest."

"That afternoon, I learned their story, their first rushed escape into brush by the well, the fear of coming back to the camp, the urging of the other women to stick together. Then they scrambled farther away. But before they really struck out on a long walk, my mother forced herself to walk back towards the village and all she saw were the dead cattle interspaced with dead men including my father. They'd gone west believing that either I was among the dead or been kidnapped. At the next village, some chose to join them. After a very long time they wound up in a long steady stream of people moving first through Darfur, and then to Chad and the U.N. camps harboring hundreds of thousands like them."

"How did your mom die?"

"Mother never really recovered and sank into a great depression. Amer became the one who held them together. Then Mother saw what was happening to the other young girls, violence in the camps directed at some of them, some becoming prostitutes. She sought a husband for Amer when she turned fifteen in order to protect her. Amer had a child that died, and then four more, two fully grown by now. Mother got to see her first grandchild before she died." David paused collecting himself. "She was out beyond the camp gathering firewood. Frequently women were attacked while doing such chores, raped at best, or killed. A young boy, an orphan she'd been comforting, went with her. When the horse came, the warrior wanted to take the boy to be a child soldier. Her anger, so deep in the core of her being, made her hold on to the boy and protect him as though it were me. That meant her death."

Liv could see David's eyes tearing up again and held his hand tightly with both of hers.

"All the feeling since then – I'm such a mess inside, so amazed and joyful that Amer is alive, that I have family, and yet I'm like a river overflowing with sadness and anger and grief at the loss of my mother."

"What will happen next?'

"I spent as much time as I could with them, thinking through how their lives might go, the danger of moving back to Sudan beforel the war is over, the difficult and dangerous life in the camp, the possibility of them coming here - but her husband won't hear of it. I had to reluctantly agree that it was still a waiting game."

"If...when the war ends, might you join them in Sudan?"

"I don't know. I'm so confused. Assuming there is peace and a referendum actually happens, and we have a country of our own - maybe I should try and be part of the new South Sudan?"

"Why wouldn't you?"

"I can't help being very skeptical, disbelieving actually that anything positive can ever come to pass among my people. The oil in the south will lead to fighting over who controls it. No sooner will the Sudanese government be done destroying us, then the Dinka and Nuer will be in a battle for leadership. I've been to enough political meetings already to know how new conflicts will arise out of old ones. The issue of controlling the oil will play out among tribal loyalties and make progress so difficult." He paused, withdrawing his hand and stretching out his arms and legs. "For now, I'll do what I can to help them supplementing their resources, and later do all I can to help them move."

Liv sat quietly. She felt his pain, his joy. She felt it all with him.

Liv was feeling that pain again when she arrived back in her own space and time. "Mom, you were out so long, I was starting to get worried! I texted you but you didn't answer."

"Oh, I'm sorry. I was thinking back to so many things, I just didn't pay attention to my phone."

"You don't like that when it's you trying to reach me."

"You're right."

"What was distracting you? Were you thinking about me? And going to India?"

Liv cringed. *I should have been.* "No, I wasn't."

"So, what was more important tonight than that?"

"Shakti, it's not about it not being very important. It's just that after a long day, my thoughts get caught up in a lot that happens, like my job, like Ryan's dad starting to mentally deteriorate, like...like refugees. Which then got me thinking about David because we've been emailing a lot what with all the news."

"Really?" Shakti came closer to her mother. "Are you thinking about going to see him again?" She'd loved being around David when she was younger and recalled wishing he could be her father. Not that her Uncle Ryan was not the best 'go to guy' and surrogate dad. Not that she didn't feel she was sort of family with Marco. But someone who would love her as a real daughter and her mom as a husband? There had only been David.

"No, not at all. There are too many other priorities to focus on right now. No, I was just remembering the time I visited him in Kenya and what we saw...Nairobi, the wild animals – actually I blame it on walking past the zoo."

Shakti flopped on the sofa, curious now about what had happened in a way she hadn't been when she was nine. "You know I really don't get why you two didn't like make something happen..." Liv returned a puzzled expression. "You know, Mom, I mean weren't you attracted to him? You went to see him in Amsterdam that time too, I remember you not taking me and I made a big scene."

"Yes, you did! All that screaming at the airport when Grandma and Grandpa dropped me off. I told them it was a mistake to bring you."

"Yeah. So. Did you ever want to marry him?"

Liv turned to make tea, wondering how simple to keep this conversation, or whether there was a teachable moment here. "Let me fix my mint tea, and if in two minutes you're still interested and not obsessed with your phone, we can talk."

Shakti was not about to let her mom off the hook. No, she would hold her feet to the fire on India and meeting her father. And while she was focused on fatherhood, she might as well learn why her mom never landed David as a father. And husband. Shakti had this vague sense that there'd been romance between them, but when she was younger, she'd accept at face value things her mother said about David not coming back to Seattle, not even to this country. And, at that age, Shakti no more thought about people like her and her mom leaving Seattle, than she thought about leaving people you loved behind. Unless you died like Great Grandma had. Shakti just took for granted that all of them would be together forever in Seattle. That was her life.

Liv brought her cup over and motioned for Shakti to make room. She lifted her gangly colt legs down to the floor and righted herself. "Okay, Mom, I'm almost fifteen. The full scoop please."

"Well, dearest, one thing I want you to know is that I have a deep and abiding love for David."

"I think I know that. Did you want to marry him?"

"That's harder to talk about. But I'll try." Liv was moving her head, doing shoulder rolls, noticing how tense she'd become since the retreat. "Yes, I thought about that the first year after he left, and maybe still for another year, about whether there was a way for us all to be together. But it was so complicated."

"Because he was far away?"

"That, but more that he had no reason to come back to Seattle to live. He's from South Sudan – do you know where that is?"

"Sort of. Africa somewhere?"

"Go get the Atlas, and we'll look at where it is." Shakti sighed at having to move her body but retrieved the oversized book from the shelf. "Here's Africa," Liv said looking at the flat spread world, and here's us in Seattle."

"I know that, Mom."

Liv was flipping to pages that zoomed in on the north central part of the continent. "And here's South Sudan."

"It just says Sudan."

"This is an old atlas, the one I had in high school. This part, down here, became its own country about four years ago after a very long war. And now there's still fighting to control it between the tribes there. That's where David's sister and her family live now."

"Why doesn't David live there?"

"Partly because he's been on a mission to make sure the horrible leader of Sudan who attacked his village when he was a boy, that the guy winds up in prison. David's avenging the death of his parents."

"Wow."

"Do you recall his friend Jonathan?"

"Sort of."

"Well, those two plus hundreds of others had to leave their villages because of the attacks and walk first to Ethiopia and then later to Kenya. That first trip I made to Kenya when you were eight, and I brought back the carved giraffes over there on the shelf for you..."

"Oh, I'd forgotten that."

"That trip I wanted to go see the refugee camp David had grown up in or one just like it, but that didn't work out." Shakti's eyes and ears were alert, getting to understand things about her mom's life she never understood before. "I did get to see some live giraffes though, lions, and all kinds of animals in the Serengeti Park – see that's here. It was incredibly beautiful."

"Was David there too?"

"Yes." Liv knew what Shakti was thinking but in no way going to ask her mother. Liv looked at her knowingly. "Let's just say I was very much in love with David after that trip."

Shakti turned her gaze away. "Oh, I get it, you needed to live here for me, and he needed to live there."

"Pretty much."

"That makes me feel terrible, you couldn't be with the person you loved because I was here."

With one hand, Liv took Shakti's forcefully, and with the other, she took her chin making eye contact. "No. Wrong. That's not the whole story. It's only a piece. It's more complicated. Yes, I didn't want to move you and me away from all the people who help us here to go live in Africa and feel like outsiders. But it was also David."

"He didn't want to marry you?"

Liv sat back releasing her hands. "It was more that he has a mission in life to get the bad guy and it dominates his life. He doesn't have time to be a husband or father."

"So, what was the Amsterdam trip about?"

"Where he works now is at the International Court and it's based near Amsterdam in a city called The Hague. And David moved there but kept traveling to Africa and other places trying to get the guy, Bashir, arrested." Liv paused, sipped some tea, and turned reflective. "Sweetie, as you get older, you'll probably hear, if you haven't already, about a man being 'not available.' David had zero time for a family."

"Why did you go then?"

"Sometimes, we, women I mean, keep hoping. I needed to learn if being there and not in Nairobi had changed anything. It would have been easier for us to move to Amsterdam. But he still really had no time."

"I never knew all that before."

"Do you understand now?"

"Yes, but why would someone want to spend all their time going after a bad guy when he could be with us?" Shakti smiled and snuggled into her mom's side. "Mom, if I hadn't been in the picture, would you have gone? To Amsterdam I mean?"

Liv didn't need to think about that one, she'd done that too many times those years. "No, I wouldn't have."

"Honest?"

"Honest." Liv wasn't about to get into the more subtle dimensions of her experiences at the time, the Nigerian professor's daughter at the dinner, Indusa, and 'the look' she gave Liv; the women at the Court and the looks and frosty greetings given her when David introduced her. She'd hashed it out with Elyse for months, examining it through every racial, feminist, societal, historical, and cultural lens. It always came out the same: those looks carried in them hundreds of years of white colonialism, of westerners coming into Africa and skimming off the riches; they carried society's suppression of black women to the bottom rungs of the racial and gender scale; they said, who are you to take this lion of Africa, of our race, and appropriate him to some backwater culture in Seattle, or to meeting the needs of spoiled Americans, when we need him to be present for us, to become a leader, to help us claim our power – and to invite one of us to be his queen? How dare you! And it didn't hurt that the professor's daughter who was in diplomatic service had a voluptuous body, and knock-out clothes; or that the women at the Court were all attorneys who had credentials creating multi-page CVs.

Reluctantly, Liv had agreed: who do I think I am? She joined their assessment: David was not destined to be with a low-key Seattleite sporting a combination of Macy's and Urban Outfitters trendiest, with her clogs and northwester. He deserved a more credentialed woman, not someone of her limited work experience and lack of a post-grad degree. At least those trips had set a fire under her, fueling completion of her marketing degree and the job upgrade at the Y. Thankfully though, those looks had given Liv clarity, clarity about her standing in the world, and David's. No match. No power couple potential like Elyse and Cory had together. Nope. What Liv had, were a few special nights with David. And her Seattle life, a daughter and family. And now Marco. Enough really.

All of which did not stop Liv from dwelling on those nights in the Serengeti with David.

They were leaving early the next morning to travel to the Serengeti Plain to view the wildlife. Liv had raised the idea before the trip, and David had jumped on it, realizing he desperately wanted to have something beautiful of Africa to savor. Neither had much money to spend on a substantial photo Safari staying at expensive tourist resorts. But David did have the benefit of a network of connections, friends, and friends of friends, who worked in the tourist industry and knew how locals could see the sights cheaply. Basically, it required a couple of vehicles, some tents, and a guide who knew the territory, especially animal watering holes, and how to behave near predatory or threatened wildlife. The two expats decided to go also, as well as a few people the guide wanted to include. Their group ended up being seven tourists, the guide, and a couple of guys in training who did the driving. Their caravan included a VW van and a pair of jeeps.

For Liv, this was an exotic adventure, the likes of which she'd never had. Yet, it co-existed with mental whiplash, as her brain coped with the juxtapositioning of her normal life in Seattle, with her experiences in Nairobi, the inhumanity of Kibera, and then the hopeful inspiration of Ingrid's microcredit program. She coached herself to simply stay open to all the stimuli and not try to really digest or analyze anything. That could come later at home.

Yet another layer of sensibility was her relationship with David. They'd fallen back into their old familiar brotherly-sisterly routines that had built up for years in Seattle. Neither was eager to make any serious physical moves toward the other in the Rescue Committee house. Becoming fully present to each other took time, holding at bey the immense differences that separated their lives, while slowly pulling away all the protective layers surrounding their deep connection to the other. That first day driving, their approaches were unsure, tentative, cautious yet caring.

On this trip, they were to share a tent together as a couple. Liv didn't know what to expect other than sleeping on hard ground. Her confidence had been eroded last night in the dinner encounter with Indusa. It had begun well enough. Her father, Professor Kindiki, was a public lawyer and instructor in international law at the University of Nairobi. David had been introduced to him by one of his professors in Seattle. The older man was more than welcoming when he learned of David's achievements. As a mentor, he made inquiries at the International Court to find work for David once this one-year investigative project was concluded. He had a keen interest in seeing David succeed, as though he was the son the professor never had.

Not that Indusa wasn't everything a father could hope for in her own right. Liv figured she was in her early to mid-thirties. Extremely well-educated including time in Paris, fluent in at least three languages. She worked in diplomacy and served already in the Nigerian embassy in Nairobi for two years. She was eager for a foreign posting, but for now was working on a team to revamp the Nigerian visa program. Tall, like David, she had the most scrumptious body, stunningly curved in every way. At last night's dinner, her bright orange mini-skirt with a yellow short-sleeved ruffled blouse, and gold jewelry, made her chocolate brown skin engagingly warm. The bronze colored high-heeled sandals provided a titillating finish to the image.

Liv wore her best trip outfit which was simply a black flowy skirt to her knees, an aqua sleeveless blouse and some black light-weight sandals. How was she to know they'd be dining at a mansion? Taking in the contrast, Liv felt akin to a Shasta daisy wilting next to a tropical orchid.

Her relatively mousy appearance was only the appetizer to an evening's meal of awkward conversation. Her responses to probing career questions were tinged with feelings of inadequacy, while missteps occurred due to big gaps in her knowledge of African politics and players. Dessert was a quiet humiliation as Indusa carried on about her work and accomplishments. The after-dinner liqueurs on the patio went sour as David inadvertently touched on Liv being a mother. While Indusa had been slyly on the attack ever since Liv arrived on David's arm, the inquiries grew more pointed as Indusa realized that Liv was a single mom, most likely on the hunt for a husband and father, and perhaps endangering others' plans for David.

"So, how clever of you to be able to survive on your own with a daughter! But perhaps that's common in – where is it you're from? Seattle? I don't know it. How do you do it all?"

"My family has been very helpful, my parents, my brother and his wife."

"And what is your little darling called?"

"Shakti."

"Shakti? That sounds Indian, why Indian?"

Liv, having concluded already this evening was a disaster, saw no reason in not boldly confronting Indusa at this point. "Her father is Indian."

"Oh my, aren't you the multi-cultural one interested in men from all over the planet!"

David was feeling awkward all evening too, especially as he otherwise enjoyed his relationship with the professor. Defensive of Liv, he struggled to curtail Indusa's behavior all night. "Yes, in her work at the International Rescue Committee, she has dealt with so many men and women from around the world and done so much. She's quite amazing." With that, he took Liv's hand and smiled at her.

The sight of his coal black hand curved around the much smaller pink fingers infuriated Indusa. It was then she seered 'the look' on Liv, the look of aggressive anger that she would never forget, emanating from deep dark eyes in a regal face. Liv took it in fully, and then moved her gaze to David, using every bit of energy she had left to smile at him, a smile of true warmth that had been missing all evening. Putting her other hand on top of his, she looked into his eyes. "We should be going. Our big trip starts early."

Setting out before the sun rose, Liv didn't appreciate what a toll the trip out would take. It didn't look that far on the map. But it was over half a day just to get to Arusha in Tanzania where they would pick up the guide and have lunch before beginning the safari into the Park. The beating sun all day, the bumpy roads, the old van in which they bounced around on torn seats, coupled with the dirt coated windows that were hard to see out of, but a necessary barrier to block the sand blowing in – this was not a luxury trip.

When they reached their first campsite, they'd already seen herds of gazelles and zebras, and breathtaking views of the plain. The group rapport was high around the campfire as night fell with much joking about sounds to expect in the night and what to do if you needed to leave the tent to pee. Liv resolved to drink almost nothing after dinner and hoped she'd sleep through the night. David wanted to stay awake and enjoy the experience of being in the wild. He and the guides stayed up quite late talking in a mix of Swahili and English around the fire, a comforting backdrop for Liv settling in. She had no idea what to expect being in the same tent as David, what he might expect, and how they would relate to each other physically. Pure physical exhaustion eliminated any over-thinking.

She was in a light sleep when he unzipped the tent and crawled in. It was a four-person tent for sleeping but not tall. A lot of the gear bore familiar American brands, stuff travelers had left behind with the guides. David left the rain flap off, wanting to have a view to the stars through the netting. The evening temperature was pleasantly cool, and their sleeping bags were lightweight and adequately cushioned by air mattresses, long enough for their upper bodies. David found it rather luxurious. Liv had been on enough camping trips in college to call it adequate. The food was stored in the van, and the guides assured them not to be afraid of anything trying to claw its way into their tent. The tents were in a circle around the fire. Sounds carried easily. As she awoke to David's presence, she heard someone in a neighboring tent snoring loudly.

David whispered, "Hi." He was also totally unsure of what this bit of privacy meant for them. Liv had put the side opening of his bag close to the side opening of hers. She'd kept on her t-shirt but had taken off her cargo pants. David was in his t-shirt and basketball shorts. There was some light from a half moon. "Are you scared?"

"Not if you're here. You faced so much all that time on the treks. You'll protect me." David settled on to his side facing her. She could see the whites of his eyes and smile, along with his lighter clothing, while he could see her skin.

"I will."

"This is weird."

"Yes, our first night alone together. Ever."

How right that it was here in Africa, his place, to share this intimacy. She lay her hand across the edges of their sleeping bags, and he placed his hand over hers. They were man and woman. But in what form of relationship? After she'd met him, for years she'd been motherly to him. Once he'd become so competent, they'd been like brother and sister. Friends. And then a year ago, they'd held hands in her backyard, sitting in plastic chairs looking at the sky, and communed cosmically merging into a yogic oneness. Yesterday, he protected her from a jealous woman's claws, as real as anything out there on the plains. "I really appreciated how you came to my rescue yesterday with Indusa. I was so miserable all evening, and felt so bad, not being more beautiful and accomplished like her, and fearing your professor wouldn't approve of me."

"I know, she was terrible. I was at a loss as to what to do. Usually, it's been me and him talking our legal talk. But recently, she's been around the house more – she may have broken up with a boyfriend. She makes me feel awkward."

"She wants you."

"I feel that. But she's not my type."

"What is your type?"

By now, both sets of their hands were layered. He smiled looking like the Cheshire cat's grin separated from any visible body. "My type? I don't know that I have a type." The smile dimmed. "I only know who I am. A nomadic tribal man who's had incredible misfortunes and equally incredible luck. For some reason, I've gotten educated beyond any expectations." He paused considering his own thoughts.

"And…" Liv wanted to know, "…what kind of woman attracts you?"

He laughed, "Such persistence!" His amusement helped drop another barrier. "Do I want to be some wealthy guy living in a place like the professor's and marrying a woman like Indusa? Not at all. I want family around me. I want days when I'm at peace with the world. I want evil to be punished. I want to be with a woman who understands that's who I am." He moved closer now and stretched one arm above her, so she could come closer to his body. He lay his other arm across her. The sound of nearby brush crunching stiffened her. "Don't worry, I will protect you."

They lay a long time like that. As the stars became brighter they heard new noises around them, some distant, some seeming impossibly close. David named each sound, all too familiar to him. "It's a hippo roaring, nothing to worry about." Later, "That's a hyena calling." Still later, there was a grunting noise that sounded close. "Likely a baboon." Slowly, he became happier and happier with the comfort of knowing that after all he'd survived, he was at home with what he loved best, the land of his ancestors. And here was this sweet girl whose gentle breathing he enjoyed immensely. For the first time in his adult life, he experienced contentment. Relishing the peace, a thought arrived: this must be how it was for his mother and father, a simple life with only temporary shelter. This must be what it was like when he was created. He was in his element.

At daybreak, as camp sounds picked up, and the sky lightened above the tent, Liv awoke first, feeling stiff all over, and pinned in place by David's arm and leg draped over her. Needing to move, but afraid to waken him, her slight muscular twitching caused his leg to lift. He turned away to be more on his back. He rubbed his face and turned his head to see her, a slowly widening smile and awakening eyes meeting hers. Then suddenly he was on her and she could feel the hardness probing her. Semi-conscious and a bit stunned, she opened her body to him. Quickly he came and lay atop her. Then raising himself on his elbow, his eyes searched every feature of her face. "You are incredibly beautiful in the morning."

He was up and out of the tent like a rabbit, leaving Liv wondering if that's how Sudanese guys always did it. Over their breakfast of coffee and sweet rolls sitting around the unlit campfire, he kept sneaking looks at her with furtive eyes, seeking an approving smile or forgiveness. As they finished up, she laid her hand on his knee and gave him a huge smile – which made him throw his head back and start laughing. Which made her start laughing. Which made Joel and Soren, still lingering with their coffee smile and ask what was so funny. Which only made it harder for Liv and David to control their overflowing delight. Finally, Liv squeezed out, "Sorry it's an inside joke!" Which caused David to stand up, turn around and let out a whoop. The guys looked at each other and shrugged their shoulders. Soren opined that there was a wild hyena in their midst and moved on.

And so the day went for the consummated pair, little touches here and there that made the other smile, body bumps as they stood and peered through binoculars and the zoom lens on Liv's camera to see the impala and giraffes better. During their long stay near a substantial watering hole where rhinos were bathing in large numbers, Liv and David got into imitating the animal sounds and taking silly action photos. None of this change in behavior escaped the Rescue Committee guys. Joel, at one point, turned his expensive camera with a telephoto lens on them and caught them kissing. "Hey everyone, look over there, I've got a rare sighting of love birds!" Which totally liberated Liv – as if she needed it – to begin to circle David, slowly flapping her arms as if in flight, and then perch on her tip toes to kiss him.

While the two of them did pay periodic attention to the splendid scenery and wildlife, especially the lion Joel picked up with his telephoto, they fell so much into each other that day it could have been Adam and Eve moving through the Garden of Eden before there was knowledge of good and evil. There was only them.

By nightfall around the camp fire, their joviality had morphed into gazes with smiles of invitation moving between their eyes. Joel couldn't resist another poke. "So, all along, I thought you two were just friends."

Liv only smiled back, while David, noticing her reticence to speak, put an end to intrusion into their special time. "Not 'just friends' Joel, but special friends who care a lot about each other."

Joel loved getting a rise. "Well, you know some of us will want to sleep tonight, so try and keep it down in your tent, okay?" The other guys erupted into snorts.

Liv sought privacy now. "See you all in the morning! Thanks for a great day," she said looking at the drivers and guide. "I've never had so much fun."

The guide responded, "We know," causing another round of good-hearted chuckles.

David wanted to give Liv some space to herself. And he wanted it too. He'd never been so light-hearted with a woman before. As he helped clean up and pack away gear and food for the night, he'd stop and stare into the darkening sky. Stunned. Feeling at one with his surroundings as though he was finally home. This was more beautiful than the place in Sudan where he grew up. But still he felt this place was home. The wide-open skies, the roaming herds of buffalo and wildebeest that appealed to his herdsman instincts, the fire sending sparks upward on a slight breeze. He wanted to stay here forever. And Liv, so incredibly strange to have her here, to be this way with her. *Is this really happening?*

Liv washed up, a bit outside the tent and now crawling inside and sitting on the mattress. A companion to him in this other world, her mind was equally stunned and silenced. Thinking could not grasp the day with him, nor hold the reality that he'd been inside her, that they'd enjoyed each other so freely and easily all day, stealing kisses, and clutching waists as they viewed the expanse of the plains, so open, so liberated. What realm of worldly delight had she entered? And if she was here, then who was that woman from Seattle with a daughter? A life that once again, as with India, was temporarily lost in transit. There was no role encumbering her in the Serengeti, no burden of choices, jobs, no family members defining a persona. Only raw life here, breathing with a beating heart.

Now this other form of life coming into the tent. The wild beasts around them would have noticed familiar behaviors, a kind of circling encounter, a patting of the ground to find the right settling spot, and then the lying together, with David circled around Liv. As the night's cool air came upon them, the heat from the other's body kept them warm. Neither wanted to sleep, it was all so new.

She turned over to face him and felt his head, then his shoulders and chest. Mindless action driven by an elemental desire to know. He followed her lead, letting her do as she would, feeling a stranger to this touching that was not pure physical drive. It was all foreign to him, this falling into, joining with a woman's psyche, a deep connectedness to what lay within her. She became playful, moving her body, nipping at him, sucking him, mounting him. Her abandonment enflamed his own force and they played like cubs hitting the sides of the tent as they rolled. Then his strength calmed her, and he shaped their bodies to enter her, their cries in coming rivalling the animal sounds in the surrounding night.

As they lay sweating, his body flattening hers to the ground, they heard Joel's voice from the neighboring tent. "Hey, keep it down in there. You're making me horny."

They exploded with laughter, then quickly muffled their mouths in each other.

The teasing began in earnest the next day, but by lunch they all took it as the new normal. Liv and David held hands, draped arms around shoulders and waists and moved into an easy couplehood. The next watering hole brought more riveting sights, as an incident unfolded of an alligator going after a cub. That brought startlingly forceful action by the pride. The fragility of life and sudden death in nature induced more reflective moments in the group.

The weight of this being their last day out and the need to return tomorrow grew heavier as the hours passed. The joviality diminished as Liv and David sensed they were being herded back to the roles they wore in 'real life' which now seemed a masquerade compared to the vitality out here. At the evening fire, the group was more somber. Soren, in some Swedish dark place, wondered aloud at the refugee work, how people were animals to each other, and the true inhumanity of supposedly civilized people. Joel knowing how fleeting love could be wondered what would become of Liv and David. "What's up for you two? Are you going to go back to Seattle at some point, David?"

Liv and he hadn't begun their re-entry yet. There had been no conversation of anything pertaining to the future. They looked at each other. He knew he wasn't going to live in Seattle again. She knew it too, especially now, here in Africa, seeing all this. David had his elbows on his knees leaning forward to poke the fire with a stick. He didn't owe Joel an answer but knew that he was a well-meaning guy. "Life these past days has been so beautifully simple. Tomorrow starts to get complicated again."

Liv suddenly wanted to cry. She rose awkwardly and said a perfunctory good night. In the tent later, they lay silently together, neither sleeping nor wanting to talk. They shifted to look through the tent net ceiling and watch the stars. 'Hold me tight, never let me go,' either might have said it.

The next day was just the initial dose of reality, leaving the plains and coming into the hustle and noise of a big city. Smells, crowds, and a cacophony of sounds assaulted them. Liv sat with her face pressed into David's shoulder most of the way in to Nairobi.

Arriving back at the house, Soren volunteered his room with a double bed to them. They'd considered going to a hotel, but that would have been even stranger. Liv's flight left in the early morning. Afraid to think about the future, to say anything, she kept her eyes on David.

That night, they loved with the desperation instilled by a dawn parting for an unimaginably long time; and they lingered so as to impress their bodies with indelible memories. Each cried at different times. David desperately wanted to comfort her but had no idea what to say. "Liv, out there going to sleep in the wild, it was the closest I've been to home since I was little. I felt like my parents were close, like I was growing into them having you there with me. So close to the earth and stars, you were my woman. I've never been so happy."

Liv sniffled, raising her eyes to his face. "I don't know what happens next. I don't even believe that I'm entitled to that happiness. Why should I get it, when it's so fleeting for everyone else? I don't know how to begin to merge our love into the life I lead." He met her gaze. "David, let's pledge to try, to try to find a way together. Maybe not for a while. But sometime. I want to pledge that to you."

"'Pledging my troth,' isn't that what people used to say a long time ago?" She smiled, but he remained serious. "I pledge to you, I make the promise that we belong together. I don't know when. Or how. I'll try."

Lying in bed, seeing the clock now registering one in the morning, realizing there was work to go to in a few hours, Liv shifted her eyes to stare at the ceiling. *We did try. It just didn't work out.*

Friday, November 13

Yes, she was going to get a seat on the bus! Thank god, Liv thought, after last night's shortened sleep, she needed to just sit and close her eyes like all the other tired people around her beginning their daily monotonous work routines.

Had it been only last weekend she'd been on retreat contemplating her stuckness? Her slow-lane life in the backwater? Now she was dealing with cross currents, having to circumvent branches and logs on all sides to alter her course. Lifting her eyes first to the gloomy sky coming over the I-5 bridge with Lake Union to the right, they moved to take in the new high-rises at the lake's south end, the site of the Amazon empire. The home of her nemesis. She wished she could just get off the bus, cross the street and go home to sleep more, instead of having to rise to the challenge of copying a successful campaign under the scrutiny of a boss being prodded to change their approach. She scolded herself for not rising to the challenge, but then sank into a darker spot: why bother, everything's always changing, now I probably need to move. An added input to her cloud of doom that chill morning was doubting that she had tried enough with David. When she entered her building, she masked her mood with waves and smiles to co-workers. At the back of the elevator she resolved to pull herself out of her sink hole by just concentrating on tasks today.

Relatively successful with that strategy, by the ride home, she prioritized her foremost task, to attend to Shakti's desire to meet her father. After a hearty sweet potato, quinoa and kale stew which Shakti only picked at – "What is this with so much kale these days?" – Liv told her she needed good energy to think about next steps for Shakti to meet her father.

"I'll eat to that!" Shakti loudly toasted Liv with a spoonful of kale. "Get on it, Mom. I'll be a good teen and do my homework right away, and you do your homework."

Liv couldn't help but toast her back, repeating, "To homework," and thinking how apt the phrase was tonight. "Okay, I'll be in my room for a while."

Liv wanted to look at the emails again and talk to Elyse. And finally get on with it and decide. Opening her journal from the last months of her pregnancy, "Conversations with an Unborn Child," she removed everything from the inner pocket: a copy of her email to Rama, his email back, and his sealed letter for Shakti. Plus a few faded photos of her time in India, of the NGO's team, with Rama in the rear squinting into the sun. A squished scrap of paper was there too. Flattening it out, she read the note she'd made when she was pregnant at her grandma's birthday party and her friend Helen had given her this advice: "never underestimate the power of love...." Liv relaxed back against her headboard and took a deep breath. Helen, she was gone too, a few years after Grandma. Liv wondered if her mom had ever figured it out, that her own mother and Helen had conspired in placing mom's unwanted pregnancy, aka Ryan, with Helen's son's family. Did Grandma go to her death with that secret? Who knew it now besides herself and Elyse who'd figured it out? Her aunt? Unlikely. Helen's son, now suffering from dementia? *Damn, am I the only family member who knows this?* It made her feel old, holding a buried family secret. She didn't like it at some level, preferring transparency in relationships, believing that to be the best foundation. Truth telling.

 Amorphous thought morphing: yes, truth telling. That's what she'd always favored in being a parent: tell the truth without blame or judgment, the mantra of the visionary from *The Four-Fold Way*. She'd treasured the book for years and frequently revisited it. You can never reach your vision if you don't know where you're starting from. Shakti deserved that, to know her beginnings so she could reach for a vision that was possible. It seemed obvious: of course, Shakti needed to meet Rama. And if she was bringing it up with urgency now, well then, Liv needed to meet her where she was. It might be one of those experiences where children think they want something, but then backtrack a little, only to get interested yet again later. Shakti could move on it now, or a year from now, who knows. But the call to do it was in the present moment; Liv's maternal duty was to respond. To show up and be present, that was the way of the warrior.

 She caught Elyse right away. "I was afraid you might be working late. Glad you're at home already."

 "Are you kidding! I'm so tired these days – were you like that? I practically threw up in a meeting today. And by five, all I could think about was getting home and lying on the sofa. This is the pits."

 "No, it's not for God's sake, Elyse. You're creating life. It needs your energy."

"I know, but I just thought things would be normal till like month eight."

"There is no normal. There's only you at thirty-six having your first child and needing sleep so life can develop inside."

"Okay, okay. What's up?"

"I've decided about Shakti meeting her father. Or actually, about me being ready."

Wow. That's huge! What does that mean in terms of next steps?"

"It means I share with Shakti the letter Rama sent to her. And whatever I know about his current situation."

"Which is?"

"Not much. He's working for the Ministry of Agriculture, and he's married with two sons." Liv paused and then her voice came low and slow, "Oh my gosh, think of it Elyse, Shakti's got two half-brothers, just like me and Ryan."

Elyse returned the latent enthusiasm she heard in Liv's voice. "Jesus. You're right. I mean you knew that. But suddenly it seems way more interesting and intriguing."

"It does. You're right, it's not just Rama, it's them too. I wonder what Shakti will do with that?"

"How are you going to open this all up for her? You know, just saying 'open it up' reminds me of Pandora's Box. What all will come out?"

Liv considered. "A full range of emotions I imagine. She's drawn to know, but then she may become afraid of how he'd accept her. Or not. If he doesn't want his wife to know, would he ever let her meet his sons? Reveal his big family secret to them? I mean as far as I know only his mother ever knew."

"How do you know she knew?"

"It's in the letter he sent back to me, enclosing the sealed letter for Shakti."

"Have you got it there? Read it to me."

"Okay, just a minute." Liv pulled the letter from underneath the journal, and began reading.

Liv,
Your letter was a total shock.
I opened it expecting perhaps a note of love. Instead, news of the baby coming.

This truly upset me. My first reaction was feeling bad that this happened. Then I was surprised you chose against abortion, not that I favor that choice, but it seems like what a young girl would decide to do. Then the whole unknown of what you will decide about raising the child – and worse, what will become of her?

It was all I could think about for many days, especially that there would be part of me somewhere that I would have no contact with.

The pain in my heart showed and my mother confronted me this week, probing at what was clouding my life.

I told her, Liv. I needed to. I haven't cried like that in a long time. I sat like a child on the floor with my head in her lap.

She has become my guiding light in this matter. We've talked more. She wanted to know about you, to see your letter. It felt right to have her counsel. She is a wise woman, Liv. She knows so much about all our family, all the family secrets. And she loves me very much and knows what I want in life. Finally, she asked if I wanted her advice. Of course, I did.

My mother said, "Let the girl decide. Let Liv decide what's best for her. If she is not reaching out to you, now or later, it's likely because she's thought things through and is making the choices she can live with. But the child, that worries me too. She may need you someday. You should stay open to the child. That's my advice."

Reading it aloud now to Elyse, they both started to tear up. Elyse said quietly but strongly, "With the condition of my hormones right now, Liv, that's a tear-jerker! I'm surprised you didn't call him or try to make something happen."

"It's so strange reading it now but notice how there is no invitation for further contact. No suggestion there could be anything more between us. And his mother nicely leading him back to a comfort zone, that if I didn't reach out, then it was okay to back off. That really struck me at the time, affirming again that he didn't think we had a future either. But my head is doing a turn-about now, just like with the half-brothers, all of a sudden, I'm thinking about what it would be like if Shakti met her other grandmother." Gentle tears were meandering down Liv's cheeks.

"I know. I get it. This isn't just our girl meeting her father, which is a big fucking deal, this is both of you meeting god knows who else."

Liv wiped her cheeks with her palms. "What do you think? Do I show Shakti everything or just the letter from her dad?"

"I don't know. I think she's mature enough, she gets adults, she gets that parents are real people making hard decisions. You're opening the box – I wouldn't try to control too much information – except then again, you don't want to give her more than she's ready for? So maybe be cautious, starting with just the sealed letter from him?"

"Yeah, I think so. That's in keeping with what I've always tried to do. Simple, focused responses, until the next question comes."

"Right." They were quiet. "So, when are you going to share this?"

"Her birthday party is tomorrow – you'll be there right? Maybe this weekend?"

Saturday, November 14

Katherine made her granddaughter's favorite for her fifteenth birthday, lasagna with meat sauce. No one in Liv's generation seemed to be much into red meat, but Shakti loved her grandma's pasta meat sauces. "She needs some iron, her body is craving it," was what Katherine always told Liv.

The house in Redmond was alive with people, the entire family and its extensions, including Aunt El and Sam, Elyse and Cory, plus Marco and Cezar. Most of them were in the family room glued to CNN's breaking news coverage of the Paris terrorist attacks at the nightclub. Liv was near Shakti who was struggling with why so many young people at the concert were targeted; Marco was assuring Cezar that assuming the Climate Change Conference was still held in Paris, the security would be overwhelming - although making it harder for the protesters which was unfortunate. "But Dad, someone in a car with an AK-47 could just mow down protesters. I don't think you should go."

Katherine was trying to herd people towards the kitchen island to get their dinner. Gary and El complied while continuing their conversation on intelligence failures. El, retired from Boeing, was pro-national surveillance systems, which Gary knew about since he had clients in his consulting business who held high security clearances, such that he too had gotten one. Marco, overhearing that conversation, leaned into Liv and whispered, "This is one way the terrorists win, turning countries into spy states."

Liv nodded, but didn't want any political talk to further detract from Shakti's birthday. "Hey folks, can I turn this off so we can focus on our birthday girl for a while?"

No objections being voiced, Elyse approched Liv and Marco. "You know, Hispanics really get into celebrating a girl turning fifteen, *quinceanera* we call it. It's gotten obnoxiously over-the-top these days, but while sweet sixteen is big in American culture, for me it was turning fifteen that was a milestone. So, I got Shakti a really special present." Elyse's eyes were sparkling with enthusiasm while her words were tentative. "I'm just not sure she'll like it. I want to take her to a downtown spa where she can choose what she wants, a new haircut, nails, massage, foot rub, whatever. What do you think? Will she go for it?"

Liv eyed her daughter's hair, a mass of curls hanging long around her face. "Maybe. Just keep the timing flexible in case it hits her wrong at first. In a week, heck in a day, she could change her mind."

"What did you get her?" Liv whispered. "Well, the big thing at home tonight is the letter from her father, which better be good is all I can say. But I got her a Kindle."

Elyse's eyes had widened. "That's pretty heavy. I hope your timing works."

The birthday cake was *tres leches*, Shakti's newest favorite since tasting it at Elyse's. With the lights off, and candles lighting Shakti's face as she bent low to blow them out, Liv was struck by how quickly fifteen years had passed. *Impossible.* Enjoying her daughter's features in the flickering lights as the crowd sang a hearty *Happy Birthday*, she saw the young woman emerging, the lovely adolescent who had her life ahead of her. *Perhaps Elyse's make-over might be a marking point for the emergence of a beauty?* A TV image interjected: what if it was Shakti who was mowed down in a theater at a concert? The celebratory moment held so much promise, yet it came wrapped in fear tonight.

Marco put his arm around Liv, sensing her spirit: each had invested their time and efforts heavily in their children, but they could be lost in just a few seconds of horror.

After everyone waxed appreciatively about the cake, now supporting ice cream for most, Gary cleared the dinner food and brought in the wave of presents. Clothes. Beauty products. Tickets from Marco for her and Cezar to go to an upcoming concert - now seeming a questionable activity. Elyse made her own gift known one-on-one hoping to get an honest reaction from Shakti and concluded that grateful words beneath questioning eyes was a decent reception. Gary went to his office to watch his computer for more news, and Aunt El turned the TV set on again. Katherine pulled Liv aside. "I'd like to talk about something, can we go into your old room?"

"Sure, okay."

Liv's old bedroom, now a guest room, was still as they'd decorated it before Shakti was born, the greens and browns with the orange silk pillow, starting to fray, and the jungle sun picture. Katherine sat on the bed and patted next to her for Liv to join her.

"This seems serious Mom, what's up?"

"Nothing that's really news to you. You know your dad and I have been talking for quite a while about our living situation for retirement."

"Right, you may move into Seattle."

"That's part of what we've decided, to not move into Seattle." Liv's face saddened. "I know honey, I loved the idea of being closer to you, but the vibe there is just not what it used to be."

"Yeah, tell me about it," Liv responded thinking of Amazon and Ian who had become the new Seattle face for her.

"We just don't see ourselves really wanting to go into the city that much. And the traffic jams we've encountered driving around checking out neighborhoods have been god awful. We started looking in areas of Bellevue and Kirkland and even at some developments down in Redmond. Also, Woodinville and Issaquah. They all have their problems with traffic. And of course, prices are so high. It's been confusing. After many, many discussions – which I'm frankly sick of at this point – when it came down to what we really want, it was being in a condo, having much less upkeep, being near the water, being able to get out to walk, and …"

"I know Mom, just cut to the chase, what did you decide?"

"We're not going far is what we decided. There are some new condos going up across the lake from us…"

"You mean here on Lake Sammamish where Aunt El is?"

"Yes, we put some money down on a place not far from here. We did it earlier this week."

Liv shifted to give her mom a hug. "I think that's great. That'll work. Why so serious?"

Katherine searched Liv's eyes, tinting green as though to match the bedspread. "This house will go on the market in January then. And the new place will be ready for us in February." Katherine moved her gaze slowly around the room. "We've done a lot of living – you've done a lot too – in this home. And it's about to become history. It just makes me feel old and sad, even while I'm really happy and pleased about the beautiful new place we'll have."

Liv got it. She looked around. It hadn't been her room in a long time but it still was intimately tied to her life. And this house with all its space, the kitchen opening to the family room and deck, this home had seen a lot of parties. An end to the era of her family life. *Damn, I may need to move too!* If Liv had ever thought of this home as a default resting place, well, forget that. "I get it Mom. I'll never have what feels like my family place to come home to again."

Walking back down the hallway to join the party and put on a happy face again, the thought struck her: is this what it feels like for refugees? *I'll never be able to go home again?* It wasn't the time or place to indulge that thought. Yet, as though reading her mind, Marco stood back among the group and put his arm around her shoulder as others were watching the news. "The National Front in France is going to use this for more anti-refugee talk, I know it."

"Those poor people who have no choice but to leave behind everything they know, at no fault of theirs, and then the world turns a cold shoulder to them."

He nodded for her to step into the dining room with him. "Have you decided about the Madrid trip?"

"I'm tilting against going."

Marco looked surprised. "You're not scared away by this terrorism stuff are you? Paris will be safer than ever when we're there."

"No, it's the latest issue around money. Not only may Shakti want to go to India next year, but I just learned..." – when was it? *Every day seems to have its change* – "anyway, I may need to move to a new place sometime in the next few months and that might take a chunk of the savings for the trip."

"Why would you move, I don't get it?"

"My brother's dad, Carl, is showing signs of dementia and Ryan needs to rethink housing. One option is his dad moves into my space. They're taking him for a doctor's evaluation soon. But if I had to move in January, no way would I go on a trip over Thanksgiving. Or if we go to India."

"You really think this is all going to come to pass so soon?"

"I just don't know. Depending on his condition, and how fast they think his mind is deteriorating...if I were Mimi, I'd be really concerned about how this would change Ryan's and her life. It may mean her not working for a while so as to be at home, at least before Carl gets to be too much to handle. There are so many unknowns. But if I were her, I'd much rather stay in my own home than move into his. So... then I'd need to go."

As Liv watched him processing this new information, a hope arose that he would solve her problems, that he'd offer to work this out together, maybe even inviting her to move in with him. In the same moment, Liv wasn't at all sure she wanted that, kicking out the long-term tenants so she and Marco could take over the house together. Her commute would get longer and more complicated with a bus transfer. And it wasn't like she cared that much for his earthy abode and its dated interior. But as they stood there, huddled away from the others, she found she was hoping for an offer of some kind, a spontaneous 'maybe it's time we lived together,' a realization on his part that despite all his intense concerns for the world's problems and people, she held a special place and he would make room for her gladly.

"You're right that apartments are not cheap. Just the other day I was looking at rents. Come January, I need to sign a new lease with my tenants. I haven't raised their rent in years, they've been so great at helping with all the work. Anyway, you may be looking at $1500 for a nice two-bedroom unit, and it would be farther out."

Liv's heart sank. She was not about to push herself on Marco and suggest that she move in, especially when she hadn't even decided if she really wanted to do that. But given the timing of the lease, she'd have to bring it up soon. Her eyes clouded over as her spirit grew heavier. "Life is so unsteady."

He wrapped his arms around her. "One thing at a time. Do you want to come to Madrid for Thanksgiving? If so, you need to buy the tickets now and commit the money it will take."

Her gut clenched. Her brain was fried. At times of indecision, she frequently reverted to simply staying open and waiting for a sign. She'd fantasized about taking in Spain and France with her multi-lingual lover, but it would take even more money to get to India. "I just don't know."

He pulled her closer. "I want you to come and join me." Seeing her indecisiveness, he added, "But I do understand about all the choices coming up."

When they kissed goodbye later that evening, and Liv began the drive home, she was frustrated. *He wants me to be a comrade, a fellow traveler, but not family.*

"How come you're so quiet, Mom?"

"Am I? It's just that I don't like thinking about moving into some north Seattle apartment complex and living without family around."

"If we get a new place, I want it to be special in some way."

"Me too." But Liv had no idea how that might come to pass. "And everything has money as a consideration. Now I'm not sure if we should go to Madrid."

"Because of the terrorist attack?"

"Not really, although Grandpa and Grandma will be more concerned. There's only so much in savings and it's expensive to move."

Shakti felt the disappointment of not going with Cezar to Madrid, although all along her mom had been non-committal about it. Now there was this danger too. *What a weird birthday.* "I feel so messed up inside tonight, like this terrible world is crashing in on our lives. How can I be happy on my birthday when all these young people just died? I don't know what to feel. I was in a good mood this morning, but now it's like how can anyone be happy any time when so much wrong goes on?"

"I know exactly what you mean. I lived through that two-sided viewer in my head for years – it's crazy-making."

"You don't feel it anymore?"

"No, no, of course I do. It's just as I've gotten older, and gone through these moments again and again – how can I be happy, when others are starving, or dying of Ebola? Or suffering from gun violence and wars of all kinds…"

"What, you get like teflon-coated and it rolls off? I don't want to be like that."

"No, that's not what I was trying to say. What I wanted to say is that you learn to be in the moment, the time and space you're in, and look inside for the response you can make here and now."

"I don't see how there's anything I can do about terrorism."

"Nor do I. But I can be the best person I can be, and try each moment to create the world I want people to live in. I can come from love, and not from fear."

"You mean like Granddad and Aunt El – I heard them talking. Auntie is really afraid."

"That's a good example of what I mean, she's coming from fear. Coming from love in this moment means that while I despise terrorism, I want to still advocate for refugee resettlement. That's what the moment is for people in Paris tonight, do you choose love or fear?"

"Like when that kid killed all those blacks in the Charleston Church and those people forgave him?"

"Yes, their reaction was to hold their own hearts in love, and not hate. You can only control yourself, Shakti."

Shakti was quiet the rest of the trip home. After unloading her birthday booty, Shakti paused at closing her bedroom door and came back to hug her mom. "I'm thinking this birthday brought some big lesson that feels too large for my head. Thanks for trying to help me make sense of it. Maybe someday I will."

That night, lying in bed, all that seemed clear to Liv was more change was coming, and she should not be flitting about spending money. No trip to Madrid and Paris. She'd let Marco know tomorrow. Honestly, she wondered if he'd miss her company. *Of course, he will. But I wish he loved me enough to invite me into his space.*

Sunday, November 15

At dinner Liv gave Shakti a heads up that she wanted to talk with her about wanting to meet her dad. "Let me clean up the dishes, and I'll come get you when I'm ready." A half hour later, Liv knocked on Shakti's door with the 'Private. Keep Out' sign she'd posted a year ago. "Sweetie, can we talk?"

A pair of determined eyes met Liv's as the door opened quickly. "What did you decide?"

Liv smiled, "Can I come in or do you want to talk in the living room?"

Shakti preferred not having her mom looking around her room, so she stepped out, shut the door, and moved to the table rather than the sofa, suggesting a more serious negotiation. "So?"

Liv met her demeanor in a down to earth way. "First, thank you for letting me have some time to think about it. I know it's been too long. And..." Liv watched Shakti's face and body movements closely to gauge her remarks, and assessed she was facing a wall of protection. "...and I've come around to thinking that if you want to reach out to your dad now, if you feel ready, I'll support you in that."

Liv watched Shakti's expression transform as features softened revealing more emotions. Her eyebrows crinkled. "You're kidding?"

"No. If you think the time is right, I'll go with that."

Shakti sat back in the chair and slumped, relaxing her shoulders and arms. The wall was crumbling. "Really? I finally get to meet my dad?"

"Yes, assuming he's ready too – this will be a shock to him."

Shakti lurched forward, arms splayed on the table. "But I thought he knew about me!"

"He does. But fifteen years have passed. So, however you or we contact him, it will be quite a surprise."

"Oh. Yeah. Okay." She relaxed again. A smile slowly unfurled across her face. She sprang up, hugged Liv hard, and then jumped, twirled, and let out a scream.

Liv had to laugh, happy to see her one-and-only so joyous. She just hoped the letter Rama wrote so long ago would not be a downer in any way.

"I can't wait to tell Cezar!"

"Darling, just sit down again. I want to give you something."

Looking puzzled, Shakti came back slowly to the table. "What?"

"Sit down, okay?"

Shakti complied, her eyes puzzled.

Liv pulled the letter from her cardigan pocket. "When I was pregnant I wrote to your father to tell him you were coming. He wrote back and sent a letter for you. Here it is." Liv slid the cream envelope across the table to her stunned daughter.

Shakti put her hand on the square envelope and raised her eyes to Liv's. "You've had a letter from my dad all these years and never shown it to me before?" The suppressed anger in her tone was all too familiar.

"Just a minute. Before you get needlessly upset about this, I've been holding it safe for you until you said you were ready. You did that a week ago. So, here's the letter." A shadow of a pout crossed Shakti's mouth, but quickly and forcefully she brought the envelope into both her hands and held it closely on her lap. Her expression was hard to read.

"What are you thinking?"

She didn't answer but rose and started pacing, first to the garden door, then back to the kitchen area. "What do you think it says?"

"I think it's going to be positive. It says, 'for my child.' That means even before you were born, he recognized you as his."

Shakti sat on the couch, holding the letter in front of her. "This is huge Mom - in case you don't get that."

"But I do get that. Which is why it took me time to think about it. You can open it whenever you want, wherever, with whomever. It's up to you."

"And then what?"

"And then you'll tell me what you want. It's really up to you what happens next."

Shakti stopped herself from saying, I need to think about it, hating the idea she'd sound like her mom. "Okay."

Liv rose to get ready for bed, sensing her daughter's need to process. She bent low over Shakti to kiss her and considered a playful 'good luck sleeping tonight,' but knew that a jest wasn't the right send-off. Awkwardly, Shakti stood up and embraced her. Liv intuited Shakti's underlying fear in her tight grasp. "I know there's a scary piece to this, so whenever you want to talk, just let me know. Middle of the night, at work, whenever."

"Yeah."

Shakti sat up in bed that night, her burnt orange bedspread surrounding her, saturated with seven years of evening fears and comforts. The tiny light next to her bed shed a dim glow. She stared at the envelope she was holding. Her mind in tumult, she tried to focus on opening it, but thoughts jostled, intrusions of her mother's having had the letter all those years, confusion about its delivery to her only now with no prior word or hint of it, and questions about what her mom and father had been like when they met. What was the attraction that brought them together and created her? Who was he today? She just couldn't bring herself to open the letter when she was this unsettled. Placing it on her bed stand, she reached for her cell and called Cezar.

"Hey, it's late, what's up?" His voice rose from the early fog of drifting off to sleep.

"Sorry. But you won't believe what happened tonight. Mom finally said I can meet my dad if I want to – and she gave me this sealed letter from him that he wrote before I was even born. The envelope says, 'for my child.'"

Cezar pulled himself upright in his bed. "No shit. What a mind-blower! Have you opened it, what does it say?"

"No, I can't bring myself to open it."

"Why?"

"I'm upset, that's why. Upset with Mom, upset at all I don't know and need to know. Afraid of what's in the letter."

"I get that." Silence at both ends. "Do you want to talk some of it through? I'm awake now."

"I don't know. I'm all tangled up inside, like I can't say anything. I don't even know what I'm feeling. Just really upset."

"You guys will be over here some night this week – maybe you should kind of be with it for a couple of days, and then we can talk here? Or I could meet you after school tomorrow?"

"I don't know. I guess. Yeah, let's meet after school?"

"Yeah, but sure you really don't need to talk now?"

"I'm a mess is all. I don't know what to say. I'm sort of mad at Mom, mad at both of them that I exist – except that's not really true. Excited too, I finally get to meet my father, except maybe he's a total jerk I won't even like who said something stupid in this letter."

"Hey, bring the letter with you tomorrow. I want to see it."

"Okay. Later."

Monday, November 16

They met the next afternoon in the back of the school auditorium stage behind the curtain. Shakti arrived first, dropped her backpack, and moved slowly across the stage towards the middle split in the curtains. She loved this stage. She'd only been back here with drama club so far when the curtains were open. She pulled them back enough to place her upper body forward and view the theater, wondering if this spring she'd land a speaking role and get to be before a real audience. The plays in middle school had been a beginning: she was good at memorizing her lines. She definitely liked the applause. The best part had been that empowering rush of using her voice to speak lines in public. It scared her, but she loved it.

Cezar appeared and joined her at stage center, poking his head out too. With his creative, dramatically oriented mind, he had an idea he was excited to share: "Let's pretend it's a play or movie. There's this huge drama about you and the letter right now. What would you want the character to do?"

Shakti backed up and screwed up her face at that. "Really? Give me a break, this is my life."

Cezar raised his hands, "Hey, just trying to help."

She began to move around the stage, obviously considering. "I'd want her to be strong. Confident – like in a way, unshakeable. Whatever the letter said, she'd know what to do." She took a deep breath and straightened her posture. "She'd be amazing." She moved quickly to grab his arm. "She'd be better than them, than her parents who got her into this."

Cezar was listening with his heart, watching her, and imagining the visuals: he saw fire, the glow of a face in a campfire speaking some powerful truth. "Now that, that sounds like you!"

"Maybe Mom should have handled things differently, maybe she did okay. There's nothing I can do about any of it now. It's just another part of our being a mom and daughter, like you having this unusual dad who lives in his garage. But I can make my own fresh start."

Cezar felt lighter. "Exactly. We all come into this world, to these sort of screwed up parents, who then screw us up – except they have some good qualities at times – and it's our turn to show we can do better." Time for a prop. "Hey, show me the letter."

Shakti went to her backpack, dug deeply into the largest pocket, and held out the letter to him. He didn't take it. He just looked. "God, that's so fucking amazing. Written all those years ago to you by this guy you don't know. I wonder if it still has his DNA on it? It blows my mind just to see it."

She pulled it back to stare at it again herself, then looked at Cezar. "I wish I knew more about him."

"What has your mom told you?"

"Not so much. Almost nothing really."

"Do you want to know about him back then when she met him? Or now?"

"All of it. Whatever she knows."

"Ask then. You're entitled."

"It would help, especially what he was like then. I mean, am I reading a letter from some dude she just had sex with because they were attracted? Or am I reading a letter from someone who was this amazing guy she was in love with?"

"That would definitely set the stage for opening the letter. Man, I'd love to write this play!" Shakti pinched his arm. "I can't help it – this is the biggest thing that's happened to you."

She blinked. "Actually, you're right."

That evening, Shakti's goal was interrogation. She brought it up right after they came down to their own flat after eating some experimental dishes Mimi and Liv were trying out for the big Thanksgiving dinner - the cauliflower in the mashed potatoes had been good. "Mom, we need to talk. I haven't opened the letter yet because I want to know what my father was like when you met him. I mean, I don't even quite remember what you were doing in India anyway - so tell me about that time and what kind of person he was."

Liv's expression brightened from general tiredness after a long day to a more open expression. She sat back down at the table with her decaf coffee and a ginger cookie. "Okay. Yes, I think that's important. Let me just re-focus okay? Can you give me a couple of minutes? Or maybe, just give me time to walk around the block and clear my brain fog from work?"

"You want me to walk with you?"

"Sure. Let's do that."

They layered on their fuzzy-lined jackets and hats and went out the side door into the usual chilly, damp evening. "Let's walk fast at first to warm up." Heading uphill got their blood moving, as did the brisk pace they set past the zoo for a few blocks before turning homeward.

"I talked to Cezar about it."

"Did that help?"

"Some. Mom, I need to know if my father was a jerk or some good guy you really loved."

That made Liv smile, and opened a gate to the past. "No way was he a jerk!" Liv slipped her arm under Shakti's, so they could be touching as they walked. She began with meeting him on her college internship with his sustainable agriculture and community building nonprofit. "I was drawn to him from the first moment I met him."

"Really?"

"Really. Maybe I knew inside he was going to be a special person in my life, in our lives. It was weird and sort of woo-woo, that feeling. It's only happened to me that once."

"Wow." Shakti suddenly felt special.

"I was there for two months and just so attracted to him. He's a natural leader. People at work and in the villages, everyone gravitated around him like he was some kind of god. Have I told you his name?"

"No. You've told me nothing Mom!"

"Rama. Rama is a very important figure in India." She stopped as they turned to go downhill under a light and faced Shakti. "There's a whole epic poem about Rama called *The Ramayana*. Your father loved that story. He even took me to see part of it on stage."

"Rama?" Her eyes looked questioning. She had a father named Rama? "Were you two in love?"

This was harder for Liv to talk about, and she chose her words more guardedly. "We were really drawn to each other. A powerful force was at work." Liv didn't want to call it lust. It had been that, but she always believed there was more to it.

"Like you craved his bod?"

Liv cracked up. "Sure, that was part of it. But I always felt there was some spiritual content to it too. Sometimes when I was pregnant and back home alone, I'd think that destiny had been at work and that you were this precious being who came of it."

Shakti knew this side of her mother and liked to mock it. Yet she couldn't help but want what Liv said just now to be true. They remained quiet as they walked the last block home. Liv stopped outside their house as though this conversation was one to be completed under the night sky in open air. "I never felt that he took advantage of me Shakti. I wanted what happened. He was and probably still is a special person. Don't be afraid of him." She wrapped her arm around Shakti's shoulders and leaned her head into hers. "I'm beginning to think this will be good."

Inside, Liv put on some hot water to make cocoa. Shakti came close. "How do we find out what he's like now? Do you know what he does? How would we reach him?"

"What I know, sweetie, is that he works for the Indian Ministry of Agriculture. He married." Liv watched her daughter's eyes dim with that. "And he has two sons, your half-brothers, just like me and Ryan."

As though a bolt of energy zapped Shakti, her face lit up. "I have BROTHERS! Oh my god! I can't believe it!"

Liv was smiling. "I know. It makes me happy to think about that. And Rama had a brother, so there are likely cousins. It's a whole family! And once you made me see it was time, and I got over my own fears, I can't help it, but I'm getting excited about this." Shakti started moving like a bouncing ball here and there, across the room, punching pillows, holding her head, smiling, laughing outright. "I just can't believe it. No way. Wait till I tell Cezar!" She reached for her cell and called him. "Get this – I have two brothers! Well, half-brothers. Can you believe it?" With that she moved down the hallway to her room to continue talking, relating all she'd learned to her best friend.

She reappeared several minutes later. "Mom, how will we get in touch with him?"

"Come, have your cooca." Although Liv was thinking a stronger sedative might be better. "I have this friend from back then who worked at the nonprofit for Rama. Arita's her name. She's my...our connection. She sees him once in a great while at events they both attend. There's this unspoken tie between them that goes back to me and you. Not that they're really friends or talk much at all. But Rama knows you're a girl. He knows I've raised you. And I know he has a nice wife and these boys, aged eleven and eight."

"They're young," Shakti said in a flat voice.

"Yes, they'd be like Jeff and Margot. In other words, like kids you could babysit." Shakti looked deflated, having initially imaged them as teens like her. "Arita and I email a few times a year. I can ask her to talk to Rama if you like. Or better maybe you can write him, and she can give him a letter from you? Whatever you think is best."

"I wonder if he's on Facebook?"

"Could be I suppose."

Shakti grew quieter now, trying to focus while imagining her little brothers. She needed to read his letter. Chances were, it would be a nice letter. She wanted a special time alone to read it. In a special place of her own. But one last question nagged. "Why was it you didn't try to be together?"

Liv was even more convinced of her answer now than she'd been at the time. "The place your father and I connected..." out beyond the field of right and wrong was how she thought of it at the time, "...it wasn't in Seattle or in Mumbai. I didn't have a desire to live my life in India, even assuming he wanted me there. Which I'm sure he didn't. He had another life ahead of him, being a man of his own place and culture and work. I didn't belong there. My home, my family, and friends, everything was here for me." Liv drifted into her own interior space, her eyes drawn inward while she spoke softly. "It's odd I suppose, since I wanted to be this multi-cultural person. But I was not about to go back to India with a baby and trap him in a marriage that he had no desire to be in. Nor dishonor or distance him from his family. Or try to make a place on my own there as a single mom, hoping he'd come around." Her reflection continued internally. *Maybe I'm a bit of a fraud and really just a homebody. Who isn't even that keen on sharing my home with a husband. Maybe I didn't try hard enough with David for that matter?* "I don't know Shakti. When you figure yourself out someday, then come back and figure me out."

Shakti saw that her mom's energy had diminished leaving her in a semi-depressed state. She hated that. "Mom stop it. Look at me. You're a great mom. You've raised me – an amazing special person – and you did it on your own. Accept that. And let me have my time on center stage without you moaning in the background, okay?"

Liv welcomed the challenge. "Okay, no whining."

When Shakti returned to her room, she still felt agitated with so much more to wonder about. Brothers, a father named Rama. She placed her laptop on her desk and googled 'Rama India' and was shown a lot of blue-skinned images. *I hope he doesn't look like that!*

She flopped on her bed. The letter was once again positioned on her night stand next to her favorite Disney characters that she wouldn't consider throwing out, a Tinker Bell plastic figurine seated in the lap of a larger Kermit the frog, who sat in front of a photo of the family on their big trip to Disneyland when she was eight. It could have been the beginning of a puja. All it lacked was a candle and incense. She slid down the bedside to reposition herself on the floor staring at the envelope. *Oh, just do it, just open it and get this part over with.*

Gently opening the seal and pulling out a single folded sheet of vellum paper, her next thought was that he hadn't written much. She unfolded it, reminding herself he was a young guy when he wrote it.

> *You are part of me now.*
> *I am part of you.*
> *You will be part of me later when you read this.*
> *My heart welcomes you with love and respect.*
>
> *Someday I hope we meet.*
>   Rama Sharma
>   Mumbai, October 2000

That's it? She re-read it. *Distant, really distant - but kind of sweet. Not really discouraging at all, he hopes we'll meet. Shakti Sharma?* Her mind emptied of thoughts, while her body became as motionless as a mannequin. After all the emoting of the past days, a peaceful stillness came upon her. The noisy birds that had been battling in her head, diving at each other and circling around, now all roosted silently in the leafy network of her brain. Quiet. Waiting. Making space for what might arise. Did she doze a bit? It was close to midnight when she began to surface. She wanted her mom and stepped outside into the dark hallway. Gently rapping on her mom's door, there was no response, so she softly opened it and came to the bedside. "Mom, Mom," she said gently moving Liv's arm laying outside the cover.

Liv moved, then her eyes startled opened. "What, what's the matter?"

Shakti pulled back the cover and came under the covers to snuggle closely. "Mom, I opened the letter."

Liv shifted around to place her head on her hand to see Shakti better. "Are you okay?"

A wan smile formed in response, as the now child-like creature continued to emerge from that empty stillness. "Yes. I'm fine. It's short. The letter." Apologetically, as though owning her father and defending his actions, she continued, "It's a little lame. But it made me really quiet. And calmed me down. It felt good."

Liv didn't want to speak for fear of ruining this moment. "What he said Mom, it was enough. He said he hoped to meet me someday."

Liv wrapped her arms around her daughter, enveloping her as tightly as she could, while tears of gratitude welled up. *Shakti will be loved.*

They unpeeled and then lay there quietly until Shakti moved and half sat up. "I feel okay. Happy. I'm going to bed now." She kissed her mom's cheek and left.

Liv lay awake a long time until her brain gave out trying to imagine what it might mean for them.

They decided that initially gathering more information from Arita was the right next step. Liv emailed her, letting her know of Shakti's desire to meet her father sometime soon in the coming year. An exchange of ideas followed on how to approach him with the news. Arita's suggestion prevailed: she would seek him out at the next sustainable agriculture event coming up in December, where he was a speaker at a break-out session. Arita as the go-between did not want to over-plan the encounter. "Let me just approach him. Maybe invite him to have tea. Just let me judge what's comfortable, and not awkward." Shakti had sat with Liv as the correspondence virtually unfolded over the course of a day and come to accept Liv and Arita's conviction that a low-key approach - see what his reaction is - was okay.

Arita provided a link to the event's marketing materials online. There was a brief reference to his part on a panel discussion: Professor Rama Sharma, College of Agriculture, Pune, and Chair of Agricultural Extension, will share an overview of the results of six experimental projects in the Tansa Valley. That sent them to the web to google and glean what they could from a few other professional postings. Not much really, as he had little presence on the web.

At first Shakti bristled with the delay of it all, even while acknowledging that it wouldn't help to shock him. Then an unexpected fear began to work on her: was she good enough? She wanted to amaze him, to be this special incredible daughter. She began throwing herself into all her school work, demanding excellence of herself in all her work. Cezar kept reassuring her, you're fine just as you are. But Liv noticed a heightened interest in her appearance, her clothes. And all things Indian. When Shakti expressed interest in reading *The Ramayana*, Liv debated internally about giving her the copy Rama had given Liv the day she left India. The one in which he wrote, *'For my Sita.'* As Liv flipped through it and came back to his message, she recalled it all too well: meeting him at the village well, making love like the gods under the Southern stars, seeing *The Ramayana* on the TV in the neighboring village, seeing another part at a theater in Mumbai – and, oh yes, the truck in the warehouse with the little lights. Holding the book transported her into a still vivid past, stored so securely that the passage of time had not marred the quality of the re-enactment. She wondered, how is it for him? *Does he remember?* In the end, Liv knew there wasn't her experience separate from Shakti's, there was only this river of life and they were both in it. She gave the book to Shakti.

"Sita?"

"It's a long story – both our lives, and the book. It all belongs to you."

Thanksgiving, November 26

The night before Thanksgiving, Mimi and Liv were making pumpkin and apple pies upstairs. Liv's spirits were in flux, a bit down not being in Madrid with Marco, but buoyed by the reception her new hair cut had gotten from everyone. She'd given up on trying to do a smooth bob that had too many cross-waves and gone instead to a curly shag. She'd never had it cut so short all over, two inches or so, but her hair had sprung back into its curls. A drizzle down effect on the nape of her neck and by her ears resulted in a totally new look for her, both sexy and womanly. Marco had raved about it, finding his hands drawn to it, which led to a playful coupling that made him sadder than her she wouldn't be at his side in Europe.

But still no invitation to move in with him. Not that she knew if she would take it, but the lack of the offer was drilling a bigger hole in her heart than she anticipated. It seemed clear, he didn't want a live-in partner, a wife-like presence in his life. From her own exploration of that territory over the years – do I need a husband? – she understood that there were many ways to create family and partnerships that weren't boxed into preset ideas of 'husband' and 'wife.' Nonetheless, she would have liked him to want her more. The absence of the invitation revealed the limits of possibility between them. She would never be the most important person in his life. They were both too centered on their children for that to be true for either one of them. But the precedence of his values and activist causes over a significant relationship, that was the killer.

Liv finished peeling and chopping the apples which had been labor-intensive compared to many quick meals she prepared. All for a single pie. "So, anything more from the doctor on Carl's condition?"

"Just that from all the tests, the diagnosis is still vague as to whether it's some form of dementia or really Alzheimer's eating away at his brain. It'll be interesting to see how he does here tomorrow around you, Shakti, and your parents."

"What should we look for?"

"Just anything odd."

"And I suppose they have no idea how quickly this might progress?"

"That's right. But more and more we're starting to plan for me not working next year, in case he's living with us."

"Will you mind that?"

"I'm warming up to the idea. I'm ready for a break from teaching. I'll be able to enjoy the kids before they start getting too old and self-conscious and withdrawn to be fun. And I may volunteer at a theater or take some classes."

"I guess I should plan for a move then?"

Mimi turned from placing the pumpkin pie in the oven. "Liv, I feel so bad about how this may play out for you. Have you thought about moving in with Marco?"

Liv didn't want to get into it. "There would be problems with that. It just might be time for Shakti and me to strike out on our own."

"Really? That seems…. I don't know, lonely? I guess because I'll feel lonely without you."

"Me too. But I need to find the upside in this, and at least I've got some time to do that."

"Any more on going to India?"

"Not yet. Maybe in a week or two we'll know more."

Mimi paused before moving on to making the cranberry sauce. "This is really pushing the envelope, but if you go, and Shakti and her father hit it off – I know, a big if – would you consider something dramatic like moving to Mumbai?"

Liv was crimping the pie crust methodically but stopped in her tracks. "No, that hasn't crossed my mind at all. My first reaction is to reject it as too wild, or frankly unappealing, or impossible."

"I know it's crazy. But with Shakti almost grown now, it just came to me, that you two could do something very different together. You're going to be one of those mother-daughter teams sharing a real life together, that's my prediction – I feel that. Honestly. And don't think small, think, 'Wow, what could an amazing sixteen-year-old and her attractive mom do together!' Maybe, just maybe, life is inviting you to a bold new start?" Mimi grew animated as she laid this out, the result of her own guilt-ridden sleepless nights, hating the idea of pushing Liv and Shakti out. She even incorporated a theatrical touch, grabbing Liv by the arm, and moving them around the kitchen and dining room, aping bystanders at the same time in awe of this duo, especially the sexy mom with the dangling curls and long earrings.

Liv cracked up and got into it which fed Mimi's positivism. "See what I mean? It's all about attitude. You used to tell me about the power of now. Well, now maybe, now IS this moment where the past has built this incredible relationship with Shakti, and the future is unknown, and everything depends on your attitude and choices."

Liv was staring intently at her sister-in-law, hearing her own words coming back at her. "I get it. I do get it. I need to be open to new possibilities. Although I just don't feel in my gut it's India."

"But stay open! Use this time, the next six or nine months," Mimi paused, "...oh my god, it's like a gestation period! Anyway, use it to think as broadly as you can. Job change. Place change. Really moving into what is going to be a great long-term relationship with Shakti."

"Once she stops being a smart mouthed, sulking, pushy, challenging teenager."

"Exactly."

That conversation generated fresh stamina for Liv's spirits, at least for a while, carrying her through the holiday gathering, where Ryan's dad had difficulty remembering Liv's name, and how Shakti and was related to her. He was obviously puzzled by the racial difference. Mimi, Ryan, and Liv found themselves frequently exchanging concerned glances, as each memory gap became visible.

Then there was her parents' conversation over dinner about the realtor they were using to put their home on the market in the coming year, and how enthused they were getting about their condo purchase. Which still carried a sad undertone for Liv, causing her yet again to lament the loss of the home where she grew up, her bedroom, and the passage of time. It was like selling an old friend. As she did her internal work to adjust to it, she grew sad from thoughts of everyone getting older, parents turning into grandparents who get old, lose their minds, and die. Combined with her overall sense of homelessness on the horizon, Mimi's beckoning light of possibilities dimmed. Liv's upbeat welcomes at the beginning of the celebration transformed into subdued behaviors by the end.

Cleaning up and putting away left-overs, she and Mimi looked in each other's eyes and slid naturally into a hug. Either could have clearly defined their joint realization: going forward in the now and leaving behind the past with healthy parents, family as they'd known it, and a home together was heavy. Loss, sadness, and projections of even more loss in the future, were the emotional left-overs of the feast. "Remind me of the power of now, Liv," Mimi begged. "How do I stay in the moment when it makes me sad?"

Liv was overcome with love for Mimi in their shared sense of loss and a shaky future. "The power of now is how much I love you in this moment. And Ryan. And the kids. And mom and dad. It's so strong, it's making me cry."

Ryan brought in more empty wine glasses. Seeing the tears, he came and wrapped his arms around them both. "Me too. I feel it too."

Friday, November 27

The Friday after brought the annual ritual at Elyse's home: she and her former bridesmaids, Liv and Selena, coming together to avoid shopping, and relax together watching their favorite Thanksgiving movie, then sharing leftovers to feed whoever showed up for dinner. Elyse's charming craftsman home in Madrona was the usual viewing site, where a three-piece, deep brown leather sofa surrounded a large screen and provided that lounge-together space that encouraged intimacy. The major difference this year was that Shakti's funk at missing Cezar had melted into a condescending willingness to join a few girls from school who were going to a movie at the mall, while Selena's son was staying over at his dad's.

Elyse was not feeling all that chipper as she drew close to the end of the first trimester. She couldn't join in the wine toast to Selena's new job as the ED of the Renton Family Service Center, the role she'd prepared for over many years. She was absolutely thrilled that all her discipline and work had led to this substantial nonprofit leadership position where she'd be more visible in the community and a real player. Plus, her Iraq vet, separated husband was doing passably well after all his treatments, job training, and enforced self-discipline, so she no longer had qualms about his fathering and the safety of her son with him. Indeed, gradually being able to transfer more parenting of her teenage son to his father was liberating her. With Elyse still looking wan from her bouts of nausea, and Liv's emotions in troubled seas, Selena was the bearer of comraderie today.

As Liv's glass of red wine met Selena's and Elyse's apple cider, Selena took them down memory lane following the cheers and good wishes. "I just can't get it into myself, my whole body, that they offered me the job. I've missed so many times in the last few years, always a finalist but never landing it in the eyes of the powers that be. You know what it's been like."

Liv thought back to her days under Selena's supervision at the family services center in Fremont, and how committed she'd been to excelling at being a nonprofit exec. "You've seen so many kinds of structural, and even overt, racism along the way, you could do a blog on that you know, now that racism is back in the national spotlight."

"True enough, a book maybe someday. But for now, I am continuing to guard my public profile – no missteps allowed for me."

"Speaking of missteps and what our white male colleagues get away with, listen to this." Liv had been waiting to share this. "At the Board retreat last weekend, Ian, Mr. Amazon, is there – he's the one who wants to decide unilaterally that our yet-to-be-even-sited women's training center is going to be all about hi-tech - the guy who shows blatant disrespect for what my department does – he shows up and pulls out of his pocket a wad of fifteen hundred dollars and lays it on the table."

That brought a spark to Elyse's face. "No way!"

"You can imagine the other Board members just looking at this grandstanding while they get their papers out or open their laptops at the table. And he just sits there smiling, with the money on the table. Finally, our Board Chair, Mr. blue-blood Stimson, sees that everyone else is ready, looks down the table and says, 'Ian, we're all curious why you've put what looks to be a sizeable amount of money on the table.'"

"So, he says – I have this third hand from our ED to Cynthia to me - he says, 'I've raised some seed money for the new training center.' Of course, the Chair is not happy that Ian's totally ignored the agenda and regular order, but he's trying to contain himself. One of the older Board members, who still uses paper a lot, she looks across the long table, maybe twenty people there, and asks him whether it's all from him. And then it gets really interesting because he says no, he just raised it this week from his staff. He'd let it be known at a staff meeting that the YWCA was building a training center and he hoped they'd support it."

The look of shock on Selena's face said it all. "How many ways can you go wrong with fundraising and management at the same time! Unbelievable. Did anyone call him on it?"

"From what I've heard, all the Board members were looking at each other and then at the Chair, but he didn't want to see his whole meeting go off-track. So, he said, apparently in a very strong way, that they thanked him for his efforts, and after the meeting they would like to make sure that those who gave would get appropriate thanks. Ian says, 'no need for that, I thanked them.' And he wanted to get Kevin's name, which he'd forgotten, so that he could come over and help a little with some communications. He thinks he can land about $100,000 in year-end donations from some other executives there."

Elyse shook her head in disbelief, while Selena spouted, "If I was ED of the Y, saw that happen at a meeting, I'd be all over the Board Chair to kick that cowboy off the Board as soon as the meeting was over. You just don't go out and get people's money without a Board-approved plan for its use in place – he could damage the Y's rep with the tech community over the long term if what he decides to promise isn't what the Board uses the money for."

"Well, Maureen may have had words with the Chair, I haven't heard about it though. But you know the Y's Board is overall conservative, and that would include processing of this in the executive committee which won't happen for another few weeks. Although I'm betting there were phone calls galore after the meeting."

Elyse chimed in, "Cynthia, you, your team, everyone must be totally up in arms against this guy."

"Of course, plus half of this short week was just everybody gossiping and wondering what it meant for us. Cynthia was in Maureen's office every day. Totally unproductive. And Cynthia hasn't like sat us down and said, don't worry, Ian's gone – because of course she doesn't know what the executive committee will do."

"If that were my new organization, no way would I let that behavior go publicly unaddressed for very long. It's trouble for morale."

"I can attest to that. I'd walk out the door if so much else in my life wasn't up in the air." With Selena's inquiring eyes, Liv gave her a brief recap of how unsettled her housing was right now, and her anxiety.

Which was a topic Elyse melded into. "I know. I'm feeling so uncertain about things right now. The doctor said I may need to stay off my feet more, she even mentioned bed rest towards the end of the pregnancy! Which seems intolerable. And then with the results of this month's city elections, I'm not sure what changes the new people who were elected will bring to our staffing. 'Turbulent times' is what my office mate said. I'm feeling off my game."

"And Cory?" Liv was pleased so far with how supportive he'd been of Elyse during her pregnancy.

"His firm just got another huge case that he's enthused about, eager to get into, so that always scares me." She looked pointedly at Liv. "You know only too well this has been a long conversation that began before we married, and, shall I say the 'negotiation' to become parents also went on forever. Frankly, me having to take it easy and then being on leave for three months, he may just lapse into…" and here her voice became imitative, "…how sweet, the little woman at home with the baby." In the meantime, what if my job gets rebundled and after maternity leave, who knows what they'll offer me. It feels like I'm sinking."

Liv put on her coaching hat, well-worn since the wedding from hell. "Elyse, stop it. You? You're never going to sink. You're like that bird, the phoenix that always takes off again. Just learn some patience and timing. By the time the baby arrives in May, and you have the summer off, you'll be ready to get back into it like always. Give yourself and the baby a break."

"I'm with Liv on that. You're resilient. You want a family. Just focus on that." Neither Selena nor Liv wanted to allude to their own history of career struggles as moms – Elyse would deal with that all in good time. Selena wanted to get out of this spirit-debilitating dialogue. "Hey, let me show you these shots from the fundraiser my new organization did two weeks ago." She pulled out her iPhone from her big orange hand bag. "That dress look familiar?"

Liv and Elyse bumped heads looking to get a good angle on the photo. "Oh no, I can't believe it! That's the bridesmaid dress from my wedding! And you still look fabulous in it – look at those Michelle Obama arms!"

"Maybe that's why they made you ED, because you're so photogenic!" Selena softly punched Liv's arm, "How dare you!"

"Just teasing. But you do look the epitome of sexy power in that dress. The wedding thing reminds me – I'll be skyping with David on Sunday."

While Selena and Liv continued talking about David, Elyse dropped off into a memory of her wedding, and the end to any meaningful relations with Cory's family. She'd been feeling bad about that now that she was going to add to the family tree. As she sat watching Liv and Selena, both moving ahead with their careers, and life expanding, especially for Selena, Elyse envied their freedom. Here she was facing a year – and Cory was talking about having two kids – so likely several years, of needing to focus on a completely different part of her life. She was already missing her ability to advance in the office this coming year. She briefly wondered, perhaps it's better to have your children younger so that once you get your career momentum going, you don't have to slow down.

"Is he still in the Netherlands?" Selena asked. "I haven't kept up with him, although I see his friends every once in a while, when I'm in the Rainier Valley. Jonathan's store is still doing well."

"We've been in touch most recently about the refugee situation in Europe. He's really depressed about that, and other stuff too. He needs to bring his sister and her kids to live with him."

"Why? My recall is foggy, but I thought she and her husband lived in South Sudan?"

"That was true up to about a year ago. But ever since they won independence, the Dinka and Nuer tribal factions have been in an off again, on again civil war. The husband got killed in a battle. At least the sister, Amer, and David were in touch right away. He got her the money to go to Kenya and share a place with some people he knew there. But he's committed to stepping up as a father to his younger nephews, and to bring them all to live with him. Or maybe that he should go to live with them in Nairobi. Anyway, he's made them all start learning English and he's been to see them, maybe more than once."

"You think they'll all wind up in the Netherlands, most likely?"

"It's not an especially good situation right now for bringing more refugees into Europe. He's researching and thinking that all through. The Paris attacks don't help."

Elyse looked concerned. "Say hello from us. Find out more. Is he still content working at the Court? I mean, is there a real chance he'd move to Nairobi then?"

"All those questions are on my mind too, for sure." Some emails to Liv included laments about the impossibility of the Court achieving justice. Here it was over five years since a warrant had been out for Bashir's arrest, and yet he continued to travel freely, no African country willing to arrest him. Liv sensed David may have slid into a prolonged depression which was replacing all the anger he'd harbored for so long. His inability to achieve his highest priority had at first frustrated him, then diminished him, and now it seemed, sapped him of vitality.

 Elyse looked at the clock. "Time to watch." She loaded her personal copy of 'Home for the Holidays' into the DVD player. Liv had seen it first at her parents' home one Thanksgiving after Shakti was born, and found it encouraging, a single mom in a crazy family winding up, well maybe, with this great guy. This might be the eighth time they'd watched it together. They knew all the lines, each had multiple favorite parts: the hilarious turkey dinner with the competing birds, one of which winds up in the uptight sister's lap, the tipsy Geraldine Chapman revealing a kiss from her brother-in-law, the snowball fight between Robert Downey Jr. and the equally uptight brother-in-law, and then of course the fact that Holly Hunter is missing how this incredibly good-looking dude is trying to come on to her. Their commentary now was an impromptu undercurrent that intimately involved them as participants and critics at the same time. Was there anything more fun than girlfriends?

Shakti was not having girlfriend fun as they drove to the movie at Northgate mall. Although 'girlfriend' is not what she would have said. She was out with her next best bestie after Cezar, Natalie. Shakti liked Natalie because she wasn't into guys that much, a good student, choosy about her friends, and overall a sweet, caring person who made Shakti feel special. Natalie also hadn't fully blossomed yet, had braces on her teeth, and a nose that for now seemed too big for her face. Like Shakti's.

 Natalie's older sister Alex was home for Thanksgiving break from Wazoo and had use of their dad's old Volvo for the afternoon. Liv allowed Shakti out in cars with other girls in the afternoons. Two of Alex's friends from high school joined them, and their conversations dominated the car talk as they rushed to catch up on the latest that they hadn't already texted and talked to death on the phone. Shakti and Natalie were used to exchanging looks when they were around this group, rolling their eyes and pretending to gag as one of the older girls' remarks would sound ridiculous or idiotic to their sharper minds. Alex paid attention to her driving, but the conversation of the other two about the love lives of celebrities morphed into who the girls were dating now and catty remarks about other teens. Shakti,

Shakti Rising

living under the cloud of waiting to hear something about her father in India, found it all trite. Now one of them was saying her boyfriend wanted her to snapshot something sexy to him, but then Alex shut her up, saying "Anna, we have children in the car!" Which caused Natalie's defenses to rise claiming moral superiority on the subject and how if Alex ever did that, and Natalie found out, "I'll have to tell Mom."

"See what you've done Anna!"

As they parked to go see the last movie in *The Hunger Games*, their chatter turned to how the heroine of the day, Jennifer Lawrence, had a bad experience with her naked photos, and the pros and cons of Snapshot.

Shakti loved the film's heroine Katniss, her look, her prowess, her courage. By the film's end, she was in that *Hunger Games* space again, where the world was evil, and it would take strong girls to make things better. She had a poster in her bedroom of Mockingjay. She'd been so into the books that Liv had read them and taken her to the first movie, becoming appalled at the level of truth young people were being asked to confront, and the foundational concept of kids killing kids because the adults made them. They'd had long discussions about it and how it made Shakti feel. Liv worried that exposure to so much evil was becoming pervasive. Whether it was more unavoidable news clips populating shows they watched, or the spread of social media, clearly in the course of one generation, new depths of human depravity were being brought to teens' field of awareness. Her own experience as a teen growing up under a President who screwed around with an intern, well, that seemed a minor immorality now. Liv felt that she, at sixteen in 1995, must have been way more naïve than Shakti was now. Shakti knew about teen suicides from bullying; child soldiers and the possibility that David's nephews might be kidnapped; terrorists who crashed airplanes into buildings, blew up trains and shot down young people at a concert; as well as the use of guns in school massacres and shootings in theaters and public places like malls. So many new ways to meet a random death. Liv as always had tried to create context and perspectives on events. But what did it say about our culture, she thought, that one even had to do this. And that a heroine today was - happily not Cinderella – but a girl who rebels in a world where adults laud children killing each other.

When the girls exited the film, they were abuzz and

drifted to the mall seating outside Starbuck's to enjoy hot chocolates and mocha lattes. As Alex led a conversation on what she loved about what Katniss did, and what she thought of the guys, Shakti's gaze traveled to a nearby suspended TV monitor. More news about the refugees. As they finished up and collectively moved to a garbage can near the TV set, Alex looked up and caught the drift. "I agree, we shouldn't take in any Syrian refugees. I mean here we are in this mall, we could just be gunned down." The TV report moved on to an update on the Paris attack leader with the regularly used photo of him looking like a crazy Mad Hatter in his winter beige hat and his bad, widely spaced teeth, a teenage jokester's face.

Natalie could not not take the bait. "Right Alex, like the shooters of the kids at Newtown, or in Aurora, or any of the gun violence attacks killing tons of people like us, like any of them were Syrians. Give me a break." This was the same debate going on in Natalie's home and she had just taken her mother's role against Alex as her father.

Shakti who'd been lost in her thoughts about Katniss, was jolted by the confrontational tone of Natalie's voice. Shakti looked at the screen again and thought of her own mother's indignation and fury on the topic the past week, how her mom had worked with refugees, how they were great people, and how wonderful David was.

As the group walked down the mall to Macy's where the older girls wanted to check out some makeup and jewelry before heading home, Shakti yearned to free herself of their mentality and this mall, and to stand for something important, like refugees, like her mom did. Her disgust with the older girls' diddling over makeup testers was palpable. Alex looked at her. "What's with you? How come you're so grumpy? Not that you're ever the life of the party, but what's your problem?" Anna piped in next, "Jealous because you don't know how to wear makeup? Honestly, if you'd spend some time on how you look, you might possibly be attractive."

Natalie jumped to her friend's defense readily, always looking to oppose her sister. "Leave her alone. She's...." Shakti was shaking her head and pleaded softly in her ear, "No, don't tell her anything about me, especially not the secret about my father." So Natalie simply said that Shakti had a lot on her mind. "We just want to leave and go home."

"Kill-joys! Well, you're going to have to wait until we finish OUR fun."

"Fine. We'll wait outside."

"Fine," Alex snapped back.

As Natalie and Shakti hung around outside watching shoppers overloaded with packages, they tried to find a nearby storefront with anything of interest to them – too bad the Apple store was on the other side of the mall. Finally, they sat on the metal benches.

"Thanks for not saying anything."

"No way. Alex is SO obnoxious now that she's in college. I thought it was bad last year. I love it when she's away, but then she comes home, and everything she says, and her friends, it's all so annoying."

"I don't want to be like them. I want to be this really smart, strong courageous person."

"Like Katniss, I know."

"Not like them anyway. This will sound dumb – and don't you ever repeat it…"

"Promise."

Shakti turned to look directly at her and spoke softly. "I want to be amazing. I want to wow my father. I want to take off…"

"Have you been watching too much Supergirl on TV?"

"No, that's lame. I guess I'm lame. Except I'm not!"

"I don't think you're lame. We're both smarter than Alex and her stupid friends. Don't let them get you down."

During the drive home, they both looked out the windows and tried to shut off the chatter about upcoming dates. When Alex dropped Shakti off, she proffered a weak 'thanks,' and walked away looking downcast. Alex turned her head to Natalie. "Remind me not to bring her with me anywhere."

Natalie ignored her.

Liv had just arrived home from the potluck dinner at Elyse's when Shakti dragged in, flinging her jacket on the nearest chair. "Hey, how was it?"

"Mom, I don't want to grow up to be the kind of girl who's into sexting and makeup and all about guys. I want to be something better than that?" Her upspeak was becoming a habit making much of what she said sound tentative to Liv.

"Better? How? Like Katniss in some way?"

"I don't know. That sounds ridiculous when you say it."

"I didn't mean it that way. Come sit by me. And tell me if these left-overs from the potluck will do for dinner for you." Shakti reluctantly sat at the table with Liv. "Tell me about the movie."

"The movie was good, although that older woman character was not good. I mean it's like the world is screwed no matter what, even when the rebels triumph, then there's still more to do. If you're up for it."

"Truth in that for sure." Liv bent over to hug Shakti, but she wouldn't have it. "Is that what's got you…you seem upset."

"I am. Alex was super nasty to me. Her friend too. You wouldn't have liked her refugee talk either."

"What did she say to you?"

"Oh, the usual snotty stuff. But it was me – I didn't really stand up for myself. I just kept quiet. Like I'm this mousy girl who can't stand up to her."

"You could try thinking that she's me and talk back to her?"

Shakti just glared at her.

"Sorry. But…" Liv groped for her point, "but all I'm saying is that sometimes you find your voice, so I know it's there. It's just a matter of developing it, knowing what you care about – like me and refugees – and finding the appropriate way to get it out."

"Appropriate? That doesn't sound like a rebel."

"Hmm, right. I meant that you have to pay attention to time and place. So where were you when Alex was snotty?'

"In Macy's at the makeup counter."

"Okay, so she was totally inappropriate insulting you in a public place like that. It's inflammatory and if you had told her off, it's a scene. So later is better."

"Like in the car which she was driving and could kick me out?"

"There's that point though when you got out. Maybe you could have called her then on her behavior in the store?"

Shakti considered. "Maybe. But I felt so small, so nothing by then."

"That's what happens." Stopping in her tracks to the oven, Liv reflected, "I'm in the same boat at work. I'm losing my voice, feeling pressed to just be the good soldier, while this bully on the Board takes over our territory. I can't seem to find the right time and place to stand for myself." They sat quiet for a moment.

"What hope is there if you're so much older than me and you can't do it either?"

Liv was asking herself, when have I had my voice and when have I lost it? "It's not like this permanent change that comes over you, Shakti, finding your voice. It's on-going, probably all our lives. I know times I've found it, and times I've used it badly, and now, it's a challenge to find it again."

"When did you find it?"

Liv positioned herself to be face to face with her daughter. "I found it for sure when I decided to have you and keep you despite voices telling me to do something else."

"Like who?"

Liv was not about to smear Elyse in Shakti's brain by noting the full court press her friend had made for an abortion. "It doesn't matter now. What matters is that I made my own choice, and that's a way of finding your voice. It doesn't have to be that you insult Alex back or tell her off. It's that you watch the company you keep. You make choices that leave the bullies of the world without any power over you."

"It just seems easier to say something back."

"True. But I can think of one time where I did that and even though what I said was right, it wasn't the right action."

"I don't get that."

"Do you recall a guy I dated named Eric?"

"Yeah, sort of – the Viking guy? I didn't like him, did I?"

"No, you didn't."

"What did you say to him?"

Liv took a breath and thought, why not. "I called him a racist at Elyse's wedding. He was my date and he made a nasty remark about me spending time with David."

Shakti had a flash of herself walking down the aisle in this polka dot dress spreading rose petals. "But Eric was your date, so I guess I get how he felt, a little?"

"That's what I mean. I should have just said something else at the time – I'm not sure what – maybe asking him what he meant by the remark to give him a chance to backtrack – although truly he was racist – but he was also a little drunk at the point. Anyway, I made a scene."

"Were you drunk too?"

"I don't think so. It's not so different than now really. I was losing my voice in that relationship, suppressing the things I cared about, and then I erupted." Liv wondered if she was at risk of an explosion at work. "Anyway, the point is, you don't have to make a scene. I could just have decided not to date him anymore. Which is what I did."

"I'm glad about that."

Liv wanted to reframe the conversation, so they could have a more upbeat end to the day. "So, here we both are trying to find our voice as challenges come up." This time Shakti let her Mom touch her hand. "We can fight these battles together, okay?"

"Yeah. Sure."

"Hey, remember whom I'm skyping with tomorrow morning?"

"David?"

"You want to say hi too, don't you?"

Shakti nodded. "Where is he?"

"Still near Amsterdam."

Liv was excited to be connecting with him tomorrow. So much had been happening in his part of the world. *Was it summer they last skyped? Before he went to see his sister and nephews in Kenya following their move?* She needed to hear him talk as his emails were always brief and lacking in the details she craved. Liv knew David was anxious about his family and focused on helping them survive in Nairobi. Which reminded her of Indusa being there. *But maybe now he was involved with someone at the Court?* Not that any relationship with a woman carried much import in his decisions.

Tonight, sitting at her computer, she saw his face next to hers in a nearby photo. The Amsterdam trip, 2009. The two of them looked happy, carefree, his long dark arm dropped over her bare shoulder. They were an odd couple, both on the surface of it, and in terms of life experiences. What they shared was years of friendship in Seattle – and then a taste of full-blooded love in the Serengeti. She looked on top of the world in that photo, taken by his roommate right at the beginning of her Amsterdam visit. Hope had inspired her to go, hope that now he seemed settled in northern Europe with a regular job, perhaps they might somehow make a future together. She'd almost finished her Master's in Marketing and Communications and was thinking of changing jobs. Shakti was eight. She'd hoped she'd like the Netherlands, maybe there would be jobs for English-speaking people, and maybe they could make something work. They would try. She'd hoped.

David had encouraged her to come. He'd been there six months, had a permanent job with the International Criminal Court as an attorney, and was immensely satisfied with the recent indictment of Bashir. With a warrant out, they just needed to get him extradited the first time he stepped out of Sudan. Finally, David would get his revenge. And while he'd been concerned about his sister's family's relocating from the camp in Chad to South Sudan when it gained its independence, perhaps that would work out for them. He too was hoping in his own subdued way, without saying too much in his emails, that the time might be ripe for a real relationship with Liv.

Did I really try? Or did I give up my voice? Did I not claim what I wanted? Or was I simply not sure our lives belonged together?

The first days had been a crazed time of sex, trips out for food, and then more sex. They'd stored their carnal energy inside for well over a year, both internally compelled to be faithful to the other. The release was like an unrelenting burning lava flow. His roommate stayed over at his girlfriend's, leaving David and Liv apartment-wide opportunities for the intimacy they craved.

Eventually they tamed themselves, and began to integrate longer outings, to tour first The Hague and then Amsterdam, less than an hour away. While her eyes feasted on the dramatic juxtapositions of venerable and modern architecture, her ears tried to attune to the babel, and noticed how everyone knew multiple languages. Their visit to his office to introduce her impressed upon her the diversity of staff working there. Many lawyers and judges from Africa, certainly an excellent milieu for David. Incredibly smart people doing critical work. As she viewed the modern chambers and absorbed David's mini-lectures on the nature of their proceedings, the heavy atmosphere of the law, thick with life and death issues, diminished her sense of self. Her own excitement at touting her master's work was quickly eclipsed by the substantial credentials and experiences of David's colleagues.

As he'd walked her around the Court offices and hallways, she'd gotten 'the look' again from a couple of the female attorneys to whom he introduced her. That look that Indusa had given her in Nairobi at the dinner party. That 'who the hell are you' look, which spoke to the obvious connection between her and David. Not that they flaunted it in public. His hand at her back as he steered her around, Liv was perhaps overly sensitive to the gaze of the two following her as they made comments in low voices.

These women, part of David and his roommate Ronald's social circle, used a party the guys had hosted later that week to continue sizing up – or down – Liv and to learn if she was a viable threat to their designs on David. If Liv hadn't been there, they would have been undermining each other's attempts to ensnare him, but with her in the picture, their pre-Davidian friendship came to the fore in a joint effort to defeat the enemy. Margreet was Dutch, a striking combination of lithe and voluptuous, while the other chunkier but sexier South African named Thabisa had a face whose beauty caused your eyes to linger.

In preparation for the trip, Elyse had shopped with Liv and together they'd settled on two alternatives: a sexy but simple black dress that showed her slim legs to good advantage in a pair of heeled sandals; and basic black slacks you could dress up with a sexy black top or cover up with a high quality casual turquoise sweater. Some rhinestone bling to make the black more fun and the Native American turquoise necklace her parents had given her one year provided the accents. For the party, she chose the slacks, heeled sandals, and black top dressed down with the sweater but elevated by the centerpiece Indian necklace, which brought out her coloring. At least with her clothing, Liv felt confident for the party. She also gathered her thoughts on the most interesting aspects and accomplishments of her work to manage the overwhelm factor induced by these accomplished legal eagles. She held in her mind her role in the micro-credit program, her work in fundraising that was growing as she became the Center's resident story teller for their communications with donors about clients, and her practically finished MA. Elyse had also provided a pep talk on taking pride in herself as an independent single mom, urging Liv to neither hide it, nor brag about it, but use it to project a maturity beyond her years.

The party crowd grew quickly to fill the apartment, with warm engagement from David and Ronald's colleagues. Ronald's girlfriend, Martine, was especially solicitous of Liv, encouraging her to share her reactions, and gently probing to learn more about her. Liv was heartened. The party was going well. She sipped her wine slowly, eating a bit along the way to maintain clarity. Martine asked Liv to help her keep watch on the food and hand out some hot shrimp *kroketten,* so she could move about the room and meet more people. Martine did not work at the Court. She was an elementary school teacher and, having dealt with her own status issues with this crowd, wanted to create a supportive environment for Liv.

Of course, everyone spoke English. But as people piled in and circulated, Liv heard Dutch, which she tentatively had concluded would be beyond her ability to learn, as even David struggled with it; French, which she recalled a smattering of from high school; and then words thrown in that sounded African. The conversation was a medley of recent cultural events - the film this one had just seen or the concert another just heard - to current events and concerns of global recession and unemployment. But the undertone of the law and the Court was a bass refrain. Those working at the court, but not their spouses and dates, began to coagulate as party central. Early on, one such discussion with a prosecutor had pulled David in. Liv wanted to show she could move in his milieu so resisted the urge to simply stand at his side and welcomed Martine's direction to keep helping and moving.

Liv took momentary refuge in the bathroom, where she took a few deep breaths to regroup. After she plumped her hair and made her curls sexier, then reapplied her peach gloss lipstick, she leaned back against the door. *This would be my world, my social interactions if I came.* Clearly, like no other she'd been in. She guessed she'd make a few friends over time. Ronald and Martine were lovely to her. But what a world of talk and languages apart from her patterns in Seattle, which felt 'down home in the boonies' in contrast to this cosmopolitan crowd. Yet, as David reminded her when she'd get like this, he was a herdsman by birth and grew up in camps. Anything was possible.

Exiting the bathroom, she headed for the tiny kitchen to see if Martine was there. That's where Margreet and Thabisa ambushed her. Without any nefarious plan or words spoken, they reverted to their natural rhythm and vibe as friends and colleagues. Neither had called a huddle with the other to name the enemy. There was no planned strategy. Their maneuvers were simply organic immune responses to a foreign agent.

As the two entered the small space, they were laughing over some witty remark they'd overheard. Liv was bent over the oven, pulling out the last of the heated hors d'oeuvres, cheesy pastry puffs. She looked up at their voices, smiled, and detected from their aura that trouble had arrived. She recognized them from the Court tour and sensed an attack. "Hi, would you like some of these? They're deliciously warm." Liv held the tray out to them.

Thabisa was laughing the most, causing her arm and hand to move and the red wine in her glass to slosh about. She was the more attractive of the two with a congruence of features and rich, sexy voice. When she wasn't laughing, which she curtailed in that moment to stare at Liv, she exuded dignity enforced by a trace of British accent. "No dear, I've had enough. Margreet?"

Margreet's face had that unattractive Dutch droop to it that did not serve her big round dark eyes well, a set of features that didn't work well together. But what Margreet had over both Thabisa's face and Liv's elegance that day was a figure to die for. Voluptuous curves punctuating a tall slim body as though she was a long sentence overburdened with commas. She wore a hot pink sheath that instantly made Liv feel as though she were dressed in mourning. "No, those little devils have way too many calories for me." Her voice was lyrical, moving in and out of multiple ranges, with rhythm and emphasis. "You have some, you're like a stick and can handle a few more pounds."

Thabisa fired the first salvo. "What have you and my man David been up to? We've missed him these days at the Court. He's such a rising star here you know. He's going to go far. Of course, he needs to work hard like the rest of us, but someday, who knows, he could be a prosecutor. You think so?" a query clearly directed at Margreet.

Liv recognized that Thabisa didn't really want to know what she and David had been doing and was quickly evaluating possible responses. Before she decided on her defenses, Margreet kept the talk moving. "Absolutely, most definitely. He'll need to learn more Dutch though, and he really needs to play the politics." Turning to cast another look of diminishment upon Liv, "You know, the Court is sooo political! David really needs to pay attention to that, whom he works with, what company he keeps...."

"Ah, yes, the company he keeps. You should talk to him about that Liz."

"It's Liv."

"Oh. Liv. Yes, you must encourage him to watch his options here, to choose his friends wisely."

"To choose a wife wisely," laughed Margreet. Then staring at Liv, "It's so very critical that he focus on his work right now, not get distracted by family. And then marry well."

"Most definitely," Thabisa echoed, "he needs to choose a woman with well-developed political connections that will favor his rise in the Court."

Margreet reverted to a familiar teasing pattern now. "Oh yes, Thabisa, no doubt a woman like you with all those familial connections to the Vice-President of the Court."

Thabisa poked her back with her elbow, and spoke smilingly into Liv's face, "Or take this one. She has deep roots in The Hague and court system here. But I, I know..." she rattled off some names, reverting into a patterned staple exchange with her friend regarding who had the best connections.

Which all afforded Liv an easy retreat. "Sorry, I need to take these around while they're still warm." She grabbed an extra pile of cocktail napkins and moved past them with her tray, looking like the maid. She heard them both erupt with guffaws. After disposing of the last of the cheese puffs, she searched out David's head and went to his side.

The conversation among him and two other older men, one from Germany, the other appearing South American, looked serious. David turned to look at her and saw that her glow from earlier in the party had faded. He took her hand and squeezed it. "Excuse me Hedrik. Let me visit with you next Monday about this. I need to pay attention to the rest of our guests too."

Liv was grateful yet noticed he hadn't bothered to introduce her in his exit from the conversation. Conflicted now, she felt a misfit in this crowd. Really, no one cared who she was. It was all issues at best, and political shoulder-rubbing at worst. She just wanted to walk out, despite how immature that would be, and so lacking in coping skills and grace.

"What's up?" David shepherded her into the bedroom hallway. "You look down."

She struggled with what face to put on, who she wanted to be in that moment, her honest down-to-earth self, or a more poised, capable woman who could deal with this kind of social challenge. "I just needed you to hold my hand. This isn't the friendliest, easiest crowd for me."

David knew it only too well. He knew beneath the 'golden boy' treatment he'd received these months, there was a whole culture of politics, connections, and approved behaviors underlying it. His habits of working hard and remaining socially unavailable had served him well so far; but he knew, as time passed, he'd have to choose how much to adapt. Now wasn't the time to get into it though. "Stick with Martine, she'll get you through this. She's had to cope too."

"Okay." She looked up at him with eyes now brighter from his support. "I love you." She hadn't said that but once before this trip. Now it was on her lips daily.

His sense of their being ensnared in a cage where they were the prey unified their spirits. "I love you too. I'm glad you're here. It helps me."

Their last evening before Liv returned to Seattle, lying in bed entwined, she'd asked, "What do you need? What do you want?" There would be finality in hearing him say what she knew the answer to be.

His response came quickly. "I need to have Bashir brought here to stand trial for his crimes against me, my family, and so many others like me. I want my sister's family to be able to live in safety. That is my life's work." He stopped with that. Liv knew him well enough to have integrated that: his past was his destiny. "What about you?"

Was that when she should have tried harder to make something happen? To link her destiny to his. To put his needs before hers? "I need to feel of a whole piece that what I do makes sense for me and for Shakti and for the others I care about. I don't feel like I fit here, not in this country, and especially not with the subculture currently surrounding your life. I'd lose myself here. I'd be too dependent on you and you'd be working long hours and traveling. I suspect we'd have conflicts. I don't want that." She began crying from the pain of truth telling. "I want someone who can be there for me and Shakti, who makes family first."

"You know I agree with you about that, the importance of family."

"Yes, and I know that's why you need to do what you said. I suppose we're both tied to our pasts by our families, and that's where our futures lie." Embracing more strongly, they held each other for a very long time.

As Liv lay in her bed in Seattle over six years later, she closed her eyes and felt that embrace, heard their silences, the words left unsaid about having separate paths, no shared destiny. All the conclusions that would have turned her tears into sobs and made her flail against him, and pound him with her fists for not reaching for a future with her. The absence of fruitless pleas for him to change – to what? Come back to Seattle? That was a voice not worth claiming. Selfish. Divisive. The voice of a needy, clingy woman who was desperate. It wasn't who she was then, or ever wanted to be. She knew those things had been left unsaid to honor the deep connection that implausibly joined their souls. No, she thought, I didn't lose my voice then. *I said what could be said, what was true, what was real, what held love.* But as she faced disruption in her patterned life now, she accused herself of lacking courage. *Why didn't I just go and try it for a year? It would have been good for us to do something brave, to force ourselves to stretch more.* Tonight, it felt like an opportunity she'd let slip away.

Saturday, November 28

At eight am her time and six pm his, they connected for their second skype session this year. Since her visit to the Netherlands, their relationship had passed through stages: at first, her frustration about it not working out made her go cold turkey and hold herself to curt emails to him. He in fact did have to work extremely hard. Trying to get other governments to extradite Bashir involved several trips to make persuasive yet unsuccessful approaches to foreign diplomats. He'd been assigned to and thrown himself into trying to learn where the Ugandan war criminal Kony was hiding and whether others in the Lord's Resistance Army were still kidnapping children. His concern for his nephews only grew more consuming. And then their father was killed. David had rushed to South Sudan and taken his sister and nephews to Nairobi and spent almost a month getting them housed with an acquaintance and helping Amer resettle into Eastleigh. Even that refugee dominated neighborhood presented urban challenges totally beyond her experience, and he'd been the one enrolling Dut and Deng, ages thirteen and eleven, into school; and arranging banking so that she could draw on a monthly stipend from a Dutch account David set up. Along the way, when Liv revealed that she was in a relationship with Marco, David moved beyond occasional one-night stands and took up first with a sweet Dutch clerk at the courts who reminded him of Liv, and more recently with a judge. While in Nairobi settling his sister, he had a sexual encounter with Indusa that left him cold. He'd been back to Kenya twice since resettling Amer and the boys and felt pressured to move there to be with them.

 Almost inevitably along their journeys, the emails between Liv and him had picked up, as he needed someone to confide in who understood his past.

 As their images popped up on the screen, he was startled by her new look. "Where's your hair?"

 "Oh, that. I cut it a while back and tried to keep it straight but that was awful. Do you like this?" she said, swiveling her head so he could see her from the side too and take in the drizzle of curls.

 "You look so sophisticated. Yes, I like it. A lot." He wished he could put his arms through the monitor and touch her face.

"Me too. So, I want to hear all about Amer and the boys – you too of course! Start anywhere."

David sat back and lowered his eyes a moment. Then, looking at the camera, "Liv, so much is changing, like tiny earthquake tremors keep happening, where first one thing changes, like with my sister, then another, like how I feel about the boys now. And then I go to work, and I get depressed because I'm a Don Quixote going after Bashir." His features squished closer together as though he was in pain. "I'm just fed up with the world. I'm not sure what I want anymore. I still want my family to be okay, I want that more than ever. Dut and Deng, they mean so much to me. I want to be with them."

"Are you going to move to Kenya then?" You could get a good job there, no? Couldn't it work out?"

David placed his elbows on his desk, hands coming together, and pressed his forehead to them. Then lowering his hands, he looked at her and spoke with difficulty. "I know that would make sense. But every time I go, I find I don't want to be in that place. This sounds weird I know. And there's no one else I can say this to...it's so painful for me to be there. To know there are hundreds of thousands of refugees in the camps, just a few hours' drive away, people like I was. And now since the al-Shabaab attack on the university, Kenya wants to push all the Somalis out, over 300,000 people. It's crazy, where will they go? When I'm there, I feel so pulled apart. Do I really want to sit in some law office in a glass skyscraper raking in the money while so many – who are just the way I was – they have so little and now are being pressured to move on? It haunts me when I'm so close to it."

"But David, that's true wherever you are. Where you are exactly right now. That reality exists every moment as you get ready for work in a nice suit, as you do your work at the Court. Is it that the court work makes you feel more like you're actually helping to change the system?"

He looked away to the right, towards his window, and then back. "Sometimes. YES, sometimes. But then there's my nephews. Do I want my family there if I can find a better place? There's still civil war in my country, I fear for my nephews growing up so near to it, of getting sucked into it somehow. After all the time I spent as a Dinka with Nuer people in the refugee camps, I can't believe - except of course I can, because of all this tribalism - but it's insane the two tribes are killing off innocents. I don't want my nephews near any of that. It makes me crazy." He pulled back now slumping a bit in his chair. "It's hard for me to say it." Then he stared right at her as though they were only a few feet away. "I'm tired Liv, really tired. I just want a normal life."

"Oh." She got it now.

Coming even closer to the screen so she saw only his magnificent forehead and sad eyes, it was as though he was whispering to her in bed. "Ever since I was still a boy, I've been struggling, trying so hard to save myself, the other children who fled, my friends, to work for justice, to be there now for Amer and the kids." Liv could see his eyes moistening, then his hand moved quickly to wipe away a tear. "I'm so tired. I want to find a safe place and rest and not be haunted by the world."

Liv was watching him intently. *Affirmations. Keep his thoughts moving.* "David, everyone, most everyone anyway, takes a rest. You've gone a very long time, like twenty-five years, without a rest. It's okay to rest, to find that safe place. That's what we want for all the refuges right? A safe place to rest, to be. It's okay that you want that." He sniffled. "Do you have any ideas what that might look like?"

"Not really. I've started to talk to attorneys I know – not staff, but ones who come to the Court on cases, civil and criminal, about what else they do. There's a guy from London who seems interested in me, my career possibilities."

"London?"

"Yes, there are a few prestigious international law firms there that have cases at The Hague. Philip's older than me. He thinks I'd love London because it's so diverse. He's invited me to visit him, meet some others at the firm, and get acquainted with the city and its neighborhoods."

"Wow! That sounds really attractive."

"It does. But it's complicated by my sister. I would want to move her and the boys there."

"Really? You think that would be better for them?"

"Not better for her. But I could be there for all of them. Be a dad to the boys. Get them in good schools."

Liv could envision it. "You know one thing I tell myself when I'm down about being in my little nook of the world here, not doing much to save the world…"

"But think of all that money you raise to help women, you redistribute resources, it's great."

"I guess. But what I was going to say is that sometimes it dawns on me, the insignificance thing, the short reach of our lives, and I'm so glad Shakti is here. To pass the torch to. Whatever I can do, she'll be better. She'll help more. Maybe an investment of your time and efforts in your nephews would be the same. They'll be the next lions of Africa and take up where you leave off."

He looked at her with brighter eyes across the virtual space. "Lions. That reminds me of our little safari." He started to smile. "What a fine time those few days were. That was a good rest. But far too short."

Liv smiled widely. "It was."

"What about you, what's happening there? How is Miss Shakti?"

"It's odd, maybe something in the stars, but I'm feeling unsettled now too." She provided a brief account of her job issues, the need to move, her parents selling their home. She moved quickly though to dwell on Shakti and the developments with contacting her father in Mumbai. "Sometime in the next week, we should hear back from my friend. Shakti and I will both be crushed if the reply is off-putting."

David's body language became more alert. "So, you may be seeing her father next year? That's amazing. Maybe you'll be the one moving south."

"Highly unlikely. It's way too soon to speculate on anything. But if I did, which I admit it's hard not to, it might mean an annual visit for Shakti there, something like that. Who knows, maybe she'll fall in love with India. Plus, she has half-brothers there, boys like your nephews."

His eyes were big now. "So much change beginning to unfold. Somehow, it makes me hopeful."

"Why? The grass is greener thing?"

"Maybe, I'm not sure. It just reminds me that when I'm feeling stuck and depressed, time will pass, and a very different future can come to be."

"Let me go wake her up, so you can say hello."

Shakti, presenting a tossled head and sleepy body came and sat on Liv's lap.

"How beautiful you are!"

Shakti stuck out her tongue. But then grinned. "David, why don't you come see us some time?"

"Well, actually I just had a different thought. We'll see how things go, okay?" They chatted for several minutes, before Shakti went to get some juice. "Liv, if you do go to India, you'll have to fly over me you know. Maybe you could have a lay-over in Amsterdam?"

Her face lit up. "Wouldn't that be fun! Now that makes me happy."

"Yes, me too. You owe me a visit."

"If, still a big if, a trip to India develops, as you say, we should stop and visit."

They smiled lovingly at each other. "I should go now. Ronald and Martine invited me for dinner."

"Say hello for me. And David, I really believe something transformative is happening inside you. Try not to get down. Just go with the flow and see what wants to happen."

Putting his hand to the screen, "I wish I could touch you."

She kissed her fingers and placed them on his.

Friday, December 4

Rama's panel presentation wasn't until the afternoon, so he'd arrived late last night in Mumbai from Pune, where he lived. Rather than stay at the conference hotel, he was at his mother's home in the old monied area of South Mumbai, formerly South Bombay as his mother still called it - SoBo to Rama's generation. This morning he planned to finalize his talk and slides.

  He was distracted though by a commitment he had made to his mother that involved connecting with Arita, very possibly at the conference. He mulled over alternative approaches to locating and then speaking with her, all the while resentful his mother had put him in this situation. He cherished his wife and boys and didn't want them to know of his American daughter's existence. It was an old secret with his mother whose non-interventionist advice had worked out. A tight family, they'd come together even more closely since his father's passing from a heart attack a few years back. When he, his brother, and sister were still producing offspring, mother had always been the one saying, "Please, a granddaughter this time, I'm tired of all these men in the family!" Not that her daughter in England wasn't as devoted to her mother as the distance permitted. But the years had brought only male progeny.

  After surviving her first bout of breast cancer four years ago, and then dealing with her husband's death shortly thereafter, Nimisha grew quieter, even morose at times. She lacked the joyfulness she used to exhibit in their gatherings. Indira, Rama's wife, was particularly attentive to Nimisha's needs despite being more than an hour away in Pune. Nonetheless, Rama worried about his mother, especially these last two months after she received the report that the cancer was back. She'd quickly gone back into chemo, but Rama and Indira shared a sense that Nimisha had less will to live, despite being only seventy. Before, they'd imagined the early version of herself going on forever. Not now.

  He and his brother had made her move out of her house and into a Malabar Hill flat after their father died. Most recently, when Rama was in town for a meeting, he took her to her chemo appointment. Afterwards, he'd fixed her tea, thinking he'd rush to get out of town. But she made him stay and have a cup with her.

An agenda was in the air, and he waited patiently. Then it came: she'd been thinking, thinking a lot over these past years, and become sharply aware that this latest bout of disease could bring her end.

He'd been quiet, beginning to internally generate the responses he usually did that minimized the threat and pointed toward a healthier future. But he waited for her to finish her words. "I'd like to see a picture of the girl. I'd like to know whom she looks like." It took no more than a few seconds for him to realize whom she'd meant. "Can you do that for your mother? Can you get me a photo?"

Dread embraced him, silencing him. He was not about to deny her. Meeting her gaze, the gaze that he associated all his life with love, he finally responded. "I'll try. But I need some time."

"I understand."

As he'd worked the angles of contacting Arita and then Liv, he'd concluded that the best thing was to maintain their go-between and not be in direct contact. He couldn't recall her face anymore, only a clear image of sun coming through her hair from behind, and a smile. Arita's email was somewhere, or he could find her easily enough online, certainly if she still worked for StreeShakti. But he vaguely recalled she'd moved on to another organization.

In the following week, as he did his first pass at prepping for the upcoming panel in December at the annual conference on sustainable agriculture, it dawned on him that he could meet her in person there. That would be better, handle it in person. Odds were high she'd be there, he'd often seen her there. And if not then he'd look her up and email her.

As he entered the Grand Hyatt Mumbai that afternoon, his eyes were in service to his mother's mission. It was only when he was up on the dais, chatting with the other panelists focused on the government's actions in support of sustainable agriculture, that he scanned the audience, and saw her take a chair at a row's end.

Arita's strategy meanwhile was to nab him quickly after the panel. After tactically seating herself, she raised her eyes and met his.

He moved and came down to greet her. "Arita, I'm glad to see you here. Would you have time to talk afterwards?"

Her eyes registered surprise, but her remarks came straight from a grateful heart. "That would be great, I was hoping we could connect here."

She had a hard time giving undivided attention to the other panelists as each took their turn, Rama first outlining the history of the Agricultural Extension's work in the Thane District, and the other two addressing recent initiatives, one north of Mumbai and the other tried elsewhere in India that they hoped to replicate. Arita's eyes kept returning to Rama, creating phrases she even jotted down in her notes to describe how he looked and acted: 'at home in a suit,' 'easy to smile,' 'still exuding leadership with his authoritative, upbeat tone,' 'bulkier around the face and neck' - she'd have to check his weight later - 'less thick hair.' *Still very attractive though.* She assessed how comfortable he was with himself, still confident and inspiring about how change would come. She wondered how he did it. She got down so easily with all the negative news, be it treatment of women, rapes, nuclear poisoning at sites in India, loss of ground water and the attendant farmer suicide rates. For her, it was a real struggle to keep showing up at the Women's Justice Movement and trying to make a difference. Rama made it sound like progress was happening for the rural poor. She wasn't so sure about that. She didn't really like that about him, wanting to label him shallow and removed from the struggles of the villages. But she felt the impact on herself even now, as she'd used to feel it years ago when Liv was there as an intern, and he was the bright star leading them on. *We do need hope to keep going.* Her spirits improved during the discussion, especially as young people in the audience asked questions at the mic near her, and she could feel their energy to create a better India.

Rama made short goodbyes to his colleagues, stopped to take a few follow-up questions from participants gathered around the dais, but kept checking to make sure she was still there. Only too happy to wait, she was buoyed that she could fulfill her mission for Liv. And Shakti. And be useful as a special emissary on such an important matter. Rama suggested they go to the hotel lobby area where you could sit in comfortable chairs and order beverages and snacks. People liked to meet there, and it took a a few minutes to find a place to sit.

Arita complimented him on his presentation and asked her own follow up question to make easy conversation. She calculated that it was best if he went first with whatever was on his mind, so she could respond to his signals. She expected it somehow related to her work.

Rama bought time with a slow, complex response to her question about water tables, while he assessed her intently. There was an edge to her. The black angular hair cut made her deep brown eyes stand out. He noticed how thin she still was compared with his own extra twenty pounds. In between his multi-part answer covering government regulatory efforts, and wide-spread support for the farming population, they placed their order for tea and biscuits. He'd considered a couple of approaches already and settled on his mother's health situation as being the most direct and compelling. "I wanted to talk with you about something personal Arita, about my mother."

Arita became totally focused, hiding her surprise. "What is it?"

"She's sick again, her cancer has come back. I don't know if you recall from my dad's memorial service, but she'd just recovered from breast cancer back then."

"Yes, I do recall your concern. She still looked peaked – of course, your dad passing relatively young didn't help. I'm so sorry to hear it's back. She's a very fine woman."

"Yes, yes she is. Always so progressive in her thinking, so supportive of Dad and his work. And me. All of us." Rama searched for his transition, relieved the refreshments arrived and he could sip his tea. "Here's the thing. She's always wanted a granddaughter and, I'm not sure if you know, but we've all had sons."

That phrase, 'always wanted a granddaughter,' reached across the open space between them as though it were a pair of arms pulling her closer. Her heart kept repeating it. Liv had to hear these words. "And?"

"And so, you don't know this, but my mother has always known about Shakti. From when Liv first wrote me. My mother counseled me. It's been our secret."

Arita tried to absorb all this. "Does Liv know that?"

"Yes, I wrote her back and told her how upset I was and that I had turned to my mother for advice."

"If you don't mind my asking, what was your mother's advice?"

"To let Liv decide." He was staring hard into Arita's eyes now, not wanted to be judged. "And so, I did."

Arita looked away. Yes, she'd admired that Liv had always been clear. Intuiting where this was going, Arita was afraid her hands might shake if she picked up the teacup. "What is your mother saying now?"

Rama appreciated the ease with which this was flowing, that Arita was so fully present to his situation understanding her role. "She would like a picture of her granddaughter. That's what she asked for. About a month ago."

Apparent now that both had waited for this personal contact, a palpable energy field encompassed them, making Arita feel she was in a bubble isolated from those sitting nearby. "And you would like me to ask Liv for a photo?"

"Yes, I would, very much." He knew she'd do it and felt at ease.

"Of course."

He wondered then – a thought neglected in his prior consideration – would Liv agree? He'd assumed she would. But after fifteen years, would she want to open this up? *She would surely want to help with a dying woman's request, no? She wouldn't have to let the girl know about it.* "Do you think she'll do it?"

Arita felt the burden of her own mission. She let her gaze travel around the lobby, not really seeing anything outside their bubble, while she considered whether to voice Shakti's request to meet him. Her intuition told her that his seeing the photo would lay the pathway, one step at a time. There was a river carrying them now, a process that was flowing. Perhaps there would be a message with the photo from Shakti?

"Arita, I can see you're not sure what to say. I don't want to get Mother's hopes up."

"I think your mother will get a photo. Do you want it sent to you first, or does she have her own email?"

Somehow the image of him opening an email with his daughter's photo hit him now in a personal way. He'd kept emotional distance from the request as though it was a sensitive transaction among family members that he facilitated but which didn't involve him. *I'm going to see what my daughter looks like, to see a face that might be mine – or perhaps it's Liv's? How will the girl look?* And then, as though with a physical blow to his torso, the realization came: there's this girl out there with a life, a real person; and I'm her father.

Arita watched the spirt flow out of his body as he sat back and looked diminished. *He gets it now, that something he's put aside is confronting him. This isn't just your mother having a request Rama, oh no, this is you having to come to terms with a full-blown young girl in your life.* "Look, when I have the photo I'll be in touch and you can tell me then where to forward it, okay?"

He pulled himself forward in the chair. "Yes. Let's do that. I think I need to be with mother when she sees it – don't you agree?"

"Yes. It may hit her hard." Arita began to gather her things. "How should I communicate with you? I mean, your wife...."

"Right, she doesn't know. I think my work email. But please be discrete, just in case."

"For sure."

Over dinner Shakti was so anxious that she only picked at her food. She knew the two-day conference in Mumbai had begun and her mom's friend was going to talk to Rama. She was on Liv right after dinner to check her emails.

Liv was quick to excuse there being none – the time difference, Arita having her own schedule, the likelihood that she hadn't cornered Rama the first day. Repeated suggestions to be patient were no longer effective. "Shakti, Aunt Mimi needs you to babysit Jeff and Margot upstairs tonight, while they check on Ryan's dad. Go help her – please!" Shakti harrumphed up the stairs leaving the doors open and commanding Liv to call her as soon as she received word from Arita.

When Liv opened her tablet to look at her emails again, she saw a fresh one from Marco. He'd left Madrid and was in Paris for the climate conference. He'd stumbled onto some people he knew from the Northwest and was hanging out with a couple of youth groups. His 45th birthday was coming up this week and he was in high spirits to be at this critical gathering. While the mainstream news about the summit outlined challenging key issues, it was nevertheless more upbeat than Marco's report that the big energy players were engaged in double talk and the media was eating it up.

After typing a short response, she returned to her incoming mail, and there it was, one from Arita. Liv hesitated, fearful to open it. She mentally braced herself and then clicked. It was short. "I talked with him yesterday and it's encouraging. Let's talk soon. Tell me when you can call me tonight (Saturday here at eight am and on my way to day two of Conference) or Sunday."

Encouraging? The fist around Liv's heart loosened its grip as she stared at the word. Should she rush to tell Shakti now or talk to Arita first thing early tomorrow? Liv leaned toward having the call to herself before Shakti was awake, to filter the information for her daughter, and shape the message. 'Encouraging' could be everything from he wants to meet her to he wants to talk to me about it.

When Shakti came tearing down the stairs as soon as Mimi and Ryan returned home, she saw her mom at the table with her tablet staring into space. "What? Did she write?"

Liv straightened her back and smiled, then left the table to come over to Shakti. "I got an email from Arita that said things were 'encouraging.'"

"What does that mean?"

"I don't know. I'm going to have to talk to her by phone to learn more. Obviously, it's not something clear and simple, like he said, yes, he wants to meet you. It's a more complicated response." Putting her arm around her disappointed looking daughter, she pulled her closer. "We knew it probably wouldn't be straightforward, right – this is huge for him Shakti, a huge shock wave from the past. He's doubtless got all kinds of reactions to it, probably not sure what his own reaction is, very possibly concerned about having hidden this from his family. This can't be rushed, sweetie. He's just like us, he needs time to think about it."

Shakti pulled back a little, unsure of her own reaction. Finally, there was movement, contact, and the word 'encouraging' described it for now. But she still didn't have an answer she could hang on to. "Mom, can't you just call her now?"

"No, she's at the conference, sitting in rooms, getting information that matters to her job, meeting other people. We have to wait until she's free."

"When will that be?"

"We're working it out. But it won't be any earlier than tomorrow morning – remember the twelve-hour difference in time?"

"Oh. Yeah." Shakti threw herself on the sofa. "Aaghh…"

"Darling, think positively."

"How am I supposed to sleep tonight?"

"For starters, don't stay in front of your screen. That will keep you up forever."

Which is exactly what she did. Googling time zones, then Mumbai, then emailing Cezar who had stayed behind in Madrid with his grandparents, then learning more about Rama and other Indian gods and goddesses, finding all of it bizarre. Except noticing that some of the images looked like her. It wasn't until one that she finally dropped off.

Liv knew she wouldn't wake up till ten or so, and emailed Arita to call her as early as possible, six or seven Seattle time, just so it was before nine.

Saturday, December 5

"Liv?"

"Oh my god, your voice Arita, I haven't heard it in so long. It's wonderful to hear you."

"I feel the same – your voice is more mature though. Is Shakti there?"

"No, she's still asleep which is the way I wanted it. In case I need to shape the news."

"I understand. So, where to start? Step by step or the bottom line?"

"Bottom line first. Is he willing to meet her?" Liv was in her bedroom with the door shut, but nonetheless using a low voice.

"I didn't ask him that – because, because you are not going to believe this – he wanted to talk to me about getting a photo of Shakti for his mother."

"What? I don't understand?"

"She's on her second bout of cancer and wait, let me read from a note I made of the conversation afterwords: he said, 'she's always wanted a granddaughter.' And Liv there are only boys in the family, his two, his brother's got three, and his sister one. And Nimisha, his mother, thinks she's dying, or at least may not have many years to live. She can't wait to see who else might still come along. She wants to see Shakti – well, a photo of her – but don't you see where this is leading?"

Liv processed. "But a photo, that doesn't mean she wants to meet her – or did he say that?"

"No. but come on, Liv, use your feminine brain: you're old and dying and you've always wanted a granddaughter – and poof, here's the photo of her, and you see features you recognize from your family."

"Maybe. I guess. But why didn't you put Shakti's request out there after he said that?"

"Liv, you needed to see his face, how I let him think he'd open his computer at work and wham, he'd be looking at his own daughter. He started off professional-like, making the request – obviously with some emotional distance from it. But by the time we finished, when I asked what email to use – the internal barrier was down, revealing a whole piece of his life he's been able to ignore. He looked like grey putty when he left, really disoriented."

"You've had more time to think this over, you know him as he is today. What do you think his reaction will be as he thinks it through?"

"Whatever his own reaction will be, he'll want to keep it a secret from his wife. He might want to put it off. But Liv, he'll be looking at the photo with another most important person in his life, his mother. Who thinks she's dying. I don't think he'll deny her anything she wants."

"Wow."

"So, I didn't ask him Liv, I didn't make Shakti's request, because we very well may not have to. His mother may make it."

"And if she doesn't?"

"Then, I'll follow up. By then, he'll have processed a lot internally. He'll have seen the photo too."

"Shakti will definitely not like the uncertainty of all this. It's so, so difficult for her to be patient."

Arita took her time responding, feeling at first slightly unappreciated for her news, but then thinking she could step out of the process. "What if, what if I send the photo as he requested; he didn't want direct contact with you. But you or Shakti put a message with the photo? Would that help?"

Liv's brain was shuffling through her favorite photos of Shakti, ready to send an album - surely the grandmother would like more than one? - but Arita's suggestion stopped the mental slideshow. "Oh. Yes. Yes, that's possible, isn't it? That would give Shakti some power in this, what photo or photos to send and whether she wanted to say something. That's good. It puts some of this back on her to confront her own uncertainty and fear. That's good, great."

"Okay, so the next step is Shakti's then. That feels right to me too."

"Arita, I am so very grateful to you. Thank you with my whole heart for guiding us. You were wise to wait this out and have a personal encounter. It's just so amazing about his mother's request, as though Shakti and her grandmother are in a cosmic convergence."

Arita was less into mystical experiences. "Thinking you're dying does open your past."

"I bet she's feeling a certain urgency – wouldn't you guess?"

"Maybe. She's back on chemo. Likely, she'll have some remission. But she won't want to wait that long."

"Once she sees her, it could move fast."

"That's my best guess too."

"Arita, if Shakti wants to talk to you directly is that okay?"

"Of course. Oh, and the full conference materials are online and Rama's headshot is there if she wants to see that."

Liv tensed. *Do I want to see that?* For a moment, she knew exactly what Rama was feeling at the thought of seeing his daughter. The person made flesh. The ideas, the thoughts rolling around from node to node in the brain, now connected to a visual image. Coming face to face with a distant past in the click of a mouse? How jarring, unsettling, a kind of grave-robbing to dig up what was buried so far under and have it rise to the surface in its present condition. A skeleton taking on modern garb and aged appropriately. A collapse of time and space that rattled one's GPS coordinates and meridian time. Like everything existed in the same moment. The power of now held all her past distilled into a single drop – what might it resurrect? Liv felt dizzy and afraid to move. No wonder Rama turned grey in front of Arita's eyes.

"I've got to run now. Stay in touch with email."

"Okay. Bye." As Liv moved from her bed to dress, it hit her that the same instability would visit Shakti, making her wobbly too. A head-spinning blow for a young mind. *She'll need to be fearless.* Shakti had been that way as a child. *And if she is afraid, I'll coach her to move through it. To love on the other side. Maybe not her father's.* But Liv knew the power of grandmothers. *Yes, her Indian grandma would want to meet her.*

Sitting at the table with a muffin, her morning coffee, and her tablet, Liv recalled what Arita said about Rama's headshot being online. Finding the conference materials and yesterday's agenda with links to the presenters' bios was easy, his name hyperlinked under "Agricultural Experiments in the Thane District." She almost clicked and then her hands retreated from the keyboard. *What do I think he looks like?* She closed her eyes and pulled herself back to her arrival in India almost sixteen years ago, recalling Arita first, her long shiny black hair and intense eyes. Then a meeting in the office where Liv studied his face and gestures. She was there again, with a clear vision of his dark hair and eyes, his authenticity with people, the leaderly presence he'd conveyed. Then his mouth, below such a long nose, speaking to her about a seed being precious. Full lips surrounding beautiful teeth and smiling warmly. A virile, muscular but thin body, in the field when he called her Sita. As she pulled the thread of the memory spool, more images came, but then she dropped the thread, too many places she really didn't want to go.

She refocused: so how has he aged? She clicked. A head propped upon a shirt collar with a tie, further supported by a dark suit. The face! A fixed smile. *Oh, so he'd put on a few pounds, fuller cheeks. Hair thinner, less forceful in defining his appearance.* She leaned back as she blew up the image. No, she liked it smaller, a head in a crowd of suits she might see at a conference. No one special. *Would I have picked him out in a crowd?* Yes, she thought, perhaps passing him and then halting abruptly to return and look again. *Still handsome.* She read his bio blurb:

> "Rama Sharma is the Chair of the Agricultural Extension program at the College of Agriculture in Pune. His own research work is in sustainable agriculture and he oversees the development and implementation of pilot programs by students. He is also co-author of a report on the state of the water table in Maharashtra. Prior to teaching, he began his career at the NGO, Improving Village Life, which successfully launched numerous pilot projects. He earned his doctorate at the Indian Agricultural Research Institute, his Master's where he currently teaches, and his Bachelor's from the London School of Economics."

A PhD too? Done quite well. Why didn't I go back to India with Shakti? She took a deep breath. *Shit, don't go there.*

Shakti appeared from the hallway in her flannel jammies, rubbing her eyes, then focusing on her mom who was closing her tablet. Her mom looked strange, maybe sad? *Is she just being serious?* "What's up? What did you just read?"

Liv breathed into a new expression and decided to short cut the predictable objections to her having spoken to Arita without Shakti. "Your grandmother in India wants a photo of you."

Shakti stopped in her tracks, scrunching up her face in confusion. "What? What are you saying?" Then, quick as a whip's crack, "You talked to her, you already talked to her without me! Mom! You know I wanted to be on the call!"

"Just cool your jets. She called very early, and I was surprised. I just let it flow. And you can still call and talk to her. But your Indian grandmother wants to see what you look like."

"What has that got to do with me meeting my father? Is she like the review committee or something?"

"No," Liv said unable not to smile. "Sit down and I'll tell you every word Arita said, including the fact that your grandmother is sick with cancer and that she's always wanted a granddaughter – and doesn't have one. Except that she does and it's you."

Shakti sat at the table while Liv rose to put on some water for oatmeal and hot chocolate. She began her account of the call, dwelling on the reasons Shakti's own request – while foremost in Arita's mind at the outset – was sent to the back burner given developments in real time. "So, the process, let's call it the process of reunion, it's underway, sweetie. And happily, the ball is not just in his court. His mother's in the game too, and she just lobbed a ball to you."

"How? Because of the photo?"

"Exactly. Do you want to send a photo is the threshold question? I assume you do?"

Shakti looked at her with puzzlement. "Mom, I have a Facebook account. It's no big deal for people to look at my pictures."

"Well, your generation is saturated with online photos, but this is different. It's a big deal for a woman say in her sixties, who's always wanted a granddaughter mind you, for her to finally get to see a picture of the one she's had but never known. That's heart-wrenching."

Shakti wasn't agreeing but she stopped responding which meant Liv was opening an inroad to her mind.

"You think it's so easy to click and view an image – well, I just sat here preparing myself to open a photo of your dad. There was something almost scary about it for me."

Shakti's nose twitched, and she tried to run her hand through her tangled bush of hair but didn't get far. "Scary? Why scary?"

"For me, it brought my distant past forward all those years - and I was scared of what it would stir up in me."

"But you did look?"

"I did."

"And, still scared? What are you now?"

"Now? Maybe stunned. Disoriented by life I guess, that we do things and then move on. But they're still there, other people's lives, your dad's, moving on too. It's heavy. It's one thing when you have pictures around you often reminding you of people you used to have in your life. But for me to see your father's face after..." after suppressing his image all those years, she thought, "...after not seeing it for all that time, it just, I don't know, I guess I felt knocked down."

Shakti, still somewhat annoyed her mother had taken the call without her, wanted to move on from her mother's overwrought reactions to life. "Show me. I want to see his picture. It doesn't scare me."

Fearless. Good. Liv opened the tablet to the headshot and pushed the tablet over so Shakti could see. "Meet your father."

"That's him? He's so normal looking. I expected him to look more... dramatic? He's just some middle-aged man in a suit."

"Look at his features – do you see yourself in him?"

Shakti moved her head closer to the screen and clicked on the image to blow it up. "Not the hair, I've definitely got yours. Maybe the rounder eye shape? And the eyebrows? What do you think?"

Liv was standing behind her now, bending over. "I think that long nose is yours... and the lips, honey, don't you think?"

Shakti kept angling her head as though she could somehow twist his head to see it from different perspectives. "I guess. The lips and chin especially, maybe the whole profile. I certainly don't get my nose from you, his seems to bend down more like mine." She pulled back, got up from the table, and viewed the photo from a greater distance, then walked up to it. "Yeah, I guess if he was standing next to me at school, everyone would think he's my dad. Although mostly they'd notice the same skin color right away."

The kettle blew interrupting their conversation. Liv hustled to make oatmeal with some apple cut up in it. Shakti pushed the tablet towards the table's center but kept the photo up, renewing it whenever the screensaver came on. As the silence lengthened, Liv couldn't predict what Shakti would say next. Once she sat down to breakfast, she paused before eating. "This is what it would be like having breakfast with my dad. This is what I'd be seeing. Sit down Mom. I want to look at you both across the table." Liv complied. "My first breakfast with both my parents in front of me." Shakti felt a wave of accomplishment, having made something new happen in her life, until a teary sadness arrived. *This is what I've missed all my life, two parents just for me.*

Liv was quiet, looking across at a ragamuffin in her faded jammies, hair like a bush that needed serious pruning, a steady pair of gorgeous blue-green eyes set off against her caramel skin. She noticed the tears being wiped away and intuited the reason. *Don't go there now, move on.* "What photo do you want to send? Should we take some new ones especially for this?"

Shakti retrieved her phone from the charger and started flipping through her gallery. Nothing seemed right. She wanted an absolutely amazing picture that would wow them. "Mom, there's nothing here that does what I want."

Liv considered a suggestion, took a breath, and dared herself to land it successfully. "What about we go to the spa, the one that Auntie Elyse picked for your birthday? We could try and get in this afternoon, get you a haircut…" Liv hesitated since this idea had been a no-go for so long, "…and you could get a facial maybe, your nails done…and a little makeup?" Liv waited for the negative blast back.

With a sneer, Shakti responded "You mean, clean me up like Natalie's sister said?"

"Just because she was mean, you shouldn't let what she said decide what you want. You seem to want a different look if none of the old shots work. You could just give it a try? Why not? Are you the one who's scared now?"

As Liv knew it would, that made Shakti mad. "I'm not afraid of anything. They need to take me as I am." She ate some, and then spouted, "But I want them to not be able to take their eyes off me." Her voice was softening, and after a few more bites, she placed her spoon down. "I want them to want me, Mom."

Liv came over and hugged her shoulders. "Of course you do. Let's see what a trip to the spa does – and I may even spring for a new top for you for Christmas, to make the photo really pop. What do you think?"

Shakti tilted her head back to stare up at Liv. "I can't believe any of this is really happening."

Liv called Elyse who arranged for a late afternoon appointment at the Gene Juarez Spa downtown where she would join them. That left time for shopping at Macy's beforehand. "What look do you want? Seems like we should shop with the photo shoot in mind, no?"

Shakti wasn't verbally responsive, but as she moved through the aisles and among the clothes racks, she tested ideas out loud. "I want to look amazing. But not shallow or flashy. Like really smart. Like they'd miss out a lot if they don't meet me."

Liv had no clue how to translate that into clothes. Mostly, as she took in the choices, she yielded to a familiar judgment: they're dressing like whores. But once she got into it more, she started pulling some items for a layered, more modest effect. "Colors? What colors are okay? Something to make your eyes stand out? Or is their color too much me and not Rama?"

"I dunno."

Confident, Liv thought. What makes a girl look confident? Expression. Posture. Which triggered her next questions about whether she wanted a full length shot to show herself completely, which might mean new jeans, even shoes.

"No, just a head shot, chest up, like what they do at school."

Finally, they settled on a warm honey-colored acrylic knit top with a U-shaped neckline that would nicely display the pendant necklace Mimi had given Shakti for her birthday, a beautiful tiger opal with matching earrings that complimented her skin and hair tones, but didn't distract from her head, which as Liv pointed out, was really where the attitude Shakti wanted to project would emanate.

Elyse was already in the spa's waiting area, when the shoppers showed up. She'd scoped out the services and timing. "A stylist I think is pretty good can fit her in in ten minutes. Then she could talk to a makeup person. And an hour and a half from now, we could all get manicures or pedicures, if we like. Does that sound like fun?"

Shakti's eyes were taking in the spa scene. She'd never been to one of these before, all these women so intently working on beauty. All the staff had big made-up faces and phony smiles, or so she thought. Slick looking products in packages stacked artfully on the lobby's shelves. Big easy chairs where women waited, skimming fashion mags provided on cube-shaped tables scattered around. She had a bad feeling about this and looked worried. "Auntie, this isn't me."

Elyse could see this didn't look like fun. "I know it isn't, but this woman who cuts hair is really good. She's not flashy or phony. I really think if you tell her what you want, you'll be happy with the cut she gives you."

"What do I say though?"

Liv interjected. "Tell her what you just told me at the store, that you want to look smart and confident, that you're going to have some very important pictures taken. And show her your top. Say that you want to look age-appropriate and awesome."

Elyse shot Liv a puzzled look. "Age-appropriate I get, but what is the stylist going to do with 'awesome'?"

"If she's good, she'll know what to do, right?"

"Mom, are you sure about this? What if it looks terrible?"

Liv placed her hand under Shakti's chin and turned her face gently from side to side. "Sweetie, you are going to look smashing."

Shakti's name was called and a big-toothed, red-lipped girl with a hot body stuffed in her black and red spa attire ushered her down a hallway. Shakti's face looked back at them buried in a head of hair that was about to be de-volumnized.

"Shall we get a snack downstairs while we wait?" Elyse was continuously hungry these days. Moving into her fourth month, it wasn't entirely clear if she was beginning to pop or just had added pounds. By the fullness in her face, it was the latter.

They opted for peppermint mochas and shortbread cookies and found a small table against the wall. Both outside and throughout this downtown mall, the shoppers were out in force. Liv felt removed from all of it. "I've been so caught up in family drama, in David's call, in Ryan's dad's situation, Marco in Paris – I haven't given a thought to Christmas."

"I have because I'm planning how many days I can take off. I'm tired a lot, Liv. I'm worried that this isn't going to pass, that my pregnancy will have issues. My OB just keeps saying 'don't be anxious.' But it's all so intense. And then everyday there's a headline or story I see about kids getting shot, refugee kids dying, autistic kids –this whole spectrum of fears that never bothered me before."

"What about your work? That's always been your focus and mainstay."

"Work? It's like how late can I go in? Will the nausea be bad? What can I snack on? And then, the issues – you know I've been all over affordable housing and transportation for years. Now, I'm paying attention to city policies that affect schools and parks. The pregnancy has changed my attitudes, my priorities. It seems like out there the world has changed, but I know it's just me inside. Which is even scarier in a way, that this little life inside me is now calling the shots."

Liv couldn't help but laugh. "Yeah, tell me about it." Elyse pouted, not hearing the sympathy she wanted. "Elyse, remember when I was pregnant, how I felt about it. You're moving into motherhood. That's what pregnancy is partly about, sure the baby has to grow, but you as a mother-to-be need time to change and evolve to welcome the baby."

Elyse was more satisfied with that response. "Still, I'm not sure I want to be so different. I liked me the way I was."

"You felt that way about getting married. Remember, the taming of the wild horse? And here we are, seven years later, and you've had a pretty great marriage as far as I can tell."

Elyse wasn't going to argue. But the reason was that not much changed when she and Cory married, except for the good: a nice home she loved, special vacations, learning to ski and sail. They'd both continued to give their all to work and been rewarded with personal successes. "We have. And the baby may change all that, mostly for me. This sounds crazy, but I think sometimes of you having Shakti when you were only twenty-two and how I thought it would screw up your life, and now she's fifteen, and you're ready to build on your career and take off. And I know this is so selfish I can only say it to you, but it's like I'm coming up near the top of a long set of stairs, and I'm almost at the top floor, and now I have to go to the bottom at age thirty-seven and start up again."

"Elyse, stop it. That's not how it will be. You're going to build your family, take it all in stride. Next thing, the kids are in daycare, then in school, you'll pick up where you left off. But you'll understand people and issues in a much deeper way. It will be good for you and your career. You'll become much more in tune as a city council member when you're also a mother."

Elyse relaxed some, already considering another cookie. "But give me this Liv, aren't you glad sometimes, I mean isolating your work life, that you've done the longest part in raising Shakti already, that the future is more back in your hands now, that you can really build your career?"

Liv immediately recalled her current dissatisfaction at work, on the upcoming need to move, on Shakti wanting to meet her father. "Honestly, I'm really unsettled right now. I don't know what's ahead. And I doubt I have much control over it. Choppy water has pushed into my little backwater cove. I'm being moved this way and that, with no sense of building anything. All I can do is focus on what matters in the moment. That's all that seems to work. Maybe you should try that?"

Elyse, rebuffed in her attempt to generate much sympathy from her friend, decided what mattered in the moment was another chocolate-covered graham cracker.

When they came back upstairs to the spa, Shakti was with the makeup aesthetician, so they went for pedicures. Returning a half-hour later to the waiting room, Liv scanned the area seeking Shakti's bushy head, often turtle-necked in her high collared green winter parka. Her eyes moved past a chair in the corner and then did a double-take. "Look Elyse, she's over there." Putting her hand to her open mouth, she exclaimed "Oh my god, she looks gorgeous!"

Waving to her and walking across the space, the two took in the substantially thinned out, but nicely fluffed ringlets, now shoulder-length, with a headband gently pulling the hair away from her face. Shakti, no longer buried in hair, emerged from an exquisite backdrop of color and curl. Her high broad forehead was fully visible. The aesthetician had her put on her new top to sample blushes, eye makeup, and lip color. Shakti wanted a soft, subdued palette including a little blue eyeliner - that she hated once on and would probably never use herself again – and a thin layer of a blush slightly darker on her cheeks than her skin tone. A barely peach matte lipstick completed the look.

She rose as they reached her and in the sweetest, almost shy way, asked in a soft voice, "What do you think?"

Their faces already said it all as they came close. "You look so..." Liv wanted to say pretty but searched for something Shakti would appreciate more, "...so amazing, like you're a together, smart, confident young woman. You're someone people will want to meet."

Elyse knew of Shakti's adulation of Katniss. "Jennifer Lawrence, step aside. Shakti is rising."

That turned her discomfort into a big smile. And that addition made Liv pull out her cell and snap.

"Mom, don't embarrass me!"

"Let the photo shoot begin. Let's go home, put on the necklace and start posing before the headband becomes annoying or you wipe off the eye makeup."

In the end, after scores of photos at home, they kept returning to the spontaneity and joy in the cell phone shot. No jewelry, no blank wall. But an irresistible face that lit up the screen.

Monday, December 7

An inert energy field of waiting followed that required even greater patience from Shakti. They sent the photo to Arita yesterday, after a prolonged discussion of what message Shakti should send with her head shot. They brainstormed mini-dialogues that might be sparked. If Shakti said, 'I'd like to meet you, Grandma,' what were the possible responses? Would Rama still show it to his mother? Would he edit something she wrote? Would he simply delete the message?

Their decision, excruciatingly debated, was that Shakti only had control over the photo. Rama had to give his mother that. And the magnetic spark was there in her half-profile, eyes spontaneously connecting with those of the witness. The invitation to meet. All that was necessary. "How soon will I hear something back Mom? Will they send me a message? What should I expect?"

"My best conservative guess is that you'll get something back which at a minimum is a compliment. Like, you're so pretty. Something like that. And then we'll figure out your next move towards meeting them. But it's better to wait for a message back."

"Ugh," came a deep emission from Shakti's chest. "I hate this."

"I know. Just try to focus on school this week. Cezar's back now, right? You have him to talk to."

The reaction of others at school to Shakti's new look, distracted her in the coming days. She'd never had so many compliments and wasn't sure what to make of it. After all, she was the very same person. Why were looks so important? But she did like the interested looks of certain boys. And Natalie kept saying that good looks were an asset in life that could make her more powerful. Shakti noticed how the popular girls carried themselves, flinging their hair around, wearing makeup, and tighter clothes. She still didn't like it, but her awareness of good looks as a source of power for women grew. Thoughts of wielding more power, in anything from relationships to future opportunities, helped break up an otherwise steady fixation on waiting for a response from India. She and her mom concocted stories of how Rama's mom lived a distance from him, that he only saw her on some weekends, that he would wait to be with her to show her the photo. When the first weekend passed though, Shakti had a melt down and assaulted Liv to come up with more options, how could she send her own message now?

Unfortunately, the more time that passed, the more awkward it felt to take their own action. Liv kept coming back to waiting. "You just don't know how the photo is working on them."

"I HATE THIS!

"I know. Hey, let's have Marco and Cezar over for dinner this week. He hasn't seen you yet, and you can wow him too."

"Give me a break."

Thursday, December 10

Marco easily was the main speaker at their dinner. Liv felt the emotional distance of his having been away for over two weeks and wanted to remind him of the attractions she offered, his favorite meal and her new sexy look. Perhaps this would be a wake-up moment for him: oh, great to travel, but there's no place like home. Or so she mused.

He complimented Shakti on her new look, although in his usual low-key fashion. Being the rebel against entrenched systems, from capitalism to male dominance, he was not one to give his power to a societally dictated set of female good looks, or to encourage women to meet those standards. Liv especially awaited his full-blown account of the climate conference. From his Facebook postings, she knew that whatever momentary joy she'd experienced about the world coming together to reduce carbon emissions, Marco had hung with youth groups who quickly provided the negative commentary on how little was really done. She braced herself for negativity and knew her Pollyannaish views were best kept to herself. What she hadn't anticipated was Marco's positive energy to move forward on 'the work,' the work of making the climate agreement a realty. Enthusiastically, he shared anecdotes about people he'd met, and how invigorating it was to be involved in this global community of change agents.

Infected by his excitement, she wanted to share that space with him. "This is all so encouraging! I'm enthused too that together we can make change. Do you already have ideas, or plans about what's next here?"

Marco's face dimmed as though a cloud moved in front of the sun. "Yes, yes I do. It's something you and I should talk about by ourselves though." He looked at Cezar who returned a knowing nod and suggested to Shakti that they go to her room and look at his photos from Spain.

"But you showed me those at school when you got back?"

"Did I? Oh yeah. Well, let's just go have our own space to talk." His eyes pleaded with her.

With a puzzled expression, Shakti headed down the hall to her room.

A mist of anxiety was penetrating Liv's skin, perplexing her. By the time the kids were into the bedroom, Liv stared directly at Marco, guessing the news before he said it. "You're going back to Europe?" Marco smiled, not happily, but with satisfaction that Liv knew him so well. "When? For how long?" She was making a quick internal audit of the winter's agenda and thinking the reconnection with India might dominate. *Don't overreact to his being away more.*

Marco leaned forward and took her hand in his across the table. "I've decided to move to Madrid." He saw first the surprise register in her eyes, then slump into sadness as the curve of her lips moved down.

"Move? As in permanently leave Seattle and go to live in Madrid?"

"Move, as in me and Cezar living with my parents, Cezar finishing his secondary school there – to the delight of his grandparents. And me being able to more easily collaborate with climate change groups across Europe, to travel more cheaply to meet with them, and take part in protests and events."

"But...but what about the work here?"

"I know. But my scope is more limited here. The real committed activists are the ones I met in Paris. Maybe I can be a connector or bring their energy here over time. I see a role to play there. I speak most of their languages. I'm older than some, more experienced in organizing. And then there's Cezar. He could benefit so much from finishing high school in Spain. Maybe do university in London or Paris, who knows. And it would be really wonderful for my mom and dad...."

"How is your dad? Is he healthy?"

"For now, the cancer is in remission. He's still writing his positive psychology books. Mom is teaching yoga. They're great. And they have rooms for Cezar and me to use, so we'd have no rent."

Liv was stunned and grasping for the mundane to hold on to. "Would you sell your house?"

"No, no I'd hold on to it and keep my tenants. Maybe ask them to get another tenant. And then the house would be self-sustaining."

No extra room at his parents. Not like he was setting up his own place a woman could share with him. A woman and her daughter. "I can't lie. Shakti and I will feel the loss – a lot." With that he rose, came, and stood her up from the table. "I know that. It's the one reason not to do this."

"But you've decided?"

"Yes. I have." He embraced her.

Whether to yield or fight it, her body was confused. As tears welled up, she found momentary comfort in his embrace.

"Liv, will you visit us?"

Like a final weak salvo from a force in retreat, the lack of commitment was clear. She'd known early on her place as third priority behind Cezar and activism. But she'd relaxed into thinking their familial housing circumstances lent a mutually agreed shape to their coupling and psychologically disabled any flashing indicators that meant 'danger, low commitment level.' *Would I visit him? Why?* Admitting the matrimonial prospect assumption buried in that question, her inner rebel protested: couldn't she have more than one man in her life? Her European boyfriend and whomever she would get involved with next in Seattle? Then panic came to the fore regarding future options: would there be any? Suddenly, Liv hated herself, her lack of independence, her letting Marco have the upper hand in this. Pulling away into her own space, dabbing at her eyes, she replied, "Visit? Madrid? It's not high on my list right now." *Make clear my own priorities.* "You've probably heard from Cezar that a trip to India may be happening. Depending."

Marco's sensitivities intuited exactly why Liv's defenses were up. Further soothing wouldn't change anything. *I'll miss her, how could I not?* When he'd think of her. Based on his weeks away, in distant space and time, he hadn't thought of her much. *She needs time, move on.* "Let's talk again soon. Come over this weekend and we'll talk about everything."

Really? What's the point, you've decided. Her eyes narrowed above a pout. "When do you plan to leave?"

"In January. We need to get Cezar there after winter holiday break and enrolled for the next semester at school in Madrid."

"So soon!" Liv's insides began to shake. "Well...I'm sure you'll be really busy but call before you go." She couldn't help turning snarky.

"Liv, don't be like that."

"Look, I'm upset. This is a blow. So just go. I don't want you here anymore."

He raised his hands as if to ward off a verbal flailing. "Sure. I understand. Really, I do. I'll call soon." He bent forward to kiss her on the cheek. She let him while remaining passive. He called for Cezar who came into the living room rolling his eyes at his dad to send the message that Shakti too had been upset. They exited like a pair of soldiers who'd had to break bad news to a family of a military loss, but who would return to their own normal comraderie only too quickly.

When Shakti came out from her bedroom a few minutes later, Liv was still standing by the table. She turned to Shakti, "The assassins have left."

"Mom! Don't be like that." Shakti made a false attempt to improve their moods. "We'll be okay. Someday we'll be all excited about meeting up with them in Spain – and David's in Europe, right? We'll like having friends over there." She shifted around to make her mom look at her. "I know. It sucks. It totally sucks." Shakti started to vent. "Here I am going through this major situation in my life and my best friend is leaving me." The tears were lining up to take the fall.

"Oh, sweetie." Liv folded her arms around her daughter. "We have each other. And our family." And without thinking it over, she continued, "And we're going to India, and you will meet your father and grandmother. We're going to make it happen."

Shakti pulled back to search for the truth of that in her mother's eyes. Seeing it, she visibly brightened. "Promise?"

"Promise."

As they stood there in a hug, Liv's brain experienced a traffic jam: why did I promise? *Will it happen? Is this how it feels to have someone walk out on a relationship? Is this what Devin experienced? Did Rama ever feel any of this for even a second? Did asshole Eric feel this sting? Had David felt any of this?* All she really knew was that this was the first time a significant other was choosing to leave her without her consent. Emptiness. Rejection. Resentment. Anger.

Liv needed to call Elyse.

It was already nine and Elyse would be in bed. Liv turned to her journal by her bedside but then back to her keyboard. She could journal to Elyse in an email and get it all out that way.

"Elyse, you're not going to believe this, but Marco is moving to Spain – soon, next month. It's all about Cezar, getting him a European education, combined with Marco running around the continent connecting with climate change activists. And no housing expense thanks to his parents in Madrid.

No, I haven't been keeping things from you, I didn't see this coming. As best as I can tell it grew out of this trip. Obviously missing in any of this grand plan is yours truly. Just like that. We're leaving. Bye.

I'm stunned. Angry. Minimized. Feeling abandoned in Seattle while another mover and shaker in my life offs to Europe. Think about that: all the men of significance to my life will be on other continents. Far away. So much for wanting to be multi-cultural, look where that's gotten me. Stuck in Seattle. At a job that's not working for me anymore. About to lose my housing next year. And the men I've loved following their destinies in other places. Shit.

Speaking of which, I see a message from David just came in. More later. Call me when you can."

Email from David:

"Hey, guess where I am! London! I've been here two days now at the invitation of that attorney I mentioned to you, Phillip Stancombe, the guy who has cases at The Hague. He invited me to his home and yesterday took me in to meet members of his law firm. They do all international, both civil and some criminal.

I'm not sure how to describe it, the 'buzz' of the place was amazing. And they were all so interested in me, the ones I met. Which included two of his other partners – there's six or seven. There are about twenty associates. He says it's going very well. We have another lunch today. I take nothing for granted, but I do think they are going to make me an offer to come work here. I'm so nervous!

Last night, Phillip sent me out to explore London, to some neighborhoods that are extremely diverse, where you find Sudanese mixing with Somalis, and Nigerians, and South Africans. It's wild! He told me to follow my nose, walk around, talk with people, and get a sense of the other

London, not the postcard city. It felt great, Liv. I walked forever. There were people from India and Pakistan too, an incredible coming together of the globe. I went to a pan-African restaurant and talked first to the waiter from Ghana, then a guy at the next table started talking to me, he was from Kenya, so we had a lot to talk about. He invited me home to meet his wife and kids. Nice, really nice. And then I walked some more. And more. Liv, I really like this city. It feels bold to type this, but I want to live here. And bring Amer and the kids here. I think this can work for us all. Imagine, ME EXCITED! Strange huh?

Have to go for the lunch now. Sorry I didn't ask about you and Shakti. Please send me news. Love, David

Little firecrackers started to go off in Liv's head. *How weird is this? Marco going to Madrid. David in London.* She closed her laptop, snuggled under the blanket, and was awake a long time. Stuck in Seattle.

Saturday, December 19

Rama hadn't slept much these past two weeks. The strange concoction of anxiety and curiosity that followed his meeting with Arita - *my life is about to get zapped, brace for it! Will she look like me?* – these were mere ripples in comparison to the emotional tsunami that came with the photo and would soon reach his mother.

He'd come in to work on a Tuesday, begun to routinely check his email, and bam, a message from Arita with the subject of 'your request.' He opened it on auto pilot and quickly grasped that all she was doing was transmitting the photo. He'd moved the cursor to the attachment, and then paused as his brain caught up with his fingers.

The pause endured. Reluctance had moved in like a fog where he'd wandered lost without context. He'd decided he needed to remember what Liv looked like before he saw the photo. No use using his search engine on her since he didn't recall her last name. The hair, he could bring that up with the sun behind her. A generous smile, lighting up the space around it. He had trouble with the eyes though – blue? The consequence of pulling these first fine threads of memory was that they didn't break but began to grow in intensity. Her in the field planting, a foot in the hole dug for the tree. Meeting at the well and going back to his truck.

He didn't open the photo that day. Or the next. Awake at night in bed with his wife cuddled into him, memories of flesh emerged, making love to Liv under the stars. The abandonment of ego and a sublime merging. He shifted his head to see Indira's. He loved her deeply. They'd made a good life. His boys meant everything to him. The beginning had been bumpy though, as she'd had to learn what he liked in bed. She was devoted to him, had consulted with her sisters, and learned - they'd made it fun. As with a line in a movie he'd seen, 'for married sex, it was good.'

But the need to open the photo, the rip cord that would pull him back in time, it was calling up images of the abandoned pleasures of youth. Reminding him that the nights he shared with Liv were among the most special. Realizing that anew scared him. He liked his life just as it was and wanted no interference from the past to disturb it.

Except now there was the photo. An image of a love child to confront. Thursday morning, first thing at work, he finally opened it.

The curls, there they were, but pulled back to show a broad strong forehead that shared the skin colors of his family. The smile! The look of her. Enticing, not in a seductive way, but so inviting, as though she was speaking to him, 'Hey, I'm here. I'm great, don't you want to know me?' He saved the photo to a thumb drive, then forwarded the email to his personal account. Only to immediately delete it there, no way would he bring this any closer to his personal life. Much better buried on his work computer and kept on a small drive he could use to show his mother.

Damn. What would Mother's reaction be? He opened the photo again enlarging it to fill the screen. She was a beautiful girl. He leaned back and saw that besides his forehead, she shared his long nose - although the face might be thinner than his. Those eyes, blue or green? Both? Maybe that had been true of Liv's? They looked so incredibly familiar. Every day before leaving work to return home, he'd stare at the photo again, contemplating when he'd show it to his mother and what his stance would be: a pretty girl, no? He'd need to disguise his own interest growing stronger with each day, wondering whether she was good at school, as good as his sons. And what did her voice sound like? Is she happy if she's grown up without a father?

Afraid of his yearning to know more, he rehearsed how to minimize the photo's impact on his mother. He'd been relieved at first to be reminded that this was a big birthday weekend in his family, with the celebration of his son Raj's tenth birthday and his cousin Satjit's twelfth. They'd all gather at Rama's brother's house in Mumbai for the big Sunday feast which cancelled out Rama's frequent weekend visit to his mother. The relief inherent in this delay returned to burden him the following week, as he waited for the next opportunity to be in her Mumbai home alone with her.

As the second week passed, his discomfort was burning up his peace of mind as though a fire had been lit that wouldn't go out. He called Nimisha Friday from work and, after the standard simple inquiries, he tried in a nonchalant manner to let her know he had the photo. "Mother, you know what you asked me to do?"

"Yes, it's been on my mind continuously. I'm trying to be patient. I bit my tongue and held back asking you last Sunday."

"The photo is here. I have it."

Nimisha was putting her hand to her mouth. Tears came fast. Feeling weak on her feet, she lowered herself into a chair.

"Mother, are you okay?"

"Yes. Yes, but it's a shock. When can I see it?"

"I'll come on Sunday in the morning. I just wanted you to know you'd see it then."

"I'm finding it hard to wait."

"Just a day really, a day and a half." Rama was worried about her state. "I've looked at it Mother. Is there anything I can say to help you with the wait?"

"Does she – what is her name?"

"Shakti."

"Shakti!" she said in hushed awe. "What a wonderful name. Does Shakti look like us?"

"Yes, in some ways. And some like her mother."

"Oh Rama, my heart is pounding! It's a good thing I have a strong heart."

"I know. It's…" his charade of casualness broke down, "…it's upsetting to see her. I can't deny it." Rama always reverted to truth-telling when it came to his mother. He'd hidden his issues with his dad from him, but ultimately, he always barred his soul to her.

"Upsetting in what way? Is she…is there something wrong with her?"

"No, not at all. It's how interesting…and attractive she looks. She has an appeal."

Nimisha smiled through the phone. "That's my girl. I can't wait now to see her."

"Sunday. Not long."

Sunday, December 20

Indira sensed that Rama was not himself that morning, yet, in her customary non-probing way, accepted that if it was anything of importance, she'd eventually learn of it. Rama did not keep many secrets from her, they were close that way. She loved him unconditionally and felt blessed to have such a happy marriage and family life.

    Rama departed at his usual time of six to drive to his mother's in Mumbai and have his special Sunday brunch with her, sometimes pancakes made of dal, cheese, and vegetables, other times spicy missal pav. Frequently, but not always, Indira and the boys went too. But he'd stressed that there was family business to discuss this Sunday and that Indira would find it tedious. Neither really liked the sterile environment of his mother's relatively new condominium building, and what worked best was to get his mother out on excursions with the boys in Mumbai. Plus, Indira had come to hate the drive – over six hours car time if they drove and returned the same day. He checked three times to make sure the thumb drive with the photo was in his jacket pocket. Since Friday night, just having it hidden in plain sight in his briefcase had made him antsy. Indira never looked in it, yet it was nerve-wracking nonetheless. He'd orchestrated his movements carefully that morning, so she didn't see him putting something from work into his jacket. How he hated this secrecy!

    Nimisha awoke unusually early at six, or so her servant thought, not realizing her mistress had been awake many times in the night and finally given up trying to sleep. She didn't know what to do with herself. She spent a long time at her puja praying to her guru and the saints. *Am I wrong to set such value on this granddaughter?* She couldn't rein in her heart's longing. All those boys at the birthday party last week only reinforced her desire. A mother, a grandmother, we need a daughter who cares for us. These boys, they're grand in their own way, so full of life and energy and mischief – of course she loved them – but after turning nine or ten they became different, noticing her less, taking her for granted as part of the backdrop to their more active lives. Their focus was on action, games, and their fathers, or each other. She was becoming wallpaper in the rooms of their lives.

Sitting before her puja that morning, calming her mind, she recalled the classical Sanskrit play *Shakuntala* that she'd always loved as a child. A tale with a flavor of Cinderella about it, the heroine is a girl raised in a forest hermitage who falls in love with a king hunting in the wood and has a child by him. A curse keeps them apart but when the curse is broken, the king returns to the forest and meets his son who takes him to his mother. They all return as a family to his kingdom.

This recollection troubled her spirit: how would next steps toward her granddaughter affect Rama? And his marriage? *My, this is such dangerous territory.* Now she was more worried than anxious to see the photo. *Lord, what is the point - if I fall in love with this girl, then what?* While she avoided consideration of next steps, she knew a stairway – up or down – was there to invite her to move beyond the status quo.

She stared out her second story window to the apartment's driveway below, wishing him to arrive. This condo living was not her cup of tea, much preferring the old family home in the hills of Lonavala. But with her husband's death, her sons had convinced her the Mumbai house was too big to maintain and that she should live simply in this modern condominium, still near to her friends and Rama's older brother, but requiring less upkeep. She felt the change as an investment decision the family made, not a housing decision to please her.

When Rama arrived punctually, she exhaled deeply. "Hello, Mother." Rama kissed her cheek as he entered. "Yes, I have it with me," he said producing the USB drive from his inside jacket pocket. "Are you ready?" Then he noticed the concern on her face, perhaps more articulated by a tightly bound scarf covering hair still growing out from the recent chemo.

Their routine was to eat first, and the servant had everything ready. Nimisha did not want to present any unusual circumstances to her, as she also worked for her other son's wife helping with the housework and meals. She was a family member in many respects going back to when she aided Nimisha in raising her own children.

Rama greeted Ubayda warmly, speaking kind regards from Indira who had also used her services before the move to Pune. While she was in the kitchen, Nimisha leaned forward and whispered to Rama, "We mustn't let her think anything out of the ordinary is going on. "

While that hadn't been one of his considerations, he immediately appreciated his mother's caution. Thus, they passed their morning meal engaged in exchanges that had a somewhat mechanical tone to Ubayda, who wondered what was different.

Fortunately for Nimisha and Rama's planned activity, the servant had the rest of the day off having already prepared food for that evening as well as a few mid-week dinners.

They were so relieved when Ubayda closed the door behind her, that she felt it as a sigh carrying her out the door. Something was up.

Rama faced his mother uneasily, his eyes searching hers. "Are you ready?"

"Yes, but I'm a little frightened. It's as though we may be going someplace we can never return from."

Rama couldn't lie in her presence. "It does, doesn't it? But we already made the choice, Mother, by asking for the photo. We can't ignore it now. Surely, we must respond in some way? We must think very, very carefully about all the ramifications. Okay?"

"Yes, most certainly. I don't want to do anything to upset your life, my dearest."

They moved down the hallway lined with family photos to the modern decor of the guest bedroom where he'd set her up with a computer. He pulled out the upholstered desk chair for her, so she could sit in front of the monitor. Rama felt around the laptop for a port and inserted the drive. Leaning over her, he tapped on the icon, opened the drive and then the jpeg image.

Nimisha gasped, her hand to her mouth. "Oh Rama! What a beauty! Look at that smile! Her coloring is so soft, like dark honey. Is this the mother's hair, those curls?"

He nodded, also mesmerized. "See my features?"

"Yes, I see our line in her." She leaned closer staring. Then she turned and looked at Rama.

And then he knew. The eyes. Shakti had his mother's eyes. The wrinkles and sags of decades contrived to hide the resemblance, but the shape was the same. And the color. Liv's Irish/Swedish genetic coding had met a like chromosome handed down from some inhabitants of the British Isles who had intermingled with Nimisha's own multi-mixed line over the span of colonialism. The submissive recessive genes had triumphed in Shakti's eyes.

They both turned to the image again, and then back to each other in unspoken recognition. Nimisha began to cry. As Rama wrapped his arm around her shoulders and held her close, she spoke her heart's desire. "I want to meet her."

Rama and Nimisha were a long time visiting, sometimes in silence. They both cried at times. But there was joy too in Nimisha's embrace of her favorite silk sofa cushion, as though she were hugging her new granddaughter. Rama was buoyed by a wave of satisfaction that he'd made his mother so happy. Their conversations were circular when it came to meeting the girl, as though they watched a carousel of considerations go round and round in front of them, each image one of Rama's family members. They got nowhere and decided they would talk while he was at work next day after they both slept on it.

For Nimisha, a new mantra was repeated with every drum beat of her heart: I want to meet her, to know her.

Rama's state of confusion was palpable throughout Sunday evening in his shortness with his wife and sons. By Monday morning, as he and Indira were parting ways in the driveway, she paused and confronted him as she rarely did. "Rama, we have to talk tonight. You are upset. I'd like you to tell me what's wrong."

That's the last thing I want to do, he thought. *I need to get control of myself.* "It's just something at work that's gnawing at me. It will pass, I promise."

That morning he re-arranged his tasks and cleared his calendar, so he could sit and think in silence. It was not in him to fight his mother's desire. He just couldn't. Her cancer most likely would return, hopefully not soon, but who could say. He wanted to let her experience her granddaughter. But he absolutely needed to totally protect his family from this unwanted intrusion. He kept testing and recycling actions that had begun to form yesterday. *Could they meet somewhere other than Mumbai? What excuse would Mother give? Could she go to see his sister in London and somehow get Shakti there?* But the thought of his sister Gauri's involvement came with RED ALERT written all over it. Heaven forbid, his all-inquiring sister should gain this knowledge. His mother had suggested a meeting at their hill home in Lonavala, a few hours' drive from Mumbai. The servants there were only hired as needed and did not have the depth of family relationships their predecessors had. *Some merit in that plan. But damn, do I need to be involved to make this happen?* How could he possibly keep it from Indira, her radar screen already sensitive to a change in his mood? *Can I stay out of it perhaps? Could Arita and Liv manage it all between them? Yes, keep me very uninformed so I don't have to think about it?* A pain gripped his heart. *Really, not even meet Shakti myself?*

Wednesday, December 23

After more conversation with Nimisha while at work, another night to sleep on it, and yet more conversation, Rama believed he had a well vetted plan. He emailed Arita to learn if she could meet with him about it. His mother wondered why this woman would be willing to assist, but Rama was confident she would. She was too much a woman's advocate not to let herself be further drawn into making this connection happen. It meant a special trip for him to Mumbai, but Indira was used to his meeting with academic and government colleagues there.

Arita agreed to meet him for lunch at a place conducive to discreet business meetings with its carpets, table cloths, and heavy drapes muffling the volume of conversations amid the well-spaced tables - a place deals were made. She'd heard of it but never been before. She wore her most professional outfit, a black suit, but her overflowing old brown leather bag nonetheless made her seem different from the high-powered business executives whose shoes shone and accessories glittered – most of whom of course were men. Only two other women were eating. "This is quite a change from my usual lunch sites."

"Actually, mine too. I still prefer a good hole-in-the-wall place with masala dosas."

"We could have just talked by phone?"

"That really gets to the whole thing I want to discuss with you. But let's order first."

Arita decided to go for it and ordered some vindaloo lamb while Rama with no appetite went for a simple lentil curry. After ordering he took a visible breath and launched. "It's about the photo. Well, not the photo, but Shakti. Since you sent the picture – first it took me a long time to get time alone with my mother to show her. Which finally happened Sunday. And the thing is..." he made sure they had eye contact, "... she very much wants to meet Shakti."

Arita gently smiled. "I don't think that will be a problem, the desire is mutual."

"But the issue is my family, Indira and the boys, and how to keep this totally confidential. I want my mother and Shakti to meet, but my wife must never know."

A more serious look replaced Arita's smile as her mind processed rapidly, grasping that she would need to continue playing a role in this. Momentarily bypassing a question about her willingness to be a go-between, she saw the crux of the matter. "Will you be meeting Shakti too?"

Rama moved his head from one angle to another, straightened his silverware and reached for water. He'd planned this out: what he needed to say for now was that it depended on several contingencies in the arrangements. "I need to keep my distance from the meeting plans and once it's set up, well, we'll see if it works out for me to be there too."

Arita scowled. "Doesn't it depend too on what Shakti wants? I mean, I'm not, emphasize not, speaking for her until I've actually put this before her - which I assume is the request you have of me, to handle all the communications, right? Which by the way, I have to consider what I'm willing to do...."

"I know. I mean that's why I wanted to meet like this."

"Okay, but just putting myself in Shakti's place, it would be really odd to travel half way around the world – again, I assume your mother isn't going to Seattle – to meet only my grandmother, but not my father? That would be very strange." Arita's voice became more emotional as she sought to frame a powerful response on Shakti's behalf. "And actually, much worse, like I was being rejected by you. I think you're either in with your mother on this – or you're out. And if I were Shakti, I might not come."

Rama surmised now that Arita knew far more about Shakti's wishes than she'd let on. But no point in going there. He and Nimisha had discussed this themselves, that she would want him there, and that she could only imagine his daughter would also. So much depended on the place and timing if he was going to keep this a secret. He was loathe to commit. The more his mother and he had talked, yes, now he too was curious to meet Shakti in the flesh. But he was deathly frightened to risk revelations of this episode from his past to Indira, worrying it would hurt her and irredeemably alter their relationship. Rama was visibly distressed avoiding Arita's eyes. He began several responses without completing them.

Neither spoke for a while. Arita's problem-solving capabilities gained energy as she slowly savored the delicious food. She did want to be helpful. She was willing to be a go-between. "Look, let me explain all this to Shakti, or to Liv. I don't know how Liv will want to handle this at her end, as she's trying to protect Shakti from disappointment. Let me lay it out and learn their response."

He could intuit the response just hearing Arita's words. He felt cowardly, unmanly: it wasn't like him to duck responsibility. He needed to make this happen but as sensitively as possible for his family. He stared at his soup. "Okay. Tell her it will be both of us meeting her, if that's what she wants. But that I need to arrange things so my wife and children are not brought into this."

Arita felt pleased. "That's much better." She suggested a time she would try to talk to Liv alone – holidays were upon them and could complicate connecting – and keep him posted. "I'll minimize contact with you, but that means you'll have to be patient. Feel free to call me if you need an update." As he finally began to eat, and she finished, the complexities at the Seattle end of things came up. "You know, Shakti's in school, so it's complicated to take her out for very long on short notice. Liv will need to consider timing, and of course the expense. It's not like she's that well off." Arita paused. "I doubt Liv will send Shakti alone, she'll need to come too. Which then involves her work schedule." Arita recalled the concern of his mother's cancer. "How soon should I say they need to come given your mother's health?"

His spirit took another blow. *Damn, of course Liv would come: I'll have to see her too. This was going to be rough, very rough.* Feeling the stress, he suddenly wanted to reset everything and just walk away.

Arita watched the visible collapse of his expression, as though air had been released from a bone structure composed of inflatable balloons. *Liv. Yes, that did add a whole other consideration. Was there any way he could meet Shakti but not see Liv? Unlikely.* Indeed, she could envision the grandmother getting interested in Liv too. *My, my, this is problematic. Too much for one meeting. Best to refocus him on logistics.* "As I was saying, this could all take time on their end to sort out, the travel and expenses."

He seized on the distraction of expenses. Flights for two, hotels, shouldn't be a problem. He knew his mother's finances quite well. She had substantial assets still from her father's side of the family. "Please tell Liv that we'll find a way for my mother to pay for the bulk of the expense. I'm sorry, I know it means more logistics to work out..."

"I'll make the offer and take it up as needed. I'm sure it will help though."

As they were leaving the restaurant's professional environment, Arita analyzed that she'd completed a deal rather successfully in a business-like manner. It crossed her mind to confirm where the meeting would take place. "I assume they'll be coming here?"

"My mother and I want any meetings to happen at her home in Lonavala. Hotels are nearby, they could stay at one of those."

Arita calculated. Best to allow two travel days each way. She'd experienced herself the terrible jet lag to Seattle years ago when she'd been an Earth Stewards exchange student, the time she'd first met Liv. A lifetime ago. And what if Shakti wanted to see more of India? Lots to figure out. As they parted company, Arita re-enforced that it could be weeks before he heard from her.

The end of December, 2015

Arita's news, conveyed in two Skype calls first with Liv and then with Shakti joining them, was like a barrel bomb being dropped, its body piercing shrapnel striking hearts and heads most assuredly but also fragmenting further into the hands-on logistical concerns about school and work, and producing periodic cries like 'my grandmother has cancer - we have to go sooner!'

From the first news, Shakti emitted what became her background refrain of the ensuing weeks, 'oh my God, I can't believe I'm finally going to meet him.' Interspersed were verses about the need to keep up her appearance, to keep her grades up, to be the best she could be. Liv might have been the rhythm section, as inner concerns jumped from high notes of happiness for Shakti to the bottom of the scale fear of seeing Rama.

They glued themselves to websites about Mumbai and Lonavala and spoke at length about how their feelings of anxiety, curiosity, and overwhelm, might correspond to feelings Rama and his mother were experiencing. For the most part, Liv was confident that this would go well for Shakti. *It can't hurt to have two other people on the planet who care about her.* And someday, perhaps Shakti would meet her half-brothers, although Arita had cautioned them regarding Rama's fear about impacting his family.

Liv quickly calmed her fear of seeing Rama as she realized she needed to be at the front end of introducing Shakti to him, for Shakti's own comfort and protection. She found she wanted to coach Rama in advance about what to say and not to say. Should she write him in advance? To provide context for him meeting Shakti, about how smart she was, what she liked and didn't like, and how not to hurt her feelings?

Meanwhile, the scheduling was complicated. Liv knew the rigors of flying half-way around the world and she felt they should take longer than a week for the trip. But perhaps not all in India. Could they stop in Amsterdam and see David? Or in London? But when could she take Shakti away from school for so long? Sooner seemed better for everyone, especially Rama's mother whom they often fixated on, wishing they knew more about her. There was a four-day holiday in February, but that meant days of missed classes. In the great scheme of life, Liv eventually concluded a smart freshman missing a week of class was not that big a deal.

As a tentative plan for a mid-February trip emerged, Liv arranged a skype session with David. It was two weeks since his last email about London. She'd expected to hear before now that he had an offer. She hoped he'd taken it.

Saturday, January 2, 2016

They skyped that night. Shakti had gone with Cezar and other friends to see the new *Star Wars* episode.

When David's image appeared, Liv felt a weight lifted. While she'd let her parents know by phone of the India developments, and of course briefed Mimi and Ryan, she hadn't been moved to call Marco or join him tonight. A chill in their connection matched the temperature outside tonight. Consequently, she hadn't had a deep conversation with anyone but Shakti about the 'great meet-up' as they called it. Tomorrow Liv would see Elyse. But at this moment her stressed soul felt more comfort confiding in David. "There's so much I want to talk about. And what about you and the job offer? What happened?" As she took in his calm facial expression and lack of enthusiasm, she braced herself to hear it had fallen through

"Sorry, earlier this week, I got it in writing, very official on firm letterhead. It's an amazing offer Liv, much more money. The firm's immigration people will handle my work visa - they have connections and can push it through quickly."

"Why didn't you email me right away? You seem so serious, not happy like I thought you'd be."

He smiled broadly now. "I am happy. Very happy that they think this well of me, that they made this offer. That Phillip made this all happen. It is amazing. And no sooner did that all settle in, then I've been thinking so much of my sister and the boys and how to make this all come to pass, so that they come to London too. The firm wants me to start soon, stay at their company apartment until my visa comes through, ease in and look for housing. They'll reimburse some of my expenses when they can legally. Imagine this: I could leave the Court in two weeks."

Liv's heart muscle relaxed. Not that London wouldn't be full of attractive women. But somehow London seemed better. Like she, never having been there, could nonetheless imagine herself in London.

"So, why wouldn't you leave soon then?"

"I'm tripping over myself, my footing is unsteady about going to Nairobi to break this to my sister. How do I bring her along mentally, emotionally to all this change? Should I go there first in two weeks to talk to her? Prepare her for yet another change just as she's settled in there? Or do I go to London and throw myself into the job and then have no time for months to go visit her?"

"Don't you speak with her by phone? Or facetime? Couldn't you begin to prepare her in other ways?"

"We haven't skyped, and she doesn't carry a phone yet. She's been focused on just getting used to urban life, and technology gives her anxiety still, like the fear of touching the wrong icon or image. And her literacy is not great."

Liv was reminded of her first job at the Rescue Committee helping refugees resettle. A quick image flashed of the unforgettable day she found out she was pregnant: the eyes of a Somali widowed mother seeking work. There was a little boy with eyes like David's. A girl too. "I get it. She needs a good IRC person to help her adjust to so many changes."

"Exactly. We need to clone you and send you to Kenya!"

"I'm going to India, David. That's my news. Shakti's grandmother wants to meet her – remember the photo I sent you? - and from what my friend Arita, our go-between, tells me, Shakti's father is reluctantly going along with this."

"Does she know he's reluctant – what's his name?"

"Rama. Not really. We just talked about it like they both want her to come, but that Rama is not going to involve his wife and sons. He's terribly concerned about their finding out."

"Man, oh man, this is huge!" How is our dear girl taking this? She wanted it to happen, right?"

"Yes, and she's totally immersed in it while doing her best to stay grounded. She desperately wants them to love her - immediately."

"Any reason that won't happen?"

"Not with the grandma. But Rama sounds very conflicted over it, so he could blow it somehow."

"What about you, are you excited to see him?" he wondered if secretly, all these years, Liv held the hope of renewing a relationship with Shakti's father. What else explained her not marrying?

"Excited? No. Anxiety-ridden? Yes. All this digging up of the past is going to happen. I'll confront again all the choices I made sixteen years ago – that's so what I do, I know I'll put myself through it, even though I wish I wouldn't. It feels like I'm being summoned to get a slap in the face."

"Really? I don't understand. Here you're bringing to the grandma this beautiful granddaughter she's longed for, right? You're bestowing a blessing! They should greet you warmly."

"Maybe. Like you say the grandma is the easier one. But Rama doesn't really want us intersecting his life. Shakti will pick up on that, and then it's an emotional setback."

"Don't over project – you know better. Just stay open and go with the flow. Keep moving, keep breathing. I know about that," he said smiling widely. But he wondered if she was afraid she'd see Rama and fall in love again. "When are you going?"

"That depends on you, remember you invited us to stop over in Amsterdam? Now it's more complicated with your move to London. Should I get a ticket with a stop to see you? Somewhere?"

David leaned forward toward the screen feeling the pleasure of her coming to see him. "This is such good news! I must make up my mind then what I'm doing – Liv, help me – how do I bring my sister along with my move to London, or more crucially, her move to London?"

Liv considered. As his sister adjusted to urban living in Nairobi, she could care less where her brother lived in Europe. Liv's own bias was clear: Amer and her sons would be much better off in the long run relocating to London, speaking English, and being comforted by the diversity of the city that David described. She 'launched,' an approach Elyse had modeled for her so many times. "I think you should make a trip now to visit them, present London as the choice you've made, and tell them how you will prepare the way for them – housing especially, schools – and that they should all focus on learning English. Get her set up and comfortable with some basic technology, especially Skype or Facetime. And then make your own move to London, find a place big enough for them to live in too, and focus on your job for a few months. Bring them at a nice time of year to a home you'll all live in together in a neighborhood that's welcoming." She paused. "What about immigration laws? What are the restraints and conditions? Will they actually be able to come?"

"Damn, I hadn't even thought about that and here I'm the lawyer."

"Sounds like your firm will help you figure that out and make it work, but it could take time. You'd best visit family now and get them aimed toward a London move, and then dig in there to make it happen."

"Okay, I'll give the Court notice I'm leaving, go to Kenya for a couple of weeks, and then move to London. Like in a month, the beginning of February."

"So, we should fly to India through London and stop on our way back?"

"When?"

"Likely mid-February, although mid-April is the fallback."

"I'll be there by February. No matter what."

Liv pulled herself back from planning mode to be in the moment: here she was face to face virtually with a man she loved. Her eyes expanded to take him in, the exotic beauty of his ebony face, its seductive curves, the wide smile between broad generous lips, his dark eyes now meeting hers. She put her hand to the screen, and he mirrored her action. "It just sunk in, we're going to be with each other. How long has it been?"

"Years. Five, six. Forever." As her face widened in a smile, the screen brightened as though the tint had changed.

"Whatever happens in India, whatever mess I'm in coming back, I'll have a shoulder to cry on." She laughed.

"Arms that will welcome and embrace you, no matter what."

"No matter what."

When Shakti returned from *The Force Awakens*, she was exuberant, in the most refreshing way a teen can be, dropping attitudes and affectations. "Mom, wait till you see it! The new Jedi is a girl – she's fantastic!" Shakti began jumping around doing athletic moves as though she had a light saber. "It was so great to watch her feel the Force. Mom, I feel it too. I want to be the best I can be and conquer evil in the world."

Sunday, January 3, 2016

Liv enjoyed going to Elyse's home in Montlake. Increasingly it had become less the perfect professor's house it had been when purchased, with well-appointed features that drew you in, the fireplace and abutting glass door bookshelves, and the craftsman touches in beautifully articulated moldings around every window, door and floor edge. Now it was more an eclectic higher-end Mexican look with mission-style furnishings from which to view enlarged photos of mountain peaks, island escapes, and flowers. The downstairs bedroom that served as an easy storage place for backpacks, cross country skis, and boots for all terrains, was slowly becoming the home of hand-me-down toys and a likely playroom near the kitchen.

The expectant mother met Liv at the door with the big news. "It's a boy! We got the results Friday!" As Elyse released their hug, she said in almost a whisper, "Imagine, I'm going to have a son. Come on upstairs and help me finish deciding on the colors for his room."

Liv knew immediately how having a boy would lessen her friend's anxieties – with a son, it would be Daddy who would need to bring him along on outdoor events, train him on all the gear, and groom him for hiking and climbing. "I know how you're thinking about this but cool your jets. You just never know. Your son could turn out to dislike the outdoors, they may not have similar personalities at all. He could be more like you. He could be whatever."

"Of course, I know that. But at least for a while, even for years, it will keep Cory more engaged, right?"

"Maybe. But a girl with some of his interests would serve just as well. Anyway, it really has more to do with Cory and what kind of father he'll be, what it means for him to have a child of his own."

"End of lecture?" Liv rolled her eyes. Elyse led on up the stairs. They entered the baby's room where paint samples had been swathed on a wall and wallpaper books littered the carpet. Elyse turned her gaze away from the wall of many colors to focus on Liv. "You're right. I know you're right. But I need these little hopes to get me through this."

"How is it now?"

"Better, but I'm still in bed early. Thank god, I have a great OB, she always takes my calls." Elyse picked up an assortment of paint chips from an old wooden child's desk which was the sole furnishing occupying the room. "Can you imagine, Cory picked up all these browns and greens? Really? A chocolate brown baby's room? He thinks animal wallpaper, sort of cartoon cows, sheep, and a red barn is the way we should go with a brown accent wall." Elyse turned to the walls in the afternoon's gloomy light. "Me, I'm calling it poop brown. Like, are we trying to match dirty diapers?"

Liv had to agree. She took the samples from Elyse. "What about a softer green, maybe a grass color? Or simply cream?"

"Too blah for me."

"Orange and yellow, with maybe lime and skip the wallpaper?" A citrus room?"

Elyse took back the samples. "Lime. I like that idea. Like a mojito. I want to have something Mexican in the room, maybe little rugs over this nothing beige carpet."

Liv recalled the seedy rugs from her old college apartment. "Yeah, that might work, if they were nice ones."

Elyse stuck her tongue out at Liv. "Let's eat something and you tell me all the details about Shakti's grandma in India. This is so incredible, I need the whole story."

While Elyse laid out a snack of tea and muffins at the kitchen alcove's round table, Liv related the conversations with Arita, and Shakti's reactions, as well as her video call yesterday with David. "Honestly, it's like I'm standing on a paddle board and waves are coming from all directions, the trip to India, Marco off to Madrid, David moving to London. Shakti wanting to be supergirl."

"Girl power, I love it!"

"Sure, me too. Up to a point. The point being if Rama is weird with her. Is she going to dive into a bipolar crash?"

"Honestly, what's he got to be afraid of? You follow all his directions, no contact outside what he orchestrates, his mom will be thrilled for sure. He's not going to weird out." Elyse sat down. "Or are you projecting your own uneasiness at seeing him?"

"Maybe. But it's a real time-space warp, no? I go off to India when I'm twenty-one, have sex with this guy, and return fifteen years later with his daughter? It makes me doubt myself again, for the first time in a long time: why did I do what I did in cutting him off? Why didn't I even try to keep up contact?"

"At the time - believe me I was listening to you - you thought there was no point, that he didn't really want you in his life, that you had no real desire to raise a child in India, possibly alone. Those were pretty sensible assessments, right?"

"Yes."

"Is it that you might be attracted to him again?"

Liv scanned her soul. "Not really. When I looked at his photo from the conference – I showed it to you – I didn't feel much at all."

"Yeah but seeing him in person – who knows. Look, it is awkward, no doubt about it. But that doesn't mean you can't come at it with a certain openness, at least for Shakti's sake. Who knows what this could mean for her? A real connection to India?"

"Not if the grandma dies. Remember, she doesn't get to meet her brothers."

"Come on, you don't know how this will unfold over the years." Elyse thought they'd wrung this out enough. "Now, you and Marco, what's the conversation there?"

Liv's lips pouted. "Not much. I feel dropped. Hurt. Down on his moving – it means the end."

"Does it have to be? From my little local perspective here, you have all these super interesting connections spanning the globe now...."

"Please..."

"Let me finish. Yes, Marco does not prioritize relationships with a woman. But he really cares for you and he's going to live in Spain – I would jump at the chance to have a friend to visit there. There's no reason you can't be more gracious about this, and for both your sake and Shakti's, preserve an open pipe line there. Start laying the groundwork for a visit. Make him miss you, at least a little. Once he's in Madrid, or running around doing his activism, who knows, he might have regrets? It's not like Livs grow on trees."

"Except we do, don't we? I'm sure he'll find someone there who's more than happy to step into a relationship with him."

"Excuse me, you overrate his good looks. A guy living with his parents? Now that's weird to me. Maybe for a girl in her twenties. But if he wants a mature, seasoned woman like he has in you? Come on."

Nothing Elyse said lit up Liv's face. "I'll take it under advisement. I mean there's truth in what you say. Especially for keeping the kids in touch, I'd hate for Shakti not to continue a long-distance friendship with Cezar." Liv stared at her cup. "How about some more tea and we move to the living room?"

"Sure."

As Liv stretched her legs and walked around looking at photos on the wall and books on the tables, she envied the settled nature of Elyse's life. Good job. Good husband. Lovely place to live. And now a son on the way.

Elyse set down fresh hot cups of tea, plumped assorted pillows against the hardwood arms of the furniture, and resumed her interrogation. "And so, you're stopping in London to see David?"

"That's the plan. Why? Do you think I should stop in Madrid instead?"

"Or both! Liv tours the world visiting boyfriends along the way. My, my, the life you're leading."

"How about, Liv tours the world meeting up with failed relationships, re-enforcing her botched life?"

Elyse gave up a chuckle. "But it's true, you're such a worldly, interesting person with all these former lovers dribbled from India to Europe. It definitely makes my existence dull by comparison."

"Dull? You're creating a human being at this very minute. You're soon to birth what will be the most important relationship in your life. Now that's the real journey. I'm a sideshow these days. Thank goodness for Shakti. My Jedi feminine force! It's about her now, her future, what she can make of life."

"God, you'll make me cry," Elyse said with a laugh. "Get off it. Tell me about David."

Liv would be lying if she didn't admit that somehow, someway she wondered if they could find a way to be together. London definitely held an allure. But she'd been burned before. "I'm thinking rationally that it never works out. It didn't work here in Seattle. It didn't work in Nairobi or in Amsterdam. Why will his being in London make any difference?" She wanted to be persuaded.

"Maybe because he's giving up on getting that Bashir guy tried at the Court? You said he wanted to claim his own life."

"Except claiming his personal life means claiming his sister and her boys and becoming family to them, a provider, and a father surrogate. Do you really think he can be a high-powered lawyer in London, take care of his family including raising two adolescent, culturally transported boys, and have any time available for a real, every day relationship with a woman?"

"It depends on the woman." Elyse was staring so hard at her it felt like a finger pointed into her chest.

"Elyse, don't go there. David's never been available, and there's no reason to think he's going to change his pattern at this age."

"I DISAGREE. You should be more open to possibilities. Everywhere. India. Madrid. London. Don't pre-judge."

Liv knew she was hearing her own lecture on the power of now. "Any other instructions for life? You're on your way to becoming a bossy mother."

Elyse recognized this possibility: she owned that side of her personality. She saw her habits of control frequently these days as she fought to keep hold of projects at work, sensing the loss of control that was coming. Indeed, bossiness was her default coping mechanism which Liv helped her keep in check. Her lips turned down, betraying sadness. "I actually feel like I'm losing you somehow. All these foreign loves are taking you time zones away. I'm afraid you won't come back to me, not in the same way. Maybe that's why I'm teasing you about it, because deep down I'm scared your life is going to change dramatically and I'll lose my best friend."

Liv instinctively felt protective. "That's crazy. I'm going away for maybe ten days and then I'll come back to the same old job, for a while anyway, and the same old house, for a while."

"That's what I mean. The ground is shifting under you. Who knows? In six months, you could be living in India. Or wherever. But not here." Elyse's face looked strained. "And just when I'll need you most."

Liv rose, came over to sit next to her friend on the sofa, and took her hand. "You're having an emotional attack brought on by your mother-to-be hormones. In six months, we'll be sitting here looking at the son you'll be holding in your arms. You'll be madly in love. And you'll be a great mom, with or without my advice." She hugged her sideways. "Best friends forever."

Wednesday, January 6, 2016

Liv bent with the wind of Elyse's advice to stay open. She invited herself and Shakti over to Marco's for one of their used-to-be regular mid-week gatherings. When Shakti wasn't applying herself to being irresistible, she was also sad about Cezar moving away. On their way over to eat, the duo were giving each other pep talks, Liv touting the possible trips ahead for Shakti to visit Cezar in Europe, and Shakti considering a possible move to Spain. "You know Spanish, I can take it, it's not that hard."

"That's true. And Spain is cheap these days. Maybe we should visit sooner rather than later." Liv wondered if she could find a job there, but concluded it was unlikely.

"A long visit would be great. Cezar told me how amazing Spain is, so many beautiful places to see."

Their relatively good spirits resuscitated the usual pleasantness of the meal. Marco was visibly appreciative, saying over their dish washing together, "It seems like you've come around."

"Come around to what?"

He turned off the faucet, and while keeping his eyes fixed on her, dried his hands and placed them on her hips. "To the change, to tending a long-distance relationship, to not cutting us off."

She liked his hands on her body, despite wanting to send a bit of a chill his way. She heard a low inner voice chanting the 'what about David?' mantra. "It's hard. I like what we've had. Now everything is up in the air for me, and when I look for a landing place, I'm not seeing it. All the terrain looks difficult."

"I know." He pulled her closer to his body, arm feeling arm, hip brushing hip. A mutual urge to merge arose. He held her neck and kissed her gently. "You never know what might happen." Rather than pushing Marco away because David was on the horizon, the immediacy of the embrace tipped the scales in favor of indulging her instincts.

Later, as they lay in bed together, he scanned the room and then returned his gaze to her. "Really, Spain will be very pleasant when you and Shakti visit us there. You know you love my parents. The city is full of art and music. You should come in the spring or fall, not in the summer, it's miserable then."

"Spring? But I'll be spending all this money on the India trip next month, unless I wait until April and stop on the way back then? It could only be for a couple of days or so?"

"No, I think you should come when we can all spend time together. Maybe travel in Spain a bit. Maybe early fall? September?"

"Marco, that's so far away. It's too hard to think about."

"Well, let me get settled there. And we'll keep talking. We'll find the right time."

Liv felt herself shutting down and lowered her eyes. He saw her spirit deflate. "I promise."

Liv heard Elyse's voice in her head: take it Liv, that's a word he's seldom used with you. "Okay, I'm sealing that promise with a kiss." Which she made as delicious as she could. *Miss me.*

Friday, February 12, 2016

Tomorrow was the flight. Given Shakti's excellent school performance of late, Liv minimized the impact of the time they'd be away on schoolwork. Tensions and apprehensions in January had been contained in part by a heavy dose of studying, in part by Shakti's girly pre-occupations and makeup experiments with Natalie, and lastly by focusing on Cezar and his departure. But the last two weeks Liv found unbearable, the inevitability of emotional outbursts manifesting in Shakti melt-downs.

At work, it just so happened that the first week she'd be gone, Kevin would be over at Amazon engaged in fundraising tasks. A big Board meeting was coming up right as she returned. She'd done as much as she could to get her own focus group work in action, scheduling sessions of potential training facility users beginning two weeks after her return. Having one of her co-workers under the evil Amazonian wing while she was gone was nonetheless disturbing. She'd kept the trip as short as she could, allowing a day in Mumbai, two plus days for Lonavala, three days in London, and four travel days to allow for the stop over, delays and jet lag upon return.

Tonight was their final night of packing, having started a week ago to gather clumps of possible clothing to take, and listing out last minute items to do. Shakti's emotions were running high, getting angry at Liv over the smallest issues and questions: 'for five days in India, do you really need three pairs of summer shoes? And then two pairs for London?' Liv was challenged enough by packing for two climates, and avoiding the burden of extra luggage, without her daughter insisting on taking half her wardrobe.

Liv's parents were coming to see them off at the house tomorrow, and Ryan and Mimi would drive them to the airport. But when Katherine heard Liv's litany of complaints over Shakti's behavior, she came tonight too. She and Mimi were finalizing Shakti's packing in the one suitcase allotted for her, giving Liv space and time to print out the boarding passes, double check passports and credit cards, assemble the camera and chargers, and finish packing underwear being laundered. Liv considered wearing summer clothes over winter leggings and then layering on sweaters under her parka for the flights over.

"You won't be able to move, you'll be like an over-stuffed rag doll with no mobility. I know I've done it." That was Mimi's advice, who had begun, tactfully of course, advocating for one more bag that would hold all the London stuff. "It'll make it so much easier to have one suitcase for both of you for London."

"Right, but one each for warm weather in India? Where's the sense in that?" Liv was determined to travel light, facilitating transporting themselves in and out of airports, changing planes, and going through customs.

Mimi went back to Shakti's room. "Failed."

Before Katherine could mollify Shakti, she turned in a rage and moved aggressively into Liv's room. "Mom, how can you do this to me? What don't you get about what a milestone this is? I need to have choices when I'm there. I've never been to these places, I want to look my best. How does one fucking suitcase matter?"

Liv had had it too. "EXCUSE ME! If that's the language you use with me, then I'm ashamed to introduce you to your father!" No sooner had she said it, then of course she realized how wrong it was to have chosen those particular words.

Shakti's system, seeking a release of the built-up tensions of the last months, exploded. "Ashamed? You're ashamed of me wanting to look nice, to have them love me? What are you? Afraid I'll love them? Are you trying to spoil this?"

Katherine and Mimi followed Shakti into Liv's room and heard the exchange. Liv wanted to scream at the absurdity and made fists at her sides, holding herself back. Katherine moved quickly to calm her while Mimi embraced Shakti. Her sobs were audible as her face squished up in pain. Mimi looking over her charge's shoulder at the mother daughter duo sitting on Liv's bed saw more tears flowing there.

Katherine opted for boldness and attempted to take charge. "Look, you've both been, and still are, under enormous emotional pressure. You need to be kind to each other, extra compassionate, beyond your usual ways." She lifted Liv's chin. "Listen to me. The bag is irrelevant. She needs to do this on her terms."

Shakti's head was lifting, turning towards her grandmother, waiting to hear her mom's response. Liv was swallowing her mother's good sense and felt terrible that the "ashamed" word had surfaced. "You're right. I'm sorry." Looking at Shakti, Liv rose and crossed the room. "I'm so sorry, sweetie."

Shakti moved into her embrace, sniffling and trying to get words out. "Me too. I'm so stressed, Mom. This is the hardest thing I've ever done."

As their hug released, Liv couldn't resist. "And you're in charge of lugging the extra bag."

Monday, February 15

Liv curled under a blanket in the plane's window seat with Shakti curled into her. They were on the last leg of their Seattle to New York, New York to London, London to Mumbai flight, somewhere over Pakistan. They'd been alternating window and aisle seats on the wide-body jet, trying to find temporarily comfortable postures for their travel-tired bodies. Liv wanted to sleep but that wasn't happening. At least the flights were on time and there hadn't been issues. Indeed, they both felt calm and spoke little. Decisions had been made. They were in process. For almost a day's worth of travel they got to step back, be still, and accept the destiny they had created.

Liv couldn't help but recall her first trip to India. *Who was that girl?* Young, idealistic about crossing cultures. That girl who with all her openness got lost in transit, as though some science fiction transporter reassembled her personality along the way. She couldn't recall any specifics of the trip over, except her first meeting with Rama in the airport parking lot under the light. *I remember the immediate connection, as though I recognized him.* It startled her more awake to hold that moment afresh. Somehow it validated her, as though there really had been no choice, there was only fate. Sixteen years ago, sometime in February, a single egg within her released to form the girl beside her. *This is destiny too, this return to the source.* Drained by thinking and rethinking the emotional mine field they were about to enter, and how best to structure – 'structure' was the operative word she used – how best to structure the meetings to create the easiest flow and the most beneficial encounters, there was comfort in relaxing into a reverie of destiny, abandoning any sense of control. Now they just needed to show up.

Which was not to say that a structure, an architecture of entry and hallways and rooms had not been set in place. They taxied after their two am arrival to the hotel Rama booked for them in central Mumbai, a pleasant three-star accommodation convenient to the city's attractions. Arita would arrive for breakfast to take them to tourist sites while their bodies adjusted to the twelve-hour time difference. Liv would plead the need for a morning nap, and Arita and Shakti would spend the morning on their own. They'd all meet for lunch and then continue together.

Liv's naptime would actually be used to visit with Rama, who'd arranged a a trip to Mumbai and then Lonavala where he'd spend the nights at his mother's. Indira easily accepted him being away a few days to escort his mother to and from Lonavola on a fabricated mission of consulting with home contractors. Liv foresaw the first sighting of him as a huge challenge. She feared stumbling over this reunion between them, especially if it was the same time Rama first met Shakti. Instead she secured this initial private meeting, the two of them alone. Rama acceded, similarly not wanting to conflate too many thoughts and feelings in a single encounter among the three of them.

He'd also gotten Liv's agreement to making Shakti wait until the next day to meet him in Lonavola. He was still anxious about an acquaintance unfortuitously intersecting any meeting in Mumbai, and remarking upon it to others, even to his wife. In Lonavala, he'd be more relaxed, more open to his daughter. He'd found during the planning that he held an affirmation of their conspiracy: yes, I do want to meet her. But fear was there as well, fear of being deemed a father. He took his parenting seriously and responsibly, not a role he wanted to take on for an adolescent he didn't know.

Seeing Liv would be troublesome. He'd come to think that he owed her some appreciation, even genuine gratitude. After all, she'd not complicated his life as a young man. He'd gone on to lead the life he chose, unencumbered except by parental wishes and his own choices. And now, quite amazingly, he had a pretty daughter of fifteen. Who would make his mother happy. *Yes, I do need to be appreciative of Liv.* He liked that it provided appropriate positive ground on which to stand with her. *I can do this.* These were his thoughts driving through city traffic to the hotel where she was staying.

Liv neglected to anticipate how joyful it would be seeing Arita in person again, sitting across the table from her, and watching her watch Shakti. Arita, hair now much shorter, dressed in western styled slacks, still projected an edge that went beyond that created by her angular features. The edge came from deep inside her eyes, critical, always assessing. Today though, she smiled often. Not like years ago, when as an intern Liv got involved with Rama. With the pregnancy, Arita thought she had failed Liv somehow, while Liv felt judged. When Liv emerged as a feminist who would keep her baby, Arita's estimation of her had grown.

Arita had risen in her feminist work with her nonprofit StreeShakti, which inspired Liv on her own nonprofit pathway. As Arita's career and courageous actions on behalf of women's causes in India developed over the years, in the context of other organizations and increasing responsibilities, Liv experienced vicarious fulfillment in their friendship. During prep time for the trip, Liv gave an informal tutorial to Shakti on their Indian friend, her activities most recently on behalf of rape victims, and the staggering amount of work that needed to be done in so many areas in India to achieve greater gender equality.

Over breakfast, Arita and Shakti clicked as she expressed enthusiasm for Arita's work. Their time in India could not have begun better.

When Liv pleaded the need to rest more that morning, Shakti was incredulous. "You're fine Mom. You don't need to sleep. Just come with us."

But 'structure' needed attention. "I won't do more than a power nap, but that will help later. And I promised everyone at home I'd let them know we're here. I need to buy a SIM card for my phone and get some messages off. Anyway, you two are a great match and won't miss me at all."

"Not true!" But Arita knew the schedule. "Shakti, we'll visit some places your mom has seen already and save new exploration for this afternoon, okay?"

"I guess." Shakti sensed something was happening offline but was enthused to dive into Mumbai and was feeling totally at ease with Arita. And maybe she'd learn some things along the way she didn't know about her dad.

The meeting with Rama wasn't till eleven. She'd texted her messages but still had time. She studied her reflection in the mirror, the pre-determined outfit for this meeting: her lime sweater set, three-quarter arm length cotton cardigan over a sleeveless shell, with a new full skirt, beige background with primitively drawn green flowers across it. An upbeat look with her beige, practical sandals, painted orange toes, and orange accent jewelry. She looked well put together but casual. What pleased her most was her haircut looking so Euro, cascading a few inches down her neck as backdrop for the fragile, dangly, gold, orange and lime earrings, a head that looked bubbly and pert with blond highlighted curls.

Seating herself in the lobby at ten-fifty against a side wall, she studied the traffic in and out, inwardly noting both how striking the business-clothes women looked – *did I dress wrong? too young? immature?* – and how more Indians looked fat to her. Obesity was spreading. *Will he have a paunch?*

She saw him first. *No paunch, thank God.* He looked just like his photo, a little more robust, maybe a second chin slightly emerging, less hair. But his strongly defined features still striking. Handsome in light brown slacks with a lavender dress shirt, cuffs rolled up. She guessed his wife dressed him.

His gaze spanned the lobby looking for a big-haired girl in a t-shirt and baggy pants. When she rose to cross the lobby to meet him, she caught his attention. He stared hard and realized it must be her. *So different! Yet the same.* Her fair skin illuminated the space. She looked mature, developed. A woman where he remembered a girl. *Lovely, very attractive.*

"Rama." No question. Certitude on her part.

"You're different." Then they both laughed. "I didn't recognize you at first." His eyes were large like Shakti's, acting like magnifying glasses moving from Liv's smile to her eyes to her hair, then stepping back to see the whole.

"I knew it was you from a photo in the conference brochure online. You look very nice in a suit." *Lame.* "I read your bio – you've really come a long way."

He hadn't taken in what she said. He drew back his gaze. "I thought we'd go down the street to a place I know. They have a nice garden café."

"Sounds good."

As he turned toward the revolving door, he instinctively moved his arm as if to guide her, a habitual gesture with his mother and wife. He pulled it back.

They were walking before she reached for her mental cue cards of pre-vetted things to say the first half-hour. "Your bio said you're with the university in Pune? How far is that?"

"You could drive it in an hour if there was no traffic, but of course that's never the case. But tell me, how was your flight?"

"Uneventful." She considered mentioning the calm that prevailed after the emotional pins and needles of preparation.

Too soon for that. "It is a VERY long trip though. Shakti's handled the time change quite well. She has boundless energy." *Too soon to bring her up?*

Hearing her say Shakti's name caused his heart to tighten. He was quiet as he pointed out the café entrance and then spoke to request garden seating.

Perhaps it's best if I let him feel his way into this. All they ordered was coffee. She looked around the patio and finally at him.

"This is so strange, that's all I'm thinking." He still had a smile that attracted.

"Yes, we've all been thinking that." As she noticed what felt like his openness, she experienced a surprising internal shift. *This is what I expected. He's facing the unknown. I have a daughter to protect whom I know intimately.* At least for now, she was the one in command of successfully docking the capsule to fathership, the mission to this meeting, beyond testing their reactions to one another. "It's been an emotional roller coaster for Shakti to be preparing to meet you. And your mother."

"I can understand that. My mother is beside herself. The photo, it made her cry."

Liv flashed to the day at the spa. *A lot went into that photo.* She needed to feel her way about how much to say about Shakti wanting to meet him and how the requests coincided. *Does he need to know that?* "Thank you for agreeing to meet me first. I felt that we needed, well, to clear some air between us, so that nothing between us would cloud Shakti's meeting with you."

"Right, I understood that. It's a shock honestly to see you. And it's good that then I can just focus on her meeting my mother."

"Rama," she said his name softly as a mother might, about to coax her child into following a preferred course of action, "...she's here to meet you too. She's wanted this for a long time. I'd hoped to send her off at eighteen to meet you, but she's a very strong soul already. At the same time, extremely vulnerable about not having known you before now."

"I'm not clear, did she always know about me?"
"Yes, I never lied."
"There was always a father in India she didn't know?"
"Yes."

He tried to imagine what that was like. It made him sad for the girl. "Does she blame me?"

"No, I have no reason to think so. If anything, she's hard on me this past year for keeping her from you."

He was clueless what to do with that. He didn't want to get into Liv's choice back then – or did he? Not now anyway. "It's difficult now. Arita's told you about my family?"

"Yes. I undersand completely how shocking this would be for them." Should she mention that she wanted the brothers to know sometime? *No.* "The arrangement you've made in Lonavala, that works well to keep things..." she toyed with saying 'secret' "...to keep things private?"

"Yes." Except for how strangely he'd acted at times over the last month. He knew Indira sensed something. "Although, I'm still anxious about it."

Liv realized in that moment that she'd been living her life out loud for all these years. No lies. No pretends. A feeling of satisfaction with her own behavior gave her more confidence. "Rama, I want to prepare you for meeting Shakti, not for your sake, but for hers. I feel incredibly protective of her, the way you feel about your family. It's so important that she feel accepted by you."

"Accepted as my daughter, isn't that what's happening?"

"Yes, and accepted as the amazing human being, divine being... you co-created."

The village, the stars, the truck, the love-making. Nodes flashed in his brain. He didn't want to go there. "I'm not sure what this acceptance means. What is she expecting?"

That you love her. "Let me talk about her, okay? She's very smart. About a lot of things in the world." This part was making Liv smile with pride. "Including terrible things. I've exposed her to a lot. And she's tried to process it. You'll find her intelligent and you can talk to her about anything. And fun, she can be fun to be around – when she's not being a typical American teenager. And she's been preening lately, wanting to look prettier. Suddenly into hair and makeup." Liv paused and assessed that she wasn't conveying what needed to be said. "All I ask is that despite all your fears about your wife and sons, that you open up to her. Really see her. Be interested in her. Affirm her."

"I do that with my boys."

"I'm sure you do. And when we knew each other, you were, and I think must still be, an amazing person yourself. People look up to you. Admire you." Liv leaned forward across the table. "She has that potential, Rama. She could be just like you in so many ways. Please let yourself see that."

Rama thought of his older boy, Raj, who took after Indira, introverted and shy - they had a hard time syncing. And his younger son, Aryan, all fire and mischief, was more like Rama's sister. His heart felt tight, afraid to open. *I don't need or want to become Shakti's father, any more than I am already biologically.*

Liv saw that a response would not be forthcoming anytime soon. "I'll have some more coffee, if you have time?"

"Yes, Sure. Waiter?" He felt the need to say something. "I can't make any promises. Right this minute – it's all removed. But I hear you. At least I understand part of what you're saying. But it's like we're in this vacuum or void. Honestly, it's not real yet for me."

"Then all I'm asking for now is that you let yourself be in the moment with her, be open, and experience her without a veil of fear between you. We're not going to disrupt your real life." Liv considered and added, "We never have."

He sensed a power across the table that didn't associate with his memories of a soft, compliant girl – except that time when she walked away from him in the warehouse. A mature, complete, forceful woman sat across from him. He liked her aura, no denying that. After so many years of being only with Indira, such an unsettling meeting reminded him of his bachelor days, how he'd been with more women. How he'd gone after Liv. No wonder they'd made Shakti.

Liv sipped and watched his face, amazed at how detached she felt from him. There's nothing here, no left-over feelings, no attraction. Since being with him, she'd had other serious relationships, plus plenty of missteps for sure, and an agonizing number of false starts. There was no innocence to be found in her internal storage units. Not that she was jaded. Just experienced. Knowing. And with her experiences had come pragmatism. There were relationships that had possibilities of working, even Marco still she supposed; and others, like with David, where she'd hit her head against a rock wall too many times. And, she'd been single parenting with all that entailed. Underneath her youthful, even slightly ingénue look today, there was no naïf. No tremors under the gaze of an old love, no, he sat across from a self-assured woman. A cloud of sadness drifted past her head, the nostalgia of seeing someone who'd been important in a prior life, but who no longer had meaning to her. *Been there, done that. What's real now?*

Rama returned with her to the hotel, planning to get some university errands out of the way before going to his mother's. Her melancholy moment was blown aside by a breeze. Satisfaction and confidence commingled as she returned to the room. *I can do this. I can help nudge this to the best possible result - if only he is still the man I knew him to be, the man who valued every seed, who liked to think he was his namesake. The man who has a mother I know I'm going to like.*

As he sat stalled in traffic, Rama slumped contemplating the challenges ahead. He'd thought he had them all mapped out and bounded territorially with a fortress protecting his wife and a drawbridge open to his mother. But where was he on the map? Was he surrounded by a moat? Or walking down a road to adventure? Or hiding out in a forest? He hadn't factored in a forceful Liv. Or a daughter who might just amaze him. A daughter he was told he might care about. And want to be a father to.

When Arita and Shakti came bouncing back into the hotel room, Liv was lying on the bed replaying her meeting and second-guessing what she'd said, to the extent she could recall what had come out of her mouth. Their first contact in fifteen years was blurry already, reduced to an emotional impact that felt like a knockout. In the minutes of his presence, it hadn't been that hard. But stepping back and taking in the singular fact they'd met again, she was immobilized by the happening of it.

"Mom, you should have come! We walked and walked, and the people are totally wonderful – they look like me! And the smells are amazing. And the colors! I have to get a sari and Punjabi before we leave."

Arita was smiling watching the girl while Liv brought herself back to the present. "Shakti is a lot of fun Liv, you've been hiding that from me."

"I told you not to sleep, Mom, you look worse now. It's better to keep going."

"You're right Shakti. But I'll rally now. Where to, for lunch?"

"I thought we'd take a cab over to where my office is, and I'll show you the place and tell you about some of our projects. There are plenty of small places we can eat around there. And then...we definitely should go shopping." She smiled at Shakti. "This young lady is going to look quite smashing in Indian clothes."

Lunching on Kati rolls and banana chips, Shakti declared them delicious. Liv intuited quickly that Shakti was loving everything Indian now, despite her stance at younger ages about wanting to eat like an American and not try that weird stinky Indian food. Shakti's embrace of her culture shot tiny arrows of fear across Liv's heart. *This won't do.* She saw she needed to accept the sudden embrace of all matters Indian – although a complaint about the pollution had surfaced – and not absorb what her daughter said as a rejection of what Liv herself had provided for her. But maintaining equanimity would be challenging.

They walked from the restaurant down streets where beggars occupied their spots, interspersed with peddlers at small tables, selling snacks and beverages from coolers, or streetside barbers trimming hair. Often there were no curbs, and in other places no sidewalk.

"We're in a low-rent district," Arita said turning to brief them. "Shakti, you need to see all sides of Mumbai, not just the nice ones we walked in this morning."

Shakti's eyes were wide. She stumbled at times as she would become focused on a beggar with an amputated limb, his tin cup rattling with change as she walked by; or a woman with a baby bound in cloth around her back reaching out to get Shakti to buy a soda. She'd not seen poor people like these before, aside from the homeless of Seattle in Pioneer Square who looked better in comparison. The next beggar wore only a loin cloth and sat on a mangled piece of foam rubber, a crutch lying in front.

By the time they arrived at Arita's offices, Shakti - and Liv too, although she'd of course seen Mumbai's underside before – was feeling dazed by sensory data and experiencing the cognitive disturbance that upsets your assumptions about life and how people live. Arita's workplace was an old bank building with a front lobby and small rooms where decades ago clerks had sat tallying ledgers of the British Empire. Posters covered the main walls, blaring calls in English and Hindi to protest and rise against every variety of inhumanity to girls and women, and championing the rights of lesbians and transgenders. The anti-rape poster dominated, highlighting organizing events against recent gang rapes. Peeking out from underneath, was the poster of Malawi calling for education of women. Shakti stared at the wall, trying to take in each one. A young assistant translated some of them: "Where are the missing girls?" had been a seminar at a university, offering the latest data on feticide. There was a clinic advertising medical services for girls, a school focused on decent education, a call to stop trafficking in village girls. Liv focused on a poster in English covering a University of Mumbai conference that was to be held on women's rights in marriage, with topics including doing away with dowries, breaking down castes, expanding property rights, improving divorce laws, and ridding India once and for all of honor killings. Shakti strayed to a bookshelf seeing titles from international organizations reporting on worldwide violence against women. She pulled one off the shelf from the United Nations, opening to the summary of statistics which blew her away: one in three of seven hundred million women who married before age eighteen, were married as children before fifteen. *I'm fifteen. What if I was forced into marriage with some old guy!*

  Arita let them stare and take it in. "If it pertains to women, we try at least to publicize it in our newsletters and blogs. Sometimes we co-sponsor events, and occasionally, we take the initiative if we see it as fundamental to the lives of most women. We're working right now to get a BBC documentary aired for International Women's Day, March 8, but chances are the Indian government will block it. It's about the rape and murder of a twenty-three-year-old medical student. Here are the flyers we had printed. You can actually get thrown in jail here if you say the wrong thing on Facebook, did you know that?"

  Liv and Shakti looked at the flyer for *India's Daughter*. "Why won't the government let the movie be shown?"

  "They're saying it will incite more violence."

  Liv began paying attention to the flurry of activity in the office. "How many staff?"

  "We're not that big, ten staff, and lots of volunteers. We're a part of many coalitions."

"How do you survive? Who pays for the space and salaries?"

"The building is owned by a wealthy widow who supports us. Our salaries come either from donations or government grants. There are a great many women in this city who care about these issues but are afraid to speak up. I know one lady who siphons small amounts from the grocery money her husband gives her to contribute to us. Some of the lesbians I know have very good jobs and give monthly. A few women who have made it in media or entertainment are more outspoken in their support of these causes. Take my partner, she's Scottish. She's got a good-paying job with an export firm. She pays for our apartment. That means I can afford to work here."

"Is there time to meet her?"

"Maybe on your last day, I'll see if I can make it happen. For now, come meet our director and some of my colleagues."

The buzz in the office was tangible. Women of all ages were moving about with tasks, on the phone, or connecting in small groups to discuss a problem. Arita introduced them to Rani, a middle-aged, polished woman in a plain Punjabi. Liv was pleased with her introduction as someone raising millions in Seattle for housing and training for women. She eased immediately into a conversation with Rani about communications and storytelling, especially as a vehicle for fundraising.

Shakti liked the order and plainness in the director's office that contrasted with the cacophony of voices emitted by the posters. Her overloaded visual sense relaxed while she listened and experienced an epiphany of appreciation for her mother's work. *She's part of this. She fits somehow. All these problems plaguing girls and women.* Shakti felt at home, like she belonged. *Mom came here when she was in college. She made me here. I'm connected to all this. I'm Indian and these are my issues too.* Gratitude welled up, not "thank God I'm being raised in the U.S." or 'so glad not to have to live here,' but *I fit.* Her energy expanded, energized to move into this time and space where the feminine force needed to rise. *Why didn't Mom just stay here? Why didn't we come back?* She watched her mother talking animatedly about the kind of housing the Y had built and the process she'd organized. In her mother's face at that moment, Shakti saw some of Katherine's too. Home. Her grandparents there. Mimi, Ryan, and her cousins. Family. *Who would my family have been here?*

How would we have survived? Would my father have married Mom? How would my life have been different growing up here? With an Auntie Arita instead of an Auntie Elyse? As they moved through the hallways and met a few more of Arita's co-workers, Shakti disengaged, absorbed by her thoughts, in the way a monsoon downpour might immobilize activity.

Using the office bathroom, Liv asked if Shakti was okay. "You got very quiet, sweetie."

"It's just a lot."

"I know. India's like that. It throws your life up in the air and the pieces come down arranged differently."

Arita aimed them for a nearby shopping district to outfit Shakti as she'd requested. But the girl's enthusiasm had waned, and a tiredness set in. Liv's energy level, now buoyant from her exchange with the Director, carried the shopping trip. She knew that a presentation of Shakti in Indian garb might help subconsciously to break down barriers. But it did take effort to go through stacks and racks in these inexpensive shops. Shakti would look great in so many of these colors. They settled on a lightweight Punjabi that highlighted her blue-green eyes with its basic teal coloring and orange scarf, and a sari in amber and gold with a green scarf.

Both Liv and Shakti were now feeling the time change as though they'd pulled an all-nighter. Which they had. It was six pm and they wanted to crash. Arita counseled them to have a light dinner in the hotel and then sleep. They should be up for breakfast and catch the cab to Lonavala by eight. The eighty-kilometer journey out of the city would take them several hours. They should arrive in time to partake in the hotel restaurant lunch which was part of their meal plan for the three days.

Rama would be taking his mother to her home a couple of miles from the hotel. The next structured meeting was to occur at the hotel in the afternoon between him and Shakti. Liv would accompany her daughter, they'd find a place to be, and both hoped that Liv would then leave so that father and daughter could find their way on their own. Not until the next day, would Rama bring Liv and Shakti to his mother's.

Tuesday, February 16

Rama was distressed. Nimisha didn't need to sense his mood as he was being extremely vocal about it as they drove out from the city. "The more I think about this meeting today the more upset I am. What am I supposed to say to this girl? We have nothing in common really. And there's this emotional elephant standing between us. Mother, what do I say?"

Nimisha's internal peace about her own upcoming meeting was being disturbed by his anxiety. "Rama, she's just a girl. She'll be so nervous to meet you. If I were her, I'd want to find a connection with you, something you can begin to share. Ask her about school."

"Oh, hi Shakti, where do you go to school?" Rama turned his head from the road towards his mother to further convey his rejection of this suggestion.

"I didn't mean right away. Why not just ask about her trip, and her reactions to Mumbai and what she's seeing? Just get her talking, and then you'll relax, you'll connect to something."

"But doesn't that ignore what's really bringing us together? I mean, am I supposed to give her a hug when I see her, like, 'ah, my daughter at last'?"

Nimisha was drawn into envisioning the scenario now, those first moments of the physical encounter. The awkwardness of it all. Except she wasn't feeling awkward at all, especially now that her hair was growing back. Ever so slowly, she was becoming herself again, only happier as she waited to meet Shakti. "Rama, is it that you don't really want to meet her?"

He looked at her again. "I really don't want or need a relationship with her. It wasn't my idea." He didn't like being harsh with his mother, but she was the one putting him in this unpleasant situation.

Nimisha received the complaint. *My, my.* She breathed deeply turning to look out the side window. *But of course, he's complicit at the source. It's his karma.* "Aren't you forgetting your role in this drama?"

She had a point. Seeing Liv yesterday had haunted him into the night. Something real and special had brought them together those nights in the field. Why should he disown that? Or, what came of it. *This is my life, my journey. I shouldn't disown it.* He had an inner mantra that at times was serious, other times funny: what would Rama do? It referred to his honorable namesake in *The Ramayana*. Rama would stand tall, uphold honor and go forth to meet his destiny. And slay the demons. Remembering that helped, and as he put the pedal to the floor to pass a truck, he felt a surge of inner strength. *This is a daunting challenge. But I can do it. I am Rama.* He placed his hand on his mother's. "I'm sorry."

She looked gently at him. "If you are the Rama I know, you'll love and respect your daughter." When he dropped her off at her home in Lonavala, she reached into her bag and pulled out an envelope. She'd sought and found it in her desk last night. It was a copy of the letter he'd written and sealed, 'For my child,' and sent to Liv long ago. "Some reading for you. Remind yourself what you thought at the time, and what this girl has read."

That morning, an hour ahead of Rama, the cab exited the Expressway, as directed by Arita, to provide its travelers with an older side road view of the countryside and its inhabitants. They stopped for some roadside drinks, both feeling the heat and wanting to take in the village they were driving through. Vendors were selling sodas and Indian snacks, all part of an informal market surrounding a larger grocery store and gas station.

Among the fruits and vegetables for sale was a large curved frying pan filled with cooked veggies and filling the air with a savory blend of spices. "What is this?" Shakti pointed at the wok-like pan.

"Oh, that's chaat, looks like one with potatoes, onion, and some chickpeas. Should we get one?"

"Isn't there anything sweet?" Shakti spied a few bags of Candyman products and picked up the éclair.

As Liv paid for it and the lemon sodas to go with it, Shakti noticed the uncovered scratched and stained boards beneath the offerings and the dirtiness of the nearby cooler where the drinks were stored. She snuck a look at the woman taking her mom's money. How rough her skin was, meeting its match in the threadbare end of her daily sari. When she smiled, her front teeth were crooked. The woman's gaze fell on Shakti who managed a quick but weak smile. Smiling back, the woman took some chikki hard candy and gave it directly to Shakti, refusing any more money from Liv. Liv and the woman bowed to each other in Namaste.

Returning to the taxi, Shakti stopped. "Mom, that woman was so poor – why did she give me an extra candy for free?"

Liv put her arm around Shakti's shoulder. "Great lesson, sweetie, often those with the least share the most."

"Really?"

"Truly. I've seen it time and time again even at home. It's those with more who can be the most fearful of sharing."

As the taxi was driving out of the village they were treated to the scene of cows in the road, one standing, the other laying there like a dog, both with their ribs painfully visible. The driver began honking, which drew a farmer's attention who came with a long stick and gently encouraged the animals to get going.

The scene made Liv happy. "I always loved the cows, that they're honored and protected from abuse."

"But they look like they don't get enough to eat."

"I know. But that's true of people in the villages too. The cows are relatively okay, people value them."

"For their milk?"

"Not only that, their dung too..." seeing Shakti's question on her face, "...poop, honey. You can burn cow patties and get heat."

"Gross!"

"Not really. It's actually very sustainable." Which reminded Liv. "Now there's something you might bring up with your dad, get him talking about sustainable agriculture, the work he does."

Shakti shot her a 'you must be crazy' look. She re-focused on the scenes they were passing through, glad to be out of the city and slums now. That slum they saw from the highway as they left Mumbai was unbelievable. She'd been shocked how it went on forever, lean-tos of cardboard and corrugated metal and tarps. Liv had warned her of the poverty, but the images of it, even from the distance of the road, drilled into her. *People really live like this?* She'd caught glimpses of children in the alleyways and wondered how long they would spend there. "Mom, do kids grow up here?"

"For however long it takes for the person, or people in the family, to somehow save enough to move into real housing. It happens, but we're talking years." *Or life times.*

As Shakti looked out at the lush green hills they were moving though now, she wondered aloud, "Why don't all those slum people just stay in their village?"

"Life isn't so great out here either. It's not like the children are going to find jobs here. The best they may be able to do is bake bricks with their families, which is hot, dirty, and unhealthy labor. Families think they can do better in the city."

"What about farming, the cows, growing things?"

Liv smiled inside. "That's actually what your father was trying to make happen when I met him. Once I helped dig out a field and plant trees. And sow seeds for crops and flowers they could sell." *And receive a seed back* was her thought about being with Rama in a field. *And my seed is right here beside me.*

For the second time on this trip, Shakti took a step closer to appreciating her mother. "How old were you then?"

"Twenty-one."

What will I be doing when I'm that age? Maybe I should be here in India helping kids. Especially girls.

In the final stretch of their journey, with the slower pace of the traffic, they marveled at the beauty of the hill country, draped in every shade of green, rich in forests, and providing relief from the rising temperatures in Mumbai. Arita spoke with joy of this place and asked the driver to point out waterfalls to them. Hoping for a generous tip, he even stopped at a scenic overlook of a verdant valley for Liv to take a few photos.

The entry into Lonavola took them on a curvy road past one modern development after another, many architecturally exciting, often with large windows aimed toward the views, most appearing expensive. From colonial times till now, Lonavala was a place where the wealthy could escape urban density and heat.

Liv wondered if one of these was where Rama's mother lived. She hadn't imagined she lived in some wealthy, suburban-feeling development. As they entered the Resort Hotel, Shakti and Liv exchanged looks of surprise that they were staying at such a posh place. The circular drive led to an open-air lobby, its louvered wooden doors folded back. It gave off a British vibe, emanating in part from a pillar surrounded by a red velvet settee, its seat and high-backed cushions embedded in a diamond pattern with metallic studs.

Their room and bathroom were quite nice, compliments of Nimisha, who'd paid for the airfare too. The generosity of this assured Liv that a warm welcome awaited them. Tomorrow would go well. It was this afternoon that felt even more stressful than her meeting yesterday with Rama had. *How will he greet Shakti? Treat her?*

Lunch was satisfying although they both found it hard to make small talk to others seeking to make fresh connections on their holidays. Returning to the room, a nap would have been excellent, but both were being kept wide awake by adrenalin in their systems. Liv half-expected another Shakti melt-down like the one before they left Seattle, so tasked her with ironing her Punjabi, well-creased from living in its plastic bag. Liv had to freshen up her own beige linen floor-length sheath that she would top with her lime cardigan again. Despite having bought her own turquoise Punjabi yesterday, she calculated that both of them donning Indian garb would be too pushy, like 'we've come dressed like natives now, so you can accept us.'

Liv urged Shakti to shower, wash her hair, and go into preening mode, all to chew up time. Still, once they were both ready, it was only three. Shakti started pacing. "This is so nerve-wracking! What am I going to say when I see him? Do I say, 'hi Dad'? Do I do nothing?"

"I could introduce you?'

"Duh. It's a little obvious Mom who I am."

"Right. Okay, so he rings to say he's here, and we go down in the elevator and walk out and he's there."

"And?"

"Yes. That IS the most awkward moment. I see that." Liv stood at the window, not wanting to crease her dress yet. Not that Rama's eyes would be on her. *Just chill.* Shakti continued moving around the room, checking her hair for the umpteenth time. "Honey, let's sit here on the bed together." Reluctantly Shakti sat down. "Remember that time when Aunt Elyse got married and the three of us were in a little room at the back of the church? You know, we have that picture at home on the shelf?"

"Sort of...I think so."

"Elyse had been freaking out a bit, anyway she was very nervous about the wedding. I was that way too. And somehow it happened that we all held hands and took some deep breaths together. We closed our eyes."

"Like when you meditate?"

"Yes, exactly. Why don't we calm ourselves that way? Hold my hand. Take a few deep breaths. Be quiet."

"That won't shut off my mind, it's practically screaming."

"Let's try though. That's the point of meditation, to still our minds. Try to be in the moment and connect with your heart. Come on, let's try."

Shakti sighed. "Whatever."

Liv rose and turned off the room lights. Sitting again, she called on her memory to say the things her meditation teachers did: take a comfortable posture, let your spine move upward, place your hands in your lap, feet flat on the floor, focus on your breath, going out and coming in. Periodically, Liv would remind them to focus on their inhalation, then exhalation. Liv felt herself becoming lighter, freer. Her head and back arched and straightened, her shoulders rolled to ease out tension. When she felt relaxed, she opened her eyes slightly to see how Shakti was. *Dear Lord, please protect her and guide her. Help her through this most challenging time. God, let him be good for her.*

Shakti felt her vulnerability. *I'm just a kid. The adults, they handed me this problem. Why can't they fix it? Why do I have to be so worried about making this man love me? He SHOULD love me. I shouldn't have to make this work, he should figure it out.* She felt helpless, a pawn in someone else's chess game. Then a calming thought arrived: she didn't have to do anything but show up. If he was a good father he'd make things work out okay; if he was a father she didn't really need or want, he'd botch it. The burden was on him to get it right. She opened her eyes to see the clock. Twenty more minutes. If he was on time.

Liv pulled herself back into the room, slowly opening her eyes, and rubbing her hands together. She stood up and flexed her body, then went and got them each a glass of water. "Better?"

Shakti nodded. Liv stayed with her thoughts that she could serve the moment best if she was fully present to it with no agenda. Show up, be present, and come from her heart. "What are you thinking, sweetie?"

"That it's up to him. He has to figure it out."

Rama dressed casually in a black polo shirt and khakis. He too had spent time calming his nerves in his room at Nimisha's before driving over. He'd given up on several first greetings and accepted it would be the most excruciating moment of his life. But it would pass, he'd take them to the covered patio of the hotel, they'd sit and have something cool to drink, and he'd simply come up with questions to ask her. He hoped Liv would stay and help guide the conversation. He was unclear what Liv meant about Shakti being a typical American teen, but that didn't sound good. Although other things she'd said meant Shakti might be someone he could get into talking to. *It doesn't have to go more than an hour.*

    Approaching the desk, he glanced in a lobby mirror and saw a tense version of himself. The clerk called the room and let him know they'd be right down. He sat down but then stood again to take a different chair about fifteen feet off to the elevator's side. There were two elevators and the doors opened twice emptying other guests. Then, they stepped out of the next one. He saw Liv first and then the girl. In a blue-green Punjabi almost as tall as Liv but looking more Indian than American. *Lovely.*

    He rose and walked toward them, Liv seeing him first. He watched the girl turn towards him and fix her gaze. She was calm. Steady. Her face open but not revealing any emotion. Liv's eyes were upon him and he felt her concern across the space while she remained still. As he came right up to them, the air was sucked out of his lungs, and his heart paused. *Mine. My child.* Just like he'd written. As his lungs filled forcefully and his heart beat again, it was as though they would burst their boundaries. The girl's eyes were holding his, those eyes reminding him of his mother's, the eyes becoming more liquid as they filled with emotion.

    In the moment, it was pure instinct. The connection would not be denied, and he pulled her into his arms, holding her close, tightly, her face pressed into his chest.

    Liv's tears came fast. *Thank you, God!*

    He slowly unfolded Shakti and looked at her. "I want to get to know you. Let's go out to the patio and sit down." He put his hand to her back to usher her, as his first question came spontaneously. "Tell me all about your trip, what you've seen, do you like India?"

    Shakti broke into smiles and laughs as she wiped away her own tears. Liv already felt they didn't need her there yet decided to stay for one drink. Just in case. Shakti started bubbling and moving like a fast-running stream, jumping from one experience to another as the nervousness she'd controlled rushed out of her. Rama got them seated at a table on the marble patio next to the colonnade in the shade, overlooking the garden and hills in the distance. Liv felt like she'd stepped into a film. Rama became all ears and eyes, taking in the qualities of his daughter, not only her animated features as she gushed, but the mind at work, her reactions and interests.

He couldn't help studying her features and then looking at Liv's. Poor child, she did have a scaled down version of his nose. Her mouth and smile were Liv's but there was a hint now and then of his sister. While the eye color was similar, Shakti's rounded shape was clearly his mother's and not Liv's sexier look.

Shakti pivoted from experience to experience, recalling after a while to ask him why all those people in the slums couldn't go out and farm.

"It's a long story of history, society, and culture. Do you know I work in agriculture at a university?"

"Oh yes, Mom told me that. But I've been talking and talking – I'm so nervous," she laughed and covered her mouth, "I should shut up."

"No, don't do that. But I can tell you a few things in answer to your question."

Liv seized this as the right moment to excuse herself to go to the bathroom. She mostly sat in the antechamber of the women's room, watching her breath, trying to ground herself. *The first time the three of us have been together – not since the man across the table and I made love and together made Shakti.* A moment long ago that set a trajectory towards the here and now. Wondrous. Scary. *Where will today's moment take us?*

The desire to drift away in her thoughts was strong and yet she needed to keep moving. She repaired her makeup to cover the mascara smudges under her eyes. Standing back and viewing the person in the mirror, she didn't quite feel inside the body returning her gaze.

Her absence meant that shortly into Rama's account of helping farmers, like Liv had years ago, Shakti interrupted in a bubbly way. "Mom told me about that. And we met Arita and went to her office. Mom fit right in."

"Your mother..." he wasn't sure what to say, "...she's a very fine person."

"Oh, she's great. I mean we have our arguments. But now I'm thinking I want to be more like her. Be like those women in Arita's office, go after what's wrong, make the world better for girls and women."

The more she expounded on her future and got into things she wanted to do, more school, studying hard, volunteering, he understood what Liv's remark yesterday: Shakti had him in her. He recognized the energy. He'd been that way himself. It was easy to connect with her, not as challenging as with his withdrawn older son, or clownish mischievous younger one. *We come from the same place.*

Liv took her time coming back, and then meant to say goodbye and go upstairs.

As soon as she returned to the table, Shakti popped up, "My turn," and hurried to the bathroom.

Liv watched Rama settle more comfortably into the wicker chair. Looking directly back, he said softly, "I'm blown away." He looked out over the garden, experiencing an opening as though he too were a rose spreading its petals to take in more sun.

"Shall I go up and leave you two to yourselves for a while? I feel like a spectator of something private."

He heard the truth in that. "I'll want to talk with you tomorrow. Maybe when we give my mother and Shakti some time alone?"

"Of course. Will you be picking us up tomorrow or should we take a cab?"

"I'll come. At ten? Mother will have lunch for us."

As Shakti rejoined them, Liv voiced her tiredness and gave Shakti a key, whispering in her ear. "You're doing great!"

It was seven before Shakti opened the door to a barely lit room and saw her mom stretched out on the bed. She'd fallen asleep following an hour of replaying the euphoria-inducing reunion that filled her with gratitude.

Shakti's entry and movements brought her awake from a light but dreamy sleep. With a fuzzy mind, she blinked several times, sat up, and turned on the bedside light. "Darling, come tell me, how was the rest of the visit?"

"He really likes me! I can tell. He listens to me and looks at me like – I don't know – it's like I'm some strange alien to him but he really wants us to like each other." Shakti was all movement in relaying this, reminding Liv of Indian goddesses with multiple arms, each one holding different significance. She expected her to start crying at some point. Or maybe get angry at something? Liv only knew there was an emotional release of energy exploding before her.

Gradually, as Liv continued with steady questions in a calm voice, Shakti's spirit settled. "Aren't you hungry now? Shall we go eat?"

"I don't think I could. Maybe." Shakti looked at Liv as though seeing her for the first time since coming into the room. "Oh. Are you hungry? Sure, let's go down. You can eat."

"Yes, I need something. You can live on air for a while my goddess, but we mere mortals need food occasionally." At the table in the dining room, Shakti nibbled a tiny bit of naan while Liv finished a plate of delicious tandoori chicken, and listened to everything that had been asked and said between the reunited father and daughter. "He wanted to know about Seattle, how we live with Aunt Mimi and Uncle Ryan, who my friends are…" Shakti slowed her account for a moment. "Mom, I hope I didn't do anything wrong, but I got talking about Cezar and him being my best friend, and how, well, how his dad is your boyfriend. Is that okay?"

Liv had authorized Arita to share the basics of Liv's single momhood, familial existence, although Marco hadn't been part of that. But she was glad for Rama to know she had a man in her life. "Sure, that's fine. Did he say anything about his wife or your brothers?"

"Actually, I did ask about my brothers. My mouth was like a fire hose, everything came pouring out, even stuff I thought I shouldn't say. Anyway, he checks the time on his cell, saying he promised his mother to be back by seven for dinner. And I could sort of see he had a photo on his phone with kids' faces, so I asked if those were his sons."

"What was his reaction?"

"He froze up for a moment. It was awkward. I said I was sorry, that I knew the rules."

"You said that? That you knew the rules?"

"Yeah. I mean that's the deal, no? He's afraid of me being a problem for his wife?"

"Right, so what then?"

"So, he took his time, asking me what I knew about his sons. I told him nothing, just that they exist and their ages. I said I was sorry again. And he changed the topic then to his mother, how I'd meet her tomorrow. He told me a few things about her, how much she wanted to meet me."

"He never showed you the screen shot?"

"Nope, he put his phone away. He did say that his mother had family photos around and I'd probably see those tomorrow."

Interesting. Maybe he'll go back and hide them all. "Well don't ask about it again, okay? There's so much going well that we shouldn't make him uncomfortable."

As they undressed, Liv was still in a daze. Every time she thought of the hug he'd given Shakti, she became very still. "Did he hug you again when he left?"

"Yes, but it wasn't like the first one."

After they each got under the sheets of their separate beds, Shakti didn't wait long to slip over to Liv's to be closer. "Mom, when he hugged me, I can't explain what happened. It was like my body was one huge firework that went off. It was the best." In the dark next to her mom's body, all was safe. She could say anything. "Mom, it felt like home, like I belonged."

Liv's chest constricted, almost painfully. *To be expected. Not dis-owning you. This is what she needs that I have never given her. Except I wanted to be everything for her.* "Good."

A while passed as they both lie awake, lost in cascading images, words, and emotions. Shakti stirred and propped herself on an elbow to look at Liv. "It just seems like you two would have gone together well, as people, as married. Why didn't you come back when I was little to see if it would work? Maybe it would have worked out?"

Those softly delivered inquiries were harsh accusations for Liv to hear. Her systems came wide awake, and instinct caused her to rise and go the bathroom to seal herself off.

"Mom?"

"I need to go."

She kept the lights off and leaned against the closed door, her body becoming chilled and shaky. *Am I to be the bad guy in this?* She wanted to go fetch a blanket and sleep on the bathroom floor with the door locked. She didn't want to go back and retrace her life's choices, to have to explain herself. Although she'd pushed her own mother once on why she'd given up Ryan. Ryan had counseled Liv about not giving up her own flesh and blood. And she hadn't. But now Shakti was accusing her, yes softly and sweetly, but nonetheless accusing her, of renouncing the flesh and blood of her father, leaving their family half-made. *I can't deal with this.* The bitter aftertaste arrived. *All I've been through, all we've brought to fruition today – and I got it wrong? I didn't do enough?*

"Are you okay?" came a tentative voice on the other side of the door.

She doesn't get it. She's been under enormous stress. Stuff just comes out. Be the grown-up. Liv opened the door, avoiding looking at her, and returned to her bed experiencing the covers as a safe place, as though she'd found a cocoon to crawl into.

"Mom?"

"I'm really, really tired. I don't feel well – maybe it was the food. I just need to rest. By myself."

Shakti crawled back into her bed, confused and emotionally askew, ending the most fulfilling day in her life with her mother distancing herself.

After Rama and Nimisha arrived earlier in Lonavala at the family's hill cottage, she'd spent the afternoon directing the maid's cleaning while engaging herself in the garden micromanaging a landscape crew she'd used before.

The home had been built in the time of the Raj in this hill station for the family of a British merchant, and then come into her grandparents' hands in the fifties. When it became Nimisha's when her parents' estate was settled, she'd thrown herself into a preservation effort. She updated appliances and furnishings, adding her favorite Indian décor, new teak carved tables for example in the living room, while preserving the ambiance of its most charming British history, including a soft cushy chintz covered sofa and comfortable wing chairs. The garden was her special love, which received her own tender care until the first bout of cancer. Having belonged to her Scottish grandmother, the home had hosted scores of celebrations and encounters that included both colonials and local Indians of importance. The generous veranda blended into internal airy spaces, while the garden also invited small gatherings to find their own niche, whether in the shaded space of a back patio off the kitchen or bench settings. This was Nimisha's respite, the place she always wanted to be now that she'd been installed in a sterile condo in Mumbai by her sons.

Nimisha went well with this space. The casual elegance here was a perfect match to her own personality and demeanor, always welcoming, and full of Indian spice. She was a gracious lady who knew how to create gracious space.

Before seven, Nimisha took a position at the front window to await Rama, eager to glean from his steps, his body movements, his demeanor, how it had gone. When he returned, she opened the door for him, searching his face with Shakti eyes that had grown old.

He'd been a nervous wreck in the car and was relieved to be on home turf. Tension he'd contained during the visit wanted to release itself in sounds and stretches and shaking. As he came in, he couldn't help but immediately orient himself to his mother's probing gaze. He knew what she needed. "She's a lovely, girl, just like in the photo. Smart, full of talk and ideas. You're going to like her. To enjoy her." He saw his mother's face relax. "Like I did."

Nimisha embraced him, "Come, let's sit and eat."

After washing up, stretching his torso, and shaking his limbs, and staring at himself in the bedroom mirror – *Who exactly are you?* - he came to the table in the downstairs dining room where a plate of food awaited him. Nimisha had sent the help home some time ago and microwaved the platefuls made up for them. She could see he was tense, constricted. "Tell me more."

Once he began, he was like a heavy stone rolling down a snow-covered hill picking up layers, and then coming to a halt. "She wanted to see the photo on my cell of the boys. I didn't want to show her, to let her cross that boundary into my life."

"And so?"

"And so, she acknowledged that she knew the rules as she called it and we moved on."

"That must have felt strange."

"It felt awful. It was all so free and open till that moment. And then I started shutting down. It dawned on me…." He turned his head to take in the credenza, he rose and went to the living room - pictures, they were everywhere. "They'll see Indira and the boys tomorrow." His voice was tightening up and rising in volume.

"Rama, Rama, come sit down. This is not such a big thing. We can simply remove these photographs if it upsets you. Except, tell me why it upsets you so much?"

"It just does. We agreed to keep my life protected. Her seeing them feels like I'm opening a gate in a fortress to let the enemy in."

"Rama, don't talk like that!"

"I know. I don't mean enemy. But like an intruder, someone who will come into my life and I'll lose control."

Nimisha knew now what the real issue was. "Because you liked her, you feel vulnerable? Like she might change your life somehow?"

"Exactly. Of course, I was very taken with her. Immediately. When she started off talking about their trip and her experiences, all my defenses came down right away." He took his mother's hand. "I hugged her like she was my own."

"She is your own."

"I feel it. Strongly. At one point, I was even talking about how I try to help farmers, and she was looking at me, her eyes all sparkly, and I could hardly get my words out as I was thinking, my daughter, my wonderful daughter. At that moment, I wanted her in my life."

Nimisha simply kept watching him as his innermost self poured out as an overflowing decanter of water across the table.

He rose again, and his voice grew stronger, his hand pulling through his hair. "This can't be. I now have a double life, and it feels terrible. I can't be honest with the family I love. I'll need to keep Shakti away from us."

Nimisha's head turned down. *What have I done?* She felt terrible. *I've meddled in his life.* "I'm so sorry. Now I wish I had never asked to meet her."

"That doesn't help, Mother." He came and knelt at her side. "The only thing that justifies this upset to my life is for you to be made happy by this. Please."

Nimisha sat quietly. "Rama, today and tomorrow, it's overwhelming. But then they'll be gone. A half-world away. Your life will return to normal."

"Yes, but then we'll never see her again. That feels terrible."

"There's time. Life will unfold in ways we can't predict." She looked at her plate, still half-full and pushed it away. "Go put away the photos. I'll clean up. Rest."

He went about the downstairs rooms picking up silver and gold framed photos from his wedding, and of the boys as they grew, then returning with second thoughts to also clear those of his brother's and sister's families. That left only historical photos of his mother and father alone, or with their relations. He held a stack of ten or so when he started up the stairs to his room with them and realized there was more family history staring at him from the staircase wall. Most of it from his mother's and father's childhood and times. But then he spied his wedding photo and one of the boys when they were toddlers. Removing these he saw would reveal the frame's outline on the wall. He began to feel pathetically silly spending time on this and dismissed those on the wall as high enough they wouldn't be seen anyway.

Placing those he carried in a corner of his gabled room, he saw the time. *Time to call Indira. And spin my white lies about helping Nimisha with contractors today.* He absolutely hated lying. Once connected to Indira, he quickly moved to eliciting accounts of everyone's day, genuinely engaging and happy to to be pulled back into his real life. After the call, what remained of the day was a sense that his real life had expanded, the way knocking down walls between the kitchen and a dining room might create a family room. This expansion of space made his whole life seem longer in history, wider in relations, and brighter as light reached across former boundaries. But it was a mess for now, as rubble from the walls kept the two rooms apart. He wanted to find big sheets of plastic to hang between them to keep one separate from the other as work continued on each side. He didn't sleep well.

Nor did Nimisha on the other side of his bedroom wall. She lay awake, at first taking herself to task for not having thought far enough ahead, feeling responsible for shaking the foundation of her son's life. *Now I've done it.* But her nature was not one to dwell on failures or missteps. Her mind shifted its focus and her heart opened to a future that was inhabited by a new active element. *Shakti.* The thought brought a smile. So indeed, her granddaughter would be true to her namesake and bring a new energy into their lives. With that she relaxed and laughed inwardly: this was to be no 'one-night stand.' There were going to be new relationships. Time and space need only be nudged to cooperate. She'd done that before, bridging gaps in her husband's family. She would do it again.

Wednesday, February 17

At breakfast they were quiet. Liv rose first, meditated seated on bed pillows on the floor, showered, and tended to ironing their outfits for today's visit. She felt confident the day would go well. Shakti would have slept even longer had Liv not roused her. She was starving so they hustled towards the day's first meal. "Are you feeling okay about today?"

A still drowsy face responded. "Yeah. I'm just really tired. I could go back and sleep more now that I'm not so hungry."

"Good. Why don't you do that. I want to walk in that lovely garden." The dining area opened generously to the colonnaded patio area where they'd been yesterday. Beyond, a bright morning sun glanced white on giant palm leaves while illuminating a panoply of greens coming from fruit trees and traditional English hedges.

They parted company, to Liv's relief. She needed to process last night. When she'd meditated this morning, her mind kept wanting to disturb her breathing and interrupt. Now she could tend to its intrusive knocking, give her laments a brief audience, and refocus on a day of promise.

The garden was charming and extensive in its three-sided embrace of the hotel. Beautifully crafted years ago with pathways of gravel, brick and stone, a formal rose garden, and perennials, some familiar, some not. The tropical fruit trees popped with intense yellows and oranges. A wooden two-seater bench with curved arms called her to sit. The sun warmed her back.

She opened her mental puzzle box and pulled out what might have been old-fashioned wooden pieces that needed to connect. For the length of Shakti's life Liv had not seriously re-examined her choice in not returning to India with her child. Not keeping up an email conversation with Rama. Not seeking to keep him engaged with her. Not asking to bring Shakti to meet him as a child. Not looking to create a real realationship out of a very short-term affair. She still felt clear that none of it would have worked. He was not interested in marriage when he met her. His family's disposition towards a wife would have had considerable influence upon him. Her only trump card would have been Rama's own character, needing to be honorable. An uninspiring foundation for a long-term relationship that required love. And more love. Always love. *I was attracted to him, but did I even really know him?* And if they had pieced a life together, or made a short-term effort at it, what would her support system have been? Arita. Period. Today, she had the luxury of being received well by his mother. Then? She might well have been a girl disrespected at best, and perhaps shunned for her promiscuity.

Her mind emptied, her eyes looked about, seeing the exquisite care apparent in the flowers of the borders and beds with their matching and contrasting shapes, sizes and colors. Liv recognized many of the flowers from gardens in Seattle, especially the rhododendrons. Her scan paused, and she rose to examine a trellis with colorful pink and purple flowers on vine-like stems beginning to climb the wires. *Sweet peas! They grow in India!* The name Liv called Shakti in her womb when she was only the size of a pea. Only later had Liv come to know the fragrant flower and bring it into her own garden. As she strolled further, an oddly misplaced fern presented itself. *That would have been me, a shade fern planted in the blazing sun withering next to a tropical bird of paradise.* She planted herself in front of it for some time. *I made the right decision. And Shakti will be helped most by accepting that construct of her life. Aim her forwards, not back.*

This assessment gained strength from an accumulated wisdom. Liv's youthful desire to be cross-cultural had been informed over the years: crossing cultures did not mean she could insert herself in another culture, simply respect and observe local customs, and expect to fit. A co-worker back at the family service center had tried for three years to do that on the Lakota Indian Pine Ridge reservation before moving on. She'd shared her limitations in being able to shed thirty years of being a white woman and become an Indian woman to her husband. At some point, internal patterns won out over her desired transformation. She was who she was, it couldn't be undone, and together she and her husband needed to create a third way. Cultural respect for Liv now included that: I can never be them. Respect the differences. Liv stood in her decision to not pursue Rama. She wanted Shakti to understand. But that could wait.

While Rama went to collect Liv and Shakti, Nimisha sat very still in the living room in her favorite blue embroidered wing chair near the partner chair of her husband. Gone four years now. Long enough that grief's intensity had faded. She'd moved into secret conversations with him that comforted. *Sudhir, what do you think of this, what I've done? Have I made a mess?* His warming smile replied, 'no more than usual, my dearest.' That curved her own lips upward. While his reactions in life to his sons' youthful escapades were harsh, he'd grown to be wiser and accept things more easily. *Do you approve of my plan?* 'Why not? But let's see the child first, consider again the possibilities.'

She heard the car and then voices as they came up the pathway onto the veranda, a woman's soft voice praising the beauty of the house. Nimisha liked sitting here in her chair to receive them, as it supported her with years of experience being steady through challenges. Yet, being who she was, as soon as they entered the corner into the room, she rose and moved quickly to welcome them.

Greeting these two significant strangers in an emotionally charged first meeting created a sudden overload of her intake ability. She became flustered as a bird startled from its branch, twittering and flitting, wanted to get them settled in the room while directing Rama to bring tea and coffee. *They're both so attractive – my, what a lovely woman Liv is! The girl, my Shakti, look at her in that Punjabi. Oh my. Oh my!* Her heart fluttered, and she felt slightly dizzy. Rama noticed and took her arm to reseat her. He'd been calmer this morning, more serious holding his attention on Shakti, realizing that this first time in knowing her would end all too quickly, and morph into a last time, at least for a predictably long time. His concern for the impact on his mother gradually passed as he saw her regather her presence while Liv took the lead in a measured way.

"You are so kind to have invited Shakti and me to visit you. And to make it financially possible for us. We're very pleased to be here meeting you. It's such a significant and moving time for Shakti - she's been enthralled with India." Liv kept speaking slowly and appreciatively, providing time for either Shakti or Nimisha to weave in and take over. Shakti looked very prim seated on the loveseat next to Liv. "Your home is so charming – when we first entered Lonavala, I thought you might live in one of those modern homes or apartments which seem a little...."

"Sterile?" Liv nodded. "Yes, I find them like that too, so different from these older homes with so much history."

"Your home reminds me of all the films I've seen about India, so perfectly designed for the hill country."

Rama was surprised how different Shakti's personality was this moment, silent, restrained, and unsure. He moved to break the ice further, speaking to her, assuring her his mother had been very interested last night to hear her stories, and encouraging her to retell her thoughts on India. Shakti's eyes got big, and she pulled her shoulders up to her ears, as though she had no clue what to say. Where yesterday talk had been spontaneous, today's conversation was laboring to take off.

Nimisha observed the nervousness move around the room, and, feeling calmer herself, wanted a closer look at her granddaughter sitting across the wide coffee table. "Shakti, you're too far away from me over there. Please, come sit in this chair next to me." As Shakti complied, Nimisha continued. "This was your grandfather's chair. We used to sit here together every evening." Shakti smiled politely. Liv began to ask about him but decided against it, opting to let these two find their way. "My son tells me you're quite the student. What do you like to study?"

Ever so slowly, Nimisha peeled back Shakti's shyness, as though using a finger nail to skin a tiger the way the god Shiva had. "Rama, why don't you get Shakti something cool to drink?"

As he left the room, Liv shifted from being a spectator to this awkward intergenerational conversation to helping it along. "Shakti, remember what we were saying about how special it was for you to have a new grandmother?"

Nimisha looked across the room at Liv. "Are both your parents still alive?"

"Oh yes, very much so. They've just retired from the computer world. They've helped me so much in raising Shakti, especially at the beginning." Liv worried that this might be difficult terrain, but she felt an acceptance coming from Nimisha that encouraged speaking freely.

"And Seattle – I've heard it's a beautiful place." Actually, she'd viewed pictures online. "Have you lived there all these years?"

"Yes, my whole life. I grew up there fairly sheltered. It was during college, I woke up to how diverse and interesting the world is." Liv relaxed, beginning to enjoy this chance to let Nimisha know more about her. "I was into studying cultural differences and that's really how it was I came to India on an internship. How I met Rama as a young college girl, here for only a couple of months."

Nimisha found Liv quite easy to converse with, so open, not embarrassed, fully present. "I loved those years of my life too. My family was well off, and I was sent abroad to study. As you say, very enlivening. I actually met my husband in school in London."

"Really? Did you marry right away or wait for a while?"

"Oh, we were terribly in love and didn't want to wait…fortunately I was acceptable to his parents despite their preference to arrange his marriage." With Rama still in the kitchen, and oblivious to Shakti for a moment, Nimisha couldn't resist leaning forward, as though she were speaking in a whisper to a girlfriend, "…I know what it is to have wanted a man." *Did I really say that?* She giggled.

Did she really say that? Liv laughed. This woman is a hoot. "You married right away then?"

"Oh yes. Of course, it meant I never finished my degree. Rama's brother came too soon."

Rama returned with pomegranate juice for Shakti who eyed it asking if it was coke. "Oh, I didn't think you'd have that in the morning." He looked at Liv.

"On this trip, whatever!"

"Okay, coke it is."

"Can I come with you?" Shakti was anxious to be relieved from her grandmother's spotlight and to be alone with her father.

Nimisha nodded. Which led to Liv moving to Shakti's place in the chair, to continue chatting away in the living room about life stories, while Rama and Shakti sat in the kitchen discussing her eating habits, her friends Cezar and Natalie, her personal likes and dislikes. And her favorite girl heroines.

Sitting closer, Liv could see Nimisha's eyes and stopped in the middle of talking about her world. "I just noticed. Shakti has her eyes from you!"

Nimisha smiled, looked at her gnarled hand, and then back at Liv. "Yes, once my eyes were as beautiful as hers, big, round, and that remarkable blue. All from an English colonial government man messing with household help on my mother's side, and, on my father's side, he was born to a wild character of a Scottish woman. She'd married an older established British business man here but chose to dally with an Indian man, likely the local librarian, and then raised the child in her household as an orphan. You know it's not unusual for such a thing to have happened."

Fascinated, Liv encouraged her to say more.

"Here, come look at these photos on the table."

When Rama and Shakti returned to the room, Liv was listening and looking at a photo of his Scottish great grandmother with her own two children and a third Indian child who was his grandfather. Liv plied Nimisha with questions about how the woman managed to conceal it, and yet how Nimisha knew today.

"Between the ginger in his hair and the fact that he inherited the Scot's fortune from her – her other children had died, one in war, one from disease – well, eventually families know these things."

Rama hesitated to interrupt and break the vibration holding Liv and his mother. But then she turned, "Rama, we're revisiting family history. Shakti, why don't you come see some of your ancestors on our side."

"Yes, sweetie, come and take a closer look at your grandmother's face – you have her eye shape and part of your eye color from her family line. And look at this lady, a great, great grandmother of yours from Scotland."

Shakti looked puzzled and stepped into the stories behind the photos, positioned between her mother and grandmother.

Rama recalled his mother's wish that there be photos taken today, and went for her digital camera upstairs, relieved that he had removed his family photos from the table. He returned to see that Shakti was now more relaxed and actively engaged in talking to his mother. He didn't want to break the spell and went back to the kitchen to warm up the food his mother had arranged for lunch, a favorite family curry dish.

When Rama returned, pausing under the arch to the room, Nimisha was asking about Liv's family, quite interested in hearing about her brother and his re-integration into the family after thirty years and how he'd been a surrogate dad to Shakti all her life. The trusting rapport that Liv and Nimisha established so quickly was a protected bubble in which truths could be shared, including some Shakti hadn't even heard before.

Liv was emphasizing what an important role Shakti played in reuniting their family with her brother, and how it affected relationships. "Shakti has been an amazing force for good in our family."

Nimisha warmed inside, so pleased to know that Liv's family had come together around her granddaughter. "That's beautiful. It makes my heart so happy to hear that."

Rama was standing listening, and he too felt the beneficial power of Liv's choice. *I didn't produce a problem, I created a beneficial life.* Good had come of he and Liv being together. He felt buoyant, as though a demon had been pulling him underwater, but now released him. Listening to and watching Liv, he imbibed her genuine positive acceptance of all that had come before. No regrets, no whining, or complaining. No hidden agenda. She was steady, self-possessed, and confident in her truth. Nothing hidden from the child. The honesty of it all relaxed him. Tension as real as shackles on his limbs unlocked itself. Standing with the truth set him free.

Rama served the lunch in the dining room. As if clucking hens, the women remained absorbed in their conversations, now of Liv's work including her years at the Rescue Committee. Liv spoke of the days Shakti used to be taken as a baby to the office and how the lost boys adored her. Nimisha, unfamiliar with their story, asked Liv to tell it. Shakti then interjected how they would be visiting one of them in London on the way back, which led Liv to talk about David's long journey. As Liv embellished his story of becoming a lawyer, working at the International Court, and now moving to London, Nimisha intuited a strong emotional connection. Eagle-like, she tuned in to Liv's enthusiasm about this David person, her admiration for him. *And do I hear something more?* Her heart beat faster to sense that perhaps a synchronistic force would aid her plan. *It may work out.*

They were all very tired after lunch, each feeling full, not just of food, but of life: Liv with a sense of completion, of having joined a curve in her life into a circle; Shakti with a sense of expanded family; Rama with the pure joy of honesty and honor; and Nimisha feeling the creative force to shape the universe. Liv agreed to visit the following morning before their return to Mumbai to begin their journey home.

Back in their hotel room, Liv encouraged Shakti to nap before dinner, but she was wide awake, her mind zipping here and there to understand better what had transpired. She hugged her pillow to have a comforting substance to cling to as her expanded universe spun around. "Mom? Do you really want to sleep, or can I ask you some questions?"

Liv turned on her side to look across the gap between the beds at Shakti. "What's on your mind?"

"Did you mean all you said about how important I was in bringing Ryan and Grandma Kathy and everybody together?"

"Yes, for sure. I wouldn't have said it otherwise."

"It's just, you've never said that to me before…it made me feel important."

Liv slipped across the space to lay next to Shakti, wrapping an arm around her skinny body. "I suppose I haven't. It's one of those things you say when you look back over a long period of time and you see it, not as separate events, but as a pattern. You see it in a fresh light."

"It made me feel like I was on some kind of special mission."

"Like one of your movie heroines?"

"Yeah. Sort of. Is that crazy?"

Liv cuddled her, enjoying the tactile give of the pillow between their torsos as though they were porcelain statuettes packed together around stuffing to prevent either damaging the other. "I don't think so. Looking back, it's clear to me, that you brought us closer. We're a really tight family compared to some." She stroked Shakti's face. "It's amazing about your eyes being hers. It draws her to you." *What a miracle!* "You know, taking the long view again, who knows what will come of our meeting her and you meeting your father?"

Shakti's eyes closed. Light drained from her face. "This is so weird, Mom. I know I keep saying that, but here I get to meet him for just a few days, and then it will just go back to how it was before? No contact? Is that what will happen?"

"I have no idea, sweetie." Liv considered the interest, even delight, she'd witnessed cross Rama's face at moments. "I think there's been a shift in all of us - life won't be the same." Liv turned to Shakti's upsetting question from the prior night. "I've thought about what you asked me last night, about why I didn't try to come back here with you as a baby and find out if Rama would marry me."

"The question that made you sick?"

Liv grinned. "I'm sorry, yes, it was a shock to my system. But I'm clear Shakti, it wouldn't have worked out."

"But his mom liked you so much today."

"That doesn't mean I would have been welcome back then. I think she liked me today because she saw a woman who was strong and capable enough to have raised you so well on my own - without altering the life she wanted for her son years ago."

Shakti wasn't totally convinced.

"What's important is now, the potential in this moment. Every decision I made meant a different trajectory for you. I didn't give you up and create an abandonment sense for you, an idea that there was some other life you should have had. By raising you as a single mom, and not trying to marry Rama – or anyone else – yes, I charted a course. Ultimately that happens to each one of us growing up, whether in the arms of both parents or not. Choices are made, jobs, where to live, staying married or divorcing, having other children, schools – all those things where the consequences create both limits and opportunities for the child. You think if your parents stay together and create your life, then 'that's the way it should be.' But in reality, there is really no 'that's the way it should be.' It could be any way and it's all part of what you're dealt - until you start laying down your own path. Just accept it. You'll do the same to your own kids. No matter how good you think it is, the life you've created, they'll find things wrong with it."

"You're so philosophical, Mom."

"Okay, let me be real. It's entirely possible Shakti that if I had come back to India, things might have worked out with your father and you would be feeling like a perfectly normal Indian girl raised in Mumbai. And yet it's possible I chose the better path. And it's possible if I had come back yet another choice would have sent us in a different direction. And what seems better to you today may not seem better five years from now. You just do what you think is right in the moment and accept the consequences. And make the best of them. It's the human condition. What's most wonderful and amazing right now is that you've expanded your family." Liv shifted Shakti's face to look straight into her eyes: "This will not be the last time you're in India."

That made her smile. "Maybe when I'm done with school, I can come here and work with Arita?"

"Hold that thought! Which reminds me I want to call her now and let her know how well it's going. And let people at home know too."

"I'll email Cezar then – he's finding this all so dramatic!"

Liv was laughing as she spoke, "You may not be a drama queen, but you're certainly queen of this drama."

Nimisha reread the draft of her letter and made fresh corrections. She wrote it out again, so she could show it to Rama at dinner. Hopefully he would acquiesce willingly in her desires. But if not? *I'll do it anyway.*

The cook had come in to prepare dinner and a few more dishes for the coming days. Rama would return to Pune tomorrow afternoon, but Nimisha would stay for a while. After she dismissed the cook and they settled into their meal, she began her queries. "What are you thinking about?"

Rama had been up in his room, checking work emails, but then drawn to study the photos of Indira and the boys stacked in the corner. "It didn't go as I thought. Shakti is so talkative with me, but with you, she was shy."

"Age differences can do that. I didn't mind it so much. She was respectful. Her mother raised her well, don't you think?"

"Yes, as far as I can tell, they have a healthy relationship and Shakti is coping well with all this."

"I know. It is a great deal to come to terms with. I liked the way Liv praised Shakti's role in their family."

"Liv has a way of speaking the truth. She doesn't lie about anything and apparently never has to Shakti. Before this all happened, if asked, I would have expected something different, a cover-up that would have gone on about how Shakti came to be."

"It's surprised me too. She's a very interesting and capable woman. I have to say I like her."

"She makes me feel bad about this all being a secret from Indira."

Nimisha heard the strain in her son's voice and looked up from her soup to see his features were taut. "I understand. Everything about you and Liv and your daughter was in the full light of day here. Somehow it was all as it should be. And to think Indira knows nothing of it, that we must keep it secret from her, that Raj and Aryan shouldn't ever know her – it's not right, is it?"

Rama stared at her and scolded her, "What are you saying? That I should return home and tell her everything?" Nimisha didn't answer right away knowing Rama's question was rhetorical. It was one he would need to return to, perhaps for quite a while. He took an audible breath and released it. "I'm sorry for attacking you. Obviously...I don't know what to do."

"I know. Just be with it." She debated internally how best to broach her letter. "Rama, you know that property my brother and I own in Goa? The one we all thought we'd use – and don't. He's been after me to sell it, and I'm ready to do that. Do you object?"

Still entangled in his own dilemma, he was unfazed by this idea. "No, not at all. You know we never object to what you do with your property. If we had come to use it, maybe – I'd thought we'd go there holidays. But for years, none of us have wanted to do that. We always find other trips and vacations we're more interested in."

"Good. Because I have a use for the proceeds of a sale." She waited to see that she had his full attention. "I want to pay for a first-class education for Shakti."

He placed his silverware down loudly. "Really?" Before a why could make it from his lips, he understood.

"It's time we stepped up for your daughter. Supported her in becoming everything she can be. I feel this strongly." She stopped herself to make space for him to affirm her. She was going to bring him along.

His mind immediately raced to the disclosure aspects of this, how to keep it secret. "But..."

"I know what your concerns are about how we do this. I need to know though whether you agree in principle."

This was his mother's way and he knew it well. Gain agreement to some family objective and minimize the details and complexities of how to make it happen. As he sat with her proposition, the truth was that nothing in him objected substantively. *Yes, of course, we should help her.* "I agree in principle."

Nimisha smiled and reached over to lay her hand on his. "I hoped you would. It makes me joyful to think about it."

"And I suppose you have planned it out?"

"Oh yes." *Your father would have liked the idea too, so like what happened to him.* "I do have an ulterior motive though also." Better to draw him in before getting into specifics.

"And what's that?"

"I was quite intrigued by the conversation about their stop in London. I'd love for Shakti to follow in all our footsteps and enjoy a British university education."

He reared back now. "Mother, there are great universities in the U.S. She doesn't need to go to school in England. Nor would she probably want to. Plus, Gauri is there, and I don't want her involved in this!"

"No, don't misunderstand me, I'm not trying to widen the audience for our family secret to your sister. But Rama, think of it, when I visit England to visit her, I could also arrange time to spend with Shakti. And you could too."

His first reaction was that his mother might not live long enough for all this to unfold, so why argue with her. Looking across at her however, she hadn't seemed this alive and vibrant in quite some time. Maybe she wouldn't be dying any time soon. "I don't know…it should be up to Shakti where she goes."

"I agree. I've written a letter to them. I want you to read it tonight, so I can give it to them tomorrow."

Following their pudding, he put the dishes in the washer, took the letter from the table, and went upstairs to study it. And most definitely think this through quietly on his own.

"My dearest Shakti and Liv, (*honestly, wasn't this a bit too loving?*)

"I have been so happy to meet you and begin to know you. As I believe you know, my health is compromised, heightening for me the importance of meeting my only granddaughter. Thank you both for making this trip.

"Beyond that, I'm so impressed with what a fine young lady you are, Shakti, and the interests that you have both in the world and its people, especially women. I would like to support you in pursuing your education. (*Nothing wrong with that.*)

"I plan to set up a trust fund for you with Rama as trustee. I have put such trusts in place for my other grandchildren and I believe that you Shakti should have one too. (*I guess she's right.*)

"It should be in place soon so that by this September it can be drawn upon for all costs pertaining to a world class education, including both prep school and university.

"Shakti, you of course have to choose, with your mother's guidance, a school to your liking. *(Good, it has to be their choice.)* I encourage you both to think broadly and to consider schools in England. That may shock you. It's a selfish request on my part. I have family relations there, and, when healthy, I'm able to visit once or twice a year. Obviously, if you were in school there, Shakti, I could visit you with greater ease and convenience…" (*and ability to conceal*) "…than if you continue your schooling in the States. (*She's right, she's never gone there and that would be strange to everyone. I agree.*) Given that you have friends in both London and Madrid, I'm hoping a time of living in Europe might suit you both. (*I could see her too when we visit Gauri, just slip away here and there.*) But again, the funds are available regardless of the location of the schools you choose.

"Please let me know your reactions to this. Assuming we go forward, I'm sure that Rama will determine a way for you to communicate your needs. Perhaps with a bank as co-trustee this can all be managed in an appropriately confidential way. (*I suppose.*)

"To conclude, I am so thrilled to be able to help in this way. I hold the hope that we have future visits and times together.

"With love, Grandmother Nimisha."

Rama smiled inwardly. *She is an amazing woman. Very wise.* He had to admit this was a fair proposal. If ever his brother learned of it, he wouldn't object. There was freedom of choice for Shakti. No suggestion they come to Mumbai again which relieved him. And some possibility that London might work out for them. He too journeyed there at least once a year to see Gauri. Importantly, he had time to consider his double life. He knew now he didn't want it to continue forever. Some contact would help him make his life whole again. And it felt right for him to have regular communitcation with her now. He was stepping into a responsibility for her life that deeply satisfied his sense of honor.

He took the letter and walked down the hallway to his mother's door and kocked. She was seated in a chair next to her bed pretending to read, but anxiously awaiting his reactions. He crossed the room and stood before her with a blank face before he knelt on one knee and looked lovingly at her. His voice was quiet and strong with emotion. "You've always been so wise about so many things. I think you've found us a way through this. I've been so anxious, even upset at times, and yet thrilled to meet her. You've made it all possible. And what you've suggested…" he handed the letter to her, "…it's right." He leaned forward and kissed her cheek.

She chuckled. "It's the shakti you know, the active feminine force of the universe."

Thursday, February 18

The next morning when Liv and Shakti arrived at Nimisha's home, she greeted them with open arms and kisses on their cheeks. "Thank you for coming again. I had many thoughts last night and I'd really like a little time alone with Shakti. Would that be okay?"

Rama was surprised by this. *More alone time with Liv? Why does Mother put me in these awkward situations?*

Liv meanwhile was eager to strengthen her daughter's connection to Nimisha. "Of course, I'd love to sit in your garden."

Shakti was unnerved but found only encouragement in Liv's eyes.

"Rama, can you bring us all something to drink?"

Liv followed him into the kitchen, content to see the rest of the home and garden. Rama appeared flustered; he'd assumed he would basically hide in plain sight in the living room while the female generational trio conducted conversation. Liv eased his tension, asking questions about its Indian décor, and exploring the inviting and sizeable garden in detail. Surely, there had to be a rose garden? More questions followed about Lonavala and his parents' lives, demonstrating how unbounded she felt – given the situation, no questions should go unanswered. "I get a sense from this place that your parents had a happy marriage, that your family relations are strong." She'd posed it as a statement testing him to add to it.

As they walked a pathway in the garden, the smell of jasmine drew her in, then an array of lilies, leading up to an artfully designed pond with a cluster of pink lotus below a small gazebo resting spot. Beyond on the other side was the rose garden which bordered their neighbor's garden. He was glad no one was there this week. "Yes, they were very happy, and despite usual family dramas – my sister was a real challenge – we all are in touch regularly and care about each other." He noticed Liv's delight in the garden and invited her to sit with him in the gazebo.

She seized on his remark about his sister to get him talking more about her, why she'd been a difficult girl to raise, where she lived? Was she married? Does she come often to see her mother? With small answers, she pieced together a few facts.

So, she has a bit of the Scottish grandmother in her, and chooses to live in London with her family, how interesting.

"She does come a few times a year to visit though. And then the rest of us usually make at least one trip to see her and absorb what's going on in England. We all have history there, a few acquaintances, although it's not the place it used to be."

"Why is that?"

"Well, you know the current news about the refugee issues I'm sure..." Liv nodded, "...but really there have been so many immigrants coming to London over the past ten to fifteen years, from everywhere, eastern Europe, the middle east, Asia, really from all over, mostly poor, but many quite wealthy from Russia and China. My sister complains about it all the time - as though she weren't an immigrant herself. But the foreign born in London are now something like forty percent she says." He weighed saying more and decided to provide a cautionary. "There's a terrible trafficking problem there, a lot of crime, so be sure to keep Shakti close."

That seized Liv's attention. She sought more specifics from him, realizing that she was holding old images of the city from film and TV in her head. She really didn't know much at all about the next stop on their way home. Their conversation began to move naturally from topic to topic as they enjoyed the comfort of the shade in cushioned rattan chairs. During a pause, Liv found she wanted, almost desperately, to know his reactions to what had transpired, what space he inhabited now that he'd begun a relationship with Shakti. "I'd very much like to know how this..." she searched for a phrase that felt soft, not 'reunion,' not 'meeting' "...this coming together has been for you."

His eyes popped in the same way that Shakti's did at times, momentarily delighting Liv. But then he took a substantial breath and appeared to relax, almost relieved to speak his mind. "It's been hands down the strangest experience of my life, like I stepped through a curtain into someone else's life. A double life is the sensation, one hidden from the other." His eyes roamed across the pond and flowers as he spoke, then fixed on hers. "That aspect of it, I don't like. It goes against my grain to have such an important relationship that my wife doesn't know about. I hate that." Liv's face, initially welcoming his truth, began to contract. "But obviously, I think you can tell, I'm also quite thrilled and excited to know Shakti. To have a daughter. Especially one so well raised, so intelligent and likable. I feel an obligation now to be a father, even in a distant way. And, I have absolutely no idea what that looks like." He laughed in discomfort. "I'm a mess."

Surprised at his honesty, Liv was grateful for what he said about Shakti. *Do I say I'm sorry for his dilemma? Do I ask if I should have done something differently? Do I try and suggest a way he stay in touch?* She said nothing. And they each sat quietly lost in their own space, as though they were meditating. Finally, the question came with a pounding heart. "Do you have any regrets? About anything?"

He stared at her with renewed intensity that was unreadable. *Do I regret seducing you?* Looking at her now he still saw the girl in the field. And he was fond of that young man he'd been. Fiery about everything. Full of idealism. Full of himself. For years, he'd gone back to their relations under the stars as a high point of being young and free. "I only regret that you were left with the burden of our actions. Not the actions themselves." His look made her eyes drop for a moment. "And you, do you have regrets?"

That brought her chin upright, and lifting her head to meet his gaze, she firmly stated, "Never." Forgetting all the difficulties of the last fifteen years, the lack of a husband and father, the tough road of single parenting, working, and needing childcare, and then the confrontations of these recent teen years, she spoke with conviction. "She's not been a burden, she's the love of my life. Dearer to me than my own life."

His heart strengthened hearing her. "Then, this is good. No regrets of the past on either side. There's only now. And the future."

"And you feeling in a mess."

"Yes, that. But I'm glad we spoke like this."

"Why?"

"It's hard to articulate, but it has to do with someday, some time, in the right place, telling my wife. And standing in who I was and who I am. Not being weak, or in regret. Maybe if I'm strong, she'll be strong too. It makes me hopeful."

Meanwhile in the living room, Shakti had gradually relaxed and become herself with Nimisha. Through poking here and probing there, she'd learned that not long before she'd been seized with the desire to meet her granddaughter, Shakti had been arguing with her mom that she wanted to meet her dad.

Nimisha was delighted by this confluence of familial and feminine energy across the globe. Shakti opened up, telling all manner of stories about her life, how her mother was always honest with her, how hard it had been for Shakti at times, and how much she wanted a dad. With just a small nudge from Nimisha, Shakti didn't think twice about revealing her mother's love life, including notable relationships Liv had tried and rejected, Eric the Viking being singled out in Shakti's mind as the worst. "In some ways, I'm lucky Mom didn't marry, because the choices I remember were not great. And my Uncle Ryan is kind of a dad to me. I love him a lot. But anyway, I'm really lucky Mom didn't marry some obnoxious man just to give me a dad."

"It must have been lonely for her at times, no?"

"I think so. But she doesn't complain about her life, not to me anyway. She does that with her best friend Elyse I suppose. But I always try to please her, most of the time, and she never seems unhappy to me. It's hard now though with Marco moving to Spain. For both of us."

"And what about this London stop over. Aren't' you visiting a man there, someone your mother is close to?"

Shakti became animated now, gesticulating more and showing her enthusiasm. "Yes, this is so great! We get to see David – the one we talked about yesterday, the lost boy. He's been our friend since I was a baby, and he's always liked me." And with that she rattled on about David, things already said yesterday, but now including how her mom loved him but could never be with him because he was always busy with his work going after this bad African guy.

Nimisha was beyond delighted with all she was learning from Shakti. *Imagine, Liv loves this man in London! My plan gets better all the time.*

Eventually Shakti ran out of steam, Nimisha changed the subject to her education. "I want you to study very, very hard and become a great woman, Shakti. Do you think you want to do that? That you could do that?"

"It's strange you say that." She wanted to add 'Grandma' but held off. She moved to the edge of the chair, her voice turning low and secretive, while keeping her eyes to her grandmother's face seeking a true reaction. "I'm always thinking about being an amazingly strong woman. I want my life to be special."

Her grandmother's face was a map of kindness. "And so it shall be, Shakti. I have no doubts." She reached for the envelope on the table next to her. It had Liv's name on it too. "This is for you and your mother to read later. I want to help you."

Shakti took it gently, stared at it, and raised a quizzical face. Nimisha yet again imprinted on her mind this youthful face in which she saw a legacy of herself and her family, her own eyes, the forehead that been her mother's, the elongated oval shape and nose that reminded her of her husband. "And, for you alone..." she reached for another envelope that bore only Shakti's name. "Here's some spending money for London. You can change it at the airport into pounds." That drew a wide smile like Liv's. "I want you to buy something you really want."

Shakti rose to move closer and Nimisha stood to receive the embrace she'd longed for all morning. "Oh, Grandma – may I call you that? – thank you so much. This will be so much fun."

Nimisha realized as they hugged that Shakti was taller than her by a few inches, and very slim under that Punjabi with the contours of her body filling out. Grateful, she was proud to have such a fine girl in their family. "Now, why don't you go get your parents and we'll say our goodbyes."

Shakti took the beginning of a step, but then froze and didn't move. Nimisha watched the girls' eyes fill with tears and one roll down her cheek, until her hand moved to wipe it away. "What is it dear? What did I say to upset you?"

Shakti in a choked voice squeaked out, "This is the first time in my life anyone has ever referred to 'my parents.'" Next, she burst out laughing, and hugged Nimisha again. "God, it's so amazing! I have PARENTS! Two of them. And for this one time, we're all here together." Nimisha watched her face continue to change, a mind unsure which thought to act upon, to cry more or laugh, or be still.

The child's gaze turned inward finding a place of darkness, a sad place, often hidden, yet part of part of the concrete foundation of who she was. She saw it beginning to crack, then break up and come apart. She couldn't move. Her bedrock identity, a child with only one parent, was deconstructing with the catalytic force of these events: a father who embraced her, who talked to her and asked questions and listened. Who liked her. They had begun something. Her home space had a life-changing addition. She had parents with an 's'. *I can say 'my parents', answer questions about 'your parents.'* She felt dizzy, as the ground shifted under her feet. She moved back to the chair and groped to lower herself.

Nimisha dared not disturb her and delicately slipped away to fetch Rama and Liv. Finding them she sensed they too were in a new place, somewhere peaceful. She beckoned them and, feeling the need to whisper, said that while she and Shakti had a marvelous time, the child was experiencing something brought on by Nimisha's reference to them as 'her parents.'

Liv entered the room first, and seeing Shakti now crumpled back into the chair, crying, rushed to her, kneeling down and awkwardly trying to hold her. "Sweetie, "I'm so sorry you had to wait so long for this." Suddenly, Liv was crying too, "But it will all be okay. We have to look to the future." Pulling back, she gently raised Shakti's chin to connect with her eyes. "You'll like having a father. It will be better now." Liv looked at Rama, claiming his commitment.

Shakti pushed herself from the chair and grasped her tightly, then slowly released and wiped her eyes. She began apologizing. Nimisha brought her tissue. Rama came close, not sure what to do. "I just love you all so much. I'm so happy we're finally a family." Which brought everyone tears and smiles, and a bear hug from Rama.

Emotional exhaustion was palpable. It was time for goodbyes. Even Shakti knew it to be so. "Will I see you again?"

Rama's heart was clear now. "Yes, we will see each other again. Many times, I think." Nimisha's heart was strong. "Read my letter. We will make it happen." Stretching her elderly spine as tall as it would go, she pronounced, "I will live to see you again. I promise."

As they finally disentangled and made their way to Rama's car to return to the hotel and a taxi back to Mumbai, Nimisha called Liv back to her side.

"Yes?"

"Liv." Nimisha had one more thing to say. "Liv, thank you. Thank you for not destroying this life. Thank you for raising her by yourself. Thank you for being an excellent mother. And thank you for bringing her here to me."

These affirmations, this spoken act of gratitude never before expressed, had no less impact on Liv than the reference to 'parents' had on Shakti. Already overwrought with emotion, Liv's face and body imploded as though from an inner collapse of structure. All those walls, made while toughing life out and defending her choices to herself and others, buckled under the unique kindness of her value being acknowledged.

Nimisha reached out to hold her while she shook. Liv's voice left her. "Breathe, dear, just breathe."

In seconds that passed as much longer to them, Liv collected herself. Holding tightly to Nimisha's hand, Liv brought it to her lips and whispered, "That means everything to me."

Later at the hotel, mother and daughter retreated to their own inner spaces, subdued, nothing left hidden or unspoken, all revealed. Their hearts were as open as the sky and overflowing with silent gratitude.

Rama drove back to his Pune home determined to find the right moment with Indira to speak the truth. Liv and Shakti moved as almost silent automatons bringing their luggage down, heading off in the taxi to the airport in Mumbai, and then boarding their flight to London in the evening. They were spent. Exhausted. Words required too much energy and would have been too weak to capture their emotionally overloaded states. Fortunately, they slept, first holding hands then releasing into separate worlds of images and people and spoken words that now began to populate their dreams.

Friday, February 19

An hour from London, Liv woke and began to rally. She was totally stiff and sore from the flight, but the day awaited them. *God, seeing David will be like having to eat too many desserts! I'm already full.*

As Shakti adjusted her body, and then bent to claim a water bottle from her backpack, she saw the letter from Nimisha shoved inside along with the spending money envelope. "Mom, she gave me money to spend in London." Opening it, and seeing the rupee notes, they were unsure how much it was, maybe $100?

"How sweet of her! Now you can do more than simply window shop."

"Yeah. Oh, and there's a letter for both of us," she said as she pulled it out already rumpled by a fold. "Why don't you read it, I'm tired."

Liv stared at the handwriting and smoothed the paper. Her heart raced at first, but then she realized it would offer similar sentiments to what had already been exchanged and that it would be special to have it in writing. And it could serve to begin what Liv planned as an ongoing correspondence. She debated opening it now, but given the days ahead with David, this letter was closure that belonged to now. As she opened it, and read the greeting calling Shakti 'my dearest,' Liv immediately shared it.

"What else does it say?"

Liv took in the first paragraph of appreciation for their visit. "She again thanks us for making the trip." Then Liv became glued to what she read, rereading sentences, then paragraphs, then the entire letter again.

"Mom, what is it? What else does she say?"

Liv was trying to process words, "trust fund," "world class education," "prep school and university," "London," "living in Europe." Stunned and speechless, she handed the letter to Shakti.

She read with punctuated questions about the same phrases Liv had read multiple times. Liv responded in a robotic voice, devoid of emotion due to continued processing – does it really say that? Did I read it right? "A trust fund means money being set aside to provide you with an expensive education. In London if you like, starting in the fall if you want."

Shakti now reread the letter but silently mouthing some of the phrases and sentences. "Mom, do you believe this? Does she mean it?"

Liv recalled Nimisha's embrace of her, both literally, and throughout their time together. She saw again the loving gaze she held Shakti in. There was Rama's commitment in the garden. There was no incongruity she could point to. From the request to come and meet Nimisha to her letter, the experiences were of a whole cloth. "She means it Shakti. She really means it."

"Why is she doing this?"

"Out of joy in meeting you."

Shakti sank into the curve of the plane's side, closing her eyes. Liv was trying to process, still stunned. "Mom, this could change my whole life. Just like Cezar going to Madrid with his dad. We could go to London."

Liv held her entire life in front of her eyes. Her parents, Ryan and Mimi, Elyse, the job she wouldn't mind leaving, the need to find new housing, the opportunity she'd longed for to live abroad in a multi-cultural environment. Now she was the one feeling turned upside down and spinning in the wind. And David. David was in London. "Did you say anything to her about David?"

Shakti saw the connection there too. "I said you loved him. But I told her more about Marco and Cezar. But Mom, the letter was there already. She'd already written it. You had already talked about David the day before, remember?" Shakti's brain was starting to engage. *Me, in Europe. Just like Cezar. How cool would that be.* "What's London like? Are the schools there that good?"

"We're about to find out."

Exiting the plane, moving through Heathrow, they found the bus to Victoria Station, where David was to pick them up. Their spirits became alert to and voracious of all things British: accents, dress, what they saw from the bus. In the early morning light, Shakti's critique began: "It seems so drab compared to India." Yet without any spoken agreement, both were determined to explore London with fervor. Liv was already wondering if she'd need to change their return date. If she was going to check out prep schools, now was the time to visit them in person.

The bus arrived at Victoria Station. Liv bought a new SIM card and texted David. His response came quickly: he had a car outside the station and could they come out on the exit to the far left. He'd meet them there.

He saw them first, the wild-haired pair in their tight jeans and bright lime parkas. He took them in, full of anticipation that he'd be spending time with Liv again after so long. Slowly sliding through a crowd coming at him, he surprised them. "Hello!" a three-way quick hug sufficed for now as he explained the need to hustle to the car illegally parked. He knew they'd met Shakti's father, and, that between that and the flight, they were likely drained. "We're going to Phillip's place now, it's in Chelsea about fifteen minutes away. I've moved over to the firm's apartment while you're here, so you each get your own room." A bit of a fabrication, as his hope was that Liv and he could have at least one night alone in the apartment. "His wife Margaret is very enthused to show you London."

Shakti leaned forward from the back seat. "We're moving to London." Liv responded to his startled expression with a "Maybe."

"WHAAT? What's this? What happened to make you say that?" He'd been wondering if their news would be a move to India, slightly, unreasonably he knew, anxious that Liv and Rama might have found some common ground. Or whatever. More reasonably, he'd realized that this short two-day visit with him would not do much in terms of a relationship with Liv.

Liv was drained but focused to ensure accuracy of what was said. Once she started relaying how well their being together with Rama and Nimisha had gone, she gained fresh spirit in the telling. "And so, Nimisha has offered, in writing no less, to pay for a first-class education for Shakti, beginning with prep school this fall. And by the way, she'd appreciate it if Shakti went to school here to facilitate further family meetings."

The more Liv conveyed, the more distracted David was from driving until he finally pulled over. "I have to stop and take this in, I can't believe it! It's too amazing!" He began grasping Liv sideways and knocking heads with Shakti. Their heads so close, their three gazes merged.

"I take it you'd like a few more friends in London?" Liv teased.

He wanted to kiss her but pulled back behind the steering wheel, looking like the Cheshire cat with his bright white smile. "This is a gift from heaven, truly."

Liv pulled back a bit too. "We still have a lot to learn before it's decided," turning her eyes pointedly towards Shakti. "We'll need to see schools, and of course, there's housing costs. And I'll need to find a job. I mean, just saying that, can I even work here?"

David knew about his own work visa requirements, and the visas necessary for Amer and the boys. But Liv would need to find work and a sponsor to stay beyond six months. "It's not a slam dunk. For Shakti, there are student visas. But your staying would take more effort, finding a job. But you'd have six months to figure it out. And I do work for one of the best immigration firms, so somehow…."

"I get it. It would take some doing. But unless Shakti decides she hates London, we're definitely exploring the option."

"Mom, I'm not going to hate London…" looking at David, "…am I?"

He leaned forward towards her between the seats. "Well, Miss Shakti, it ain't Seattle. It's a very intense mix of people from all over the world. It reeks history and glamor while immigrants suffer in the streets, and often do not endear themselves to the locals. It makes me crazy sometimes. But, so far - I really like it!" He turned and started the car again. "I know under all this news, you are exhausted. Let's get to Phillip's, and let you rest a bit."

He parked the car on a tree-lined street of not overly impressive three-story older townhomes. From the outside Liv thought it looked nice enough, unaware of the multi-million-euro value of a place like this. She grew more impressed, entering the totally remodeled space filled with expensive furnishings and colorful modern art. Liv moved in a daze, smiling on cue as she met Margaret, Phillip already gone to the office. Liv's first impression of her hostess was positive, sensing a dynamic force. Plans for their time were quickly laid out by this attractive woman in her fifties who looked and sounded straight out of the BBC productions Liv watched. Liv interjected that they did want to check out prep schools, and would it be better to do that first? And should she change her flight home on Monday, or would there be enough time?

Margaret adored David and during the weeks he'd stayed with them, she'd squeezed out enough of his past to know that this woman was no ordinary friend, but a very special lady in his life. With great delight, she quickly came to terms with Liv and her daughter coming to reside in London. Margaret was a take-charge kind of person who'd had her own career in journalism – how she'd met Phillip decades ago during an interview - but now lent her talents to sitting on boards. With her own children out of the house, she'd been at loose ends and looking for a new project. Something connected to romance made her tingle all over. "I think another weekday would definitely help if we're looking at schools – but first let's see what I can make happen today." Meanwhile, she noticed the residue of weariness in their eyes. "Yes, and let's get you something to eat, and a bit of a nap, before we launch our activities." While they had tea and toast, she began setting appropriate expectations for Shakti. "Mind you, you may have to wear a uniform. And the teens here in these schools may come off snobby until you get to know them."

Liv managed to get a word in, "She's right, Shakti. Changing schools at sixteen is no cake-walk, let alone changing cultures."

Shakti glared back, aware they were with strangers.
"What?"
"Later."

The simplicity of the morning snack to tide them over contrasted with the glamor of the townhome itself. The kitchen was cream and pink with upholstered chairs in the nook looking out on the small charming garden beyond the French doors. Throughout the first level of the home, the emphasis on beautiful wood floors and cream walls left an expanse of space for decorative carpets, leather furniture, well-selected antique tables, and large artwork. While Phillip's practice of law was lucratively successful, it had been the wealth in Margie's family that had enabled the purchase when mum died. And then remodeling, when her father passed on. The entry foyer was dominated by a long glass table with a floral arrangement that looked real even in this dismal time of year.

Over the snack, Liv learned of the status of Margaret's children, the daughter now off at Cambridge, while the son had his own place. As Margaret showed them to their upstairs bedrooms on the third level which her children had occupied, Liv admired the exquisite dining area, noting the highly reflective quality of the well-polished table centered with an arrangement of candles in exquisite glass holders. Across was adjoining space for the piano whose music could entertain guests in the nearby living room. The second floor was dominated by a large master bedroom adjoining a study for Phillip, and a small TV room.

Liv felt like a poor cousin come to visit. *This is where David is living? How amazing.*

Margaret suggested a short power nap for them, and after pointing out their bathroom, ushered Shakti into a small refurbished playroom, now a guestroom with a single bed, while Liv was given the daughter's room. David had been staying in the son's room, but extremely appreciative of Margaret's hospitality to his friend, pled the need to stay at the firm's apartment so that he could get some work done while Liv was in town. Phillip gave David a reprieve on one due date to free him up, but he needed to meet another deadline from a demanding partner he sought to please. Indeed, he'd already had too little sleep going into today due to deadlines at work. Staying among his friends with Liv in town would draw him away from his commitments. All of which Margaret had taken at half-value, sensing there was perhaps some relationship tension that was causing David to give Liv her own space. She wasn't quite clear yet as to the source of the tension: was it David not wanting to get sucked into something so soon while he had his mark to make at the firm and his sister to care for on the horizon? Or was it that this interesting young woman was holding back? The situation was all too delicious, and Margaret was looking forward to getting into their heads to figure it out over the next few days. This whole move possibility made it even juicier! She was keen on observing a bit of romantic drama.

For ninety minutes each took a power nap, dropping off quickly, and then awakening late morning to feel like it was time for dinner. Each opened their eyes to the same thought: where am I?

Liv's waking was abrupt. She felt first the comfort of the fine linens, then propping herself up an elbow, was drawn to the beauty of a gorgeous armoire reflecting light from its middle-mirrored panel. *London. David's friends.* How other people lived, that's right, these old places don't have so many closets. She was clearly in a girl's room, a pinky mauve not so different from the colors she'd chosen for her own high school bedroom. But plush. Real hardwood furniture in a French country style. Space, probably the size of two bedrooms at home. *Imagine growing up in a well-to-do family like this in Europe.* This whole home reeked culture, old wealth and new. She wondered what Shakti's reactions would be. *Would she want to step into a world like this? Shakti going to school here? David? Can I really do this?* A tsunami was rolling into her backwater of a life these last few days and carrying her out to this huge river of activity, where everyone she knew except Shakti was left behind, and all these foreign strangers were moving her along. It didn't feel like her life anymore. They were all pushing her towards some new future. *Who are they, Nimisha and Rama, to be pulling Shakti away from me? I raised her by myself and now they want her in London – and am I supposed to change my whole life for them, leave the family and friends I love, to come here to start over? Because they want it?* Then she realized: *and what if I can't find a decent job? And I can't live here. And Shakti's in school and I have to go back to Seattle!"*

She sat up as the adrenalin flooded her system, realizing all the calculations that now complicated her life, the geographic challenge of keeping Shakti at some ease of proximity to her new birth family members, a decision about high school and whether to seize the offer now or have Shakti to herself a few more years in Seattle. And, even if she liked the idea of a move to London this year because of David – was it doable?

In the room down the hall, Shakti's awakening was groggier. She knew she was someplace she'd never been before. The room was weird, old-fashioned looking. *Mom? Where's Mom?* That brought her more awake, and as she moved to get up and pull her parka on, she recalled it all. Sitting on the bed, her feet cold, pulling on socks, it was all coming back. *David.* This place he was staying. *London.* She went to the window which overlooked a courtyard two stories down and saw a skyline of roofs. Nothing like the sights and sounds of India. She missed it already. And her father. *He was so cool! I want him in my life. More than anything. If it means living here in this cold, stuffy place, I'll do it. Just to see him once a year.* Seattle seemed incredibly far away, as though she'd stepped out of her life already. Her cousins, Uncle Ryan and Aunt Mimi, Grandpa and Grandma. *They're me. And now I'd be somebody new. Do people really do that? Leave everything they know and start up in a faraway place?* She thought about her heroines from the movies, how they moved around so many places, flying here and there in space systems, meeting all kinds of obstacles with courage. A rush of excitement came as she contemplated her own coming of age, meeting her challenges, becoming strong, becoming a woman who moved around the world. With a first-rate education, surely, she could help make the world a better place? She'd outdo her mom. *Mom. She'd be here with me, wouldn't she?* The muscles around Shakti's heart tightened. *She'd have to be here.* The imperative to talk to her mom seized her. She moved quickly to the end of the hallway abutting the stairs and cracked open the door she knew her mother was behind.

Liv was trying to meditate on the bed with the comforter loosely around her shoulders. Shakti sat next to her coming under the puffy shelter to lean into her. "Honey, did you have a good nap?"

"Oh yeah. But now it's weird waking up in this strange place."

Liv wrapped her arm around her. "For me too."

"Mom?"

"What?"

"You're not going to send me to school here and then go back to Seattle, are you?"

"I don't think I could do that." Immediately, Shakti's spirits lifted, as did Liv's, grateful her daughter seemed to care they still be together. "I couldn't bear it."

"We're in this together?"

Liv squeezed her. "At least for now. If I can't find work and be allowed to stay, then you wouldn't leave me and Seattle until college, that's what I'm thinking. By then, we both might be ready."

"Mom, I know I'm difficult for you sometimes. But I don't ever want us to be apart."

Thank you, God, I needed that. "Now that we have the most important thing settled, let's go out and see London and figure out what's possible, okay?"

David, anticipating their need for rest before they launched into sightseeing, planned on getting straight to the office and putting in a full day. He was committed to being a success at the firm, as much to justify Phillip's faith in him as for his own sake. He put in long days on his assignments, while boning up at night on commercial law he didn't know. Phillip assured him that he would always have a share of criminal international work but coached that he needed to expand his portfolio into commercial matters. The opportunities to work on cases where banks were committing crimes harming the public appealed to David.

In many ways this was the change he'd needed. He'd been stuck in a karmic groove at the International Court. Both relief and a certain freedom arrived with his leaving it. Not that the firm didn't come with substantial constraints on his time and position him in a milieu not always to his liking. Thank goodness though for Phillip, steady in his encouragement and kind. A truly fine human being under his British façade of aloofness and practicality.

David's spare hours were also spent on continuing to navigate the system on his sister's behalf. The visit to Nairobi a month ago had gone better than expected. Amer was guardedly experiencing a stronger sense of security beyond anything she'd known in decades. She was sleeping well and less worried about her boys who were quite excited by their schools. They were doing so well living with his friends that David wished he didn't have to uproot them. If she stayed, she too needed schooling or training to find a decent job, and he would need to start finding her their own apartment soon. But that was true too if she came to London.

To his surprise, what became the most decisive factor was how in two weeks he'd grown so close to his nephews. He wanted to be with them, to be a father to them. When he'd made the case to Amer for her moving to England, he'd put his love for the boys front and center in a way she hadn't resisted. At the same time, he'd realized that if visas were impossible, then not so far down the road, he might be compelled to move to Kenya. Right now though, prospects for their visas were good.

He'd been thrilled when Liv arranged to stop and visit. Despite the five-year gap since they'd last been together, she remained a center of gravity for him. Their shared history grounded him. He loved her in a simple way, perhaps as his father had loved his mother. He knew Liv'd moved on after their own failed attempts to create a future together. Marco, yes, he knew about him. As time passed and David's frustration grew with his own commitment to revenge, he suspected he'd made a mistake in not being more flexible, in not being open to multiple commitments. Even now, the possibility that he would have to multi-task his life between a demanding firm and his family stressed him. He was just so used to doing one thing and doing it with all his attention. His survival mode. Like walking a thousand miles. Like studying law. Being focused was central to his identity.

The idea of Liv moving to London was a shock to his system. His instinct was to discount it: surely something will get in the way of it. When he'd left Liv to rest, he'd told himself not to think about it. He had his office work plan to tend to, needing to finish the draft brief he'd promised to Arthur for a sex trafficking case. Then he could enjoy seeing London with Liv. Show her where he was planning to live, so different from Phillip's neighborhood, and perhaps with time to be alone together.

He didn't want to count on that, yet nonetheless hoped they could be as they were years ago, their bodies glued together, reading each other's thoughts. He'd not have to mind about Marco, as that was a consequence in part of choices David made himself. No one else had come along to move into the central chamber in his being, not the sweet court clerk, nor Sylvaine after that. The relationship with her, while dramatic at times and lasting several years, was one based on sexual need, respect, and ultimately convenience. Ten years older than he, she was a judge, equally committed to certain goals. They'd met each other's needs. But a lasting, ever-present, loving relationship with a woman? It was not to be in his life. Love would find its outlet with Amer and her boys.

Reaffirming his work prioities, he sat at his computer this morning, ready to execute his plan for improving the brief. The tiredness from only a few hours' sleep last night hit him, and he sought another cup of coffee. Which opened the space just enough for an uncharacteristic straying of his mind back to Liv. Which upon returning to his desk, sent his fingers on the keyboard to the firm's research archive on visas. His own visa had been so slickly handled he barely knew the process. He was learning much more about asylum, refugee, and child visas now, ways to relocate his family here. The boys could make it on a child student visa and Amer should be okay until the youngest reached twelve. But the refugee visa offered permanence. It wasn't them however that took him to the archive.

What would it take to get a work visa for Liv? He confirmed that Liv could have a six-month visitor visa, but a work visa was trickier. Basically, she needed to have a job offer to work in the UK that met specific requirements including a healthy salary level. And she had to have the offer in hand before she arrived. *Would she really give up her job for six months to come here, seek work, and if fortunate enough to obtain it, then return home to come yet again?* He stared at the screen rereading the text and then settled back in his chair, propping his chin with one hand as he considered.

Just when he concluded that he was wasting precious work time on something he had no say in, as he sat in a limbo between ending his own research and finding energy to work on the brief, there was space for a voice to creep in and confront him. *What if she came?* He had difficulty imagining it, resisted spending time considering it, stood and went for water, and returned only to look at the black screen and hear it again. *What if she came?* The proposition triggered fear at first of being torn between his family and Liv. And then he saw her smile at the train station, so like the smile he recalled when he stepped off the plane in Seattle to make a new life. When she had been there for him and his friends, his angel. *Everything she did for us then, she could help me do now for Amer and the boys.* It was part of who she was to reach across culture and history and lack of shared experiences, to smile, to help, to be gracious and practical. The realization that she could indeed help him recreate his family life here stunned him. He sat for a long time doing no work.

Margaret was abuzz as soon as Liv and Shakti went to rest. Not a moment to be wasted. She knew the schools and was clear that Shakti should go to one of the international ones. Two or three she had a real sense of from stories that the spouses of Phillip's partners shared over the years. Of course, her own children had had friends at them. A couple of schools were not far from their home, and there was one out in Middlesex if Liv wanted to consider that.

Marg, as her friends called her, was eager to get to know Liv better, already intuiting a certain softness about her, but wanting to get a sense of the attraction between her and David. Maybe Marg could help them. The board work she'd tried out the last two years in do-gooder groups hadn't really engaged her passion, nor her desire to be more hands on helping people. Phillip's mentorship of David enthused and pleased her with the personal connections they were all forming. And what little she knew of Shakti's situation already fed her imagination. *Life is getting interesting.* She needed this, to help real people, and not become some stuffy bored wife of a successful solicitor.

When Liv and Shakti came into the dining room calling her, Marg stuck her head from the kitchen and beckoned them to the breakfast table. Liv visibly lit up stepping into the sunny charming kitchen again and looking out on the courtyard, imagining eating out there on a sunny summer day.

"I'm thinking a quick brunchy thing before we take off. How do you like your eggs?"

"Oh, please don't wait on us. We can just have bread or cereal. Really."

"Nonsense. I love making eggs. It's my favorite meal. Fess up you two, how do you like them?"

Once they were all settled in eating their scrambled eggs with ham and mushrooms, and brioche with jam, Margaret launched in a manner highly reminiscent of Elyse. "I've been on the phone already with one school. And I'm waiting to hear back from the other. I thought we'd go ahead and get guided visits, so you could get questions answered and not simply stare at buildings. And of course, there will be materials, brochures, applications for you to take."

Liv focused her attention to get quickly in the flow of all this, watching Margaret's energetic slim figure first darting here and there in the kitchen and pantry, while emitting this organizing force. Her shoulder length brunette bob with bangs covering her brows, running unbroken with her glass frames, was colored and highlighted. It framed a remarkably pointy face, nose and chin, but well-structured cheekbones too. All of which communicated an intentional architecture directed at creating a purposeful life.

Marg was trying to gauge Liv's reaction as she spoke but was struck most by the round eyes of Shakti that seemed to pop with the school update just delivered. "Oh dear, have I done too much?"

The sincerity of her efforts yielded generous smiles. "Not at all, we're just still in a state of shock with this whole development. It was only on the plane that we read the letter from Shakti's Indian grandmother offering this opportunity to her - it's very, very new to us. Exciting, but scary too."

Marg's wall phone rang and in no time arrangements for them to visit two schools today and one on Saturday were made. "Another option I could pursue is a visit to a boarding school, perhaps on Monday, one that's not too far away – would you like that? Of course, we'd need to change your flight."

Shakti lost her smile with that and Liv responded quickly. "Probably not. We want to be together, living together, if we do this in the fall. Which is a big if. It seems so soon to make such a big change."

"That's fine. I'm sure any of these three schools will fill the bill, if not this year, then next. And of course, there are others that you could look at on the web once you're home."

As Liv's brain waves moved in circles, Marg began herding them to change for the first visit, demonstrating an affiliation to an English sheepdog. David checked in as they were leaving, and Marg instructed Liv to have him come for dinner at seven. Which left Liv to wonder if Margaret would allow time for David and her to make their own schedule. But for now, it was a day to go with the flow. As Marg drove through Kensington Gardens and into Paddington, then farther north to the American School, keeping up a steady stream of information about the sites, Liv was reminded of a poem Marco kept on the wall in his garage room near the computer. The poem by Goethe, about jumping in the river and providence carrying you. *This is how it feels.*

The first school visit was to a pleasant complex where the enrollment was predominantly American. A rather gushy dean of student admissions met with them and escorted them through the buildings. As classes changed and they observed the flow of students, Shakti felt comfortable. The accents sounded familiar, the attitudes struck were no different from what she knew, albeit with a heavy coating of affluent entitlement. Overhearing one exchange in a bathroom reminded her of some of Natalie's sister Alex's older friends, snotty, boy crazy, makeup obsessed. She left feeling that these kids were not that different from what she knew lay ahead of her in Seattle. She'd be fine with it.

They immediately drove to the next school also in the Paddington area, and arriving early, hung out in a nearby coffee shop. In debriefing their first visit, Liv and Shakti were positive, noting that the curriculum looked challenging enough. But Marg picked up on their lack of enthusiasm. "I'm glad we went there first. Not to offend you, but if your purpose in coming here is to get a world class education, that place is just too American for my taste. I think you'll find the next one more stimulating because it's more international."

While they waited for their three pm appointment, Marg used her natural interviewing skills to draw them out. She'd been a journalist, free lancing for specialty women's magazines and *The Guardian*, where she enjoyed a small following for her human-interest stories. She built trust quickly, slipping into details of people's lives with ease. She knew how to take something simple and obvious – 'how was it visiting with your grandmother?' – and draw out the story. And what a story emerged! By the time they were off to their next meeting, Marg had a whole new take on Liv, realizing the path she'd walked as a single mom, and the emotionally challenging experience they'd just been through.

As they walked to the administrative offices of the International Community School, Shakti was immediately attracted by a bulletin board with Malala's photo on a poster. She'd just been at the school last weekend speaking on girls' education. "Mom, look, she was here!" Liv and Shakti had followed her story from the gunshot to her head to her recovery in London, all the way to the Nobel Peace Prize. As they glanced over the other myriad posters and notices, they saw more speakers and events that drew them in. As Marg called to them that they'd be late, the mother-daughter duo exchanged a knowing look.

This time it was the head of school herself, Dr. Neseem, who met with them. She didn't like to see too many Americans admitted but being Pakistani, she was intrigued by Shakti's name and claimed this interview for herself. "Good afternoon, I'm so pleased to meet you and that we could accommodate your schedule. I understand you're here for only a short time."

"Yes, we're on our way back from India and only able to stay a few days. The idea of my daughter Shakti coming to London for school in the fall – well, it came up rather suddenly."

"Splendid. And how did you find India? Where were you?" She was curious to see if Shakti would speak up for herself so posed the question directly looking at her. Of course, often the students were shy in interviews, but she was always looking for a special intelligence or connection in the students admitted.

Shakti was not shy. "We were in Mumbai and Lonavala. In Mumbai we met my mother's friend and she showed us her nonprofit office, and it was all about women's issues, so many terrible things going on in India. And it made me want to go back there and work someday to make it better. The way Malala does. She's one of my heroes."

"Oh, you probably saw, she was here last week. Fantastic, really. Amazing. You know she lives here and has started an organization, The Malala Fund. The girls were all so thrilled to meet her. Now they're doing a fundraiser for her."

"I want to give something, Mom," Shakti said, reaching into her purse for the money Nimisha had given her.

Dr. Neseem thought, aha, she'd be a fit. "Well, that can wait. Let's have a look around first. And then I've arranged for you to attend one of the last classes of the day, if that works for you. Usually, that's a good way to give potential students a feel for how we teach here."

Shakti smiled. "What class will it be?"

"It's one on global history. Our view is that far too much history gets presented from the shall-we-say colonial perspective, and one of our many fine professors chooses different countries each year to use as a filter to world history. Students always rave about his classes."

Liv and Marg exchanged a high-eyed look, sharing telepathically the same thought. Marg spoke it, "I wish I could go!"

"I know," Dr. Neseem confessed. "With a staff prerogative, I have sat in at times and always learned something new myself."

As Shakti entered the upstairs classroom, the head of school spoke softly to the professor, who looked at Shakti with interest. As other students filed in, he asked who would sit with their visitor and give her some context for their class today. Being Year 12 students, they were older than Shakti. An Indian girl rose quickly, came towards her smiling, and led her to the back of the room where there were extra chairs.

"She'll be done, Ms. Anderson, in forty-five minutes. Let's return to my office and I'll go over our materials with you." Dr. Neseem made a point of the fee schedule to see if there was any reaction to that. But Liv blithely ignored that part and focused on the International Baccalaureate curriculum. "You're welcome to wait for your daughter outside my office, but there's quite a nice café around the corner and I'd be happy to send Shakti over when class is done."

Marg interjected, "Yes, we know it already."

"Fine. And then please be in touch about your plans. I suspect your daughter would be quite challenged and happy here."

As they walked to the coffee shop, Liv was atwitter. "I loved the vibe, what can I say! It's more like what I would want for myself if I could start over."

"Yes, and I think Shakti made a strong impression - you're raising a champion for women."

Liv's smile came from gratitude. Once seated, it poured out. "I want you to know how very, very much I appreciate what you've done for us, all in less than hours. You've been so welcoming. I'm embarrassed that I've been slightly out of it – the India visit was emotionally charged and wonderful, yet totally exhausting. It's hard for me to stay focused. But I'm getting with the program and you've been lovely. So good to us."

Marg's face sparkled. "Why, thank you Liv for saying that. That is one thing I do love about Americans, you say what's in your heart more often and much better than we Brits. For me, this is fun!" She held back on speaking negatively of her own child Sarah, but really it hadn't been since she was fourteen that she'd been civil to Marg. Every time she returned at university breaks, Marg tried hard to strike the right note. But she felt ignored at best, or the recipient of contempt at worse. Her friends said it would pass. Just give it time. "I'm envious of the relationship you have with Shakti. You seem so close."

"I suppose a one-parent family can do that. If it doesn't tear you apart."

"Well, let me raise my teacup to you Liv. And now tell me more about your own work."

With that, they were off and running, Marg extracting all she wanted to know about Liv's professional background in nonprofits, Liv warming to her even more as she received the gift of being listened to, of being welcomed as someone who was interesting to this extremely capable British woman. When Shakti showed up an hour later, Marg was acknowledging internally that Liv was not just a pretty face, but a woman of substance.

Shakti's energy walking in conveyed how totally enthused she felt about the school. "Mom, I have to go there! It felt so right to me. That girl who helped me, Alison, she gave me her email and said I should write to her."

Liv and Marg exchanged gleaming smiles. "What was the class about, sweetie, I'm curious."

"It was so interesting, all about when India became independent, and separated from Pakistan. The professor was doing several lectures on it because of Malala's visit. It was awful though, extremely bloody. All the Hindu versus Muslim stuff, I don't get it. It made me wonder, Mom, is my father Hindu?"

Liv had no idea. Rama seemed secular. She was trying to recall Nimisha's place and what it showed but came up empty. "I'm not sure, but likely I suppose."

"I'll have to write him and find out." That made Liv wince internally, as she didn't know quite how that would work. "But anyway, just being there, it made me want to become so smart about the world. I would love to go there, Mom."

Liv, acutely aware of the need to set appropriate expectations, put her hand on Shakti's. "Remember what we talked about this morning. We're doing this together. Or have you already changed your mind about that?"

Shakti gave Liv her give-me-a-break look. "Mom, you need to be here, so I can come home every day and tell you all this stuff I'm learning. And to go to events too. We're in this together. But no way do I want to spend three more years at Ballard High School, dealing with the people there. Especially now that Cezar's gone."

Liv briefly explained to Margaret, who then cut to the chase. "Well then. It's decided, no? We must find you a job here, Liv."

Liv and Shakti both had to laugh audibly at the force of Margaret's personality. As though just when they were sinking in the river, a nice big tree limb came along to be their life raft. By the time Shakti had a hot chocolate and biscuit, Liv and she began to fade back into Indian time. Marg suggested yet another nap for them and saw that she would have almost two hours to pull dinner together. *Lovely.* She'd make something simple and spend time gathering her own thoughts about what was beginning to be a most synchronistic meeting with this American mother and daughter.

The chopping of veggies to roast took the most time but then with them and the pork loin in the oven, and couscous a five-minute last thing, she settled in the breakfast nook with her notebook, a running commentary on all the creative thoughts that visited her day. The notebook's pockets served to collect eclectic ideas and articles to form her mental scrapbook. They also housed her own work, a few thoughtful pieces she'd written by hand about what it meant to be fifty-five, for the rose to be losing its bloom, the sense of still having energy and intelligence to bring to some effort, and the unhappiness that Sarah kept her distance. Ruminations on her board work were there too. Clippings of articles or photos that particularly attracted her attention. Tentative blogs on an array of topics – she hadn't settled on a theme or personal way to launch a regular blog.

Most recently she'd been looking at the Sudanese community because of David's presence in their lives. A substantial diaspora existed due to decades of immigrants arriving who were professionals of all kinds but layered also with less educated refugees from rural areas. Marg was becoming more cognizant of the basic tools immigrant women needed, especially literacy. And microfinance helped. But she'd sensed the stirrings of a need for something more, especially as stories from so many communities involved women struggling against male oppression. Even more, each community of immigrants catered to their own people of course. Shouldn't they be crossing cultures now? London life was becoming so fragmented, with too much 'us versus them.'

Shakti and the girls her age were going to be different, better, Marg thought. But what about all these older, already mature women in London? Did life have to end with family for them, in their narrow native ghetto-like communities? Wasn't there a next level of participation they could reach for? Something across ethnic lines? Or were they too stuck? Seeing the diversity in that classroom today, girls from all parts of the world, likely five continents represented, they'd grow up learning how to speak across ethnic boundaries and in some cases to lead more horizontally – social media of course playing a key role. And a common language, the great gift Britain had given to the world. These young women would know so much about crossing cultures, and the issues arising in almost every latitude and longitude of the world. Their skill sets would be much more robust than those of the women whose shoulders they stood upon. Yes, what about the mothers? The older women in London, confining themselves to the communities of birth, while their girls would become global citizens and leave them? Could nothing be done to expand their role?

    She really needed to set the table, tidy a bit, open some wine. She knew her mind would keep working behind the dinner scene. By morning, perhaps sleep time would generate the next big idea.

David was there by seven, satisfied he'd done good work on the brief, but now tired. By contrast, Liv and Shakti coming off their second naps of the day were fully alive and extremely upbeat, full of the day's news to share with him.

    "Darling, did you have time to look at the visa situation for Liv today?" Marg had given that task to Phillip on the way out the door that morning.

    "Oh damn, I forgot. But I can have a look tonight after dinner."

    "No need," David piped in, "I researched it this morning." Everyone was all ears as he explained the need to receive a job offer in England before coming into the country to get a work visa.

    "So, I need to either convince people on the net that I deserve a video interview, or return at some cost to be here to do interviews? And then go home again?"

    "That's right. I'm saying that though without having consulted with our immigration department. But, it's all pretty clear on the government's website."

    Shakti's expression dimmed. "Does that mean we can't do it?"

    Liv was about to put the same question, but before she could alleviate Shakti's concerns, at least for the moment, Marg jumped in using a rather commanding tone. "Now surely, Phillip, people at the firm can make something happen...."

"I promise, I'll look into it tomorrow. Liv, please leave me your cell number in case someone needs to get more information from you."

Liv nodded, wondering if she was about to incur legal fees, but this all seemed cozy and among friends for now.

Marg wanted to blow away the gloom that was rolling in and leaped to the topic of tomorrow's schedule. "David, are you available all day? Right now, I have one more morning appointment for Shakti…" whom Marg saw looking quite deflated across the table, "…if nothing else, so that she can reaffirm the International Community School is the one she wants to attend."

Shakti, acknowledging what she saw in her mother's aspect, concluded, "If it works out, and that's a big if I guess."

"I'd like to check in tomorrow at work, just to know that what I've turned in is satisfactory, and that everything is okay through Liv's departure date. I expect I could meet up with you all at lunch?"

"Perfect. I heard today that Shakti has some spending money. If she agrees, I was thinking I could go on a bit of a shopping spree with her." Marg looked at Liv. "If both of you would indulge me and give me the joy of shopping with and for a most beautiful young woman?"

"I was hoping to have some time alone with David," Liv spoke up. "We've hardly had…"

Marg interjected quickly. "But of course, darling. You and David go have a lovely rest of the day catching up, and Shakti, if she agrees, will come with me to feed my need for a girls' thing. Will you give me that?"

Shakti smiled, knowing full well this was all about alone time for her mother and David. Which she hoped would make it easier for her to come to school here. "It's not like I have a ton to spend, just whatever my grandmother gave me. It's still in rupees."

"Not a problem, love. We'll get that changed and I know just the areas my daughter likes to shop. And some stores that are not that expensive."

By the end of the wine and a scrumptious torte Marg had picked up at the café, David's drowsiness from the the meal compounded with his lack of sleep last night. Shakti was summoned to help clean up. Phillip excused himself to his study upstairs while Liv moved towards the living room. "Finally, we're almost alone. At least for a few minutes."

"And we're clear from lunch on tomorrow. What do you want to see?"

"You. Be together. Catch up. Relax. I've been on this hyper emotional track for over a week now, and I just need to chill. It's not physical tiredness so much. Just all my inner wiring is tangled up with processing the visit to India, and now this whole school thing. And…" her voice lowered, "Margaret."

"Has she been too much for you?"

"All in all, no. She's been a saving grace really, facilitating our visits, shepherding us around. She's making our time here incredibly productive. Except I'm worried already it could lead to a huge disappointment for Shakti."

"I don't think I'm up to figuring it out tonight. But tomorrow, maybe we can come up with ideas for how you get a job here."

She snuggled under his arm that had been draped across the back of the couch. "Just hold me."

As Shakti left the kitchen and saw them quietly cuddled, she motioned back to Marg to be quiet. Moving quietly upstairs. Marg paused before losing sight of them. She experienced a not unfamiliar moment of clarity, which Phillip would usually label with a warning: watch out, Marg's just resolved to make something happen.

Liv's eyes were resting as she began to feel truly present to the moment when she felt his head jerk. He'd nodded off. He rubbed his eyes and focused on her. "Sorry, I only slept three hours last night – I was trying to finish some work."

"Home with you. Tomorrow will be our day."

"And Sunday too."

She kissed him gently at the door. After checking in on Shakti, already asleep, she climbed into bed, exhausted by the intensity of life. Her mind wanted to view each big thing of the last week, acknowledge it, make peace with it, and put it on a shelf. Her last full thought was the need to somehow convey all these things to her family and Elyse. Surely, she was forgetting someone? *Oh, Marco.* He already seemed like a past life.

Saturday, February 20

The third school, the International School of London, a half hour west from Chelsea, was impressive, but turned Shakti off. Too many Arabs and Chinese looking way too rich, and no opportunity to connect with a couple of Indian guys she'd seen from a distance. And no visit to a live classroom given it was the weekend. Debriefing over lunch, Liv was taking note of the marketing approach of each institution. "That head of school at the International Community School yesterday, she really knew how to draw Shakti in with the personal touches, enabling her to clearly visualize being in a classroom there. Very smart."

Shakti texted her new friend from yesterday, Alison, that the school today didn't excite her.

David texted them to begin lunch without him as he finished a last minute redraft of his brief. by 1:30, he'd taken the tube to join them. They were done eating when he arrived to order a panini sandwich.

"Ah, the life of a lawyer," Marg commented, "I know it well."

"Me too," Liv echoed. "A bit anyway, as my best friend's husband is a workaholic anti-discrimination attorney in Seattle. Good thing she has her own career. Their first child arrives in May, and it remains to be seen how each will adjust." That sparked David's interest in getting a more detailed update on Elyse and Cory, and then he brought up one of his last experiences with them in Seattle, their wedding.

"Yes, the wedding from hell." Whoops, Liv realized she wasn't about to explain that remark to any of them right now and quickly steered the topic back to Shakti's money and shopping. "Where will you go to shop?"

"Oh, we'll head over to Soho likely, a lot of trendy shops there, some decently priced – plus there will be sales wherever we do go."

"Well, have at it anytime you want to take off. We'll stay and let David finish his meal. I could use another coffee to get past the need for a nap today. I'm looking forward to walking the streets of London."

"David, make sure you take her tubing too! We're for sure going underground to travel for some of today. It'll be fun for Shakti."

"Let's go then…" Shakti searched for what to call Marg.

"Love, call me Auntie Margy. That way you won't mind me doting on you the rest of the day as I fully plan to do."

Before leaving, Marg bent towards Liv's ear. "And don't worry about tonight, Shakti and I will entertain each other." Liv shifted her face to catch Marg's twinkling eyes. "See you in the morning, Liv." The shoppers waved goodbye, and then Marg returned once more to mention there might be rain tonight, and did they want her brolly?

After lunch coffees and small tarts arrived. Liv's and David's gazes became more linked to each other, each finally able to take in the physical reality of the other: he seeing her fair skinned face perched above a black turtleneck surrounded by a trendy circular scarf in green, orange and black. Her hair was so different now, a curly cap of curls cascading down over her ears in a way that made David want to reach out and finger them. She was freshly surprised by his lips, probably twice the height of hers and even more substantial compared to Marco's thin, more delicate mouth. The eyes that bothered her mother – he always looks sad to me was how she put it. There was perfect proportionality of the broad and high forehead, the wide nose and lips and the strong jaw. She'd always come back to thinking of him as art, the human form as art.

Liv broke the silence. "Amazing, no? We're here. Together. In London of all places."

David reached across the table to take her hand from the base of the cup and hold it. Questions about their future hung in the air between them. But Liv was tired of thinking life through. Being here, with his hand on hers, it was a physical respite. Words, thoughts, conversation – it would all be exhausting. *Let him figure it out.*

David's reluctance to speak came in part from a sense of peaceful attainment. In this moment, he was in the right time and place with the right person. Nothing more was needed. The cockney-accented waitress finally brought the check, wanting to collect her tip before she left, wondering what was being communicated by these quiet customers through a handhold. It seemed profound in some way, like going into church, so she resisted speaking and simply slipped the bill on the table.

Which did rouse David and cause him to pay, signalling to Liv they should return to the street bustle. Exiting, David gained his bearings, looked at Liv, reached out for her hand, and they were off to a tube station. First, he wanted to show her the neighborhoods he was considering living in, so she could see them in the light of day. He'd begun looking at places to rent between Paddington and Brent Park where he felt comfortable – and more importantly, his sister would feel comfortable among a fairly substantial Sudanese population, intermingled with a full collage of Africans and East Asians. Not the best of neighborhoods by the standards of his firm's associates, but David loved it and knew Liv would be her most wide-eyed. And potentially helpful in thinking space issues through with him. Later he'd bring her back to the Thames at night to walk the river a bit, perhaps show her the firm, eat somewhere along the way. Nearby would be the firm's apartment they would have to themselves.

They exited at an underground station near a park where he already imagined his nephews playing basketball in the future. While the day still had a winter chill to it, the sun on a bench invited them to sit. Cuddling up to him, Liv reminded him "I need to hear about your Nairobi trip…the last we emailed you said you went and it was good. Tell me about it."

He wrenched his mind back to his trip last month. What did he really need to say? "I'm ninety-nine percent sure I can make this happen Liv, that Amer and the boys will be here sometime in the summer."

"No kidding?"

"No kidding."

"So Amer is okay with relocating yet again, no resistance there?"

"Reluctance, yes. But Liv…" and now he shifted to really look at her, "…Liv, I feel so much love for them, expecially the boys. It blew me away when I was there. Amer, I care deeply for her as my sister, I'm responsible for her, but she's harder to love in a way. She can be harsh at times. She's not the easiest person to warm up to. But for me, I feel it so strongly, I must raise Dut and Deng. It's my responsibility. And I want to."

"But not in Nariobi? Why are you so clear about that?"

David turned his gaze towards the expanse of green lawn before them. "Because Phillip's been so good to me. Because I like being a London lawyer. Because this city is seducing me." He paused. "Because I too want a world class education for my boys. I want them to know the whole world. This may sound silly, but I can't help thinking of my life in stages, in walks of a thousand miles. I walked a thousand miles to survive. Then it felt like I walked just as far to get to this place, here on this bench in this park with you." His arm draped around the back of the bench squeezed her closer to him. "And now, the next stretch is to give back, first to them, then to my country somehow, sometime in an unknowable future. And it may not be me who does it. Maybe it will be through them."

The simple sound of his strong voice in his well enunciated English brought back a distant conversation. Liv smiled recalling that time at her dinner table. "And you'll be their ancestor, walking invisibly with them, helping them?"

"What?" he looked at her eyes sparkling in the sun. "Oh that. Yes, that walk too."

"It's odd, but one reaction I've had to being at these schools with Shakti, is that now it's all about her." He looked disbelieving. "I know, I know, I'm only thirty-seven, but maybe, maybe the rest for me, is all about launching her to go places I'll never go, to right wrongs I'll never deal with. All those bright, engaged students made me feel old."

He laughed and rocked her a bit in his strong encircling arms. "Oh, we are so old, you and I, and there's nothing left of our lives but our children!"

She pushed him away, grinning widely, and rose to stand in front of him. "Okay, let's walk then. Show me where you're going to house your boys."

As they moved along, David pointed out a few apartment buildings he'd already been in. Plain, older. "The main thing I'm trying to decide on is whether I get a studio for myself now, and then scramble when they arrive to find them something very close. Or just take a two-bedroom flat now so I can already be making it ready for them. And then when they come, I can sleep on a couch or sleeping bag or whatever until I find a studio nearby."

"Are you talking furnished or unfurnished?"

"Well, most are unfurnished although some studios I saw had the basics."

"For me – you know I'm a make-a-nest mom, I'd argue for the two-bedroom and start furnishing it while you wait for the visas to come through. I think it would help them if you could skype – are they set up to do that now?" He nodded. "Good, you could skype and show them, this is your new neighborhood, here's your building, this is your room. And then you'd all be together those first few weeks till you found the right place for yourself as nearby as possible."

"It's quite a bit of rent difference though, I'd feel like maybe I was wasting money."

"But time it. When you know it will be eight weeks or so, get serious about it. Till then, won't Phillip and Margaret let you stay?"

"Yes, I think they would. I get that they like having me in their life now that their own nest feels empty."

"Exactly, and you can't tell me Margaret wouldn't have fun helping you find good but inexpensive furniture for your sister's place. Really, it's funny, but on the one hand, I definitely feel genuinely welcomed and appreciated by her, while on the other, it's like we're projects for her to grab hold of while she figures out what this stage in her life is about."

David stopped walking. "Yes, that's it. You are as astute as ever. That captures what I've been sensing. When I arrived, she went out of her way to investigate everything Sudanese about London. Which honestly is quite a history. People think it's just about immigrants fleeing the war, but no, we have a very large population here and the older ones are often established professionals. I just met another Sudanese lawyer last week, a much older guy. He has kids at Oxford. With the war refugees, there are several community support groups too. And Margaret already has figured out some group that Amer would likely be comfortable meeting."

"You think it's because she's an empty nester?"

"Yes, but not just that. I think what we're experiencing is the way she was bringing up her kids - and why they're not around much. I met the son once, Gerald, and he implied that his sister didn't come home more because she couldn't stand her mother trying to organize her life, solve her problems, and manage her."

"Interesting. She does have a lot of time on her hands."
"You should check out their library. On one of the bookshelves she keeps all her magazine articles. She showed me a couple once, the ones she was most proud of – one was about female genital mutilation. Liv cringed. "I know. It makes me glad I don't come from a people who do that. I'm sure it still goes on in London here in the Muslim communities."

They'd come a way walking, and David paused. "There's another area farther out I want to show you – shall we walk or take a bus?"

"Oh walk, for sure. Walking a great distance with you is quite appealing." She stood on her tiptoes and pecked him on the cheek. As she started to move away, his long arm encircled her tightly and he bent his lips to hers in a long kiss. Just then two women in burkas walked by. Becoming aware of them, Liv gently pushed David away. "Somehow, public displays of affection don't seem right here."

He looked at the back of the dark blue triangles bobbing along the sidewalk. "That doesn't seem quite right to me either."

And so, they walked. And walked. The parade of world differences continued, until Liv realized at one busy intersection that even with her fair skin, holding hands with this African giant, they didn't stand out. They were part of the wallpaper, blending in, no more striking or unusual than anyone else. And the languages she heard in passing! Repeatedly she queried David to identify them. And yet, everywhere she looked there was English. This plethora of differences, superficial or deep, somehow worked. She tried to study each person in his or her particularity, but her visual scanning, moving from individual to individual, was being stretched to the point her introverted wiring began to reach overload.

They checked out an apartment building along the way but found it too challenging to engage in a task involving external conversation with a rental agent that took them from their inner connection. David explained that rents in this area were taking off and he might need to live farther out. They returned to walking, adrift in the world diaspora, until as dusk fell they turned to each other and voiced their overlapping needs, 'I need a snack,' 'I'm hungry again.' The global array of ethnic restaurants surrounding them resulted in David suggesting an African place, with Liv leaning toward Italian comfort food. They compromised on

Indian because Liv was already missing it, and David hadn't had it since Nairobi.

The Indian food and ambiance provided the perfect venue for Liv to respond to David's questions about her trip. The spicy smells evoked meals with Arita, with Rama and Nimisha, and their encounters, yet with many specifics, who said what in what order and in which conversation. already slipping away. Nonetheless, the retelling began to channel her to the critical residue, like pan drippings being scraped into a sauce that was now becoming the story of 'what happened in India.' "Despite my concerns and his own stated apprehensions, in the moment, he was a father meeting his daughter and he loved her." And "The grandmother and I got along quite easily, so well that I must admit to a fresh seed of doubt as to whether she would have rejected me at the time." And "Shakti was so natural with him, chattering away about her life."

This seasoned sauce of concentrated events enabled David to understand at a deeper level how emotionally challenging the encounters had been. "What about you and him, what was that like?" He could ask that now, feeling more confident after so many small, loving gestures from Liv that she still loved him, that Rama or Marco were not holding her heart. David was seeking what he had never grasped for in his life: confirmation that a woman deeply loved him.

She paused eating, her eyes shifting upward and away as she formulated her answer, yet another fresh distillation of what transpired. "It's hard to find the words to talk about it. There were times when I was in a time warp, me meeting him again after all this time, older and gone our separate ways; yet at the very same time, on the other side of a thin veil, we were there in the reality of fifteen years ago, when a young girl was attracted to this guy, and wanted to be with him. As though in a closing and opening of our eyes, we could be in that other time and space again, like in a parallel universe, and our time together was still there." Her eyes turned to David, "Do you understand?"

He nodded. He'd had that feeling here often, being in a swank office or the posh firm apartment. A blink away he was alert in the desert on night watch while Jot and the other young boys tried to sleep.

"It wasn't just me, I mean Rama said he felt he had a double life now. Although what he meant is the secrecy from his family of a thread of his past which just showed up. Which hopefully, the secrecy, won't last. But now Shakti, she's beginning a new life that in a few years will make her upbringing in Seattle, and her family there seem so removed. I guess what I'm trying to say, is that somehow the past is always there in the present moment if you let it be. It's everything you've ever done or decided or been that's brought you to this very moment...." Her eyes locked on to his. "...and then everything to come is anchored in what we choose now."

"What about Marco, Liv? What do you choose now?"

Intuiting his drift, she smiled and began eating again, a bit flirtatiously with a sexy look and smile now and then, postponing the moment of reconnecting with him, simply to enjoy the anticipation of it more before releasing it. It was then that Sara Bareilles' lovesong, *I Choose You,* began to drift into her consciousness. *Later. Not here. Not now.* Instead: "I have to choose between schools in London this fall for Shakti, which scares me - or holding steady in Seattle. I mean it occurred to me, there are expensive private college prep schools there, and we could delay any separation until college."

"What scares you? I don't understand."

"I'm scared that I would come for six months hoping to find a job, having no income, not finding a job, and then having to leave Shakti here and return – to what? I'd be devastated. Plus, my personal finances would be in the tank until I found another job in Seattle. And I don't even know where I'd live."

"You really think you'd spend six months here and come up empty-handed?"

"That, or with a job that didn't pay enough to meet the criterion." David understood that concern: in a conversation this morning, an immigration attorney warned there were rumblings about increasing the salary requirement. "I have no idea what to think, or what's realistic. Do British NGOs or companies hire many Americans? I just don't know."

He didn't know either. "I see the dilemma."

"I'd be risking a lot, and could wind up unsuccessful, separated from my daughter who'd be living a life I want her to have, and that I wish I could have too, but stuck in what now feels like the back waters of Seattle."

"On the other hand, it could work out great. You'd come, say in August, with some basic things, get a job offer within a few months, return to Seattle to pack up, and job offer in hand, return here."

"I know. It seems doable. But then what am I living on all that time? I don't have much left in savings right now. My parents would have to help me pay rent here, put out for flights, all my living expenses. That's not right."

"I bet you could stay for free with Phillip and Margaret. You could be her project." That brought guffaws from both sides of the table. "And I know she has connections in good places."

"I'm not going to ask, David. I think I'd lose her respect if I asked about all that."

"Hmmm. Not as simple as it appeared on the surface."

Liv kept hashing it over, while David's mind wondered if either as his fiancée or spouse, Liv could stay based on his long-term work visa. He'd spent that extra time at the office this morning exploring this option with one of his immigration colleagues. Gleaning his interest in the American woman, Theresa brought it up first, posing the question whether marriage was in the picture. She needed to research it more, but she thought it was a possibility, the main complication being David's own work visa status might impede Liv's ability to take a job. Right now, David didn't want to bring it up as it only created a larger field of uncertainty.

And more deeply, he'd been taken aback by the idea that he might marry, a prospect new to his mind. As he watched Liv's graceful gestures, listened to her melodic voice, and experienced the comfort of a history they already shared together, he began to warm to the possibility, seeing it come into focus with images of them all together. *One big family.* It made him smile across the table at a glum looking companion. "Let's walk off this meal along the Thames and see the lights on the river."

Liv brightened. Her sensory overloaded head hurt from clashing into all these considerations about next steps. Once they arrived at the Embankment station via a longish underground ride, the cool night air and sparkling river lights lifted her spirits. Liv noticed how talk of the future eclipsed the joy of the moment in being with David. Breathing deeply, she closed her eyes, then opened them to the river's movement, and brought herself fully into the place and time. She kept looking up to find a good angle to see Big Ben itself, while feeling the pull to cross the river and ride the London Eye ferris wheel. "Can we do that?" David checked his watch, thought it too late, and suggested they save it for when Shakti was with them.

They arrived near Westminster Palace and the base of the iconic clock just in time to hear it chime the quarter hour. Nine fifteen. One point of time. She withdrew her arm from David's and shifted to face him. "There's only now, David. That's all that's real. That one moment the clock is ticking away going from nine fifteen to nine sixteen." She moved closer and slid her arms around his torso padded as hers was by a parka. His eyes held steady with hers. "You asked me before what I choose. I wish I could sing my favorite song to you, but I'll simply say it instead." Her voice, soft in a higher range, choking midway as her eyes moistened, and ending in a broad smile, pulled the words from a heart that had lain nights alone listening to the song and wanting it to be true for her. Just once, and only once forever after.

> *"My whole heart*
> *Will be yours forever*
> *This is a beautiful start*
> *To a lifelong love letter*
>
> *Tell the world that we finally got it all right*
> *I choose you*
>
> *I choose you."*

Their kiss lasted much more than a moment and fresh hunger arose. "The firm's apartment isn't far from here. Let's go."

They hadn't gone far when the rain began, gently at first, insubstantial enough to make them forego the tube, but then with blocks left to go, a heavy downpour began. They reached the shelter of the condo building out of breath, their hoods soaked along with their pant bottoms and shoes. The building befitted the historical neighborhoods surrounding the courts but was renovated. The firm owned a fully furnished studio unit on the tenth floor, pleasantly comfortable but not overdone. They quickly peeled off their wet pants and socks, David hanging them in the bathroom, leaving them both top-heavy with clothing, Liv with her big scarf and turtleneck and bikini underwear and David with his work shirt and cardigan atop some boxer shorts. Laughing, Liv prompted him, "Can you get me a long shirt or something else to put on? She felt un-composed and wanted to use one of those fluffy towels in the bathroom to take the chill off. "And dry socks. And maybe put the tea kettle on?"

"Do you remember this?" David was handing her a flannel shirt, red and green and white plaid that he'd worn to death in Seattle.

She took it and eyed its faded colors. "I sure do. You used to live in this shirt those first winters in Seattle. I'm surprised you still have it."

While she patted her legs and feet dry in the bathroom, pressing the towel into her wet hair, and slipping her long, narrow feet into his even longer gym socks, David put on his basketball shorts and an old Mt Rainier t-shirt. He crossed the room to the kitchenette to fill the kettle. When she joined him at the stove holding her hands over the heat, she noticed the shirt. "Is that from that trip we all took once? There were like seven or eight of us in two cars? We took you guys up to see the snow since Seattle didn't have any that first winter."

"Right, that trip. It was so amazing seeing snow. Even this winter, people complain when it comes. But it's beautiful. Peaceful. Comforting, like I'm being tucked into bed under a fluffy quilt."

Liv shifted her gaze to the alcove of the studio where the bed nestled into a corner with pillows galore and a fluffy white comforter. "That's what I want, that comforter." She scurried across the room, lifted it and sat herself propped against the pillows and headboard. The view from the bed out the window was of endless dots of lights out to the horizon shimmering in the rain. "So, this is how a lost boy lives today."

David brought the mugs of tea and Liv eagerly sipped hers to warm herself inside out. He crawled in under the comforter next to her. "I know. The time warp thing."

She reached over his body to set her mug down and snuggled now, pulling the socks off to let her feet feel his legs. He dimmed the light next to the bed. "Remember that first morning you made love to me? That quick in and out? How funny it all became with our tent love in the wild?"

David rejoined in a falsely sober tone, "Yes, the infamous morning attack of the panther on the gazelle. I recall it well. I was desperate to have you, but so unsure of myself."

"But then remember the next night, how wild we were like animals. And that guy, how he teased us later, talking about animal sex in the Serengeti?"

David needed no reminding; the memories were strong. "That was the craziest time, to be so unsure and then so liberated from all thoughts and conventions."

"In a way, it's the peak moment of love, isn't it? To go from the uncertainty, the mystery of not knowing – does he want me? – to affirmation that this person really desires you."

He moved to twist and look at her. "But does that mean our peak moment is past? It's all downhill now?"

Her face lost its distant look of reverie and became sober. "No, because so much is still unsettled."

"You said under Big Ben that you choose me. Is that not settled?"

With her most wickedly amused eyes, she whispered, "I need to hear the response." As he tightened his embrace, she said, "In words."

Pulling back, he kept his hands on her shoulders while closing his eyes. *Do I really need to think about this? Isn't she my family already? We are so close to making this work. This is right.* These spontaneous affirmations neither surprised him nor raised doubts; they had history. Wasn't this union, first clear as they sat in the evening chill one night in Seattle, holding hands and cosmically communing, wasn't this a moment suspended in time for all too long? Opening his eyes to a face tinged with trepidation and using a voice appropriately strong and deep for a ceremony, he vowed, "In this moment, and for all time into our ancestor life, I choose you."

Her smiles and tears arrived together as she pulled him into full body contact. He pushed their torsos down the bed together. He wiped her tears with a deep laugh. "Don't cry. It will be fun I think. No?"

"Yes, yes, yes. Somehow, we'll do this, and it will be very fun." Which was a remarkable affirmation from Liv who had always said she didn't do fun. She pulled the comforter up quite high now over their heads, and whispered, "Let's do the tent thing again."

"Ah yes, me lion and you lioness." She made a soft feline roar, pretending to hold him at bay, only inciting him to prevail.

Thus it was, fifteen years after they met, half of that being friends, two years of being long distance lovers, five years of emails and skyping, and less than twenty-four hours together in London, under a makeshift tent, their destinies finally fused.

Sunday, February 21

As the sunlight brightened their bed the next morning, Liv was immediately concerned that she hadn't texted Shakti the night before. When she went to her phone, it was almost dead. But there was a text that reassured her, coming from Shakti at ten pm. "I hope this means you and David are having a great time. I have! I've brought Auntie Marg up to speed on all she's been missing."

It took time to pull themselves together to leave, as they kissed and fondled and poked and tickled each other into their clothes. In the lobby as they headed towards the glass doors, David stopped. "I forgot. I reserved a rental car for us today, so we could get out of London and see some English countryside."

"You drive?"

"I learned in Brussels. Although this other side of the road thing requires attention."

They found a chain café on the way and stopped for coffee and sweet rolls. Leaning close across a small table, Liv almost whispered, "David, does what you said last night still hold? I can't be telling Shakti we're coming for sure if you have any second thoughts. I'm willing to take risks to be with you, but I don't want to jerk her around."

"My dearest, darling, sweetest Liv, we will find a way for you to stay. And no matter what, I will do whatever it takes to keep us together. Accept it."

"And Shakti and your sister and nephews?"

"Yes," he grinned, "...instant family for both of us."

They arrived to pick up Shakti after texting Margaret not to fuss about them. "Right then, I'll feed Shakti. But you must all come for dinner."

"If we must, we must!" said Liv as David drove. "We have our orders."

Shakti greeted them with enthusiastic hugs searching their eyes for signals. She and Marg had chatted the night before that love was in the air.

"What? Why are you looking at me like that, sweetie?"

"Oh. Nothing." Then biting her lip, "You know."

Liv blushed, knowing full well that Shakti could always tell when Marco and her mother made love. Cezar and she used to giggle and make jokes about it. She looked toward David. "Say something."

David could only back up in a laugh himself. "Your mother and I had a most splendid time walking the streets of London all night long."

"Right. In the pouring rain."

Marg came to greet them, also fluttering at their arrival, eyeing each closely as though they were newlyweds returning home from a honeymoon. "Thank you ever so much for letting me have your daughter for a day. I haven't had so much fun in many a year, not since my Sarah was a teen."

"What did you all do?"

"What didn't we do! Shakti, why don't you show your mother the clothes you bought." While she ran to her room, and the others settled into the living room, Marg chuckled her way through an account of their time. "My lord, I had no idea you Americans were into such kick-ass heroines! Over dinner - we ate out at this funky spot Shakti chose - we got into talking about them. I was feeling ignorant, what with Sarah and I not being so chummy these last years. I'd lost touch. Shakti was convinced I needed to get with it, and we wound up streaming *The Hunger Games,* so I could see her idol Katniss – which by the way, I thought the premise was shocking and certainly a piercing critique of our times."

"And I made her promise to see the new *Star Wars* and check out Rey." Shakti said, as she brought three plastic bags of clothes down the stairs. "Mom, this stuff was on sale and I was able to get so much with Grandma's money." Shakti held up a pair of leggings, brown cords and black leather pants - "Fake, Mom!"- and then showcased two whore-like tops to go with them. From the last plastic bag, Shakti pulled a smashing black purse, real leather, but with lots of buckles and paraphernalia. "This is just like the one Alison had."

"That's an amazing amount to have purchased with what Nimisha gave you," Liv said looking to Margaret.

She gave an acknowledging glance that disclosed her complicity in adding to it. "We did have fun, didn't we?"

"Oh yes, auntie!"

"Oh, and I have to finish. After dinner, after we watched the movie and I was expressing my surprise at how strong, and well, storm-trooper-like, girl role models are these days, Shakti used her phone to show me this Taylor Swift young woman doing, what was it? Yes, her *Bad Blood* video. Have you seen that?"

"God, yes!" Liv looked at David who was clueless. Time to move on was in his eyes. "Well, our news is that David has a car for the day and we're going for a trip. What do you suggest?"

Marg considered. "You could do Oxford or Cambridge and surrounding areas. Each is only an hour away. That would definitely provide a long-term vision of where Shakti may be headed."

"Are they nice towns for tourists?"

"Oh yes, fun to poke around, especially Oxford. And now that I know Shakti better, my guess is she'd prefer Oxford, more going on there. And in that direction, you could see Stratford-on-Avon if you have time and Mr. Shakespeare interests you." Marg took in Liv and David suddenly thinking what a fine Othello and Desdemona they would make.

"Does that sound good, Shakti?"

"Sure."

Once headed out of London, GPS guiding their way, Shakti leaned forward. "So, anything you guys want to tell me?" David and Liv exchanged glances, but neither spoke. "It's our last day of this trip Mom, and I'm sad, like all the excitement is over, and we have to go back to boring old Seattle? And I don't even know if I get to come back here in the fall?"

Liv felt it too. How could so few days turn her life inside out and upside down? She exchanged another sober look with David. *I'm afraid to promise.*

He saw her hesitancy. "Shakti, how would you like it if we all lived together here in London, you, your mom, and me?"

"That's easy, I'd love it!" My dad would be in India and you'd be my other dad too, just like Uncle Ryan, right Mom?"

"That's right, sweetie."

Shakti sat back looking down at her lap and touching her new leather bag. Then she lifted her head smiling and speaking with her first try at an English accent. "I think it would be splendid. Marvelous really."

Oxford proved to be the fun outing Marg claimed. Shakti was in awe of the place, staring at every edifice, loving the dining hall made famous in Harry Potter. They took a guided tour, punctuated by David's projections of his nephews being there, and Liv marveling at the architecture, and its history and notable graduates. Over stout beer in a pub, Shakti googled to learn more. "Mom, we would save a lot, really a lot of tuition, if I graduate from prep school someplace in the UK."

"Good, yet one more reason to risk it."

"Risk what, Mom?"

"Don't doubt it, we are coming. This summer sometime. But we don't have it figured out yet how I get to stay beyond six months."

"You need to get a job, right?"

"Yes, if I'm lucky and then I'll have to leave for a while to get our stuff back home and then return, job offer in hand."

"Don't worry about it." Liv was taken aback by Shakti's confidence. "Aunt Margie's working on it. She'll figure it out." Liv's wide eyes grew tall as she stared at her daughter, then David.

He shrugged. "I told you so. You're a project."

Marg was busy all day, not with the dinner which she ordered in from her favorite caterer, but in jumping into the 'to do' list of her new venture. Bursting with energy to get started, she was delighted to feel at her age that she too might be a kick-ass heroine. She'd been scribbling ideas on scraps of paper the last two days and now she sat in the breakfast nook with her scrapbook journal, her latest jottings, and a large sheet of drawing paper to do her mind map. She needed to determine what was at the center of her thoughts. She knew one vein feeding into the heart of it - organizations like the Sudanese ones she'd learned about that helped migrants and newcomers to acclimate by getting connected to those in their ethnic community. She'd googled a bit and saw that there were nonprofits focused generically on integrating refugees and migrants and these were ethnically based organizations. She labeled this vein the 'integration of new comers.'

Another vein was what she was calling 'second tier connections/bridging community differences.' Bridging from just your own community of difference into being more integrally connected to London, to its issues, its development in the face of all these migrant challenges. She believed it would take strong leadership from within communities to really build those connections, not a colonial mindset emanating from white

Londoners organizing them. Which of course pointed to a problem that would need addressing in that she was a white Londoner trying to figure this out. And then there was the 'Liv' vein, her experience in fundraising, communications and marketing, along with refugees and women, and how that would play into this. Marg put herself on the map too as a 'chief storyteller,' recognizing her own journalistic talents. Of course, there was a 'women' vein. Marg firmly believed based on the history of the war in Northern Ireland and its resolution, that it would take peacemaking skills in women, the biochemical relational makeup of women, to bridge community differences. A mother suffering from a son's death in a gang war understood the pain of a mother on the other side. 'Skills' was a last vein, what were the skills women needed to take a greater leadership role?

She began surfing the web next, finding British community leadership programs like 'Step Up' in Manchester. But that had been a one-time shot it appeared. She'd really need to go interview those people. 'Engage! London' too, while focused on professionals, had an interesting model with projects that intrigued her. She got into the American community leadership models and had a field day tracking through those sites. She added a vein of 'knowledge of community issues' and the need for speakers to come in.

Phillip came in for lunch and looked over her shoulder. "What the devil are you up to woman?"

Marg accepted his comment as a clear invitation to launch, to begin to speak it out loud, to explain the work she was gravitating towards. She became increasingly animated, in a way he hadn't seen since her writing days, standing as she heated some soup for them, gesturing to the lines on the mind map coming to a center place as she toasted bagels, and finally sitting down to land it. "I want to start a women's community leadership program." Quickly she grabbed her pen and wrote that at the center of the veins.

"Does this have anything to do with our American visitors?"

"Of course, Phillip, don't be coy. They've spurred my thinking along, the schools we visited where the young will get all this," she swung her arm dramatically across her map, "...all the knowledge and skills they need. But what about women who are older, living the realities of family and cultural changes, trying to make peaceful communities where their kids can grow up without assaulting each other, where they can get more involved in local politics, keep learning, not just become some old ladies letting a world they neither understand nor appreciate pass them by? What about them?"

"As you are feeling, perhaps? Are you sure this isn't a wealthy white woman's perspective?"

She loved that about Phillip, he didn't indulge stupidity. "I know what you're saying, dearest. But I'm sure I'm on to something. Our city has taken in so many from so many places, we're at risk of multicultural suicide. Obviously, we would need focus groups. We'd need the potential community leaders telling us what would work for them. For example, I'm saying, 'women's leadership,' and maybe they'd want men involved. Although it's hard to imagine some of the most traditional Muslim women dealing with that. This is going to require a lot of interviewing, learning the specific issues that cross community and neighborhood lines. And then testing program designs. There's a tremendous amount of this that's gone on in the States, really a lot to draw from." She paused. "Which leads me back to Liv."

"I sensed that was coming."

"I'd need a colleague, Phillip. Why not? She has great relevant experience. There's at least six to nine months of program design work. Then promotion and enrollment with a lot of logistical stuff which is not my cup of tea. For me, it would be creating the board to run it – imagine what an amazing multi-ethnic board I'd need to build." Her gaze traveled in space to a future world.

Phillip coughed. "And then they would need to get along. That would be real work with all those large feminine egos – I know some of them from my work."

"Yes, I suppose it would." Marg was still. "The people I'd want on the board are already leaders but would probably need some skill training themselves to learn how to lead together with other strong players, to develop a collective leadership. It's complicated, I recognize that, getting powerful women to agree."

"Yes. Something to think about. You could be creating a big headache. And after a while, they might very well not want an American directing or managing the actual program."

"Phillip," Marg pulled her eyes from her vision to really focus on him, "...she just needs the offer. I could form the nonprofit, you know a community interest group, and make the offer. And the board would just have to live with it for a while, enough time for Liv to get grounded here."

"And the funds?"

"Initially, some of what mother left me. It's just sitting there, barely earning interest. It could be an investment in my last career. And Liv would be calling on corporations to get funding. And I'd go after individual donors."

"I can see your mind has been extraordinarily active, no wonder you've been up early and to bed late these days."

She cleared away their lunch plates and bowls. "So, what do you think?"

"Does it matter?"

"Yes, you'll have to live with my new career."

Phillip stood and came to her, loosely placing his hands on her waist. "To pull it all off well, it will take a person of indefatigable organizing energy, passion, and an underlying kindness and compassion." His smiling eyes held hers. "Who else but you?"

A wave of euphoria swept over Marg that settled into focused energy later that day, spilling out a new list of to do's, people to contact, and even a draft job offer.

When the three travelers returned, it was Shakti who bounded out to the kitchen to give Marg the thumbs up sign, move into video dance moves, and conclude with a 'we're coming!' As Marg raced out to greet Liv and David, Shakti leapt ahead, "I told her!"

"Marvelous, congratulations you two!"

They were all smiles. "Yes, you're going to be seeing more of us. I've decided to take the risk of getting Shakti enrolled here and coming, believing I'll find a job."

Marg came closer, arms open. "May I?" Liv moved into what felt like a motherly embrace. As Marg pulled back, she beamed at them, "Anyone hungry?"

"Starving," came Shakti's immediate response. "We walked everywhere in Oxford, it was awesome."

"Do tell me more as we get dinner on the table." Phillip joined them, and sensing celebration in the air as a Prosecco cork popped, learned the news. As the stories of the day trip spilled out around the dining room table, Marg waited for the right moment. "I've had quite the day myself working on my...dear, what shall I call it?"

Phillip had cautioned her to underpromise and overdeliver and was pleased to have some say in how this came out. Looking back at Marg with their shared secret in his eyes, he made the lift off. "Let's call it Marg's next career." Turning to the others, he amplified, "Margie's been in a bit of a transition you know with the children away at university. And"...he looked directly at Shakti, "...your visit has inspired her to think more creatively about what she cares about and what she'd like to do."

"Yes, so I'm going to be looking at the possibility..." Phillip nodded at her choice of words, "...the possibility of forming a community leadership program, aimed perhaps at immigrants, women in particular."

"I'm so happy to know our visit stimulated your thinking Margaret, you've been so generous and kind to us. Say more," prompted Liv.

"Well, it's all tumbling about in my head right now. It will require more research, talking to people..." she nodded to Phillip, "...but honestly I think I'm on to something, about getting, for example, Sudanese women leaders in the same space with say Romanians, and Poles, and Syrians."

At this David was shaking his head and interjected somberly, "Good luck!"

"Yes, darling, I know it's a challenge, the traditional English ways are getting thrown out all over the country by Poles pissing in our squares, while those wealthy Russians and Chinese make housing unaffordable. But perhaps we could figure out how to tackle some community issues together? They tried something like it up in Manchester and I'll be investigating that. And there's an interesting program here called 'Engage! London'..."

"It's interesting you mention that, darling. Our firm's administrator was in that program one year. He quite enjoyed meeting and getting connected to other professionals."

Liv was listening intently, knowing this was what Shakti referred to before. But she wasn't hearing how she might connect to it. The talk however reminded her that Cynthia was in Seattle's Leadership Tomorrow program this year. "My boss is in that kind of program this year. I've seen the materials for it and of course, she comes back and tells us about it in staff meetings. She's quite enthused about being with this group of mid-level community leaders from business, government and nonprofits."

Marg was ready to pop her own cork. "Do say more Liv, this is so interesting for me!"

Liv didn't know a whole lot more but recalled that the Mayor had spoken to the group and her boss had met him. She didn't recall if there was a project involved. "I do recall Cynthia saying that this was just one of hundreds across the country."

Marg was having a hard time containing her enthusiasm. "This is so exciting! Liv darling, could you do me a huge favor and do a little research on these programs, send me everything you can about this?"

"Sure, I'd love to. It's the least I can do to thank you for all your kindnesses."

"Oh, fiddlesticks to that, I've loved every minute. But I would love to have..." she felt Phillip's eyes upon her, "...I want very much to keep up with you about this."

"Definitely, me too."

Later as Liv brought their plates back to the kitchen, Marg looked to make sure Phillip had gone to the living room with David. "Liv, Phillip doesn't want me committing to this yet, but here's what I'm hoping." Liv brought her full attention to Marg's face. "It's that we'll both do some investigation on my idea, and I'll go ahead and form a nonprofit and start getting this going. And..." Marg stared into Liv's eyes steadily now, "...I want you to set up the program side of it. I'd run the board, but at least for a while, you'd help me make this happen." Marg watched for Liv's reaction and was pleased to see her muoth drop and her eyes grow grow tall with interest.

"Margaret, oh my god, I'd love to do that. But I have to get a real job to stay here past six months."

"That's what I'm trying to get to, dear. I need to convince Phillip – who's about 75% on board right now – that we can make this happen together and that the organization I create can make you the offer you need."

Liv's immediate reactions combined her eagerness to find a job solution with her characteristic reluctance to lead, as though no sooner did her spirit rise and affirm this opportunity than some constricting tentacles encircled it. Her introversion. *If only I were Elyse! How can I take on something this daunting when*

I don't even know this place and its people? Liv shifted and moved slightly away.

    Marg could see that an internal demon had gotten hold of Liv's thoughts. Experiencing her own moment of panic, Marg spoke with a soft yet commanding edge, "Liv, we can do this!"

    What am I going home to? She immediately saw the evil Amazonian's face, the techie who was undermining her focus groups, taking charge of her prerogatives to lead the training facility campaign. *Damn. This is my opportunity to help create something of my own. In London of all places. Working across cultural boundaries.* Suddenly, it was as though Elyse came out of the shadows and stared at Liv with a 'come to your senses' intensity, then slapped her face to knock out the demons. "Girlfriend, just do it!" came Elyse's voice as though she stood there. *If Shakti can stretch, then so can I.* Lifting her shoulders, and turning to face Marg, Liv heard herself say to her own amazement. "Of course, we can do this. I can help you research and design a prototype. I can run your focus groups. I know how to be with immigrants. I know what helps women and their families. I can tell the story to donors of what we're doing and raise the money." Her distinctive smile shone and soothed Marg's worry. "Of course, I'd loved to work with you!"

    Reassured, Marg moved closer. "That sounded triumphant!"

    Elyse's voice came again: claim it, make it yours. Liv took Marg's hands in hers. "As life would have it, I'm actually the perfect person to help you make your idea happen. I've been in training for this in so many ways. I'm the perfect nonprofit woman to make it happen."

Monday, February 22

The farewells the next afternoon were filled with hopes and dreams that would have been inconceivable two weeks ago. The night before, which David happily spent with her at Phillip and Marg's, Liv sneaked in a few emails, letting her mom and Mimi know that the trip had been 'beyond belief' and that there was too much news to share in an email. She let Cynthia know she wouldn't be in Tuesday due to 'unavoidable' delays.' Shakti meanwhile had lost no time letting Cezar know she was going to be living in Europe too, which brought a prompt inquiry from Marco, his first in weeks. Liv replied that it was incredibly true but too involved to share details yet. Someday she'd share the news of David with him, but she wanted to think that through carefully, in terms of the tone she struck.

Again, as during their prior flights, they each entered their own encapsulated world of thoughts. Shakti captured it best when she said, "It's like our down time these weeks is when we've been up in the air flying."

It was true, with both holding, processing, and filtering memories to share upon their return from the future to the past. At first, not that they would have admitted it, the regret in having to leave overshadowed enthusiasm to see the people they loved. That only lasted till New York where the transition into the U.S., the sense of being two little pixels in a huge world, awakened in both an eagerness for seeing those who would be greeting them. "I'm excited now to see everyone again, Mom. I feel completely changed, so different than when I left." She was wearing her faux leather pants and her fingers at times massaged the buckles, zippers, and baubles on her new purse.

Liv was transformed also. *I have a future I didn't have when I left. I have one foot in it already, one leg slipping under the time warp veil.* Emotional good-byes lay ahead. It would be hard on her mom and Mimi and Elyse, especially with the baby coming. That thought tamped down Liv's enthusiasm for her new life, and opened space to grieve, yes, grieve, for the ending of what had been. Of course, they'd plan visits: mom and dad could definitely do Europe once a year. She and Shakti would return once a year. Perhaps Elyse and the baby could come? Mimi would need a break from caring for her father-in-law. Somehow, they'd keep themselves connected. Thank god for technology! BUT, it will never be the same again. The loving support they'd given each other all these years, the family rituals, the continuous weekly interactions. Liv pulled out a tissue from her bag.

Shakti noticed. "Mom, are you crying?"

"A little."

"Why? Are you missing David already?"

"No. I'm just beginning to say good bye to life as we've known it in Seattle."

"I get that."

"It really was a pretty good life, wasn't it?"

"Oh MOM! Of course, it was good. We always had each other." She smiled in that way that looked just like Liv. "And it's going to get even better."

Liv would have eased out the telling of their adventures, retelling each step chronologically. That was her intention, as they sat gathered at Mimi and Ryan's, her dad having picked them up at the airport around dinner time. Again, their biological clocks were going to need serious re-setting as they lived their second thirty plus hour day over a period of four days. At first, the deluge of observations came, how happy everyone was to have them back, dying to hear everything, Liv deflecting and asking what had happened while they were away, appetizers being served in the living room, presents from India being given, Katherine and Mimi a bit shy about asking probing questions yet eager to hear about new and old connections and the feelings that accompanied them.

Liv had secured Shakti's cooperation in talking about India first. Camera photos from Nimisha's triggered outbursts and repeated sharing, blowing up of photos, and commentary on shared looks. The questions flew to Shakti about how she felt about meeting her father and other grandmother. Liv was happy for her to chatter away about it all, how easy it had been to be with Rama, how much she loved India, its people, sights, colors and smells. When they asked about Nimisha, Liv said more, providing family history behind Shakti's eyes, and sharing the visit to Lonavala. Everyone wondered about Liv's reaction to seeing Rama, but no one dared to ask that question in the big group.

A pause came after about an hour, which Shakti decided to fill. "Are you going to tell them, Mom?"

As eyes focused on Liv, her mother spoke her fear. "Don't tell me, you're moving to India?"

I might as well get to it. "Actually, Mom, not that far. Only to London."

That news exploded the conversation and brought a volley of questions. Shakti finally stood up to take charge. "Here's the deal. My new grandmother is setting up a trust fund for me to get a world-class education and she'd like it to be in London, so she could visit me there – and my father would come sometimes too – and so we looked at schools with this nice lady, Auntie Margie, and we found one I want to go to if they'll let me in. I'll go in the fall and Mom of course will come with…" she took another deep breath, "…and in order to stay she needs a job which Margaret is going to give her, and we're going to live there…with David and his family." Turning to Liv, "did I get it all in?"

Liv wasn't sure whom to look at as she viewed the group's almost orchestrated mournful reaction. Her parents' mouths were open and dropped. Mimi's face was screwed up in a large question mark. Ryan and the kids just looked stunned. "Yes."

Gary placed his hand on Katherine's shoulder, softly saying, "What a blow." Mimi and Ryan turned to each other, and he put his arm around her.

Shakti was not about to let the moment last long. "Aren't you excited for us?"

Katherine took a deep audible breath, already seeing the future her darlings would have, knowing how absolutely right this was. She rose and embraced Liv, then looked in her eyes. "Finally, my Liv. Finally. Everything you've wanted and deserved." Tears began to flow indiscriminately. "I couldn't be happier for you and Shakti."

Mimi approached. "Say it again, when will all this happen?"

"Probably late summer. I have a lot to do to help Margaret get a nonprofit going so I can help run it. And David has to get his sister and her boys settled first if possible. They're coming from Kenya."

That sent Mimi's and Katherine's hands to their mouths. The men were silent. Jeff and Margot swiveled and went pouting toward their rooms, with Shakti trailing.

Gary rallied then and came to Katherine's side. "Well, we're all going to be seeing a lot of Europe I guess!"

Mimi looked at Ryan, who cracked a weak smile. "You've been wanting to see Viking land."

More questions percolated: who was this Margaret? Were Liv and David getting married then? Was this nonprofit idea on solid footing? Slowly, people peeled off – Ryan to comfort Jeff and Margot, sad already about their diminished grandfather living with them instead of Liv and Shakti, and and now lamenting about their cousin's departure and how nothing good ever happened to them. Mimi moved robotically to finish getting dinner on the table. Katherine continued probing Liv about both Rama and David.

Shortly after dinner, Liv pleaded the case of their very long day and the need to rest. When she gratefully slipped into her own bed, her last thought was having to go through this again with Elyse.

Tuesday, February 23

Liv was glad she'd allowed this day for them to deal with jet lag and to take a mid-day nap. She called Elyse at work just to let her know they were back and to set a time to meet. Elyse was enthused to hear all the good news that Liv kept alluding to. Even with her current nine pm bedtime, Elyse suggested dinner out the next evening, always happy to not cook on a weekday night. But Liv didn't think sharing all this in a restaurant setting was a good idea. Plus, she needed a few days herself to settle in. To Elyse's dismay, they wouldn't have their visit until a Saturday lunch at Liv's. In the meantime, Liv was to call Elyse at home with 'appetizer' news. Which worked for Liv who knew that all the events of India would be both juicy and palatable to her.

When Mimi returned from teaching school, she invited Liv up for some tea. "That was like a bomb dropping yesterday."

"I know..."

"We get it, honestly we do. But it's a shock to my system how this trip to India has just blown everything out of the water. I feel like I need a life raft."

Liv sat quietly, unsure what to say. "What's the latest on Ryan's dad?"

"It's still looking like something needs to change early summer – but don't think you don't have a place here till you go to London. I'm sure we can double up to make room for him."

"Thanks. That helps. Are you really ready to take this on? Staying home with him?"

"I've committed to it to Ryan, that I'll make a good faith effort to make this work. And Ryan has given Jeff and Margot their marching orders about helping when they get home from school if I need them to do more. That's why they were so upset yesterday. Let's face it, we'll all be going from having people we love living with in the house to caring for someone with dementia. I keep telling myself it will be a growth curve for me. By summer, I'll have a course to go to at least once a week, something to look forward to. I'll have more time with Margot while she's still at this lovable age." Liv was feeling Mimi's challenge – and pain. "I guess even knowing you wouldn't be in the house anymore, I imagined you living close and our still being together. And that I could always pick up the phone and tell you that he was making me crazy." A small laugh escaped her, and her theatrical background made her lighten the moment as she pretended to pick up a cell: "Liv, I just had to chase him down the street as he wandered off! He's making me crazy too!"

"I'm sorry."

"Sorry? Why should you be sorry? You've been a single mom all these years, doing your level best to raise Shakti, and support your family." She came close and put her hands on Liv's arms, "I don't want you to be sorry, I want you to be happy. Really happy! But I'm going to miss you terribly."

That evening as Liv completed unpacking, she saw Nimisha's letter again. *My God! I need to write her back about everything! And fill Arita in too.* She began with her, writing a long email about Nimisha's offer and what transpired in London. She shared Shakti's visits to the schools and emphasized her wanting to follow in Arita's footsteps. For now, she limited her comments about David and the potential job, as she felt the pressing need to establish a communication link with Nimisha directly. Liv begged Arita's help this one last time in contacting Rama and making this connection.

By the morning, Arita had already responded: Rama had contacted her first to provide Nimisha's new email address. Liv worked the rest of the week composing the most appreciative letter she could to Nimisha, including a contribution from Shakti to it. She went into some detail on their investigation of schools and sought to reconfirm that this fall would not be too soon for a tuition payment.

At work, Liv guarded her conversations, revealing much less about her trip than was concealed, and calculated to give no indication a move was in the works. Finally, she composed a longish email to Marco focused on Shakti and staying in touch with Cezar given their likely move. She left it to Marco to inquire about David if he cared to. Perversely, she didn't mind if at some point in future communications she was able to drop her coupling with David as lightly and with as little preparation as Marco had let her know about the move to Madrid. She was not above tit for tat.

Saturday, February 27

When Liv opened the door, her eyes traveled immediately to Elyse's baby bulge that had popped out considerably. Elyse followed her gaze. "It's the fat clothes I've begun wearing, it makes it look bigger."

As they hugged, Liv felt the baby pressed into her body. "Only three more months! How's it been going?"

"I think something about the size has gotten Cory's attention finally. He's more solicitous. And he's committed to taking the first two weeks off, even moving some things off his calendar. I'm encouraged. And don't you think about being out of town in early May. You're my backup."

Just as Elyse had been there with Liv at Shakti's birth, Liv had already promised to be as supportive as possible. "You know I'll be there a hundred percent for you."

Elyse situated herself at the set table. "Alright, hand over your phone so I can see pictures."

For all her forethought on how to best inform Elyse of the move – perhaps a launch as Shakti had done with the family? Or was it best to dribble it out? – Liv knew Elyse favored directness. Already Liv was on the defensive due to intentionally withholding news of the move in their phone conversations this week. Liv handed over her cell, and while she ladeled soup into bowls, Elyse enthusiastically commented on each photo as her thumb flicked from one to another. "This is your friend Arita? Wow, India does look interesting. Oh my, so this is the grandmother! I do see the resemblance. My god, Rama is a handsome dude! I know you already said there was nothing there for you, but he is handsome. Jesus, look at David! You should have a pin-up gallery! I can't wait to hear how he is. Who are these older people at this dining room table?"

"Oh, that's Margaret and Phillip, the place where we stayed. The lawyer who helped arrange David's job offer and is a mentor to him."

"Got it. Oh, look how sweet you and David and Shakti look in this one – where's that?"

Liv peered over her shoulder. "That's a place in Oxford, the day we got out of London."

Elyse kept staring at that photo and then put the phone down. "You look like a family in that last shot. How did it go with David?"

"Really well. What you just said, about us looking like a family..." here Liv reached across to touch Elyse's arm, and in a low, slow steady voice said, "...we're going to do it, it's finally going to work, we're going to be together."

Incomprehension, then fear registered on Elyse's face as her arm instinctively moved to protect the baby. She was speechless as her mind stopped working. Then Liv watched Elyse's eyes begin to demonstrate that mental calculations were resuming. *He just took a job and is not coming back here. She's moving there. It's finally going to happen with David. After all this time. Finally.* Liv watched light come back into her friend's eyes. Elyse tapped the phone again to look at the last photo. *That's it. It says it all. Look how happy they are.* Elyse pushed the phone back towards Liv. "When?"

"Mid-summer, August maybe? Before school starts. There's a lot that needs to come together, but... we're going. For sure."

"Damn. Just when I'll need you most, girlfriend, to help me become a good mother, you decide to take off."

Liv shoved herself out of her chair to kneel at Elyse's side. "Isn't it amazing? All this time." Liv put her ear to the baby. "I can hear his heartbeat."

"He knows I'm upset and he doesn't want me to do anything rash."

"Well, haven't we got the lines of communication with baby wide open now!" Liv listened again. "He's calming down." Liv rose and retook her seat. "Let's eat our soup while it's still warm."

"Just say it again, that you'll be here in May."

"Absolutely. And for June and July likely. Enough to see you tightly embedded in your new network of mothers."

It was true. Laurie, the wife of Cory's closest climbing buddy Steve, was pregnant with her second. Elyse's best friend at work was delivering next month. Selena had remarried and was talking of having another child before she turned forty. Tessa, Elyse's sister, already had two. "You know me, Liv. My brain is wildly excited for you and David and Shakti – honestly it hasn't fully absorbed how truly happy I am for you. It's my heart." Elyse paused and stared into Liv's soul, as best friends do. "I don't want to see you go." The tears began. The soup turned cold as they lost themselves in their world of memories, of all the daily life they'd shared for so long. Between some audible sobs, Elyse squeaked out, "It's like the baby will come but you'll go and somehow...that wasn't supposed to happen."

"You'll come see us, won't you?"

That brought Elyse out of it, causing her head to straighten up while she wiped under her eyes. "Of course! When?"

"When there's decent weather, maybe next spring, before the baby starts to walk though - that could be challenging on a long flight."

Elyse eagerly eyed the grilled cheese sandwich and chips Liv served. "Will you be getting married? Has that been decided?"

"At some point. We're committed to each other and a life together. There's stuff to work out though, especially with his sister and her sons coming about the same time, before the school year begins. He's going to have to be there a lot for them. And you know what demands law firms make. Meanwhile, I'll really have to up my game and skill set to be successful. There'll be a lot going on the first year we're there."

Talking with her mouth partially chewing, Elyse reverted to her usual role. "I was just thinking, you haven't lived with a guy since college. There's always that getting adjusted to things you didn't know about the person. You probably don't see it, but you've become terribly independent and used to running your life. You'll need some taming – just as I did!"

Liv smiled with acknowledgement of how Elyse had had to adjust her priorities, and become a helpmate to Cory. "You're right, and I don't have a clue yet about the sister, or how she'll react to me. But I know he'll be there for her. He really loves his nephews and wants to be a father to them."

Red flag. "That's a wrinkle for sure, like maybe competition for his time."

She's right. "It's going to be a huge learning curve for us all. So yes, I think we'll marry, just not right away. Unless a serious obstacle gets in our way."

"It's good that's not the only reason you're going. You'll have you own life still." They grew quiet. "I desperately want to hold on to my own life too... but Liv, remember how before Shakti was born, you got so close psychologically to her too?"

"Yes." Liv recalled her journal.

"I feel it. I feel so many things, incredibly protective, determined to give him a great life. I think I'm losing myself to the baby."

"Yeah, I know how that feels, so close to the baby within. It's quite an experience isn't it!"

"But then they grow up and push you away and yell in your face. And become their own person. Like Shakti is - what about her and you, what have all these developments done to your relationship, especially her meeting Rama?"

"We've gone through so much these weeks, really the last few months. But lately, it's like we're together every step of the way. I feel closer to her than ever right now."

"And Shakti?"

"She was emotionally saturated and overwhelmed on parts of the trip, but with this school in London thing happening, sometimes it's like we're sisters. She's full of herself and all she's going to do, and yet still happy to have me there, keeping her grounded. All of this has moved her beyond where she was, being so snotty with me. She's more mature now."

"Amazing. Whatever the course of love with David, you and Shakti are off on a big adventure then. Nice. I like that. What's the next big thing that will happen?"

"Landing the job offer from Margaret – and making sure Shakti has a school to go to. And then David and I figuring out the housing mix, especially whether when he moves out from the place he's going to rent for his sister, he'll get a studio, or we'll live together."

"You need to really think that through, Liv. In advance, you just won't know how the sister will react to David dragging her to London, only to immediately get involved with this American girl."

Liv valued that insight: perhaps saving money by quickly moving in together wouldn't be the best way to start a relationship with Amer? "Good point."

"There will be so many demands on everyone's time those first months. Integrating your life with David's may need to be gradual."

"I hadn't really thought it through yet - but maybe a place of our own, just Shakti and me, is a better first step for the transition. So much else will have changed." Liv surveyed her cozy burrow in her brother's house that she and Shakti had inhabited for seven years. "Maybe having our own space would make for a more solid landing pad."

Elyse was enjoying a reprise of her advisor role to Liv. "Think about it some more. It's much more complicated than simply looking at costs."

Sunday, February 28

Liv met her mom at the Bellevue condo she and Gary had purchased. Compared to Liv's apartment, it was plush. Two bedrooms with real wood cabinetry, moldings around all windows and doors, cam lights, built in bookshelves, beautiful parquet floors. The location was good for hopping on the highway over Lake Washington and making the western trek to Phinney Ridge and Ryan's place. "On a good day, midday, I can make it over there in about a half hour, much easier than coming off Sammamish hill."

"You know, I'm feeling really bad about leaving them – you too of course! But I'm counting on you to come see us at least once a year."

"For sure. Wait till you talk to your dad. You know with retirement, he's been looking for something to dig into. And he was thinking it might be his Scandinavian roots. With your news, now he's talking naval history from the Vikings down to the British Empire. I keep telling him he has to include Mediterranean trade too, so we can visit warmer places. There's a new kind of fun to be had with your move, honey." Despite Katherine disliking the idea of being so far from Liv and Shakti, she refused to voice it.

"That's comforting to hear. It's different though for Mimi. They won't have the money to be coming over. And the whole thing with Ryan's dad – it's a bummer."

Katherine, having stepped up as much as she could for her own parents' passing, changed perspectives. "It's a bummer for him too, sweetie. It's not fun getting old, losing it in one way or another. Doubtless, in his better moments, Carl is extremely depressed. And I give Mimi and Ryan a lot of credit for facing the situation and being responsible. She has her kids, it will be good for them too, to learn how to care for people."

"I know. Still, it's going to be hard, and I regret already not being here to support them."

"Liv, listen to me. There will come a time when you'll need to be here for me and dad. You'll get your chance to show you can step up. You did it with your grandparents. You'll do it again."

I guess? Long distance makes that hard to think about though. "Let's move on Mom and get on with packing and throwing stuff out at home."

After decades in the Redmond house, one side of the garage had become a fortified wall of boxes, meaning one of their two cars always stayed in the driveway. "This? This is where you want to start?"

"I don't want to move any of this, Liv. We need to winnow it down before I start filling the garage with stuff we do want to move."

An hour into it, they came to the boxes moved from Liv's high school bedroom when it was redone, the year Shakti was born. They opened a box filled with an assortment of teenage girl paraphernalia: mementos from events, a few small stuffed animals and figurines, yearbooks, and photos of Liv and Devin. "This is painful. I don't want to go through this now to find maybe two things I want to keep."

"Simple then, just put it in your car! Or else I toss it all. But just remember, you're moving too."

Later in the kitchen having a snack, Liv tried to express how this time warp thing kept coming up for her, sensing the past as so distant, another life time, but totally present too. "I looked at that photo of me and Dev when we went to the senior prom – I could feel the dress, Mom. I remembered how we used to look into each other's eyes forever. And now, I'm going to be with David in London, and he's got his own time warp, moving among all these wealthy attorneys, but really a kid who can still smell the cattle he grew up with."

"Mind blowing. I know. I feel that way too, being retired now. I've become invisible. Totally irrelevant after all those years of directing projects and people. I'm not who I was."

"Does it get you down?"

"Sometimes. But I try hard to focus on how liberating it is. For one thing, I'll have time to help Mimi and be there more for their kids. Margot is still such a lovely child to be with. I want to take her on outings, play with her more. What's the point of feeling sad about these big life transitions? I like to think that as a mother and grandmother I helped pull you and Shakti into futures that are now blossoming. But at the same time, you both pulled me into a future where I have a relationship with Ryan and his family. And Shakti is pulling you already into a new time and place, and then you'll both pull dad and me forward into trips to so many places - all with stops in London."

"There's a reverse to that though, all the things we've missed out on because of choices we made – maybe I should have moved to India after Shakti was born?"

Katherine contemplated Liv's question as they moved back into the garage. "Perhaps, but why dwell on that? There's no avoiding changes and transition – why not put the best face on it we can? Who does it serve to be negative? Me? You? I've come to believe there's only one way to be and that's positive."

"In that line of thinking, Elyse's baby is certainly taking her to a new time and place, that's clear already. There will be Elyse as I've known her through school and work, and Elyse as a mother."

"Exactly. It's what happens to us all. Carl and his dementia will pull your brother into a different kind of lifestyle, at least for a while. But that's payback, no? If Carl and his wife hadn't adopted Ryan, well, who knows what situation he'd be in, but he wouldn't necessarily have all of us and his boat business that Grandpa helped with." Katherine opened another box and with fresh energy began tossing old pre-electronic file folders from her first job into garbage bags. Pausing over an old resume of hers, she was drawn again to ruminate. "It's odd really, how we go along for years and think nothing is happening, but it's not true. People around us are shifting and changing all the time and we're absorbing all of it, tiny little ripples, and then a giant wave comes and it lifts us up and it's like, wow, I've got a different life. When did that happen?"

"Maybe the time warp is a long evolving tube of life, and it starts doubling back, and parts of it lay next to each other, or twist over each other? It's good, I guess? Like waving to your past across the thin skin of the tube, 'Hi, used to be you!' But it does make me feel disjointed at the same time, as if I'm not just one person, but have multiple lives."

Scanning her decade-old resume, she laughed at her litany of early IT certifications, catching a mental glimpse of a dress she wore back then. *When's the last time I wore a dress?* "Life after life after life...so it seems at times."

"What holds us together?"

"Our memories? Our story?"

Considering the truth in that made Liv feel even worse for Carl's loss of his past. She vowed to treasure her memories and keep her life intact. "I'm taking that memento box with me, Mom."

March and April

In the following weeks, Liv heard from Nimisha, joyful about their move to London, and ready to pay application fees for Shakti. Liv meanwhile googled a few more prep school possibilities, checked them out with Shakti, and pushed her to accept that she might not get into the one she loved. Liv was determined she apply to three schools.

In addition to transcripts and forms to be completed, each school required answers to essay questions. One question asked what long-term plans or aspirations the applicant had and how the school's curriculum would support those. Liv advised Shakti that building on the foundation of her strong freshman high school grades so far, this might be an answer that would cement her admission, if crafted well. Given the expense Nimisha was going to, it was actually a very important question to answer no matter what – although Liv secretly acknowledged she had no idea what she herself would have written at fifteen. Shakti applied herself to this task while working assiduously to get straight 'A's for the semester. She was determined to get into the International Community School and have Alison as her first friend.

Liv used most of her spare time to research community leadership programs, assess materials and designs of programs across the U.S., and interview directors by phone during her work hours, behind her discretely closed door. She stayed in weekly contact with Margaret, sending summaries of each week's efforts and results. At her end, Marg was interviewing people from the Manchester and London programs, as well as potential board members, along with identifying firms that might be willing to sponsor the program and checking if any local government funding might be finagled.

By the end of March, Liv was anxious to send in Shakti's applications. She'd already exchanged emails with the admissions officers, explaining their extraordinary circumstances of a trust fund and trying to build relationships long distance. Fortunately, the head of the community school they'd met recalled Shakti quite well and was encouraging: there were always a few people moving away on international assignments each year and leaving openings in the school.

As Liv assembled the packets for mailing, triple-checking them against the requirements, she read Shakti's essay one more time. They'd debated how much to say in response, how explicit to be. Shakti favored a simple paragraph of wanting to be a champion for women in the world, but Liv made her write more. Then Shakti insisted that her poem also be included. Liv was unsure the first time she read it a week ago, weighing perhaps what it lacked in artistic worthiness against an expression of her daughter's passion. "Shakti, when did you come to write this?"

"It started in my head that day in Arita's office. And then I thought about it on the plane rides. I know it's not really a poem. It's just something that I want to say. I discovered a lot on the trip, more than Dad and Grandma Nimisha. I discovered a lot about myself."

Liv kept silent to encourage Shakti to reveal more.

"I discovered there's this really strong fire in me. I even see it sometimes."

I rise up...

I sleep with the fetus who is never born, life crushed because she is a girl.

I am born into the arms of an impoverished mother, whose breasts cannot sustain me.

I ache with the pains of an empty stomach and suffer the lack of medicine to protect me.

I yearn with the girl wanting to go to the school her brother goes to.

I make bricks with the indentured natives.

I struggle to learn to read and do numbers with no books.

I scream with the trafficked girl, bargained away by her parents for a TV.

I bleed and stink as a young woman when my culture mutilates me.

I protest my arranged marriage to a man my father's age.

I am trapped into the pattern of my mother's life, confined in a burka.

I am so frightened by the noise and explosions of war that tear my country apart.

I lay down in a mass grave next to my parents, pretending that I am dead too.

I fight to the death against my rape by thugs.

I pass my days in a dead-end refugee camp.

I flee to another country only to be forbidden entry.

I cry for my own child lost along the way.

I wake up then to the revolution that must happen.

I stand with the nameless to never be known other than as a number.

I liberate myself from the bondage and shackles of culture and class and history.

I rise up with my sisters to create a better world.

I rise up with my sisters.

I rise up!

Shakti watched Liv read it again. "I just want them to know I care about all these things. It goes with the essay where I imagine working at Arita's nonprofit."

"I think the school where you need to be will value your passions. Let's get these sent now." For the first time, and subject to repeated retractions over the coming years, only to be reaffirmed as many times as taken back, Liv heard a voice. *Your work as a mother is done.*

The river kept flowing and carrying them forward. By the end of April, Liv's offer from Margaret came in a formal looking email attachment on letterhead, with the original to come snail mail. Marg had formed a nonprofit called Community Leadership London, and offered Liv, beginning in September, the post of Program Director at a salary of thirty-five thousand pounds. In the email Marg said that advice from Phillip's firm was that the government would be upping the salary requirement, so she went ahead and locked in the higher number to ensure that Liv would get a long-term work visa. But Marg also relayed his concern: 'You two have to prove yourselves now,' and she'd assured him that 'indeed we will!' Further, she was planning that they take an entire year from September into August, to finish all the prep work to start the program. Marg would focus on board formation, roles, and fundraising, while Liv developed the prototype program to test with focus groups, as well as a marketing plan. Together, they'd work on the business plan. "Roll your sleeves up!"

Reading the offer over and over, Liv experienced her destiny opening before her, a call to a totally new future. Initially, she'd been bothered by the offer to be only program director, not executive director. Marg anticipated that concern in what she wrote: if this was going to be long-term, they best not force an American on the board members as ED. Liv would have a chance to prove herself; or if not her cup of tea to manage the whole thing, enjoy the substantial work of program direction. Which would be augmented by trips annually back to the States to do further 'research in person.' Marg did think of everything.

Liv knew very well what directing the program would mean. She'd have the lead role in landing a successful program design, filling the classes, and making it work interpersonally for the participants, as well as logistically. That fundraising and board development stayed with Margaret suited Liv quite well, given she was stepping out of her geographical comfort zone and existing network of donors. Marg was aiming for a board of mostly powerful women, talented in their own ways, and well-connected to assist in bringing in money. The program's participants would be Liv's constituency to serve.

Considering all aspects, Liv found she had to agree with how her benefactor was structuring this startup. Indeed, being program director of a learning endeavor the like of which she'd never run, would be more than enough to take on for several years. She'd have her skills challenged to gain the trust of community leaders and secure enrollments. Already, she identified the need for a group of local diverse experts to serve as a curriculum committee. And Liv would need to facilitate building that at the outset. Fortunately, she could envision herself doing these tasks. As she researched leadership skills, she'd often measure herself against the approaches advocated, recognizing as she, Elyse, and Selena had before: Liv herself would never be an extrovert leading the charge, inspiring others to make things happen. No, Liv belonged with the introverts who led from behind, facilitating people coming together, and bringing their own leadership skills to the group. Collective leadership. That's what she'd read about, it was precisely what she was convinced this program would need, and she would strengthen her facilitation skills to make it happen. She'd already enrolled in a three-day facilitation workshop.

In yet other email exchanges with Marg, they discussed the current landscape in Britain, the concerns regarding accepting more refugees, the upcoming vote on the UK leaving the European Union, and whether any of this made any difference to Marg's vision of the organization. The need to bring people together to solve local problems was a constant theme. Heartened by the election of a Muslim Mayor, she was already planning a meeting with him.

In the following weeks, in emails from David, she learned that the visas for his sister and nephews were moving along. He'd travel to Nairobi in late July or early August to bring them to London. In phone calls, they discussed timing, when it was best to secure rental units, and whether David and she should live together from the outset. With further counsel from Elyse, Liv decided: they all needed space to land their separateness, and from there, feel their way to coming together.

Shakti's acceptance letter to the International Community School came the same day in May as Elyse's baby was born.

Friday, May 6

Elyse called at six am. "We're on our way to Swedish. Come as quickly as you can." Liv was her Lamaze coach given that Cory's schedule was just too tight to make every training session. In a class where they were not the only female pairing, the instructor leaned over them at one point and said, "Men need good women, but women need their girlfriends." Elyse hadn't minded. Liv being there for her at the birth created a symmetry of shared experience that would bind them forever. As Elyse moved through a long labor, Liv couldn't help but recall her friend at her side during Shakti's birth. They spoke of how strange it was that with all their closeness, one had her child at twenty-one, the other at thirty-seven. One was now stepping into the fullness of her professional life, while the other was experiencing a contraction. Liv fell into envying the sweet baby years ahead, while Elyse envied Liv's liberation. Such different paths for two so close. Liv thought of a child, a seed, holding a new life for her friend, a life she couldn't predict. Elyse thought of the destiny delivered by a seed planted sixteen years ago. Their children were pulling them into the future.

As Liv saw Elyse struggling with the pain – she asked for an epidural – Liv wondered, will I have another child? By David. Would he want that as parenting his nephews gave him a new role? Would she want that? Just when her career might really take off? Would it be an issue?

Meanwhile Cory took turns breaking Liv and was by Elyse's side as she fully dilated.

The baby was long at twenty-two inches, clearly headed for his father's height. In recovery, the baby wrapped tightly and lying on Elyse's stomach, Liv saw the wonder and joy in Cory's face. *He's going to be fine. A great dad.* The intimacy of their new family made Liv step back farther, until finally she excused herself to go bring Shakti to the hospital. As she walked out to the car, she was content with their separate destinies. *I may be leaving her, but I'm leaving her with her hands and heart full.*

Sunday, May 15

"Happy first-time Mother's Day, Elyse!" Liv had visited her and the baby so many times already, but today she would be with her own mom here at Mimi and Ryan's house with all the grandchildren. "What's Cory doing for you?"

"It's frosting on the cake. You know how great he's been this week with baby Will, and then today he made this really yummy breakfast and produced a beautifully framed picture of the three of us that looks like one you must have taken?"

"I can't deny it; he and I did have a little conspiracy going."

"Oh Liv. I'm just so..." another time she would have said 'fucking happy' but it didn't fit, "...so absolutely, totally happy. I'm in love with Will, and Cory is too."

"I'll say! I just hope you're ready for the camping trips coming up."

"Now don't go spoiling my day."

"Hey, I've got to run. Looks like Shakti has arrived here at the kitchen table with a present."

"Love you. Best friends forever."

"Always."

Ever since completing her school applications, Shakti had been either putting her efforts into her grades or continuing what Liv called her 'depressing research' into a host of women's issues. She was systematically creating her own wiki covering every wrong perpetrated on women in the world today, now into categorizing things across pre-birth, children, adolescents, womanhood, and old age. Liv was concerned the fixation was unhealthy, asking her why she was doing this. "Because I'll want this later when I'm writing papers. And I'll sound more intelligent in class." Liv took to sending links to Shakti about the great things girls and women were doing. "You need to know this side of it too, so you can inspire others. Telling the truth is not enough – you need to give people hope. You can't leave them in the desert, you have to lead them out."

Shakti was excited this morning, bouncing around in the t-shirt and gym shorts she'd slept in, with a gift in her hands. "Mom, open it. I got you a great present. It's for your new office in London, to hang on the wall."

Liv unwrapped a large metal frame, ten by twelve that had a gold piece of paper with something called a 'Proclamation' on it. She saw that Julia Ward Howe had authored it in 1870.

"Read it out loud, it's beautiful. She was an abolitionist and wrote it after the Civil War, trying to establish a Mother's Peace Day, the beginning of Mother's Day."

Liv read the first line. "Arise, all women who have hearts," and immediately choked up.

Shakti took it from her. "Okay, I'll read it. I've read it so many times, I can do it dramatically now." With sweeping gestures and a strong voice, Shakti read, "Arise all women who have hearts, whether your baptism be that of water or tears! Our sons shall not be taken from us to unlearn all that we have been able to teach them of charity, mercy and patience. We women of one country will be too tender of those of another country to allow our sons to be trained to injure theirs." She interjected her own thoughts as she read, "It's like your new job, Mom, how you're going to get different ethnic women to get along so that their communities work better. Read how it ends: 'In the name of womanhood and of humanity, I earnestly ask that a general congress of women without limit of nationality may be appointed...to promote the alliance of different nationalities, the amicable settle of international questions, the great and general interests of peace.' Isn't that what you and Auntie Margie are all about?"

She placed the frame on the table and made Liv push her chair back so that she could sit on her lap. Wrapping her long, thin arms around Liv's body, it was as though she was finding her way back into her mother's womb to begin their love anew. Genes replicating, hearts attuning, blood flowing. Separating, yet fulfilling mutual growth, one shaping the other, until even standing alone, their bond was so strong they were inseparable in spirit. Shakti relaxed as Liv's arms encircled her. "Do you love it Mom? It's so you!"

Liv tasted her salty tears. Easing their torsos apart, in a blurry vision her eyes lingered on Shakti's features, finding Katherine here or Nimisha there – or herself. A past replete with love from others supported this child. An adventurous future beckoned, going forth with women she had yet to meet. And in this blissful shared moment, Liv had her daughter to herself. "I do love it. It's so us, sweetie...going forward...women together."

Did you miss the beginning of Liv's story?

Nonprofit Girl Trilogy, book one

Nonprofit Girl

Finalist, Indie Excellence Book Awards, Women's Fiction
Finalist, American Fiction Awards, Family Saga

If you had an unwanted pregnancy, what would you decide?

When Liv, 21 and about to graduate into a career of nonprofit work, returns from India and discovers she's pregnant, she needs to make choices that will define her life. What should she tell her live-in boyfriend Devin who is not the father? Does she want to have an abortion as her best friend Elyse urges? If not, will she give up the baby as her mother Katherine did? Set in Seattle, with flashbacks to her time in Mumbai and affair with Rama, watch Liv's new-found feminism shape her decisions. And hear a legacy from the women in her family that gives her the courage to stand for her own values.
This coming-of-age story begins the *Nonprofit Girl Trilogy* that evolves into a family saga spanning 15 years and populated by strong women of all ages.

Shakti Rising

Nonprofit Girl Trilogy, book two
Karma Blues

Would you settle for the man who's available, or hold out for the one you really want?

Against the backdrop of building her nonprofit career, Liv yearns for a mate, and struggles with a litany of ill-fitted suitors. Just when she's ready to abandon the man quest, her best friend Elyse's wedding news results in Liv meeting Eric, a fine Nordic specimen with darker undertones.

As Elyse fears losing her life in marriage to a workaholic attorney, Liv pushes herself to explore the possibility of coupling with someone who compromises her interests and values. Meanwhile, an old friend, David, whom she first came to know as a refugee from Sudan, crosses her path again, rekindling suppressed interest on both sides. Emotions intensify leading up to Elyse's wedding, as control dramas unfold and past lives intersect, culminating in a fiesta party that crashes. Badly.

You can begin the *Nonprofit Girl Trilogy* here as past is blended with present.

290

About the author:

Ann uses her own nonprofit career experiences, travel to India, and volunteer work with the International Rescue Committee in Seattle, her home of thirty years, to context the inner explorations of those affected by adoption. Having her own adopted son who met his birth family has attuned her to the emotional cross-currents surrounding unwanted pregnancy.

Currently residing in the Washington, D.C. area, she's taught business courses at George Washington University and uses her J.D. to be a citizen advocate with RESULTS to help alleviate the worst aspects of domestic and global poverty.

You can learn more and contact her at www.nonprofitgirltrilogy.com

If you would like to blog about your personal motivation or inspiration for being a nonprofit girl or woman, please contact Ann at www.nonprofitgirltrilogy.com

Visit me on social media

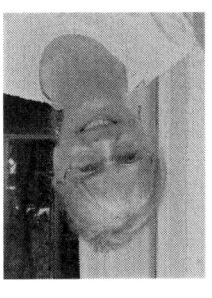

Made in the USA
Middletown, DE
07 January 2019